THE BEST AMERICAN MYSTERY STORIES 2011

THE BEST AMERICAN MYSTERY STORIES 2011

EDITED BY

HARLAN COBEN

SERIES EDITOR OTTO PENZLER

CORVUS

First published in the United States of America in 2011
by Houghton Mifflin Harcourt.

This edition first published in Great Britain in 2011
by Corvus, an imprint of Atlantic Books Ltd.

9 8 7 6 5 4 3 2 1

A CIP catalogue record for this book is available from
the British Library.

ISBN: 978-0-85789-501-1 (hardback)
ISBN: 978-0-85789-503-5 (tradepaperback)
ISBN: 978-0-85789-502-8 (eBook)

Printed and bound in Great Britain
by TJ International Ltd, Padstow, Cornwall.

Corvus
An imprint of Atlantic Books Ltd
Ormond House
26-27 Boswell Street
London WC1N 3JZ

www.corvus-books.co.uk

Contents

Foreword

MANY OF THE GREATEST NAMES in the mystery genre have appeared on the pages of *The Best American Mystery Stories* during its fourteen-year history, including Elmore Leonard, Michael Connelly, James Lee Burke, Dennis Lehane, Laura Lippman, Jeffery Deaver, and Lawrence Block. Too, many of the major authors of literary fiction have contributed outstanding work to the series, including John Updike, Jay McInerney, Roxanna Robinson, Russell Banks, Alice Munro, and, of course, the incomparable Joyce Carol Oates. I would make the argument, however, that one of the greatest strengths of the series has been the stories of relatively little-known writers who have graced its pages, many of whom have gone on to enjoy warm critical attention as well as popular success.

Stories by these authors are seldom found in the pages of such acclaimed purveyors of contemporary fiction as *The New Yorker, The Atlantic,* or *Harper's Magazine.* Most of the early work by these hugely talented writers has been discovered in the pages of literary journals, those labors of love produced in such modest numbers that very few readers ever get to see them, and a few in electronic magazines.

Here was the introduction to a large readership of Scott Wolven, whose "Controlled Burn" was initially published in *Harpur Palate* and collected in the 2003 edition of *The Best American Mystery Stories.* This, and subsequent stories also published in *BAMS,* got him a book contract with Scribner's *(Controlled Burn: Stories of Prison, Crime, and Men).*

Tom Franklin's "Poachers" was found in the pages of *Texas Re-*

view and appeared in *BAMS 1999*. The story went on to win the Edgar Allan Poe Award from the Mystery Writers of America and a book contract from William Morrow for *Poachers: Stories;* it was later selected for *The Best American Mystery Stories of the Century*. Franklin has gone on to write several novels, including *Crooked Letter, Crooked Letter,* which was nominated for an Edgar as the Best Novel of 2010.

"All Through the House" by Christopher Coake was chosen for *BAMS 2004* after its first publication in *The Gettysburg Review;* it became the centerpiece of his Houghton Mifflin Harcourt collection, *We're in Trouble*.

It is profoundly gratifying and humbling to know that this series can have such a powerful impact on the world of mystery fiction and the enormously talented writers who toil in its gardens. One can only wonder if some of the contributors to this volume will go on to follow in the footsteps of Coake, Franklin, and Wolven to find similar much-deserved success in their mystery writing careers.

While it is redundant for me to write it again, since I have already done so in each of the previous fourteen volumes of this series, it falls into the category of fair warning to state that many people regard a "mystery" as a detective story. I regard the detective story as one subgenre of a much bigger genre, which I define as any short work of fiction in which a crime, or the threat of a crime, is central to the theme or the plot. While I love good puzzles and tales of pure ratiocination, few of these are written today as the mystery genre has evolved (for better or worse, depending on your point of view) into a more character-driven form of literature, with more emphasis on the why of a crime's commission than on the who or how. The line between mystery fiction and general fiction has become more and more blurred in recent years, producing fewer memorable detective stories but more significant literature.

It is a pleasure, as well as a necessity, to thank Harlan Coben for agreeing to be the guest editor for the 2011 edition of *The Best American Mystery Stories*. Putting aside virtually everything on his very crowded plate, he delivered the work on schedule, thereby causing champagne corks to pop and hats to be flung in the air at Houghton Mifflin Harcourt as the very tight deadlines have been met. Sincere thanks as well to the previous guest editors, beginning with Robert B. Parker, who started it all in 1997, followed by Sue Grafton, Ed McBain, Donald E. Westlake, Lawrence Block, James Ellroy, Michael Connelly, Nelson DeMille, Joyce Carol Oates, Scott Turow, Carl Hiaasen, George Pelecanos, Jeffery Deaver, and Lee Child.

While I engage in a relentless quest to locate and read every mystery/crime/suspense story published, I live in terror that I will miss a worthy story, so if you are an author, editor, or publisher, or care about one, please feel free to send a book, magazine, or tearsheet to me c/o The Mysterious Bookshop, 58 Warren Street, New York, NY 10007. If it first appeared electronically, you must submit a hard copy. It is vital to include the author's contact information. No unpublished material will be considered, for what should be obvious reasons. No material will be returned. If you distrust the postal service, enclose a self-addressed, stamped postcard, on which I will acknowledge receipt of your story.

To be eligible, a story must have been written by an American or a Canadian and first published in an American or Canadian publication in the calendar year 2011. The earlier in the year I receive the story, the more fondly I regard it. For reasons known only to the blockheads who wait until Christmas week to submit a story published the previous spring, this happens every year, causing much gnashing of teeth as I read a stack of stories while my wife and friends are trimming the Christmas tree or otherwise celebrating the holiday season. It had better be a damned good story if you do this. Because of the very tight production schedule for this book, the absolute firm deadline is December 31. If the story arrives two days later, it will not be read. Sorry.

O. P.

Introduction

I HATE THIS PART.

You should skip it. I'm serious. You know what this is, don't you? This is the part of a story collection where the editor writes some faux-deep, pseudo-erudite essay on the larger meaning of the short story. It is, quite frankly, an irrelevant exercise. The collection is about the story, not my view of it, and thus this introduction becomes the literary equivalent of a bad overture at a musical: It gets you in your seat, but if you're already seated, you just want the curtain to open. It stalls. It annoys. Even the best introductions, no matter how well done, are a bit like a toupee. It may be a good toupee. It may be a bad toupee. But it's still a toupee.

It is also pretty ironic when you think about it—an excess of words to introduce a form that relies on the economy of them. A novel is a long-term commitment. A short story is more like a heady fling—intense, adventurous, emotionally charged, and, when I was young, embarrassingly quick. Okay, forget that last one. The best short stories, like those high-octane lovers, never fully leave you. They burn, linger, haunt. Some sneak up on you in a subtle way. Others are like a punch in the gut—sudden, spontaneous. They knock the wind out of you.

One of my favorite rules of writing comes from the great Elmore Leonard: "Try to leave out the parts that readers tend to skip." If you learn nothing else from this introduction—as if you're really learning something—please make sure you keep this rule front and center in your thoughts. The best writers do. The best writers ask themselves on every page, every paragraph, every sentence, every word: "Is this compelling? Is this gripping? Is this absolutely necessary? Is this the best I can do?" (So, too, do the best readers, but that's for another time.)

That doesn't mean you can't have larger themes, descriptions, well-defined characters, or explore matters of great import. You can and you must. All great stories—long and, yes, short—contain those elements. You will, in fact, witness many examples in just a few turns of the page. Again, my job here is to delay that sense of satisfaction, I guess, by pointing out the obvious in wonderful, economic storytelling, so let us continue.

What Elmore Leonard means in the above quotation, of course, is that every word must count. The writers included in this collection are masters at this. In the pages after this intro, you will find no navel-gazing, no endless descriptions of winter weather or dithering on about worldview, no fashionable "look at me" acrobatic wordplay that amounts to nothing more than proving that someone bought a brand-new thesaurus and isn't afraid to abuse it.

What will you find, then? In two words: great storytelling.

The writers in this varied and brilliant collection—a heady blend of household names, veteran scribes, and promising newcomers—have taken Elmore Leonard's credo and fed it steroids and raised it to the tenth power and then driven it out to a dive bar by the airport and given it an unlimited tab. Yes, I know that makes no sense, but horrendous analogy aside, you're in for a treat.

Here, my good friend Otto Penzler and I have assembled the "best of the best" in mystery short stories. We often wax nostalgic about some past era, some now-gone golden age of—take your pick—music, literature, cinema, art. Let me give you the good news here. We—you and me, dear reader—are living in the golden age of crime fiction. I do not say this lightly. Never in history have so many authors "dunnit" with such variety and such skill.

In this collection you will find every sort of hero, every sort of villain, every sort of setting, every sort of crime, every sort of solution, every sort of surprise. To paraphrase the old saw, these stories will make you laugh, they will make you cry, they will make you cringe in fear, they will become a part of you.

All of which brings me back to Elmore Leonard's rule. Do you see something worth skipping? Cut it. Cut it off at the knees. Like, to give you an immediate example, this introduction. Cue the maniacal laughter. Fool. If you had skipped this part, you'd already be lost in one of the best mystery short stories of the year. Instead, alas, you're stuck with me.

But not for much longer. Turn the page, dear reader. These will be the last wasted words you will read in this collection. Go. Enjoy.

HARLAN COBEN

The Best American Mystery Stories 2011

BROCK ADAMS

Audacious

FROM *Sewanee Review*

SHE WAS A PICKPOCKET.

She haunted the subway station on Thirty-fourth and Holloway, where every morning Gerald waited for his train on the same cold concrete bench. He watched her through thick glasses. She was young, frail and thin, waiflike, with short shaggy black hair, and she moved like a ghost, drifting in and out of sight as the crowd milled about.

She made him look forward to the mornings. She made him feel sparks. Watching her was the only time that Gerald had felt alive since he found Dolores, his wife of fifty-three years, face-down in her Cheerios on a Sunday morning, dead from a stroke.

Gerald's pickpocket wore black leggings covered by a short blue-jean skirt. She wore two jackets, Windbreaker over denim—lots of pockets, Gerald figured. Sometimes she wore sunglasses, even though she was underground.

She was good, crafty and swift and clever, and not greedy—you get caught when you get greedy. Gerald learned her patterns as he watched her on the way to work.

Not work really. After Dolores died, and after the funeral and the family and the random visitors bringing potluck stuff over to mold in the fridge, he found himself alone in the house. He had been retired for nine years before she died, and they had never done much of anything. They never traveled or went to parties or joined any clubs. But they were in the house together, living close but separate lives, side by side. She was there, a constant, a daily affirmation, like the soreness of his right rear molar or the ingrown toenail on his middle toe—a part of life.

Once she was gone, there was nothing there but an empty house and a lot of hours between waking up and falling asleep. Gerald cleaned and straightened until there was nothing left to clean and straighten; then he tried to get his job as a building inspector back, but the contracting business had moved on, far on, from the last time he worked. The site was now run by a kid who had been an intern when Gerald retired. He had laughed and put his hand on Gerald's shoulder when he brought up returning to work. Gerald watched the light drain from the kid's eyes, watched the uncomfortable tension slide in, when he realized Gerald was serious. The kid forced the smile back onto his face. "We'd love to have you back, Gerald," he said, "but it's just not safe to have a seventy-four-year-old on a construction site."

Gerald had smiled and nodded, shook the kid's hand. His hand seemed old and callused in the young man's grip. It felt bulky in his pocket as he walked away from the site. Gerald's hair was white by now, even though he parted it the same way he had when he was thirty. His skin was weathered and wrinkled. Everything around him was new. He didn't fit.

He took an office downtown, a small dusty room with a big window that was full of sun and blue sky in the mornings. He told people he was going to be a freelance writer. He didn't write much—a humor piece for the local tabloid, a few halfhearted attempts at a memoir; mostly he looked out the window and breathed in the musty air. He just liked the rhythm it gave to his life, this waking up and getting ready and going to work and coming home, although every morning it got harder to get off that bench and onto the train. And then he found his pickpocket.

She followed patterns that no one but Gerald knew. She entered from the south entrance, the one with the stairs, rather than the escalator. She skipped down the stairs and moved close to the tracks, leaned her back against a cement pillar. She faced straight down into the black hole of the tunnel, but her eyes darted around—light, searching. She stood at the pillar a few minutes. When the first train came rumbling up the tunnel and the crowds pressed right up to the edge of the track, she drifted in, melted right into the throng, and when the doors hissed open, she made her move. Gerald had seen her unzip purses and unhook wallets from chains while the crowd jostled and shoved. She snatched a silver fountain pen from a stockbroker's breast pocket, plucked a small jewel out of an Indian woman's scarf. Then, as the crowd disappeared behind the sliding doors and was shuttled away from her, she slipped her prizes deep in her jacket, slid out the north entrance, and was gone until tomorrow.

She was interesting, a diversion for a while, until the day she pickpocketed the cop. The cop was young and nervous-looking, and he stalked around the station every other day and ran out the bums who begged for change. He stood over a bum on a Wednesday morning.

"Got to move along, buddy," he said.

The bum looked up at him. "Come on, man," he said.

"No panhandling in here."

"Cut me a break."

"Don't make this hard," the cop said. He wore a heavy utility belt loaded down with radio and gun and baton and other cop stuff. Everything was held down by leather straps with snaps on them. He unsnapped the pepper spray. "Just move along."

The train rumbled in and the doors opened and the crowd sardined its way into the waiting cars, and as Gerald watched, his pickpocket wove her way in between the people and up behind the cop, nicked the pepper spray right out of his belt, and scuttled on out the north entrance. The cop reached for his belt, fumbled thin air, looked down with confusion.

"Watch out for those damn ghosts," the bum said, laughing, grinning a dirty-toothed grin.

Gerald fell in love with her that morning.

Gerald stood at the edge of the crowd with his hand against a pillar. He ran his finger over the cold, gravelly cement. The subway station always smelled of metal and soap, of machines and people just out of the shower. A thin man in a suit stood beside Gerald, one of those phone earpiece things attached to him, making him look like a robot. He yelled at whoever was on the other end of the phone, like he was yelling into thin air. Two kids with lunchboxes sat side by side on a bench. One punched the other on the arm, and they both laughed.

All around Gerald the crowd hummed, feet clicking and sticking on the cold ground.

She came in through the south entrance, her sunglasses on, her jackets zipped up against the November cold. She leaned against her pillar. Gerald watched her out of the corner of his eye. He could feel her looking around, looking at him. He slid his hand further up the pillar, his jacket falling further open, his wallet inching out of the inside breast pocket. An inch and a half of leather showing now. She had to see it.

The train snaked into the station. The doors opened. The crowd surged and shoved around him; he looked at her pillar, and she was gone. A woman with a bagel smushed into him, got cream cheese on his coat.

"Sorry," she mumbled without looking at him.

The crowd pressed him into the car and the doors shut behind him. Warmth was everywhere, coming from the car's heater, coming from the bodies pressed against each other. The odor of coffee on the air. Gerald felt his pocket. The wallet was gone.

The train began to move and the station slid away outside the window. Gerald watched his pickpocket as she edged through the crowd toward the north entrance.

He held on to the metal rail above his head and smiled as the train plowed into the darkness. Graffiti raced by on the tunnel walls. He closed his eyes and pictured his girl, climbing up the stairs and into the cold hard air of the city, scooting along the sidewalk, head down, hands in her pockets while the wind whips her hair around. She turns down an alley and tucks herself into a corner behind a dumpster. She unzips her coat, pulls the wallet out, and opens it, rifles through it, stares. No money, no credit cards, no ID. Just a piece of paper. She holds it in her little pink fingers. One side says *BUSTED*. She flips it over. *So audacious. Find me tomorrow.* She huffs, pouts, crumples the paper, sticks it back in her pocket. She fumes. A tiny ball of fire.

Gerald smiled and felt his feet rocking with the train.

She was there the next morning. She leaned against her pillar, her arms crossed, her top teeth biting into her bottom lip. She stared at Gerald. He sat on the bench and stared back while people cut back and forth between them. The subway came and went. She let the crowd and all their wallets and purses and jewelry walk right by in front of her. Then the station was nearly empty: the cashiers were changing shifts, the cop was heading out the north entrance, and the pickpocket padded across the concrete, the soft pat of her shoes echoing around the station. She stopped in front of him and crossed her arms again.

"What was that all about?" she said.

Gerald smiled at her. He put his palms on the bench and leaned back, crossed one leg over the other. "Surprised?" he said.

"Are you going to turn me in?"

"I wasn't planning on it."

"Then what do you want?"

He looked at her feet. She wore black ballet slippers. "I see you every morning," he said. "Just wanted some company, I suppose."

"Are you trying to hit on me?"

"No."

"How old are you?"

"I'm not trying to hit on you."

"Okay." She looked around the room. A janitor was wandering around with one of those grabber-claw things, picking up coffee cups and fruit-bar wrappers. She sat down beside Gerald and pulled the crumpled piece of paper out of her pocket. She looked at it, flipped it over, turned it between her fingers. "What does *audacious* mean?"

"You've never heard it before?"

"No."

He took the paper from her. "It means daring, bold."

"So audacious."

"Yup." He handed the paper back to her. She folded it up and slipped it neatly into a pocket. She looked at her feet. Pushed her hair back behind her ears.

"I'm Gerald. What's your name?"

She licked her lips. "You think I'm audacious?"

"I do."

"So just call me Audacious."

"You don't have a name?"

"Not that I'm going to tell you."

"Well, Audacious is a little long for a name."

"So shorten it then, whatever. I'm not telling you my real name." She stood up.

"Shorten it? Like Audi?"

She stood in front of him, zipped her jackets up, first the denim one, then the Windbreaker. "Like the car?"

"As in short for Audacious."

"Fine then. Audi." She turned around, headed for the north entrance.

"See you tomorrow?" Gerald said. His voice bounced off the walls of the station.

She tucked her hands into her jacket and walked out of sight.

He brought her coffee the next morning. Audi stood across the station and stared at him until the train left, then came and sat down beside him. Didn't say a word.

"I thought you'd like it sweet. I put lots of sugar in it. Lots of cream," Gerald said.

She took it from him. "Thanks," she said. She took a sip, licked her lips. "You know, this is two days in a row I've missed a score because of you."

"Whoops."

"You're going to have to help me out if you keep this up," she said. She smiled at him. The gums above her top teeth showed pink and tender. Her dark eyes sparkled. Gerald felt himself filling up inside.

"I brought you coffee," he said. "What else do you want?"

"I'll think of something."

For two weeks she was there every morning. Gerald missed his train to talk to her. He showed up late to the office every day. Not that there was anyone who would notice.

Audi told him about herself. She was twenty-two years old, had been fending for herself for the last six years. She ended up on the street when her boyfriend left her. He owned a house, begged her to move in. She did, and a month later he'd had enough of her.

"Get your shit and move out—that's all he said to me," Audi said, turning her coffee cup around in her palms. "I knew my parents wouldn't let me back in; they were all pissed off that I left in the first place. So I went downtown to stay with one of my girlfriends. She said there wasn't room, and that was that. I started sleeping in here." She waved her arm, gestured to the cavernous space.

"In the station?" Gerald said.

"Over behind those vending machines. It's warm back there, the machines make it warm, and there's space. And the cops don't look back there."

"Not the most comfortable place in the world, though."

"No." She drank her coffee and looked at the vending machines. "But I hung around here enough that I figured people out. And started stealing their stuff. It's easy. And I got enough to pay a sixth of the rent at this place." She told him about the apartment, a place downtown where she stayed with a half-dozen other people her age, the population of the apartment constantly in flux as people disappeared and new ones showed up. She slept on the kitchen floor. Rent was cheap.

"And you're happy there?" Gerald said.

"No."

She leaned forward, her paper cup dangling from her fingertips. She scrunched her face and looked at the ground. Her jackets bunched up around her shoulders, her back. Gerald held his hand behind her, an inch from her back, thought about it, watched her, and finally rested his palm flat and gentle against her jacket.

"You know, I've got extra space, if you ever need somewhere to stay," he said.

"I'm not going to have sex with you."

"I'm not asking you to."

"You're old enough to be my granddad."

"Probably so."

He left his hand on her back while another train came and went. Audi was gone the next day. He sat on the bench with a cup of coffee in each hand and watched four crowds get into four trains. Then he went home.

The city turned dark, gray, and frigid as the month wore on. The streets were slick and the tall buildings looked like they were cut from wet cardboard and stuck against the sky.

Each morning Gerald sat at the station, scanning the platform for her, searching the overcoat-wearing, briefcase-toting crowd. He noticed women with their purses hanging loose and open from their shoulders. Men shouting into cell phones while their briefcases sat unwatched beside them. A treasure trove of targets. But no Audi.

Gerald watched through the window of his office as the winter came in fast and cold. The snow blew in sideways and piled in dirty drifts along the edges of the rooftops. The pigeons at first huddled together in the rafters and eventually disappeared altogether. Gerald tried to fill the hours in the day. He balanced his checkbook. He did crossword puzzles. He wrote, toying around with different stories, far-fetched tales with beautiful female pickpockets as the leading characters. Mostly he just looked out the window. He wondered if Audi's apartment had a heater. He wondered if she'd really had an apartment to begin with.

He went by the market near his house every day on his way home. He liked putting his hands on the fresh vegetables, weighing the ripe fruit. He walked slowly, taking his time, planning his meals as he wandered the aisles. This took time. Bringing it all home and cooking something also ate up the evening. By the time everything was eaten and cleaned up, it was almost time to go to bed, and another day was over.

A week before Christmas, he was sautéing onions when he heard the knock. He left the onions sizzling in the skillet and went to the door. Audi was there, the wind blowing cold and wintry around her, her hands deep in her pockets, her ballet shoes wet with dirty snow.

She looked at the ground, made patterns in the sludge with her toe. "Hi," she said.

"Hi," Gerald said. He stepped aside and she came in.

He put on a pot of coffee; then he made a huge omelet with eight eggs, green peppers, onions, chopped-up smoked sausage. Audi sat at the kitchen table with her hands folded in front of her and didn't speak. She watched him cook. He cut the omelet in half with the spatula and put half on a plate and set it in front of her. He sat down with the rest of it and began to eat it right out of the skillet. Audi stared at her plate.

"You don't like eggs?" Gerald said.

"They're fine," she said. "It just looks pretty. I don't want to mess it up."

"It's just an omelet."

"It's been a long time since I've had an omelet."

She ate, and she told him the story, how she'd come home to her apartment and found the door boarded up, how she didn't even know who the landlord was, how she had no idea what happened. She found one of her roommates on a bench at the park. He told her the rest.

"Drugs or something," Audi said. "The guy said that the cops came and busted them, and after that the landlord kicked everybody out. Boarded the place up. Said she'd had enough of renting to worthless kids."

"Shame," Gerald said. "Not really your fault."

"Hmm."

She finished her plate, and he took it from her and put it in the sink. He poured her a cup of coffee and sat back down at the table. She held it tight between her hands.

"How did you find my house?" Gerald said.

"Followed you one day, a few weeks ago." She pushed her hair back. Looked from the cup to Gerald and back again. "You said I could come if I needed to."

"I know I did. And you're welcome to. I just wondered how."

"I don't want to impose."

"You're not."

She drank the coffee. "The food was good," she said.

They sat at the table in silence and drank their coffee. The snow started to come down again, edging against the windowsill like silent white feathers. Frost coated the glass. The heater kicked on with a groan, and the warm air blew through the kitchen. Audi squished her shoes against the tile.

"You want some dry clothes?" Gerald said.

She nodded. Gerald left her at the table and went upstairs. He had a walk-in closet in his bedroom; the right side was full of his stuff, on the left still hung all of Dolores's clothes. He hadn't known what to do with them. Her shoes were lined up neatly against the wall, except for a pair of heavy brown boots—the last shoes she'd worn—thrown haphazardly in the corner, exactly where she'd left them. He took a selection of shirts and pants and carried them back downstairs.

Audi was sitting on the couch in the living room when he got back. Gerald laid the clothes out on the coffee table in front of her.

"So retro!" she said, fingering the frilled sleeves of a scarlet blouse. "Where'd you get all this stuff?"

"It was my wife's," Gerald said.

Audi nodded and looked at the clothes.

"She died a few years ago," he went on.

"Of what?"

"Stroke."

Audi picked up a pair of brown slacks and stood up. She held the slacks in front of her and looked down, lifted her leg, twisted her toes. "Do you miss her?"

He nodded. "Often."

"I'm going to put these on," she said. She took the scarlet blouse and the brown slacks and went into the bathroom. She was in there a long time. Gerald turned on the TV. A rerun of *The A-Team* was on. Mr. T beat someone up. Gerald turned down the volume.

"What was her name?" Audi said. She was standing in the doorway, looking slim and clean and young in his wife's clothes.

"Who?"

"Your wife."

"Oh. Dolores. Her name was Dolores."

Audi looked at her reflection in the dark window. "Very pretty," she said, flexing her arm, turning around and standing on her tiptoes. The snow fell quiet and heavy.

She stayed in the guest bedroom that night. He took the sheets down from the top of the closet and made the bed while she stood in the doorway and watched him. She grinned at him.

"For a guy you're pretty good at that."

"I had to learn," Gerald said. He tucked the sheets under the corners of the bed.

"My ex-boyfriend was terrible at it. He always made me help him." She sat down on the end of the bed. "It was a huge pain in the ass."

Gerald propped the pillows against the headboard. "There's a TV," he said, "if you want to watch TV, but I don't have HBO or anything, and I don't know where the remote is."

She crawled up to the top of the bed and settled back into the pillows. "I'll be fine," she said. "I think I'm just going to go on to sleep. I'm tired." She smiled at him. Her skin was fair and her cheeks were flushed and pink. Her hair fell over her eyebrows and spread out behind her on the pillow.

Gerald backed out the door. "Okay, then," he said. "Good night, then." He pulled the door to behind him.

The next day he woke at seven and got dressed. He cracked the door into Audi's room and peeked inside. She lay asleep, under the covers, except for one leg, a long fleshy leg that hung out and down to the floor, bare and pink. Dolores's pants were on the floor beside the bed. Gerald looked at Audi's skin as she shifted in her sleep. He shook his head and shut the door.

At the office, for the first time in weeks, he found himself compelled to write. He took his latest attempt at a memoir out of the drawer and read the first page. The writing was pedestrian, dull. The scene was a boring one, a school play, from ages ago, from third grade. He folded the pages in half and threw them in the garbage and slid a fresh sheet into the typewriter. He began to write, this time starting the story with Dolores's death. He wrote with fire, the words crackling like lightning across the page. He saw himself rolling over to the empty part of the bed, relishing the space, nuzzling into the pillow as the sun made its way through the windows. Then rising late, stumbling downstairs, where Dolores's hair was splayed across the table, her hands dangling limp and straight down at her sides, milk dripping slowly onto the tile.

And then came Audi, a ball of fire in the empty house. He put the paper away and headed home.

She was there when he got back. She was on the couch in another outfit of his wife's, an old sweatsuit. She had cooked popcorn and was cuddled up under the blankets, watching TV.

"Enjoying yourself?" Gerald said.

"You know it."

He sat down beside her. She scooted closer. She took a pillow from the end of the couch and set it in his lap, laid her head on top of it, and turned on her side to keep her eyes on the TV. She was watching a music video.

"What did you do today?" Gerald asked her.

"This," she said. "All day. Bummed around. It was great." She laughed. It was the first time he'd heard her laugh, a tinkling wind-chime sort of sound that started in her chest and bounced its way across her tongue. It put tingles in Gerald's spine. "How about you?" she said.

"I did some writing."

"What about?"

"About you."

She turned over on her back and looked up at him. "You're writing about me?"

"Yup." He watched the TV. The band was playing in a warehouse. He could feel her eyes on him, cold and intense.

"You better write me exciting. I don't want to be a boring character."

"You're not."

"And I better be pretty," she said. Then she turned back to the TV.

She stayed with him. He went to his office and wrote, and came home and talked to her about his day. He spent all day looking forward to his time on the couch with her, to the feeling of the weight of her head on his lap, the feeling of her breath so near his face.

He stayed home on Christmas Day. He was cooking biscuits when she came downstairs, slow and sleepy-eyed.

"Merry Christmas," Gerald said.

She sat down at the table and yawned. "Don't say *Merry* Christmas," she said. "It sounds so commercial."

"What do you want me to say?"

"How about *Happy* Christmas, like you say for every other holiday?"

"Fine, *Happy* Christmas. Honey or jelly? On your biscuits."

"Honey."

"Good choice." He put the biscuits in the oven and took the honey from the cabinet and set it on the table in front of her. "They'll take a few minutes to cook."

"I got you a Christmas present," she said. She looked at the table and wrung her hands. "I'm not sure if you'll like it."

"What is it?"

"You promise you'll like it? Or at least say you'll like it?"

"I promise I'll at least say I like it."

"Smart-ass," she said. She ran upstairs and came back down with a brown paper bag and handed it to Gerald. She sat back at the table and waited.

Gerald opened the bag. There was a picture frame inside. He

pulled it out. Inside the frame was the piece of paper that he'd left for her in his wallet, the side with the *audacious* bit on it. She'd taken colored pencils and traced over all the creases from where she'd crumpled the paper up; then she'd colored the sections all different colors. It looked like the dry, cracked ground in the desert would look if someone attacked it with a paintbrush. The word *audacious* was traced in brilliant red. The colors were amplified behind the glass of the frame. Gerald turned it between his fingers.

"You like it?" Audi said.

"I love it," Gerald said. He propped it up on the table in front of him.

"You promise?"

"I love it." He looked at her. She was blushing, her face turned away from him. "I didn't get you anything," he said. "I can get you something."

"You don't have to," she said. "You've done plenty."

They spent the entire day on the couch, watching the Christmas shows—Rudolph, Frosty, Island of Misfit Toys—until it got dark outside and the snow started to fall. Gerald went upstairs and got into bed. He closed his eyes.

He didn't know how long he had been asleep when Audi came in. He felt her as soon as she came into the room. Gerald watched her. She was wearing a T-shirt and panties. She tiptoed across the carpet to the side of the bed, then she pulled the covers back a bit and slid under them. She cuddled up close beside him, put one of her bare legs across his. Her legs felt smooth and soft. She pulled Gerald's arm up above his head and put her head on his chest, wrapped her arm across his stomach. Gerald felt her hair on his chin. He felt her eyelashes on his chest. His muscles tensed.

"You've been really sweet to me, Gerald," she said.

He let his arm drop slowly. He brought it around her and pulled her close to him. She wrapped her leg around him and squeezed back.

"I could fall in love with you," she said.

"No, you can't," he whispered. He breathed in her hair; she smelled of honey and apples and skin. Then he kissed her on the top of her head. She looked up at him, her eyes dark points in the dark room. She inched forward and kissed him on the mouth, twice, feather soft. Then she laid her head back on his chest and fell asleep. Gerald stared at the ceiling and listened to her breathing.

He woke up and the sun was bright on her face. He shook her. She stirred and batted her eyes and looked at him.

"Hey," she said.

"Get up," he said. "I want to take you somewhere. Late Christmas present."

She rolled off him onto her back, bunched the covers up over her face. "I'm still sleepy," she said, her eyes peeking out above the bedspread.

"You want me to make you some breakfast?"

"Make me some more biscuits," she said. "Just do it quietly." She grinned at him, then she flopped over in the bed and covered her head with the pillow.

Gerald walked downstairs and looked in the refrigerator. He was out of milk. He put on his boots and his coat and his hat and walked outside. The air was crisp and stung his nostrils. The sun glinted off the icicles that hung from the eaves of his house.

He put his hands in his pockets and walked up the street to the market. The electric doors slid open and bathed him in warmth and fluorescence. He smiled at the cashier and walked to the back and took a carton of milk from the shelf. He turned it over in his hand, checked the expiration date. He looked at the back of the carton, where they put the announcements about missing children. Audi's picture was printed in smudged ink beneath the nutrition information.

Gerald stared at it. Her eyes looked back at him from the cold cardboard. Nikki Tyler, age sixteen, runaway, missing for a year. Height. Weight. Parents' number and address. Her parents live just forty-five minutes outside the city, less than an hour from Gerald's house.

He put the carton on the shelf and chose a different one, one with a picture of a little black boy on the back, and bought it and took it home.

Audi was on the couch watching *The Price Is Right*. "Took you long enough," she said. She had the blankets tented around her, just her head sticking out, her eyes intent on the TV. Her nose was small in profile, her lips thin and pink. She turned to him, smiled. "You miss me?"

Gerald shifted the milk from one hand to the other. "Terribly," he said.

He cooked the biscuits, and they ate some in front of the TV; then they packed a lunch and got in the car and headed north on the interstate. The roads were empty. The new snow was flat all around them, mostly smooth, but whipped by the wind in some places until it looked like peaked meringue. The sky was deep blue and far away. Audi pressed her nose against the window as they drove.

"Where are we going?" she said.

"*Ultima Thule,*" Gerald said.

"What?"

"End of the earth."

They pulled into a parking lot beside a huge frozen lake. Gerald got out of the car and opened the trunk and took out a blanket and their food. They set off toward the lake. Gerald stepped gently off the sand and onto the ice; it held firm.

"Careful," he said. He took Audi's hand in his. They walked across the ice, their footprints sitting deep in the powdery snow.

"It's like walking on the moon," she said, her hand tight in his, warm, her eyes scanning the blue horizon. Her feet were soft on the ice.

A hundred yards offshore, Gerald spread out the blanket and sat down. He handed Audi a sandwich. They ate and looked out over the lake. The ice was cracked and shattered not far from where they sat, and beyond that there were huge gaps with water in between them. Silvery blue and white floes were broken off and drifting beyond, spaced farther and farther out toward the blue horizon.

"I used to take my wife here," Gerald said. "She liked it. She said it was like the world was trying to stay together, but it was too much. The pull of whatever's outside the world was too much, and it made the earth just break apart and float away."

"That's very pretty," Audi said.

"She said when we were here, she felt like we were sitting on the very edge."

Audi nodded and chewed her sandwich. She took Gerald's hand

in hers and held it in her lap and squeezed it tight. The air was still and cold. Water birds cackled at the edge of the lake. The ice cracked and groaned.

"Audi," Gerald said, "what are you going to do?" He watched the birds as they pecked around in the snow. He felt Audi looking at him.

"What do you mean?" she said.

"I mean, with yourself?" He felt her put her other hand on his, closing his rough hand in her fists. "Don't you miss your parents?"

"They were mean to me, Gerald."

"Were they really? Is that why you left?"

She squeezed his hands. "I'm not going to lie to you," she said. They watched the ice float out over the deep water.

They headed home as the sun started to go down. The sky was cloudless and clean; the sun turned the horizon a bright yellow-orange as the light reflected off the snow and the ice. Audi leaned back in the passenger seat and shut her eyes.

"I'm stopping up here at this rest area," Gerald said.

Audi mumbled something, her voice heavy with sleep.

"You got to pee?"

She shook her head. Gerald pulled off the interstate and into a parking place at the rest area. He left the engine on, with the heater running. He used the restroom and came outside and stood in the cold, watching his breath form clouds in front of his face. In the parking lot a family rearranged the contents of their van.

Gerald shook his right leg, then his left. They felt stiff from the drive. He took some long steps around the rest area. He wandered over to the drink machines and bought a Coke. He opened it and took a sip and walked back to the kiosk with the map and the advertisements. He looked over the ads for car insurance and get-rich-quick jobs. In the top right corner were six pieces of paper with pictures of people on them, fliers advertising missing children, the rest-area equivalent of the back of a milk carton. Audi's was in the middle. He read her parents' address again, looked back at the car in the parking lot. The headlights were on and steam was easing out from under the hood. In the woods behind, the snow lay heavy on the limbs of the trees. The branches crackled with ice.

Audi slept in the passenger seat. Her mouth was open slightly and her right temple leaned against the window. She had her legs tucked into her chest and her arms pulled inside the sleeves of her shirt. Gerald turned the heater up and looked out the window. The dark in front of him grew brighter as the inky night slid past, and then the city rose up glowing and hard in front of them. He left the interstate and headed into the neighborhood.

Gerald drove slowly, scanning the dark houses for the address. The houses were small and weathered; the streets were lined with ghostly bare trees. The wind picked up outside and tossed snowflakes off the ground and into the air. It ripped and whistled around the car. Audi woke up. She yawned and scratched her nose, looking around. She stared out the window.

"What are we doing here?" she said.

Gerald didn't say anything. He turned the brights on to see through the swirling snow.

"Gerald. Where are we going?" Audi was glaring at him, her eyes piercing neat holes in the side of his head.

"I'm taking you home," Gerald said.

"I don't live around here."

"I'm taking you back to your parents, Nikki."

Audi sat up straight in the chair. "You son of a bitch," she said. "You knew? How long have you known?"

"Only a little while —"

"Have you been planning this? Is this your trick? Your trick to get me back to my parents?" She climbed onto her knees in the seat, one hand on the dashboard, the other on the headrest, and put her face close to Gerald's, yelling at him. "They rewarding you or something? Are you some sort of bounty hunter?"

"I only found out today," Gerald said. He stopped at a stop sign and looked at her. "I just found out."

"I don't want to go back. I told you they were mean to me."

"I know."

"They were awful! They never let me do anything. They wouldn't let me see my boyfriend. They locked me in my room. They locked me up, Gerald!" She was raving, her breath hot on Gerald's ear. "They were so mean. I told you they were mean."

Gerald sighed. "I know, Audi, but you've told me a lot of stuff."

"You son of a bitch."

"I just want to do what's best for you," he said. He started to pull forward.

"Stop the car," Audi said.

"What —"

"Stop the car!" She yelled it right in his ear. Gerald stopped and Audi sat back down in the seat. She looked out the windshield. The wind rocked the car and the snow made wispy patterns in the dark air. "Who the hell are you to say what's best for me?" she said.

Gerald sat quietly for a moment. The engine vibrated; snow melted on the hood. The air from the heater felt fusty and warm on his face. "I don't know. I don't know."

She didn't look at him. She stared down at her shoes. After a while she said, "You don't want to keep me?"

She was so small in the chair. She had her knees pulled into her shirt again.

"You know I can't, Nikki," Gerald said.

She turned to him. Her eyes were wet pieces of coal. "Stop calling me that," she said. She opened the door and the cold swirled through the car. She got out and zipped her jacket tight around her and slammed the door behind her. She walked up the street.

Gerald reached across the center console and struggled to roll the window down. "Nikki," he yelled after her. "Nikki, hang on. Audi! Audi." He checked the intersection and put the car in gear and swung around the corner after her. She was hurrying along the edge of the street, her feet tromping through the matted snow along the gutter. Her head tucked tight between her shoulders, hands deep in her pockets.

Gerald slowed beside her. "Audi, come on," he said.

She walked faster. The wind was high and the snow blew like a white sandstorm through the darkness. Street lamps lined the road, casting cold yellow pools of light on the asphalt. Audi walked through one; Gerald saw the snow stuck in her dark hair. She looked up at him, her eyes black, so black and cold. She began to run, cutting across a lawn, ducking between two houses.

Gerald got out of the car. The wind hit him and blew his coat open, blasting his chest, the cold stealing his breath. He ran a few steps. His legs were stiff from the drive, stiff from the cold, stiff from seventy-four years of life. Audi was just visible at the dark edge of an anonymous backyard. Gerald called out to her again. He stepped out of the light of the street lamp and into the hard winter dirt in front of the house. He stumbled, put his hand out to catch himself. His old heart pounded in the cage in his chest. When he looked up again, Audi was gone, disappeared into the dark, into the wind and the cold.

When Gerald got home, the house was empty and quiet. Upstairs Dolores's clothes, the ones that Audi had worn, were scattered across the floor. The bed was unmade. He left it all there. In the kitchen the remains of the biscuits sat in the sink. His Christmas present, Audi's artwork, *audacious,* lay on the kitchen table. He picked it up and carried it into the living room and propped it on the TV.

He looked at his gift. The colors were still vibrant and glowing beneath the glass. The lines were fine but dark where Audi had traced. He pictured her small fingers, spending hours meticulously following the paths already set into the paper. Her lines followed those paths, the ones that split out in a thousand directions, one way leading to three more, each of those three leading to three new ones, on and on, the paths circling each other and spreading out and falling together again, a patchwork of possibilities spread across the once-blank field of the paper.

He had thought of the other possibilities, of course, all the other paths. The other lives that he might have lived had always hidden somewhere in his subconscious, specters of other Geralds in other worlds where things were not the same. Worlds where he did other jobs, lived in other cities, married other women. Worlds where Dolores wasn't dead, worlds where he'd never even met her. All the different paths, and now these new ones: he catches Audi out there in the snowy night, before she disappears into shadow, and she sobs into his chest, and they get back into the car. They go on living together, but for how long and for what purpose and under what pretense, he doesn't know. Or maybe he adopts her, but that one could never be. Her parents would keep looking for her. They'd never allow it.

And the last one, the one he felt in his stomach and pushed aside with his brain. Her leg wrapped so tightly around his. Her lashes on his chest. *No,* he thought, shaking his head. *No.*

All those different paths, traced so carefully with delicate fingers.

The wind had died down, and the snow was falling again. He wrapped himself up in a blanket and sat down on the couch and closed his eyes. The heater clicked on. Gerald listened to its ticks and pings and rumbles as the heat moved through the empty rooms.

ERIC BARNES

Something Pretty, Something Beautiful

FROM *Prairie Schooner*

WE DIDN'T START breaking into houses to steal things. The four of us started breaking into houses simply to see what would happen.

By the time we were eighteen, we were still doing it because none of us had found any reason to stop.

"Now," Will Wilson whispers, waving me forward, then silently pushing me over the high windowsill of another house we've broken into in Tacoma.

When we were little kids, like eight or nine years old, my friend Teddy and I would walk home from Sherman Elementary together collecting bottle caps and Popsicle sticks and cigarette butts. We searched the grass and the sidewalks, under bus stop benches and around paper boxes, keeping what we found in secret pockets we made in the lining of our jackets. Teddy and I would walk home in the rain, racing the cigarette butts and Popsicle sticks along the narrow streams of water in the gutters; then days or weeks later, when it was dry, we searched for the butts and sticks in the stiff, matted mess around the sewer drains.

Teddy and I were best friends.

On rainy days back at Sherman, Teddy and I built dams during recess in the dirt near the long-jump pit. The rainwater ran through the pit in a shallow, foot-wide stream as it flowed along the far side of the schoolyard toward a big iron drain. Other kids came out to make dams too, but Teddy and me were always the first there, building the main dam, a tapering arc six inches high and five feet across, leaving the other kids to make small dams and beg us to release some water.

I remember being out there in my corduroys and nylon coat, wet like everyone else. None of us wearing raincoats. It's as if it rained so much no one bothered to fight it. Except Teddy. Teddy always wore one of those bright yellow slickers, curls of black hair bursting from beneath the yellow hood. Scraping more dirt toward the dam with his yellow rubber boots.

And as recess went on and our dam got to be seven and eight inches high at the front, now ten feet around, the kids below would always start their really loud yelling, wanting us to break our dam, to let the water rush down and wreck theirs. But Teddy and me always held out, even when one of the kids tried to kick a hole in our dam—one of the hyperactive kids, usually, the ones that every day had to go to the nurse's office to take their medication. The ones like Michael Coe, who we weren't friends with then and didn't ever want to have to talk to.

I had to push Coe away once, after he tried to kick at our dam. He was a low, heavy kid with a buzz cut and tight T-shirt. I knocked him into a small mud puddle, and he went into this frenzy, whipping himself in circles and screaming and his face turning red. Coe told on me, and the teacher made us put our desks together for a week, and that, we always said, is how we became friends. Although, really, that is how Coe started following Teddy and me to my house after school, showing up uninvited when me and my babysitter and Teddy were playing Wiffle bat baseball or eating bologna sandwiches. How, after a while, Coe started bringing his new friend Will Wilson over to my house.

But on those rainy days in the dirt, when the bell to end recess would finally ring, on those days Teddy would only then begin to smile, carefully moving to the very front of our big dam, the other kids now yelling happily and jumping up and down and Coe and the hyperactive ones turning in fast circles, flailing their bodies onto the hard, wet ground, the teachers a hundred yards away, screaming at us from the dry doorways, and Teddy with the tip of his round, brightly booted yellow foot, he'd make just a nick in the dirt of our dam and the water would begin to trickle out.

And Coe and the other hyper ones would be breaking their thin little dams even before the water had reached them, the water flowing faster through the now bigger break in ours, Teddy pacing back and forth, staring and watching and smiling.

And sometimes I thought I wanted to smash the wall of our dam, jump on it with my wet sneakers and let the water rush down. But I never did that to Teddy.

And I remember now a day when I looked past the kids around us, seeing some new kid leaning against the high chainlink fence, watching us all and smiling too. Smiling like Teddy was. Smiling like he understood something more. Although now, when I think of him, I think of Will Wilson in that first moment, and he had a lean face, older, eighteen, not eight.

Will Wilson did look young then, I know. He'd been just a child. But I can't remember that so well.

But I remember standing next to Teddy, so satisfied with him. Teddy, my best friend, dry beneath his coat, me wet and warm in the rain, both of us watching our dam in the schoolyard, smiling as it went through its slow self-destruction.

Old Town was the wealthiest area of Tacoma, an area that we some-times drove through just to look at, to see it. And as I cross that sill into the darkness of this house in Old Town, I see the black shapes of unseen furniture, gray light from a window. Touch my feet to a wood floor, then carpet, feel around me the full and spreading silence, and even then I can't explain it, can only sense it and want it, but from that moment, like the first moment we ever entered a house, the break-in is about the violation itself, the entering of a space that isn't ours, that is protected not by guns or bars or even locks but by an assumption of safety. An as-sumption that we—with one easy motion—have taken hold of and de-stroyed.

And like most every time before, I now turn to Will Wilson, standing with him in the shadows of a wall, the two of us smiling as we think of the owners and their children upstairs asleep. Oblivious to it all.

When we were seventeen and eighteen, we'd wake up at Will Wilson's house. It was a house on an empty road between two neighborhoods, some unplanned midpoint between subdivisions. It was like a lot of places I remember in Tacoma, one of those for-gotten roads lined by high fences and tall, overgrown bushes and lit just barely by intermittent streetlights. Sometimes there'd be a store, a corner store with faded advertisements for cigarette deals and inexpensive beer, and in a few places there'd be duplexes or

old storefronts, doors that faced these forgotten roads, dark doorways that looked abandoned until you looked close and you saw
something, mail in the mailbox or the flickering blue light of a TV
behind a curtain or a tricycle pressed against the side of the building, and you realized that someone was home.

It was always damp in Will Wilson's house and it smelled bad,
and you'd wake up on the thin hard carpet feeling sick and like
you'd never slept at all. His stepdad was always teaching himself
to play the guitar, this bright pink guitar he'd bought at a pawn
shop and that he'd rigged up to run through the old console stereo
that filled one wall of the living room, which was one of only a few
rooms in that whole house, so a lot of the time I'd end up sleeping against that hard wooden stereo with the tan cloth over the
speakers. I'd wake up hearing the feedback still ringing quietly
from the speakers, my face against the floor and having to pee,
feeling cold and wet in my jacket, wet maybe from the night before
out in the rain or just wet from the air in the house, with the curtains pulled shut and the floor and couch almost damp when you
touched them. I'd wake up in the silence, turning over and staring
up at that gray ceiling sprayed rough with texture and mixed with
the thousand glimmering bits of pink and green and gold, lying
there feeling so gray through my body, hurting, and wanting to
throw up, and staring up at that ceiling and now hearing the buzz
from the speakers next to me and hearing the others sleeping in
the room and remembering all that beer we'd drunk and the half
gallon of gin and the dope his cousin's friend had had, because
you couldn't not remember it, every drink and all that smoke now
so deep in every part of your body, turned sick now and dying,
and for me staring at that ceiling glimmering pink and green, I
could remember every drink and every breath of smoke and would
feel it still, wondering now if I was really sick or just stoned or
drunk, all of it turning bad through the end of the night, that
fight in your mind that you'd forgotten in the drinking and smoking and that had finally just sunk you, so you'd only known to
drink more, drinking through the smoking hoping another drink
would make you feel like you had when you'd started, that soft,
warm moment of the first hit of the pot and the first sip of the
first drink. But now it was lost, everything awful, and worn, and
gone. And I'd sit up finally, among my sleeping friends, finding

Will Wilson sitting up, on the couch, sipping a beer, staring at me, gray eyes in a leathered face, nodding at me like he'd never gone to sleep.

Bad things had happened. I'd feel my hand then and know we'd gone out and fought. Know we'd driven to each corner of Tacoma. I'd close my eyes and see dark figures tearing at each other, hidden faces in the black backyards of the houses we'd passed, faces turning gray as they ran in groups through the pale white light of empty parking lots.

And I'd blink my eyes and know there'd been a dream I'd just woken up from, that I couldn't quite remember, a dream of the hidden faces in groups, in backyards, roaming.

Bad things had happened. We'd started here and ended up here, on this floor, in the quiet of this small, forgotten, almost unidentifiable home.

"What happened?" I'd ask Will Wilson then, my mouth hurting just to speak.

And he'd sip beer. "Fuck you," he'd say, swallowing. "You know. You know what happened."

"Hung over," I'd say, and close my eyes, touch them lightly with one hand, then another, pain shooting through my eyes to the top of my head, my neck, the front of my chest.

"Fuck you," he'd say. "You were right there."

And I'd still have my eyes in my hand, pressing just that bit harder, the pain going white, with the other hand finding a Valium in the pocket of my jeans, slipping it across my lips, biting it once before swallowing it down.

And I'd be nodding now. Saying, "Right," realizing my face was damp too, like the carpet and my jacket and the insides of my jeans, and I'd know that I was damp from this house we were in and from the rain we'd run through and from the sweat of all that we'd done. "Yes," I'd say. "Yes, you're right."

Coe's low, heavy body is moving so gracefully in the dark, silently bouncing on couches, stretching out easily on carpets, walking quietly across dining room tables. He is trying to circle the room without stepping on the floor, hiking up his badly fitting jeans as he noiselessly leaps from a piano bench to a radiator to a TV on a rolling stand that he uses to pull himself three feet before the cord goes tight. And only when he seems on the verge of thrashing

*about and finally making noise does Will Wilson step in front of him and
grab his face at the jaw, shake it: No.*

Often the four of us don't speak at all. We just move our lips or point.

The guy was still smiling as I broke his first finger. My hand already
holding his thick, wet hair, pulling his head back and another finger back, and I was pulling him to the ground, the side of his head
smacking loud against the sidewalk, the second finger breaking
easily in my hand.

When I was a child, one night I watched my dad lean over the
kitchen sink, washing blood from his swollen face as I stood near
my babysitter. *There's nothing you can't do in a fight, Brian,* he said to
me quietly, his voice slowed and heavy. Long hair in his blue eyes.
Pushing his fingers along the thin lines leading to his lips. Twenty-
two years old. Maybe twenty-three. *You just want to win, Brian. You
just want to hurt him.*

I was hitting this guy in the face now, striking his nose, his eye,
his cheek. We were in front of a mini-market near school, and it
was raining, hard, after school and this guy, eighteen, he'd pushed
Teddy hard into a door, being cool in front of his friends, this guy
from school who'd tried to push Teddy around a few times that
week, and today I'd told him to fuck off, and he'd turned to me,
smiling, leaning close and pointing his finger in my face, smiling
down at me, a foot or more taller.

"Fucker," I said quietly, feeling the light rain against my lips as I
spoke. Breathing steadily, finding a rhythm between my words and
motions. Feeling all that anger, feeling it run through my chest
and arms and hands.

And I turned slightly as I swung, seeing Teddy standing near the
window of the store. Watching.

And the guy's friends, they hadn't moved.

Will Wilson had shown up. Standing near Teddy. Not smiling,
just watching. He carefully sat down. Cross-legged on the wet sidewalk. Watching.

The guy rolled away from me, standing and turning and trying
to find me, his right eye covered with blood and the left side of
his face bleeding too, his twisted hand wiping at his good eye, and
when he saw me he came at me. Not wildly. Moving forward, saying, "No," and breathing hard. Swinging straight and almost hitting me again. "No."

I hit him in the throat and he leaned over. I moved to my left. Watching him gag. I kicked him in the chest.

"Don't ever," I said. Spitting blood from my lips. Tasting blood in my throat. "Don't ever fuck with my friend."

Teddy had stepped forward. Standing on the curb, a few feet away. Watching.

The guy's nose poured red and yellow. He sat up. I knocked him onto his back.

My hands were wet with spit and blood and rain.

I was tired. I was mad.

The guy looked toward his friends, three of them standing on the sidewalk. He stared at them for a moment but didn't ask for help. Didn't expect them to do anything.

I hit him in the ear. His face hit the street. He was laid out on his side. In a moment, he asked dully, "Why won't you stop?"

I was tired. I was mad. I didn't know why exactly.

Will Wilson stood up now. I turned to look at him, and behind him, in the window of the store, I could see my reflection. Hair so wet in the rain. Hair that hung straight past my eyes.

Will Wilson was standing. It was time to go.

The guy was screaming, blood and spit spraying across the street.

I walked to the curb and kneeled at a puddle, rinsing my hands in the cool rainwater. Two fingers on my right hand were numb and bent. I turned my face to the sky, let the rain run down my eyes and neck. Wiped the water away before again rinsing my hands in the puddle. Again wiping at my face before the three of us met up with Coe and we all walked home, fourteen, and none of us had a car.

Teddy is standing at a window. With his curly hair turned gray in the darkness, his soft and round face turned pale by a streetlight outside, Teddy looks like an aging man. Some old guy at his window. With nothing to do but stare. For a while I'd thought Teddy stood at the windows because he was watching for the police. But one time he tells me he is just seeing what this family looks at during the day.

Will Wilson is going through cabinets, drawers, seeming to count the forgotten records and books.

Coe is rolling, on his side, across the couch.

And years later, when I find myself thinking about the break-ins, I know that what I liked most was watching the three of them in a house that was

ours. I bounced soundlessly on chairs playing tag with Coe, stood next to
Teddy staring out at the night, searched through closets and drawers with
a smiling Will Wilson. But I now mostly remember watching through the
shadows, seeing my three best friends doing a careful and silent nighttime
dance.

Maybe because they're too small to park in or too far from the
house, but the garages behind a lot of the houses in Tacoma's
blocky, sprawling neighborhoods often stand unused, the swinging
door left open, the small panes of the windows broken by neighborhood kids. And beginning in the middle of our senior year, Will
Wilson, Coe, Teddy, and I had started burning these garages down.
At two or three in the morning, we'd sneak along a dark alley with
a can of gasoline, pouring it against the inside base of the wooden
walls, making a big pool in the center of the smooth, concrete slab.
Lighting the gas, the four of us throwing matches while watching
the alley and the surrounding houses, the garage igniting in front
of us like a huge gas oven, the walls burning with low flames, the
pool in the center burning with flames three feet high.

We'd burned nine by the end of May. Six days from graduation,
we burned another one. The next day, we made the newspaper,
a small article about what fire officials believed was a pattern of
arson. The police had been consulted. Officers on patrol in Tacoma's North End would be checking alleys.

We went out that night at two A.M. in our black sweatshirts and
gloves and ski masks and found a garage on Cheyenne Street only
ten blocks from the last garage we'd burned.

Will Wilson went to check if the house was dark.

"Shit," Teddy whispered to me in the dark. "Shit. This is serious.
They've got to be watching, Brian. Fuck, Brian, fuck. This is serious, Brian."

"Well," I whispered. "Fuck. Well."

Will Wilson came back, matches in his hand. There were paint
cans and a can of paint thinner in the garage. There was also a
lawn chair, an old croquet set and a cardboard box full of books.
We spread out the junk and books and some boards from the stairs,
then poured thinner and gas over it all.

Coe was bouncing on his heels, circling in place.

Will Wilson held a book of matches out to Teddy and me but

didn't look at us. We were all near the entrance, and Will Wilson lit a match and tossed it, then another, the gas catching. Teddy kept looking over his shoulder, glancing down the alley.

"Come on," Will Wilson said, still not looking at Teddy and me, just flicking matches across the floor, small blue fires now burning in four or five places.

And finally I took a match from Will Wilson. Lit it and threw it because Will Wilson wanted me to. But most of all I lit it because I wanted to be a part of this. I wanted to see what would happen.

Blue flames had spread across much of the floor. A small pool near the books ignited.

I lit and threw another match.

And Teddy was starting to go down the alley and Will Wilson turned quickly, grabbed him hard by the neck, pulling Teddy close to his face. "Come on," he said quietly and held up a lit match for Teddy.

The books were burning orange and red, the wood catching now. The plastic seat of the lawn chair burning bright, shining on Will Wilson's face and Teddy's face and sending a foul smell through the garage.

"Come on," Will Wilson said, and then smiled and took a high voice. Whining, *"This is serious."*

And Teddy did light a match and did throw it then, lighting another and another, tossing each into the already hot fire, the tiny match flames disappearing in the gold and growing light, but Teddy just stared at Will Wilson, not scared, not weak, just staring, Will Wilson holding him by the neck and not once looking at the fire behind him, whining over and over, *"This is serious. This is serious."*

And then a white police cruiser turned down the alley and hit its lights.

And Teddy's pool of gas was burning yellow, blue, and white.

We ran. Through alleys, across yards, over fences, and through hedges. Ducking behind houses, running along streets, trying to make our way toward a huge, wooded park where we could hide.

Fifteen minutes later, with two cops on foot behind us, the sirens of three cruisers screaming near us, Will Wilson and I were sprinting toward the park, Teddy and Coe probably already in there, the

two of us crossing a brightly lit street, aiming for the low white wall
that bordered the park, the park here sweeping in an arc a half-
mile around, sloping a few hundred yards deep like a quilt of thick
green trees and bushes, stretching three quarters of a mile uninterrupted to the waterfront. And as I ran across that pavement with
a cop car skidding to a stop near me, both doors opening, two
more men jumping out, I saw the glow of lights from the unseen
mills and oil plants five miles away where right then my dad was
working.

And I do remember wondering if the police would shoot an ar-
sonist.

Will Wilson and I hit the low fence, stepping off, jumping, floating for that moment, silently flying into the park. We hit trees,
then bushes, finally sliding across the wet, steep ground. We were a
hundred feet down before I looked back. Another hundred and
we stopped sliding, seeing the pinpoint of searchlights waving back
and forth above us.

It only took twenty minutes to find the base of the Proctor
Bridge, where Teddy and Coe were waiting.

We climbed up the dirt hillside, the bridge's heavy concrete sup-
ports stretching out over our heads, hearing all around us the low,
numbing sound of the rain against the leaves. We reached the wide
dirt ledge just below the surface of the bridge, the four of us sharing from a bottle of vodka that we had hidden there.

"God," Will Wilson said, "God." He somehow seemed so thin in
the dark. A bare, hard person drinking next to me. "They were
chasing us. Everywhere we went they were chasing us. And it was
beautiful."

The four of us never called anything beautiful.

He told Teddy and Coe how the two of us split off from them,
crossing through yards and over fences, and he was drinking and
saying *beautiful,* and finally he sat down in the dirt and I realized
Will Wilson was drunk.

And I watched him and I remembered how, when we were running, he'd split off from Coe and Teddy, touched my arm, pulled
me with him. Taking the two of us down an alley he knew, toward a
street we'd been on a hundred times.

A brightly lit street that led away from the park. Where the three
police cars had been waiting.

Will Wilson hadn't made a mistake. He'd just tried to draw out the chase. To make it more dangerous for me and him.

Will Wilson was getting bored.

I watched him now. Even in the shadows under that bridge, I could see his eyes staring out behind half-closed lids. His usually hard face gone somehow soft. I don't think I'd ever seen him drunk. I'd seen him drink twice as much, but I'd never seen him drunk.

"It's coming to an end," he said slowly. "We'll get jobs. And sooner than you think, it'll all come to an end."

We hear the steps upstairs and my legs go blurry, then numb. I'm pulling in air as slowly as I can, turning left, seeing the door I can run through if the voice comes any closer.

"Colleen?" the voice says. "Colleen?"

Coe is crouched low on the floor. Teddy stands at the door. Will Wilson stands at the foot of the stairs.

But then it is quiet, a door upstairs closing. And I look at Will Wilson and he is smiling.

"Almost," he whispers. And he smiles even more.

Teddy and Coe are already starting to climb out the window, Will Wilson next. And as I turn to lower myself over the sill, I think about Will Wilson standing at the foot of those steps, Will Wilson like always starting to think of another way, another step, another thing we can do to find something more. And as I drop to the ground I glance back in the house and I see a woman sitting in the dark kitchen off the wide living room, her eyes barely white in the darkness of the house, staring at me as I still hold on to the frame, having watched the four of us wander through her first floor. Not saying a word, Colleen just a silhouette in a far corner chair.

Teddy had come by to pick me up. He wanted to go for a drive. The two of us used to go for drives a few times a week. We were thirteen and neither of us had a license, Teddy using his cousin's Volkswagen Bug as just me and him went driving around Tacoma.

As we'd turned fourteen, though, I was less interested in driving with Teddy, wanting instead to go by Will Wilson's house, wanting to see what he had going on. And Teddy always agreed.

We were eighteen now, and it was a few days before we all were going to graduate, then leave for summer jobs in Alaska.

We drove in Teddy's white Dodge Dart, the June night air swirling cool around us in the car.

And Teddy then quietly told me he was thinking about going to college when we got back from Alaska. Trying to get into Washington State University, in eastern Washington, three hundred miles away.

And as he told me this I nodded and was quiet.

We were crossing along the waterfront at low tide, the wet and salty, heavy bay smell pouring through the windows. And the silence, not speaking, it was a kind of answer. Teddy, who'd never thought school was important, needed my encouragement to go to college. Teddy, who seemed bound to Tacoma and Will Wilson as deeply as me, needed my support to leave. Even to Seattle. Especially to eastern Washington. Teddy was trying to make a break. But that night I gave him nothing.

Teddy and I drove up McCarver Hill toward our small houses above Old Town, silently driving past the steplike rows of nice homes, the reflection of the yellow streetlights glowing on the hood, the reflection of a house window sometimes even shining on our windshield. McCarver Hill, which we'd ridden up on our bikes when we were ten years old, back then talking about being little kids, saying, do you remember that bush on that corner where we found that whole box of Popsicle sticks? Do you remember the day we skipped school and walked through that alley and then that alley to cross just an edge of the gulch, going to the waterfront with the sand and the rock crabs? Saying, do you remember the lady who lived in that house, who gave everyone the cocoa on snowy days? Do you remember that kid in the window of that house, how he'd smoke pot and stare, just stare out his window for hours, how he was there at the start of that walk and when we got back? Do you remember racing sticks down this hill in the rain, this very spot on this very block, me and you chasing boats, right here, right there, eight years old and passing through this place, me and you in a race at one hundred and twenty-five miles an hour?

But that night on McCarver Hill, I just stared at the road. And, still, said nothing to Teddy.

The car stopped in front of my house. The engine still running. I was about to open the door when Teddy said quietly, "Will Wilson was blowing up some old toaster this morning."

Teddy didn't talk for another moment. I held on to the door handle, thinking Teddy must have something more to say. Will Wilson was always blowing things up.

"And an old gas can," Teddy said quietly, "and this little black-and-white TV. Two M-8os each. He called me at six this morning. Said he was blowing stuff up. Told me to come over."

Teddy was leaning against his door, turned as if looking toward me but staring out the windshield toward my house. The light from the radio glowed above my knee.

"It's like I can't say no," Teddy said. "Going over there at six. I'd rather be in bed. But I can't say no."

I didn't say anything, just looked out the window. I could feel Teddy staring. Wanting me to agree.

"He was talking about break-ins and all," Teddy said, his voice loud now and awkward. "I don't know. It's like he's maybe pushing for something more. When we get back from Alaska."

I stared ahead, the intersection glowing pale yellow from a streetlight, the roads leading into it all lost in shadows. "Like what?" I asked.

"I don't know. He was just talking. All quiet like he gets. Taping M-8os to this toaster. He unscrewed the back of this TV. You should have seen that TV go."

"What was he saying, though?"

"Like, I don't know," Teddy said, turning the radio up slightly. "I love this song."

"Come on, Teddy," I said.

"Just more, you know? When we're in the house. Things he's thinking about for when we get back from Alaska. I don't know. He blew up an old wooden mailbox. It caught fire."

I sat in the car, staring at the shadows beyond the intersection. I knew Will Wilson was making decisions. Will Wilson was thinking, wishing.

Will Wilson was getting bored.

Teddy's face looked a little pained, talking now like he was answering a question. "More," he said, shrugging. "Just doing more. I'm not sure about it. Like, I don't know. He was saying stuff. While, like, he was blowing these things up. Six A.M."

I lowered my head. Saw my feet. "Come on, Teddy."

"Just saying," Teddy went on, but getting quiet now and his

voice evening out, not struggling. "When we're in the house. Doing more. I'm not sure about it, Brian. Like, I don't know, Brian. Like waking people up."

The four of us leave the houses almost completely undisturbed. Even Coe is always careful to return furniture to its place. I think the owners woke up in the morning and never knew anything had happened, maybe wondered weeks or months later, How long has that lampshade been crooked? Is this where I left my shoes?

Teddy had been wrong. Will Wilson didn't want to wake people up when we got back from Alaska. Will Wilson didn't want to wait even that long.

One night later, we were in a house in Old Town, the four of us standing against a wall in the living room, after hours of near silence under that bridge near the park, under there quietly drinking, and I was blurry now, and slowed and focused from all the drinking, watching the lights on the ceiling now, light from the bay that flickered up through the windows, white, white flashes in a room that was dim violet from a streetlight outside, and I think I knew it was different when I saw Will Wilson pull a bottle of bourbon from a liquor cabinet, take a drink, and we'd never drunk in a house, never stolen anything. Coe was smiling, drinking, and I was watching Will Wilson, in his gloves like we always wore, with a ski mask in his pocket this time, and passing the bourbon to me before he put the mask over his head.

"Let's just see what happens," Will Wilson said.

And I knew what would happen. Knew we would do anything. Knew we would not stop. I knew we had so lost ourselves to whatever was possible. And so I was watching Coe and Will Wilson move and I was drinking from the bourbon, and I looked around for Teddy. He was staring out a window. And for a moment I thought I'd stay with him. For a moment I thought I'd grab his arm, pull him with me, and we would run from here.

Because I knew I would do what Will Wilson wanted.

And because I knew I wanted it too.

I found Will Wilson and Coe on the second floor, already turning down a hall, at a door in their masks, Will Wilson turning the knob, and there would be chaos soon, and violence, and power and fear and anger, and I drank from the bourbon, still in my hand, drank again from the bourbon and heard the screaming.

Screaming downstairs. People screaming downstairs.

Will Wilson and Coe had gone in the room. But downstairs there were people screaming and alarms going off, and I looked back down the stairs, saw Teddy standing there now, looking up at me, and I was glad he was there, glad and I smiled, at Teddy, my friend, and I saw that a flame had sprung out from his hand, Teddy looking up at me, Teddy flicking matches toward the stairs, the steps going blue, then red, then gold.

He'd poured something on the stairs. He was lighting them on fire.

I could smell the smoke already, the flames climbing toward me, heat all across my body, Teddy disappearing from the foot of the steps, the downstairs turning gold, the smoke alarms screaming up at us, and I ran into the room with Will Wilson and Coe, could see out the window, see people outside, one last person running out of the first floor, and then I remembered someone should have been in this room. But there wasn't anyone except Will Wilson and Coe, which seemed strange, I thought, and I was drunk and confused and scared, but I couldn't help but think it, couldn't believe that Will Wilson had been wrong. There was supposed to be someone in here.

Smoke alarms were going off upstairs too now, all screaming together.

I turned to Will Wilson and Coe, standing in the dark, watching out the hall, Coe bouncing, and Will Wilson looking around now, out the window, toward the hall, saying something I couldn't hear in the noise of the alarms and the fire now spreading up the stairs.

"How do we get out?" Coe was saying, loudly, and he was bouncing up and down even harder.

Will Wilson turned to me, his eyes staring out of the mask. "Where the fuck is Ted?"

"I don't know," I was saying. "We have to get out," I was saying.

Will Wilson hit me, in the face, so hard and so fast, and I was on the floor and couldn't hear and couldn't see and couldn't breathe.

I could see him before I could hear anything, blurry and above me and his mouth moving and I'd never been hit so hard.

"Where the fuck is Ted?" Will Wilson was screaming.

I was talking, I thought, saying, "I don't know," but I couldn't hear my voice. Couldn't feel my mouth or lips.

"How do we get out?" Coe was yelling.

Will Wilson hit me again and it was white and black and gone and there was a smell then, I remember now, a smell of air and water and rain against my face. But in a moment I could see again and the smoke was in the room. The fire in the hall.

Will Wilson was gone.

"He left," Coe was saying, quietly or maybe I still couldn't hear. "Oh my god, he left."

The smoke was getting heavier. The flames had reached the hall. Coe was bouncing against the walls. "How do we get out?" he was saying. "How do we get out?"

I stood and felt the blood across my nose and mouth and my head spun and I threw up, fell down again. I crawled to the window and looked out. There were about five people in the street.

Coe was hitting the wall. Coe was spinning in place. "How?" he was screaming, "how?"

"We have to climb down," I tried to say, but I still couldn't hear my voice. "Okay, Coe? We climb and then we run."

Coe kept hitting the wall. I tried to stand but threw up again, my head spinning and my neck all sickly numb.

And then Coe started running. Through the smoke. Into the hall. Into the flames.

Trying to make it downstairs.

Maybe he was thinking he could make it to the door. Maybe he was afraid to climb. But probably he just wanted to find Will Wilson. To see how Will Wilson would finally make this work.

Once, in a house, I leave Will Wilson in a kitchen as he slowly makes his way through every drawer and cabinet, pass Coe in the dining room climbing across a fireplace mantel. I'm looking for Teddy and find him in the living room, a wide, tall room with windows open onto the bay and the bright ships and the lights of the neighborhoods all around us, and he is climbing up the windows, in bare feet with his toes just balanced on the thin frames of the windows, fifteen feet in the air now, and he is looking out of a skylight, his hands touching the panes of the glass, his face close to the frame.

"What are you doing?" I whisper, as loud I can.

I can see he is talking, but I can't hear him.

"What are you looking for?" I ask again.

He is talking, his fingers running along the edges of the skylight, his head turned upward, and I think I hear more the echo of his voice, coming back to me off that window, and I've never known if he knew I was there.

"Something pretty," Teddy whispers, "something beautiful."

I knew Coe would die. Like all of them. All of them would die.

I climbed out a window, dropping to a covered porch, then jumping to the ground. I turned to the now ten people in the street and they stared at me and I fell on the ground, dizzy still, vomiting again, and they hadn't moved.

But when they did, I stood and I ran. Down an alley, through yards, across parking lots, finally into the park, across it, finding my car on the other side.

I was already packed for Alaska. My clothes and tent and sleeping bag.

I was in Bellingham by dawn. I crossed the border into Canada on foot. Stole a car. Stole a truck. I rode three freight trains, riding blind first north, then east, then west again. I did not hitch a ride. Did not eat in restaurants. Did not sleep in any motels. I broke into grocery stores at night. And I'm sure no one ever knew I'd been there.

I rode the ferries as much as I could. Sometimes north, sometimes south. But I was on the Aleutians within two weeks.

Alaska is a very big place.

Within two years I was living in Arizona. Within three years I was out in New Hampshire. And that's a long way from Tacoma.

These things are not so hard to do.

Once, in a house, Coe almost breaks a dining room table, falling off of it onto Teddy, and when we get outside, six blocks away, walking quietly like we usually did, Teddy then turns on Coe, in one motion hitting him in the face, falling on him, hitting him still, and Will Wilson steps back and smiles, and I step back and watch, and Teddy is saying something to Coe as he hits him again, something about trying to be more careful, about not fucking up all the time, about thinking about what he was doing.

It was years before I managed to find an article about the fire. I drove to Tacoma just to read the stories. The only risk I ever took. Reading old newspapers in some cubicle in the bright light of a silent library.

Will Wilson had managed to live.

There were only two bodies in the house. Ted Selva. Michael Coe. Another kid had been seen climbing out of the house. When they identified the bodies a few days later, the police soon learned that the four kids ran as a group. That William Wilson and Brian Porter were gone.

Two cars from Tacoma were soon found near the Canadian border. There were stolen cars found farther north into Canada.

Both kids, the police said, had probably gone into Alaska.

And sitting there in the library, I was leaning back now, looking around, expecting to see Will Wilson in a cubicle near mine. Reading about the four of us. Leaning back in his chair too, looking around for me.

Michael Coe had died in the smoke, was found lying at the foot of the stairs.

Ted Selva appeared to have been beaten badly before he died. Four fingers snapped. A few ribs fractured. His chin and eye socket broken.

There was no manhunt. No detectives who ventured north. "Pretty soon," a policeman said, "they'll show up back here in Tacoma. Bragging about what they've done. Looking for a warm bed. They're half scared out of their minds right now, alone up in the woods somewhere. They'll come back home."

Will Wilson is out there. Living some life.

And driving through Tacoma after I left the library that day, I thought about how, when I got in my car after the fire, my backpack next to me, my money in my pocket, how even then I knew I wasn't just running from the police. I was running from Will Wilson, Coe, and Teddy. They were dead, I thought. But it didn't matter. I knew I had to run. Running from my three friends and the life we'd had, a life I would not have been able to end.

And now I'd spent five years forgetting.

But Will Wilson is still out there.

He could find me, I suppose.

Or maybe I could try to go find him.

LAWRENCE BLOCK

Clean Slate

FROM *Warriors*

THERE WAS A STARBUCKS just across the street from the building where he had his office, and she settled in at a window table a little before five. She thought she might be in for a long wait. In New York, young associates at law firms typically worked until midnight and took lunch and dinner at their desks. Was it the same in Toledo?

Well, the cappuccino was the same. She sipped hers, making it last, and was about to go to the counter for another when she saw him.

But was it him? He was tall and slender, wearing a dark suit and a tie, clutching a briefcase, walking with purpose. His hair when she'd known him was long and shaggy, a match for the jeans and T-shirt that were his usual costume, and now it was cut to match the suit and the briefcase. And he wore glasses now, and they gave him a serious, studious look. He hadn't worn them then, and he'd certainly never looked studious.

But it was Douglas. No question, it was him.

She rose from her chair, hit the door, quickened her pace to catch up with him at the corner. She said, "Doug? Douglas Pratter?"

He turned, and she caught the puzzlement in his eyes. She helped him out. "It's Kit," she said. "Katherine Tolliver." She smiled softly. "A voice from the past. Well, a whole person from the past, actually."

"My God," he said. "It's really you."

"I was having a cup of coffee," she said, "and looking out the window and wishing I knew somebody in this town, and when I saw you I thought you were a mirage. Or that you were just somebody who looked the way Doug Pratter might look eight years later."

"Is that how long it's been?"

"Just about. I was fifteen and I'm twenty-three now. You were two years older."

"Still am. That much hasn't changed."

"And your family picked up and moved right in the middle of your junior year of high school."

"My dad got a job he couldn't say no to. He was going to send for us at the end of the term, but my mother wouldn't hear of it. We'd all be too lonely is what she said. It took me years before I realized she just didn't trust him on his own."

"Was he not to be trusted?"

"I don't know about that, but the marriage failed two years later anyway. He went a little nuts and wound up in California. He got it in his head that he wanted to be a surfer."

"Seriously? Well, good for him, I guess."

"Not all that good for him. He drowned."

"I'm sorry."

"Who knows? Maybe that's what he wanted, whether he knew it or not. Mom's still alive and well."

"In Toledo?"

"Bowling Green."

"*That's* it. I knew you'd moved to Ohio, and I couldn't remember the city, and I didn't think it was Toledo. Bowling Green."

"I've always thought of it as a color. Lime green, forest green, and bowling green."

"Same old Doug."

"You think? I wear a suit and go to an office. Christ, I wear glasses."

"And a wedding ring." And before he could tell her about his wife and kiddies and adorable suburban house, she said, "But you've got to get home, and I've got plans of my own. I want to catch up, though. Have you got any time tomorrow?"

It's Kit. Katherine Tolliver.

Just saying her name had taken her back in time. She hadn't been Kit or Katherine or Tolliver in years. Names were like clothes;

she'd put them on and wear them for a while and then let them go. The analogy went only so far, because you could wash clothes when you'd soiled them, but there was no dry cleaner for a name that had outlived its usefulness.

Katherine "Kit" Tolliver. That wasn't the name on the ID she was carrying, or the one she'd signed on the motel register. Once she'd identified herself to Doug Pratter, she'd become the person she'd proclaimed herself to be. She was Kit again — and, at the same time, she wasn't.

Interesting, the whole business.

Back in her motel room, she surfed her way around the TV channels, then switched off the set and took a shower. Afterward she spent a few minutes studying her nude body and wondering how it would look to him. She was a little fuller in the breasts than she'd been eight years before, a little rounder in the butt, a little closer to ripeness overall. She had always been confident of her attractiveness, but she couldn't help wondering what she might look like to those eyes that had seen her years ago.

Of course, he hadn't needed glasses back in the day.

She had read somewhere that a man who has once had a particular woman somehow assumes he can have her again. She didn't know how true this might be, but it seemed to her that something similar applied to women. A woman who had once been with a particular man was ordained to doubt her ability to attract him a second time. And so she felt a little of that uncertainty, but willed herself to dismiss it.

He was married, and might well be in love with his wife. He was busy establishing himself in his profession, and settling into an orderly existence. Why would he want a meaningless fling with an old girlfriend, who'd had to say her name before he could even place her?

She smiled. *Lunch*, he'd said. *We'll have lunch tomorrow.*

Funny how it started.

She was at a table with six or seven others, a mix of men and women in their twenties. And one of the men mentioned a woman she didn't know, though she seemed to be known to most if not all of the others. And one of the women said, "That slut."

And the next thing she knew, the putative slut was forgotten

while the whole table turned to the question of just what consti-
tuted sluttiness. Was it a matter of attitude? Of specific behavior?
Was one born to slutdom, or was the status acquired?

Was it solely a female province? Could you have male sluts?

That got nipped in the bud. "A man can take sex too casually,"
one of the men asserted, "and he can consequently be an asshole,
and deserving of a certain measure of contempt. But as far as I'm
concerned, the word *slut* is gender-linked. Nobody with a Y chro-
mosome can qualify as a genuine slut."

And, finally, was there a numerical cutoff? Could an equation be
drawn up? Did a certain number of partners within a certain number of years make one a slut?

"Suppose," one woman suggested, "suppose once a month you
go out after work and have a couple—"

"A couple of men?"

"A couple of drinks, you idiot, and you start flirting, and
one things leads to another, and you drag somebody home with
you."

"Once a month?"

"It could happen."

"So that's twelve men in a year."

"When you put it that way," the woman allowed, "it seems like a
lot."

"It's also a hundred and twenty partners in ten years."

"Except you wouldn't keep it up for that long, because sooner or
later one of those hookups would take."

"And you'd get married and live happily ever after?"

"Or at least live together more or less monogamously for a
year or two, which would cut down on the frequency of hookups,
wouldn't it?"

Throughout all of this, she barely said a word. Why bother? The
conversation buzzed along quite well without her, and she was free
to sit back and listen, and to wonder just what place she occupied
in what someone had already labeled "the saint–slut continuum."

"With cats," one of the men said, "it's nice and clear-cut."

"Cats can be sluts?"

He shook his head. "With women and cats. A woman has one
cat, or even two or three cats, she's an animal lover. Four or more
cats and she's a demented cat lady."

"That's how it works?"

"That's exactly how it works. With sluts, it looks to be more complicated."

Another thing that complicated it, someone said, was if the woman in question had a significant other, whether husband or boyfriend. If she didn't, and she hooked up half a dozen times a year, well, she certainly wasn't a slut. If she was married and still fit in that many hookups on the side, well, that changed things, didn't it?

"Let's get personal," one of the men said to one of the women. "How many partners have you had?"

"Me?"

"Well?"

"You mean in the past year?"

"Or lifetime. You decide."

"If I'm going to answer a question like that," she said, "I think we definitely need another round of drinks."

The drinks came, and the conversation slid into a game of truth, though it seemed to Jennifer—these people knew her as Jennifer, which had lately become her default name—it seemed to her that the actual veracity of the responses was moot.

And then it was her turn.

"Well, Jen? How many?"

Would she ever see any of these people again? Probably not. So it scarcely mattered what she said.

And what she said was, "Well, it depends. How do you decide what counts?"

"What do you mean? Like blowjobs don't count?"

"That's what Clinton said, remember?"

"As far as I'm concerned, blowjobs count."

"And hand jobs?"

"They don't count," one man said, and there seemed to be general agreement on that point. "Not that there's anything wrong with them," he added.

"So what's your criterion here, exactly? Something has to be inside of something?"

"As far as the nature of the act," one man said, "I think it has to be subjective. It counts if you think it counts. So, Jen? What's your count?"

"Suppose you passed out, and you know something happened, but you don't remember any of it?"

"Same answer. It counts if you think it counts."

The conversation kept going, but she was detached from it now, thinking, remembering, working it out in her mind. How many men, if gathered around a table or a campfire, could compare notes and tell each other about her? That, she thought, was the real criterion, not what part of her anatomy had been in contact with what portion of his. Who could tell stories? Who could bear witness?

And when the table quieted down again, she said, "Five."

"Five? That's all? Just five?"

"Five."

She had arranged to meet Douglas Pratter at noon in the lobby of a downtown hotel not far from his office. She arrived early and sat where she could watch the entrance. He was five minutes early himself, and she saw him stop to remove his glasses, polishing their lenses with a breast-pocket handkerchief. Then he put them on again and stood there, his eyes scanning the room.

She got to her feet, and now he caught sight of her, and she saw him smile. He'd always had a winning smile, optimistic and confident. Years ago, it had been one of the things she liked most about him.

She walked to meet him. Yesterday she'd been wearing a dark gray pantsuit; today she'd paired the jacket with a matching skirt. The effect was still business attire, but softer, more feminine. More accessible.

"I hope you don't mind a ride," he told her. "There are places we could walk to, but they're crowded and noisy and no place to have a conversation. Plus they rush you, and I don't want to be in a hurry. Unless you've got an early afternoon appointment?"

She shook her head. "I had a full morning," she said, "and there's a cocktail party this evening that I'm supposed to go to, but until then I'm free as the breeze."

"Then we can take our time. We've probably got a lot to talk about."

As they crossed the lobby, she took his arm.

The fellow's name was Lucas. She'd taken note of him early on, and his eyes had shown a certain degree of interest in her, but his interest mounted when she told the group how many sexual partners she'd had. It was he who'd said, "Five? That's all? Just five?" When she'd confirmed her count, his eyes grabbed hers and held on.

And now he'd taken her to another bar, a nice quiet place where they could really get to know each other. Just the two of them.

The lighting was soft, the décor soothing. A pianist played show tunes unobtrusively, and a waitress with an indeterminate accent took their order and brought their drinks. They touched glasses, sipped, and he said, "Five."

"That really did it for you," she said. "What, is it your lucky number?"

"Actually," he said, "my lucky number is six."

"I see."

"You were never married."

"No."

"Never lived with anybody."

"Only my parents."

"You don't still live with them?"

"No."

"You live alone?"

"I have a roommate."

"A woman, you mean."

"Right."

"Uh, the two of you aren't . . ."

"We have separate beds," she said, "in separate rooms, and we live separate lives."

"Right. Were you ever, uh, in a convent or anything?"

She gave him a look.

"Because you're remarkably attractive, you walk into a room and you light it up, and I can imagine the number of guys who must hit on you on a daily basis. And you're how old? Twenty-one, twenty-two?"

"Twenty-three."

"And you've only been with five guys? What, were you a late bloomer?"

"I wouldn't say so."

"I'm sorry, I'm pressing and I shouldn't. It's just that, well, I can't help being fascinated. But the last thing I want is to make you uncomfortable."

The conversation wasn't making her uncomfortable. It was merely boring her. Was there any reason to prolong it? Was there any reason not to cut to the chase?

She'd already slipped one foot out of its shoe, and now she raised it and rested it on his lap, massaging his groin with the ball of her foot. The expression on his face was worth the price of admission all by itself.

"My turn to ask questions," she said. "Do you live with your parents?"

"You're kidding, right? Of course not."

"Do you have a roommate?"

"Not since college, and that was a while ago."

"So," she said. "What are we waiting for?"

The restaurant Doug had chosen was on Detroit Avenue, just north of I-75. Walking across the parking lot, she noted a motel two doors down and another across the street.

Inside, it was dark and quiet, and the décor reminded her of the cocktail lounge where Lucas had taken her. She had a sudden memory of her foot in his lap, and the expression on his face. Further memories followed, but she let them glide on by. The present moment was a nice one, and she wanted to live in it while it was at hand.

She asked for a dry Rob Roy, and Doug hesitated, then ordered the same for himself. The cuisine on offer was Italian, and he started to order the scampi, then caught himself and selected a small steak instead. Scampi, she thought, was full of garlic, and he wanted to make sure he didn't have it on his breath.

The conversation started in the present, but she quickly steered it back to the past, where it properly belonged. "You always wanted to be a lawyer," she remembered.

"Right, I was going to be a criminal lawyer, a courtroom whiz. The defender of the innocent. So here I am doing corporate work, and if I ever see the inside of a courtroom, that means I've done something wrong."

"I guess it's hard to make a living with a criminal practice."

"You can do okay," he said, "but you spend your life with the scum of the earth, and you do everything you can to keep them from getting what they damn well deserve. Of course I didn't know any of that when I was seventeen and starry-eyed over *To Kill a Mockingbird*."

"You were my first boyfriend."

"You were my first real girlfriend."

She thought, Oh? And how many unreal ones were there? And what made her real by comparison? Because she'd slept with him?

Had he been a virgin the first time they had sex? She hadn't given the matter much thought at the time, and had been too intent upon her own role in the proceedings to be aware of his experience or lack thereof. It hadn't really mattered then, and she couldn't see that it mattered now.

And she'd just told him he'd been her first boyfriend. No need to qualify that; he'd truly been her first boyfriend, real or otherwise.

But she hadn't been a virgin. She'd crossed that barrier two years earlier, a month or so after her thirteenth birthday, and had had sex in one form or another perhaps a hundred times before she hooked up with Doug.

Not with a boyfriend, however. I mean, your father couldn't be your boyfriend, could he?

Lucas lived alone in a large L-shaped studio apartment on the top floor of a new building. "I'm the first tenant the place has ever had," he told her. "I've never lived in something brand-spanking-new before. It's like I've taken the apartment's virginity."

"Now you can take mine."

"Not quite. But this is better. Remember, I told you my lucky number."

"Six."

"There you go."

And just when, she wondered, had six become his lucky number? When she'd acknowledged five partners? Probably, but never mind. It was a good-enough line, and one he was no doubt feeling proud of right about now, because it had worked, hadn't it?

As if he'd had any chance of failing . . .

He made drinks, and they kissed, and she was pleased but not surprised to note that the requisite chemistry was there. And, keeping it company, there was that delicious surge of anticipatory excitement that was always present on such occasions. It was at once sexual and nonsexual, and she felt it even when the chemistry was not present, even when the sexual act was destined to be perfunctory at best, and at worst distasteful. Even then she'd feel that rush, that urgent excitement, but it was greatly increased when she knew the sex was going to be good.

He excused himself and went to the bathroom, and she opened her purse and found the little unlabeled vial she kept in the change compartment. She looked at it and at the drink he'd left on the table, but in the end she left the vial in her purse, left his drink untouched.

As it turned out, it wouldn't have mattered. When he emerged from the bathroom he reached not for his drink but for her instead, and it was as good as she'd known it would be, inventive and eager and passionate, and finally they fell away from each other, spent and sated.

"Wow," he said.

"That's the right word for it."

"You think? It's the best I can come up with, and yet it somehow seems inadequate. You're—"

"What?"

"Amazing. I have to say this, I can't help it. It's almost impossible to believe you've had so little experience."

"Because I'm clearly jaded?"

"No, just because you're so good at it. And in a way that's the complete opposite of jaded. I swear to God this is the last time I'll ask you, but were you telling the truth? Have you really only been with five men?"

She nodded.

"Well," he said, "now it's six, isn't it?"

"Your lucky number, right?"

"Luckier than ever," he said.

"Lucky for me too."

She was glad she hadn't put anything in his drink, because after a brief rest they made love again, and that wouldn't have happened otherwise.

"Still six," he told her afterward, "unless you figure I ought to get extra credit."

She said something, her voice soft and soothing, and he said something, and that went on until he stopped responding. She lay beside him, in that familiar but ever-new combination of afterglow and anticipation, and then finally she slipped out of bed, and a little while later she let herself out of his apartment.

All by herself in the descending elevator, she said out loud, "Five."

A second round of Rob Roys arrived before their entrées. Then the waiter brought her fish and his steak, along with a glass of red wine for him and white for her. She'd only had half of her second Rob Roy, and she barely touched her wine.

"So you're in New York," he said. "You went there straight from college?"

She brought him up to date, keeping the responses vague for fear of contradicting herself. The story she told was all fabrication; she'd never even been to college, and her job résumé was a spotty mélange of waitressing and office temp work. She didn't have a career, and she worked only when she had to.

If she needed money—and she didn't need much, she didn't live high—well, there were other ways to get it beside work.

But today she was Connie Corporate, with a job history to match her clothes, and yes, she'd gone to Penn State and then tacked on a Wharton MBA, and ever since she'd been in New York, and she couldn't really talk about what had brought her to Toledo, or even on whose behalf she was traveling, because it was all hush-hush for the time being, and she was sworn to secrecy.

"Not that there's a really big deal to be secretive about," she said, "but, you know, I try to do what they tell me."

"Like a good little soldier."

"Exactly," she said, and beamed across the table at him.

"You're my little soldier," her father had told her. "A trooper, a little warrior."

In the accounts she sometimes found herself reading, the father (or the stepfather, or the uncle, or the mother's boyfriend, or even the next-door neighbor) was a drunk and a brute, a bloody-minded

savage, forcing himself upon the child who was his helpless and un-
willing partner. She would get angry, reading those case histories.
She would hate the male responsible for the incest, would sympa-
thize with the young female victim, and her blood would surge in
her veins with the desire to even the score, to exact a cruel but just
vengeance. Her mind supplied scenarios—castration, mutilation,
disembowelment—all of them brutal and heartless, all richly deserved.

But her own experience was quite unlike what she read.

Some of her earliest memories were of sitting on her father's
lap, his hands touching her, patting her, petting her. Sometimes
he was with her at bath time, making sure she soaped and rinsed
herself thoroughly. Sometimes he tucked her in at night, and sat by
the side of the bed stroking her hair until she fell asleep.

Was his touch ever inappropriate? Looking back, she thought
that it probably was, but she'd never been aware of it at the time.
She knew that she loved her daddy and he loved her, and that
there was a bond between them that excluded her mother. But it
never consciously occurred to her that there was anything wrong
about it.

Then, when she was thirteen, when her body had begun to
change, there was a night when he came to her bed and slipped
beneath the covers. And he held her and touched her and kissed
her.

The holding and touching and kissing were different that night,
and she recognized it as such immediately, and somehow knew
that it would be a secret, that she could never tell anybody. And yet
no enormous barriers were crossed that night. He was very gentle
with her, always gentle, and his seduction of her was infinitely gradual. She had since read how the Plains Indians took wild horses
and domesticated them, not by breaking their spirit but by slowly,
slowly, winning them over, and the description resonated with her
immediately, because that was precisely how her father had turned
her from a child who sat so innocently on his lap into an eager and
spirited sexual partner.

He never broke her spirit. What he did was awaken it.

He came to her every night for months, and by the time he took
her virginity she had long since lost her innocence, because he had
schooled her quite thoroughly in the sexual arts. There was no

pain on the night he led her across the last divide. She had been well prepared, and was entirely ready.

Away from her bed, they were the same as they'd always been.

"Nothing can show," he'd explained. "No one would understand the way you and I love each other. So we must not let them know. If your mother knew—"

He hadn't needed to finish that sentence.

"Someday," he'd told her, "you and I will get in the car, and we'll drive to some city where no one knows us. We'll both be older then, and the difference in our ages won't be that remarkable, especially when we've tacked on a few years to you and shaved them off of me. And we'll live together, and we'll get married, and no one will be the wiser."

She tried to imagine that. Sometimes it seemed like something that could actually happen, something that would indeed come about in the course of time. And other times it seemed like a story an adult might tell a child, right up there with Santa Claus and the Tooth Fairy.

"But for now," he'd said more than once, "for now we have to be soldiers. You're my little soldier, aren't you? Aren't you?"

"I get to New York now and then," Doug Pratter said.

"I suppose you and your wife fly in," she said. "Stay at a nice hotel, see a couple of shows."

"She doesn't like to fly."

"Well, who does? What they make you go through these days, all in the name of security. And it just keeps getting worse, doesn't it? First they started giving you plastic utensils with your in-flight meal, because there's nothing as dangerous as a terrorist with a metal fork. Then they stopped giving you a meal altogether, so you couldn't complain about the plastic utensils."

"It's pretty bad, isn't it? But it's a short flight. I don't mind it that much. I just open up a book, and the next thing I know I'm in New York."

"By yourself."

"On business," he said. "Not that frequently, but every once in a while. Actually, I could get there more often, if I had a reason to go."

"Oh?"

"But lately I've been turning down chances," he said, his eyes avoiding hers now. "Because, see, when my business is done for the day I don't know what to do with myself. It would be different if I knew anybody there, but I don't."

"You know me," she said.

"That's right," he agreed, his eyes finding hers again. "That's right. I do, don't I?"

Over the years, she'd read a lot about incest. She didn't think her interest was compulsive, or morbidly obsessive, and in fact it seemed to her as if it would be more pathological if she were not interested in reading about it.

One case imprinted itself strongly upon her. A man had three daughters, and he had sexual relations with two of them. He was not the artful Daughter Whisperer that her own father had been, but a good deal closer to the Drunken Brute end of the spectrum. A widower, he told the two older daughters that it was their duty to take their mother's place. They felt it was wrong, but they also felt it was something they had to do, and so they did it.

And, predictably enough, they were both psychologically scarred by the experience. Almost every incest victim seemed to be, one way or the other.

But it was their younger sister who wound up being the most damaged of the three. Because Daddy never touched her, she figured there was something wrong with her. Was she ugly? Was she insufficiently feminine? Was there something disgusting about her?

Jeepers, what was the matter with her, anyway? Why didn't he want her?

After the dishes were cleared, Doug suggested a brandy. "I don't think so," she said. "I don't usually drink this much early in the day."

"Actually, neither do I. I guess there's something about the occasion that feels like a celebration."

"I know what you mean."

"Some coffee? Because I'm in no hurry for this to end."

She agreed that coffee sounded like a good idea. And it was pretty good coffee, and a fitting conclusion to a pretty good meal.

Better than a person might expect to find on the outskirts of Toledo.

How did he know the place? Did he come here with his wife? She somehow doubted it. Had he brought other women here? She doubted that as well. Maybe it was something he'd picked up at the office water cooler. *"So I took her to this Eye-tie place on Detroit Avenue, and then we just popped into the Comfort Inn down the block, and I mean to tell you that girl was good to go."*

Something like that.

"I don't want to go back to the office," he was saying. "All these years, and then you walk back into my life, and I'm not ready for you to walk out of it again."

You were the one who walked, she thought. Clear to Bowling Green.

But what she said was, "We could go to my hotel room, but a downtown hotel right in the middle of the city—"

"Actually," he said, "there's a nice place right across the street."

"Oh?"

"A Holiday Inn, actually."

"Do you think they'd have a room at this hour?"

He managed to look embarrassed and pleased with himself, all at the same time. "As a matter of fact," he said, "I have a reservation."

She was four months shy of her eighteenth birthday when everything changed.

What she came to realize, although she hadn't been consciously aware of it at the time, was that things had already been changing for some time. Her father came a little less frequently to her bed, sometimes telling her he was tired from a hard day's work, sometimes explaining that he had to stay up late with work he'd brought home, sometimes not bothering with an explanation of any sort.

Then one afternoon he invited her to go for a ride. Sometimes rides in the family car would end at a motel, and she thought that was what he planned on this occasion. In anticipation, no sooner had he backed the car out of the driveway than she'd dropped her hand into his lap, stroking him, awaiting his response.

He pushed her hand away.

She wondered why, but didn't say anything, and he didn't say anything either, not for ten minutes of suburban streets. Then abruptly he pulled into a strip mall, parked opposite a shuttered bowling alley, and said, "You're my little soldier, aren't you?"

She nodded.

"And that's what you'll always be. But we have to stop. You're a grown woman, you have to be able to lead your own life, I can't go on like this . . ."

She scarcely listened. The words washed over her like a stream, a babbling stream, and what came through to her was not so much the words he spoke but what seemed to underlie those words: *I don't want you anymore.*

After he'd stopped talking, and after she'd waited long enough to know he wasn't going to say anything else, and because she knew he was awaiting her response, she said, "Okay."

"I love you, you know."

"I know."

"You've never said anything to anyone, have you?"

"No."

"Of course you haven't. You're a warrior, and I've always known I could count on you."

On the way back, he asked her if she'd like to stop for ice cream. She just shook her head, and he drove the rest of the way home.

She got out of the car and went up to her room. She sprawled on her bed, turning the pages of a book without registering their contents. After a few minutes she stopped trying to read and sat up, her eyes focused on a spot on one wall where the wallpaper was misaligned.

She found herself thinking of Doug, her first real boyfriend. She'd never told her father about Doug; of course he knew that they were spending time together, but she'd kept their intimacy a secret. And of course she'd never said a word about what she and her father had been doing, not to Doug or to anybody else.

The two relationships were worlds apart in her mind. But now they had something in common, because they had both ended. Doug's family had moved to Ohio, and their exchange of letters had trickled out. And her father didn't want to have sex with her anymore.

Something really bad was going to happen. She just knew it.

A few days later, she went to her friend Rosemary's house after school. Rosemary, who lived just a few blocks away on Covington, had three brothers and two sisters, and anybody who was still there at dinnertime was always invited to stay.

She accepted gratefully. She could have gone home, but she just didn't want to, and she still didn't want to a few hours later. "I wish I could just stay here overnight," she told Rosemary. "My parents are acting weird."

"Hang on, I'll ask my mom."

She had to call home and get permission. "No one's answering," she said. "Maybe they went out. If you want I'll go home."

"You'll stay right here," Rosemary's mother said. "You'll call right before bedtime, and if there's still no answer, well, if they're not home, they won't miss you, will they?"

Rosemary had twin beds, and fell asleep instantly in her own. Kit, a few feet away, had this thought that Rosemary's father would let himself into the room, and into her bed, but of course this didn't happen, and the next thing she knew she was asleep.

In the morning she went home, and the first thing she did was call Rosemary's house, hysterical. Rosemary's mother calmed her down, and then she was able to call 911 to report the deaths of her parents. Rosemary's mother came over to be with her, and shortly after that the police came, and it became pretty clear what had happened. Her father had killed her mother and then turned the gun on himself.

"You sensed that something was wrong," Rosemary's mother said. "That's why it was so easy to get you to stay for dinner, and why you wanted to sleep over."

"They were fighting," she said, "and there was something different about it. Not just a normal argument. God, it's my fault, isn't it? I should have been able to do something. The least I could have done was to say something."

Everybody told her that was nonsense.

After she'd left Lucas's brand-new high-floor apartment, she returned to her own older, less imposing sublet, where she brewed a pot of coffee and sat up at the kitchen table with a pencil and paper. She wrote down the numbers one though five in descending order, and after each she wrote a name, or as much of the name as she knew. Sometimes she added an identifying phrase or two. The list began with 5, and the first entry read as follows:

Said his name was Sid. Pasty complexion, gap between top incisors. Met in Philadelphia at bar on Race Street (?), went to his hotel, don't remember name of it. Gone when I woke up.

Hmmm. Sid might be hard to find. How would she even know where to start looking for him?

At the bottom of the list, her entry was simpler and more specific. *Douglas Pratter. Last known address Bowling Green. Lawyer? Google him?*

She booted up her laptop.

Their room in the Detroit Avenue Holiday Inn was on the third floor in the rear. With the drapes drawn and the door locked, with their clothes hastily discarded and the bedclothes as hastily tossed aside, it seemed to her for at least a few minutes that she was fifteen years old again, and in bed with her first boyfriend. She tasted a familiar sweetness in his kisses, a familiar raw urgency in his ardor.

But the illusion didn't last. And then it was just lovemaking, at which each of them had a commendable proficiency. He went down on her this time, which was something he'd never done when they were teenage sweethearts, and the first thought that came to her was that he had turned into her father, because her father had done that all the time.

Afterward, after a fairly long shared silence, he said, "I can't tell you how many times I've wondered."

"What it would be like to be together again?"

"Well, sure, but more than that. What life would have been like if I'd never moved away in the first place. What would have become of the two of us, if we'd had the chance to let things find their way."

"Probably the same as most high school lovers. We'd have stayed together for a while, and then we'd have broken up and gone separate ways."

"Maybe."

"Or I'd have gotten pregnant, and you'd have married me, and we'd be divorced by now."

"Maybe."

"Or we'd still be together, and bored to death with each other, and you'd be in a motel fucking somebody new."

"God, how'd you get so cynical?"

"You're right, I got off on the wrong foot there. How about this? If your father hadn't moved you all to Bowling Green, you and I would have stayed together, and our feeling for each other would have grown from teenage hormonal infatuation to the profound mature love it was always destined to be. You'd have gone off to college, and as soon as I finished high school I'd have enrolled there myself, and when you finished law school I'd have my undergraduate degree, and I'd be your secretary and office manager when you set up your own law practice. By then we'd have gotten married, and by now we'd have one child with a second on the way, and we would remain unwavering in our love for one another, and as passionate as ever." She gazed wide-eyed at him. "Better?"

His expression was hard to read, and he appeared to be on the point of saying something, but she turned toward him and ran a hand over his flank, and the prospect of a further adventure in adultery trumped whatever he might have wanted to say. Whatever it was, she thought, it would keep.

"I'd better get going," he said, and rose from the bed, and rummaged through the clothes he'd tossed on the chair.

She said, "Doug? Don't you think you might want to take a shower first?"

"Oh, Jesus. Yeah, I guess I better, huh?"

He'd known where to take her to lunch, knew to make a room reservation ahead of time, but he evidently didn't know enough to shower away her spoor before returning to home and hearth. So perhaps this sort of adventure was not the usual thing for him. Oh, she was fairly certain he tried to get lucky on business trips—those oh-so-lonely New York visits he'd mentioned, for instance—but you didn't have to shower after that sort of interlude, because you were going back to your own hotel room, not to your unsuspecting wife.

She started to get dressed. There was no one waiting for her, and her own shower could wait until she was back at her own motel. But she changed her mind about dressing, and was still naked when he emerged from the shower, a towel wrapped around his middle.

"Here," she said, handing him a glass of water. "Drink this."

"What is it?"

"Water."

"I'm not thirsty."

"Just drink it, will you?"

He shrugged, drank it. He went and picked up his undershorts, and kept losing his balance when he tried stepping into them. She took his arm and led him over to the bed, and he sat down and told her he didn't feel so good. She took the undershorts away from him and got him to lie down on the bed, and she watched him struggling to keep a grip on consciousness.

She put a pillow over his face, and she sat on it. She felt him trying to move beneath her, and she watched his hands make feeble clawing motions at the bedsheet, and observed the muscles working in his lower legs. Then he was still, and she stayed where she was for a few minutes, and an involuntary tremor, a very subtle one, went through her hindquarters.

And what was that, pray tell? Could have been her coming, could have been him going. Hard to tell, and did it really matter?

When she got up, well, duh, he was dead. No surprise there. She put her clothes on, cleaned up all traces of her presence, and transferred all of the cash from his wallet to her purse. A few hundred dollars in tens and twenties, plus an emergency hundred-dollar bill tucked away behind his driver's license. She might have missed it, but she'd learned years ago that you had to give a man's wallet a thorough search.

Not that the money was ever the point. But they couldn't take it with them and it had to go somewhere, so it might as well go to her. Right?

How it happened: That final morning, shortly after she left for school, her father and mother had argued, and her father had gone for the handgun he kept in a locked desk drawer and shot her mother dead. He left the house and went to his office, saying nothing to anyone, although a coworker did say that he'd seemed troubled. And sometime during the afternoon he returned home, where his wife's body remained undiscovered. The gun was still there (unless he'd been carrying it around with him during the intervening hours) and he put the barrel in his mouth and blew his brains out.

Except that wasn't really how it happened; it was how the police figured it out. What did in fact happen, of course, is that she shot her mother before she left for school, and called her father on his cell as soon as she got home from school, summoning him on account of an unspecified emergency. He came right home, and by then she would have liked to change her mind, but how could she with her mother dead in the next room? So she shot him and arranged the evidence appropriately, and then she went over to Rosemary's.

Di dah di dah di dah.

You could see Doug's car from the motel room window. He'd parked in the back and they'd come up the back stairs, never going anywhere near the front desk. So no one had seen her, and no one saw her now as she went to his car, unlocked it with his key, and drove it downtown.

She'd have preferred to leave it there, but her own rental was parked near the Crowne Plaza, so she had to get downtown to reclaim it. You couldn't stand on the corner and hail a cab, not in Toledo, and she didn't want to call one. So she drove to within a few blocks of the lot where she'd stowed her Honda, parked his Volvo at an expired meter, and used the hanky with which he'd cleaned his glasses to wipe away any fingerprints she might have left behind.

She redeemed her car and headed for her own motel. Halfway there, she realized she had no real need to go there. She'd packed that morning and left no traces of herself in her room. She hadn't checked out, electing to keep her options open, so she could go there now with no problem, but for what? Just to take a shower?

She sniffed herself. She could use a shower, no question, but she wasn't so rank that people would draw away from her. And she kind of liked the faint trace of his smell coming off her flesh.

And the sooner she got to the airport, the sooner she'd be out of Toledo.

She managed to catch a 4:18 flight that was scheduled to stop in Cincinnati on its way to Denver. She'd stay in Denver for a while, until she decided where she wanted to go next.

She hadn't had a reservation, or even a set destination, and she took the flight because it was there to be taken. The leg from To-ledo to Cincinnati was more than half empty, and she had a row of seats to herself, but she was stuck in a middle seat from Cincinnati to Denver, wedged between a fat lady who looked to be scared stiff of something, possibly the flight itself, and a man who tapped away at his laptop and invaded her space with his elbows.

Not the most pleasant travel experience she'd ever had, but nothing she couldn't live through. She closed her eyes, let her thoughts turn inward.

After her parents were buried and the estate settled, after she'd fin-ished the high school year and collected her diploma, after a real-tor had listed her house and, after commission and closing costs, netted her a few thousand over and above the outstanding first and second mortgages, she'd stuffed what she could into one of her fa-ther's suitcases and boarded a bus.

She'd never gone back. And, until her brief but gratifying re-union with Douglas Pratter, Esq., she'd never been Katherine Toll-iver again.

On the tram to baggage claim, a businessman from Wichita told her how much simpler it had been getting in and out of Denver before they built Denver International Airport. "Not that Staple-ton was all that wonderful," he said, "but it was a quick, cheap cab ride from the Brown Palace. It wasn't stuck out in the middle of a few thousand square miles of prairie."

It was funny he should mention the Brown, she said, because that's where she was staying. So of course he suggested she share his cab, and when they reached the hotel and she offered to pay half, well, he wouldn't hear of it. "My company pays," he said, "and if you really want to thank me, why don't you let the old firm buy you dinner?"

Tempting, but she begged off, said she'd eaten a big lunch, said all she wanted to do was get to sleep. "If you change your mind," he said, "just ring my room. If I'm not there, you'll find me in the bar."

She didn't have a reservation, but they had a room for her, and she sank into an armchair with a glass of water from the tap. The Brown Palace had its own artesian well, and took great pride in its water, so how could she turn it down?

"Just drink it," she'd told Doug, and he'd done what she told him. It was funny, people usually did.

"Five," she'd told Lucas, who'd been so eager to be number six. But he'd only managed it for a matter of minutes, because the list was composed of men who could sit around that mythical table and tell each other how they'd had her, and you had to be alive to do that. So Lucas had dropped off the list when she'd chosen a knife from his kitchen and slipped it right between his ribs and into his heart. He fell off her list without even opening his eyes.

After her parents died, she didn't sleep with anyone until she'd graduated and left home for good. Then she got a waitress job, and the manager took her out drinking after work one night, got her drunk, and performed something that might have been date rape; she didn't remember it that clearly, so it was hard to say.

When she saw him at work the next night he gave her a wink and a pat on the behind, and something came into her mind, and that night she got him to take her for a ride and park on the golf course, where she took him by surprise and beat his brains out with a tire iron.

There, she'd thought. Now it was as if the rape — if that's what it was, and did it really matter what it was? Whatever it was, it was as if it had never happened.

A week or so later, in another city, she quite deliberately picked up a man in a bar, went home with him, had sex with him, killed him, robbed him, and left him there. And that set the pattern.

Four times the pattern had been broken, and those four men had joined Doug Pratter on her list. Two of them, Sid from Philadelphia and Peter from Wall Street, had escaped because she drank too much. Sid was gone when she woke up. Peter was there, and in the mood for morning sex, after which she'd laced his bottle of vodka with the little crystals she'd meant to put in his drink the night before. She'd gone away from there wondering who'd drink the vodka. Peter? The next girl he managed to drag home? Both of them?

She thought she'd read about it in the papers, sooner or later, but if there'd been a story it escaped her attention, so she didn't really know whether Peter deserved a place on her list.

It wouldn't be hard to find out, and if he was still on the list, well, she could deal with it. It would be a lot harder to find Sid, because all she knew about him was his first name, and that might well have been improvised for the occasion. And she'd met him in Philadelphia, but he was already registered at a hotel, so that meant he was probably from someplace other than Philadelphia, and that meant the only place she knew to look was the one place where she could be fairly certain he didn't live.

She knew the first and last names of the two other men on her list. Graham Weider was a Chicagoan she'd met in New York; he'd taken her to lunch and to bed, then jumped up and hurried her out of there, claiming an urgent appointment and arranging to meet her later. But he'd never turned up, and the desk at his hotel told her he'd checked out.

So he was lucky, and Alvin Kirkaby was lucky in another way. He was an infantry corporal on leave before they shipped him off to Iraq, and if she'd realized that she wouldn't have picked him up in the first place, and she wasn't sure what kept her from doing to him as she did to the other men who entered her life. Pity? Patriotism? Both seemed unlikely, and when she thought about it later she decided it was simply because he was a soldier. That gave them something in common, because weren't they both military types? Wasn't she her father's little soldier?

Maybe he'd been killed over there. She supposed she could find out. And then she could decide what she wanted to do about it.

Graham Weider, though, couldn't claim combatant status, unless you considered him a corporate warrior. And while his name might not be unique, neither was it by any means common. And it was almost certainly his real name too, because they'd known it at the front desk. Graham Weider, from Chicago. It would be easy enough to find him, when she got around to it.

Of them all, Sid would be the real challenge. She sat there going over what little she knew about him and how she might go about playing detective. Then she treated herself to another half glass of Brown Palace water and flavored it with a miniature of Johnny Walker from the minibar. She sat down with the drink and shook her head, amused by her own behavior. She was dawdling, postponing her shower, as if she couldn't bear to wash away the traces of Doug's lovemaking.

But she was tired, and she certainly didn't want to wake up the next morning with his smell still on her. She undressed and stood for a long time in the shower, and when she got out of it she stood for a moment alongside the tub and watched the water go down the drain.

Four, she thought. Why, before you knew it, she'd be a virgin all over again.

DAVID CORBETT AND
LUIS ALBERTO URREA

Who Stole My Monkey?

FROM *Lone Star Noir*

Port Arthur

Can you really make it stink?
— *Beau Jocque and the Zydeco Hi-Rollers*

LOOKING BACK LATER, Chester could not convince himself he'd heard the sound at all, not at first, for what memory handed up to him was more sensation than sound, the tight sawtooth grind of a key in a lock, opening the door to hell.

They were midway through a cover of "Big Legs, Tight Skirt," Chester caressing the custom Gabbanelli Cajun King he used for the night's first sets. Saturday night at the old Diamond 21, some of the dancers in western getup, down to the Stetsons and hoop skirts, the rest in the usual Gulf Coast duds—muscle shirts, ass-crack jeans, shifts so cellophane-tight a blind man would weep— the cowboy contingent arrayed in three rows for the line dance, the others rocking to their own inner need, women holding the hair off their necks, men combing back damp locks, the band double-clutching but bluesy too, John Lee Hooker meets Rockin' Dopsie with a tip of the hat to Professor Longhair. Yeah—'fess, chile. Midnight in East Texas, the music savage and hip, the band hitting it good, the room steamy, the dance crowd punchy from the beat but craving more, always more.

But the sound. It came from outside, no denying it now, that distinctive growl, like the sulfurous thunder-chuckle of the devil himself—a rear-mounted diesel, rebuilt Red Diamond in-line six. Chester even caught a scent of the oil-black exhaust and the muffled scattershot of spewed gravel as the bus tore out of the parking lot.

No, he thought, blinking like a man emerging from a silly dream. Two-toned copper and black, a perfect match not just for the gear trailer but his ostrich-skin boots—100 percent personal style, that bus. Last gasp of the days when oil money ran flush, when Chester had a nice little stilt home in Cameron Parish (before the hurricane took it to Belize, that is), when the clubs were paying sweet money and Beau Jocque was still alive and touring the country and a good two-step chanky-chank band could make beaucoup cash dollars. That bus was just about it for the Chester Richard empire, the final signature on a bleak dotted line.

But that wasn't what broke his heart.

Lorena, he thought.

His fingers stopped their flight across the mother-of-pearl buttons as a drop of sweat, fat as a bumblebee, splashed onto the accordion's Honduras rosewood. He wore a tight leather apron-vest, cut and sized in Lafayette so the bellows didn't pinch his nipples. Underneath, his chest was a swamp.

The rest of the band, oblivious, pushed on, the dancers unfazed too, a whirlwind thrall of spins and dips and shuffles. He glanced into the mold-speckled mirror above the stage as though the smile of some last hope might reveal itself. Fog hazed his reflection.

Turning his back to the dance floor, he waved the band to a stop. Geno, his frottoir man, lost the rhythm with his spoons. Skillet, the drummer, faltered when the rubboard did. The tune stumbled and fell apart.

"You didn't hear that?" They stared at him gape-eyed. "Someone just stole the motherfucking Flyer."

Two hours later he sat in a nearby diner, waiting for Geno and Skillet to return with a car, the night pitch-black beyond the screens. One fan hummed in the doorway to keep out the wasps and skeeters, another sat propped on the ancient counter to whip the soupy heat around, the air thick with the smell of sweet crude off the ship channel. The cook was in back puzzling out the walk-in's condenser. A plain bare bulb swam overhead in the breeze, casting a dizzy light.

Chester, craving a pinch, leaned back in his chair, shirt cling-ing to his skin as he pretended to listen. The woman did go on. If he only had some Red Man. Hell, any chaw at all—he'd take gas station rubbish right now if it had some mint in it. All the other club patrons had trudged on home, demanding their cover charge back, getting half, everybody ripped off one way or the other. But this woman here, she'd elected to stay.

He remembered her from the first set, waltzing with the others in the grand counterclockwise circle, her partner a doodlebugger wearing throwback pomade. Small wonder they'd parted. Coppery freckles dusted her cleavage, which from time to time she mopped with a white paper napkin. Her hair was the color of bayou am-ber and she wore it swirled messily atop her head, strands curling down like so many afterthoughts, a pair of chopsticks holding it so. Another time and place, he could imagine himself saying, *I bet you taste just like rice pudding, sha.*

Chester had suffered three marriages, survived as many divorces, more time spent with lawyers, it seemed, than in love. He had a wandering eye and a ravenous crotch and a Category 5 temper, his love life a tale of wreckage—one judge had nicknamed him Hur-ricane, given his knack for sheer, mean, indifferent destruction. No woman could endure him for long, but few could resist him neither. Like fortunetellers staring into a glowing ball, they could sense within him a tragic, beautiful, lonesome soul. Hell, he was the crown prince of lonely; open his heart you'd find a howling wasteland, make West Texas look like Biloxi. And the ladies could not resist that—*I'll soothe you, sugar. Save you.* But no bride, no groupie, no rice-pudding blonde with chopstick hair had ever hon-ored his longing, or yielded to his touch, like Lorena.

"Mr. Richard," she whispered, pronouncing it *richered,* like some-thing that happened when money landed in your lap, "I have been a hopeless fan ever since that night at Slim's Y-Ki-Ki Lounge in Opelousas, that first night I heard you, heard you and your band." Her hand rushed across the table like a hawk toward his. "I've been on my share of tailrides and I've been not just to the Y-Ki-Ki but Harry's Club over in Beaux Bridge and Richards Club in Lawtell, the Labor Day festival in Plaisance . . ."

Chester, cocking an ear for sounds of the car, shook himself from his thoughts. "Let me stop you, darlin' dear."

She clutched his hand as though afraid it might escape, her eyes a pair of low-hanging plums; their skin a telling contrast, hers creamy and white like egg custard, his the shade of caramel.

I must be hungry, he thought.

"I have never," she intoned, "never heard a man play as wild, as free, as hard as you."

He could no longer see her face. His mind's eye conjured Lorena.

She was a custom Gabbanelli, not unlike the one he'd been playing onstage when the music stopped, but finer, older, one of a kind. Handmade in Castelfidardo sixty-five years ago, during the war, she'd been bought by his granddad for twenty dollars and a pig.

Chester thought he'd seen one of the Cheniers play one just like her at the Acadiana music festival, and the prospect had coiled a skein of fear around his heart. But no, theirs lacked the purple heart accents, the buttons of polished bone, much more. And sure enough, Lorena proved her royalty that day. An accordion war, oh yes, him and Richard LeBoeff at the end, Chester taking the prize with a fiery rendition of an original he'd penned just the night before, titled "Muttfish Gumbo." Next day, the local headlines screamed, "The Jimi Hendrix of the Squeezebox," and there she was, in the picture with Chester: Lorena. Who else was worthy to share his crown? He grinned, in spite of himself. What would Granddad think of that?

He'd been a marksman in the 92nd Infantry, the fabled Buffalo Soldiers, moving up the Italian peninsula in '44 while most white troops got shipped to Normandy for the push to Berlin. He hefted Lorena on his back like a long-lost child as the Mule Pack Battalion marched up alongside Italian blacksmiths and resistance volunteers, South Africans, Brazilians, trudging across minefields and treadway bridges, scaling manmade battlements and the Ligurian hills toward von Kesselring's Gothic Line.

He endured the march up the Serchio Valley, survived the Christmas slaughter in Gallicano, suffered the withering German 88s and machine-gun fire as the 92nd crawled across the Cinquale Canal. Throughout his boyhood, Chester sat beside his granddad's rocker and listened to his tales, enthralled, inspired, and each one circled back to guess who? The accordion became his granddad's prize, his lucky talisman, his reason for fighting, and he named her

Lorena, same as his girl back home, the one who refused to wait. In time, the beautiful box with all that luck inside became the real Lorena, the one who was true.

And she was a stone beauty—pearl inlays, seasoned mahogany lacquered to the color of pure cane syrup, the grille cut lath by lath from brass with a jeweler's saw, double reeds made from Swedish blue steel for that distinctive tremolo, a deep mournful throbbing tone unmatched by any instrument Chester had ever heard. She had the voice of a sad and beautiful thrush, the tragic bride of a lost soldier. And yes, Granddad had come back from that war lost. The accordion became a kind of compass, guiding him back, at least halfway.

In time, Granddad passed her on to Papa Ray and he in turn handed her over to Chester, the prodigy, the instrument not so much a gift as a dare. *Be unique and stunning and wise,* she seemed to whisper, *like me.* And that was the full shape of the inheritance, not just an instrument but a sorrow wrapped in warrior loneliness. Chester treated her like the dark mystery she was, never bringing her out until the final set of the night, queen of the ball—which was why she'd been in the bus, not onstage, when the Western Flyer got jacked.

Chester glanced down at the table, saw the woman's fingers lacing his own, felt the nagging heat of her touch. "Darlin' dear," he repeated, snapping to. "As I have told you at least twice now, and which should be obvious to a fan as devoted as you claim to be . . ." He lumbered to his feet as, at long last, the headlights of Geno's Firebird appeared in the lot. "The name is pronounced *Ree-shard.*"

She cocked her eye, a dark glance, the rice pudding curdled. "Oh, boo."

"Adieu."

"Boo!"

He tipped his hat and hustled into the night.

Inside the car, Chester collected a pearl-handled Colt .45 from an oilcloth held out to him by Skillet, who kept for himself a .44 Smithy and a buck knife big enough to gore a dray. Geno carried a .38 snub-nose and a length of pipe. You play enough bayou jump joints and oil-coast dives, you habituate your weapons.

Geno, sitting behind the wheel, glanced over his shoulder at

Chester, who straddled the hump in the backseat. "I'm guessin' there ain't no guesswork to who took the bus."

"No." Chester dropped the magazine on the Colt, checked to be sure it had all seven rounds, plus one in the pipe, slammed it home again, then tucked the pistol under his belt as Geno slipped the Firebird into gear and took off. "I think not."

Skillet, true to his nature, remained quiet. Black as Houston crude and wiry with cavernous eyes, he'd been hit with a fry pan in '77, still had the telltale dent in his skull. Geno, plump as a friar with slicked-back hair, kept up a low, tuneless hum as he drove. He was the band's gadfly mystic, always wandering off on some oddball spirit craze, and he'd recently read somewhere that you ought to chant "Om" to get right with the cosmos. Apparently, though, he'd snagged some cross-signals, for the effort came out sounding like some rural Baptist dirge, hobbling along in waltz time. Chester almost asked for the radio, then reconsidered. Who knew what sort of ass-backward mojo you'd conjure, stopping a man midchant?

They pulled over for food at an all-night canteen on the Port Arthur outskirts: crawfish étouffée, hush puppies, grilled boudin sausage. Using his fingers to scoop the food from its white cardboard carton, Chester dug in, reminding himself that vengeance is but one of many hungers.

"Boudin," he said. "Proof that God loves a Creole man." To himself, he added, *Let's hope some of that love will hold.*

They took Route 73 to catch I-10 near Winnie, figuring the thief was heading west. He'd mentioned home was El Paso, just across the border from Ciudad Juárez, murder capital of the planet.

His name was Emigdio Nava but he went by Feo, the Ugly One. The handle was not ironic. Small and hunched but muscular, arms sleeved with tats, he had a scrapper's eyes, a mulish face, the complexion of a peach pit. He'd approached Chester about two weeks back, at a private party they were playing out on the levee road in East Jefferson Parish. He invited himself back into the greenroom between sets and sat himself down, a cagey introduction, smile like a paper cut. Everybody in the band figured him for a dealer—except for a few old locals too big to unseat, the Mexican gangs ran practically everything dopewise now—but he made no mention of such.

He did, though, have an offer.

"Want you to write me a song," he said, whipping out a roll of bills. He licked his thumb, flicked past five hundreds, tugged them free, and handed them out for Chester to take. "For my girl."

Chester glanced toward Skillet, by far the best judge of character in the band. He'd played up and down the coast for over thirty years, headliners to pickup bands, seen everything twice. It took a while, but finally Skillet offered a nod.

"Tell me about your girl," Chester said, taking the money.

Her name was Rosa Sánchez but everyone knew her as La Monita, Little Monkey. Again, Chester learned, irony was not at issue. Feo showed him snapshots. She was a tiny woman with un-naturally long arms. Her small round face was feathered with fine black hair. An upturned nose didn't help, though the rest of the package was straight-up fine. And being clever and resourceful, or so Chester surmised from how Feo told it, she turned misfortune to her advantage. A hooker who worked near the ship channel, she gained the upper hand over the more attractive girls by, more or less, outfucking them.

Geno, catching a glance at the picture, muttered, "Ain't we funky."

Chester cut him with a look.

"We got this tradition in Mexico," Feo said, ignoring them both. "Ballads. We call them *corridos*. It's how we sing the praises of the outcasts, the unlucky ones, the tragic ones, but also the bandits, the narcotrafficantes, the pandilleros. Anyone who understands what it means to suffer, but also to fight." The dude had picked up a bit of a Texas accent, and it was weird, hearing the Mexican and the Texican wrestling in his voice. Gave him a case of the mush-mouth.

Skillet watched him like a cat perched beneath the humming-bird feeder.

"You people," Feo continued, "have such a tradition also, no?"

"Called *raconteur.*" Chester too could be a man of few words. You people, he thought. "When do you need this by?"

Feo rose from his chair, that slashing smile. "How hard can it be?"

Harder than Chester thought, as it turned out, but he'd taken the money and so was stuck. The problem was simple: how to pen something apt that wasn't at the same time offensive. It proved the better of him — he put it off, scratched out a few sorry lines, cast them aside:

> Only the homely
> And the angels above
> Know how to suffer
> The pain called love

Mama would shoot me dead onstage, he thought, if I dared sing that out loud. She'd been a torch singer famous up and down the bayou country, Miss Angeline her stage name. She'd died when Chester was seven, the cancer setting a pattern for women he'd lose.

Seeing that Chester was suffering over the lyrics, and sensing in that the chance for some clowning, Geno tried his hand too, singing his version over lunch, a plate of fried chicken and string beans with bacon:

> She is my monkey
> I'll make her my wife
> Gonna be funky
> For the rest of my life

Chester glanced up from his own plate, jambalaya with shrimp and andouille. "You looking to get me killed?"

Geno veiled his grin with a shrug. "Not before payday, no."

Two nights later, Feo showed up unannounced at the club they were playing, gripping an Abita beer, working a path through the crowd to the bandstand. He offered no greeting, just gestured once with a cock of his head.

Desperate for an idea — something, anything, quick — and unnerved by the small man's stare, Chester turned to the band and counted off the first thing that popped into his head:

> My monkey got a cue-ball head
> A good attitude and them long skinny legs

No sooner did the lyrics escape than he felt the sheer disastrous lunacy of what he'd done. And the band hadn't played the tune since forever, execution falling somewhere between rusty and half-ass, a dash of salt in an already screaming wound. The gleam in Feo's eye turned glacial. The bottle of beer dropped slowly from his mouth, and the mouth formed an O, then reverted to slit mode as he vanished. Chester thought maybe that would be it, a feeble wish, but then he spotted him at the bar between sets, and at the end of the night, like a bad itch, he turned up again, drifting across the parking lot as they loaded up the Flyer.

Approaching Chester: "Got time for a word, cabrón?"

Chester led him off a little from the others, not sure why. "Nice night—no, mon ami?" Cringing. Lame.

"You were supposed to write me a song."

The boys in the band sidled up, watching Chester's back.

Chester worked up a pained look, phony to the bone. "I thought I did."

"That thing you played?"

"It's called 'Who Stole My Monkey?'"

"Bartender tells me it's an old tune, written by some dude named Zachary Richard. Not you. You're Chester."

"He's my uncle," Chester lied.

"Still ain't you."

Chester tried an ingratiating smile. "How's about a few more days?"

"And you insult my girl too?" Feo held Skillet and Geno with his eyes, warning them that he could take all three. "You diss me twice? Know how much money you could make writing me love songs, güey?"

Got a fair idea, Chester thought, just as he knew how many grupero musicians had been murdered the past two years by cats just like this. The situation had snuggled up next to awful, but before he could conjure his next bad idea, the Mexican turned away. Chester saw a whole lot of luck heading off with him.

Over his shoulder, in that inimitable mush-mouth Texican-Mexican, Feo called out, "Fuck all, y'all!"

Inside the car, Geno broke off his solemn humming. "I'm also guessin'," picking up his thread, "that we ain't gonna call the law on this."

"If we were—" Chester began.

"We'd a done it by now."

"Correct."

You don't call the law to help you fetch a stolen bus when there's an ounce of coke on board, not to mention a half-pound of weed, a mayonnaise jar full of Oxycontin, and enough crank to whirl you across Texas a dozen times and back. Small wonder we're broke, Chester thought. They'd stocked up for the road, a lot of away dates on the calendar. Sure, the stash was tucked beneath false panels, nothing in plain view, but all it took was one damn dog.

Getting back to Geno, he said, "Long as you're in the mood for guesswork, riddle me this: think our friend the music lover, before skipping town, scooped up this chimp-faced punch he loves?"

Geno's eyes bulged. "In our bus?"

"He'll ditch it quick, trade down for something more subtle. Or so I figure. Skillet?"

As always, silence. In time, a stubborn nod.

True enough, they found the Flyer with its distinctive black-and-gold design sitting on the edge of the interstate just outside Houston. Maybe he feigned a breakdown, Chester thought, stuck out his thumb, jacked the first car that stopped. Maybe he just pulled over to grab forty winks.

"Ease up behind," he said, drawing the .45 from under his belt. "Let's see what happens."

Geno obliged, lodged the tranny in park. "You honestly think he's up inside of there?"

"That's one of several scenarios I could predict." Chester let out a long slow breath. "What say we not get stupid?"

Chester kept the gun down along his leg—wouldn't do for a state trooper to happen by and spot two armed African American gents with their fat dago sidekick sneaking up on a fancy tour bus in evident distress. They lurked at the ass end of the Flyer, waiting to see if the old in-line six turned over, a belch of smoke.

Geno glanced at his watch. "Wait too long, we'll be dealing with po-po."

Chester felt the engine panel, noted it was cool to the touch. "I'm aware of this."

"Like, Rangers."

"Indeed."

"Just sayin'."

"Duly noted."

They ventured single file along the bus's passenger side, Skillet in the lead, his crouching duck-walk straight out of some Jim Brown blaxploitation joint. Chester, lightheaded from fear, began imagining as a soundtrack a two-step rendition of the theme from *Shaft*.

Reaching the door, Skillet tried the handle and found it unlocked. He let it swing open easy. A glance toward the driver's seat—empty—then a glance back toward Chester, who nodded. Crouching, pistol drawn, Skillet entered, the others right behind.

The stillness was total, all but for the buzz of flies. No one there, except for the seat at the back, dead center. She wore a black miniskirt with a crimson top bunched in front, no stockings, shoes kicked off. Long skinny arms you couldn't miss.

Geno put words to the general impression. "What happened to her fucking head?"

Chester searched for Lorena while Skillet probed the hidey-holes, unscrewing the panels, bagging the dope he found untouched within. Geno kept an eye out for troopers. Chester could feel his heart in his chest like a fist pounding on a door, sweat boiling off his face, but the accordion was nowhere to be found. Thief wants me to follow, he thought, that or he's got a mind to hock her.

Despite himself, he glanced more than once at the headless corpse, sitting upright at the back, like she was waiting for someone to ask her the obvious question: *Why?* The woman he loved so much, Chester thought, paid five hundred cash for a song, then this. Only way it made sense was if she was just a means to an end. And the end lay somewhere west.

Geno, suddenly ashen, said, "That Mex is tweakin'," then stumbled off the Flyer and vomited in the weeds. Jackknifed, short of breath, he mumbled, "Oh Lord . . ."

A moment later, like a sphinx handing up its riddle, Skillet finally spoke: "'Less you wanna get us all sent up for that girl's murder," he told Chester, "might be time to make a call."

In Houston they phoned the Port Arthur police, reported the bus stolen, fudged a little about when and where, claimed no notion of who—they didn't want some cop getting hold of Feo before they got their chance—then dialed every local pawnshop, even called the Gabbanelli showroom, putting out word that somebody might be trying to offload Lorena on the sly. If so, a reward would be offered, no questions asked. But they got no word the Mexican had tried it yet. Still, the phone lines would be ringing all the way across the state. If he stopped to unload the accordion anywhere along his jaunt, they'd hear, unless Feo sold it to a private party.

"Which," Chester noted despondently as they resumed the trip west, "I figure he might well do."

"That'd be my plan," Geno acknowledged.

"Just drive," Chester said.

They were screaming past a little town called Johnsue when the cars showed up, two unmarked sedans, recent model, U.S. make. The men within remained obscure behind tinted glass. One car tore ahead, the other locked in behind. A window in the lead car rolled down, an arm emerged, gesturing them to the berm.

Geno glanced back over his shoulder. "What you want me to do?"

This business just ain't gonna turn easy, Chester thought. "What I want and what's wise would seem to be at odds at the moment." He let out a sigh and pushed the .45 under Skillet's seat. "Pull on over."

Skillet and Geno tucked their weapons away as well, as two men emerged from the lead car; the crew behind stayed put. The visitors wore identical blue sport coats, tan slacks, but they walked like men who spent little time in an office. The one who approached the driver's window did so almost merrily, an air of recreational menace. The other had shoulders that could block a doorway, a bulldog face, that distinctive high-and-tight fade, fresh from the Corps.

The merry one glanced in, studying each man's face, one at a time, settling at last on Chester. "You wanna un-ass that seat, big fella?" He grinned, cracking gum between his molars.

Chester opened the door and bent Skillet forward as he struggled to unfold into the sun, while Mr. Merry Menace leaned on the Firebird's fender, arms crossed. His wraparounds sat crooked on his face.

"Understand you've made some inquiries regarding a certain Emigdio Nava." A whiskey baritone. "Mind telling us what that concerns?"

Us, Chester thought. "He stole an instrument of mine."

The man cocked his head toward his partner, who just continued to glare. Turning back: "Instrument?"

"You knew we've been making inquiries, I'd guess you know
about what."

The smile didn't falter. The man repeated: "Instrument?"

All right then, Chester thought. Way it's gonna be. "Accordion.
Belonged to my granddad. Serious sentimental value."

A loathsome chuckle. "Sentimental value. Touching."

"Can I see some identification?" Chester said.

The man pushed his wraparounds up his nose. "I don't think so.
No."

"You're not the law."

"Better than the law, most occasions."

"Such as this?"

"Oh, this especially."

The sun-baked office bore no name, just another anonymous door
in an industrial park ten blocks off the interstate. Four men not
much different from the first two emptied from the second car,
another two waited inside. They put Chester and Skillet and Geno
in separate rooms, each one the same morose beige, folding chairs
the only furniture, to which each man got bound with duct tape. A
silver Halliburton case rested in the corner of Chester's room, and
he doubted an item of luggage had ever terrified him more.

Mr. Merry Menace snapped on a pair of latex gloves. "So you're
musical."

"Look," Chester said, his mouth parched, "no need for this, I
told you—"

The fist came out of nowhere and landed like a sledge, the latex
chafing his face like tire rubber. He heard the hinge crack in his
jaw, a phosphorescent whiteness rising within his mind, blotting
out the world. When the world came back, it came back screaming—Geno, the next room over.

Chester shouted, "I'm telling them everything!" but all it earned
him was a crackback blow, knuckles busting open his cheek.

"You talk to me. Not them."

Chester shook his head, gazing up through a blur. The trickle of
blood over his stubble itched. "Why do this?"

"What was it like, finding your bus by the side of the road, Feo's
little ape-girl inside?"

Chester shook his head like a wet dog. "You know."

"Oh, I know. Yes."

"He said he loved her."

"Love?" The man's smile froze in place. "She stood up to him, only woman who ever did, so it's said. He put up with it. That's love, I suppose. Up to a point."

"Why—"

"Cut off her head?" A shrug. "Style points."

Chester coughed up something warm, licked the inside of his cheek, tasted blood.

"They hurl severed heads onto disco floors down Mexico way, Chester, just to send a message. It's how vatos blog."

"I don't—"

"I'm gonna make it simple, okay? There are forces at play here. Secrets. Schemes and counterschemes and conspiracies so vast and twisted they make the Kennedy hit look like a Pixar flick." A gloved finger tapped Chester's brow, tiny splash of sweat. "Bottom line, you're dispensable, you and your two wack friends. I'm doing you a favor. Whatever business you have with Señor Nava, it's hereby null, moot, done. Tell me I'm right."

"I don't understand."

An open-hand slap this time, mere punctuation. "He's a poacher. Understand that?"

Chester inhaled, his chest rippling with the effort. "I grew up in Calcasieu Parish. I know what a poacher is."

"Not that kind of poacher. He's Mexican military, Teniente Nava, trains infantry, automatic weapons. When he's not recruiting assassins for the Juárez Cartel."

Chester swallowed what felt like an egg. "That's got nothing to do with me."

"Not now."

"Not never. All I want is Lorena."

The man glanced to his partner, eyebrow cocked. Perplexed.

Chester sighed. "My accordion,"

It was like he'd admitted to sex with a fish. "Damn," the man said. He barked out a laugh. "You *are* sentimental."

They were escorted all the way back to the Houston city limits, then the two cars broke away. Message delivered, no further emphasis required. Skillet held a wet bandanna to the gash on the side of his head. He'd about had it with being hit on the skull. Geno, glancing up into his rearview, face swollen and colored like bad fruit, caught Chester's eyes, held the gaze.

"Say the word."

Chester had never killed a man—thought about it, sure, even plotted it out once. Now, though, he felt as close as close got. Feo had to pay. Pay for the theft of Lorena, pay for what Geno and Skillet had just endured, pay for the girl in the back of the Flyer. Feeling within him an invigorating, almost pleasurable hate, he imagined it was what his granddad—tongue unlocked by a jug of corn, Lorena resting in his lap—once described as the sickness at the bottom of the mind. He confessed to killing barehanded, last days of the war, his unit charged with cutting off the German retreat through the Cisa Pass. Low on ammunition, they didn't dare call in air or artillery support; the white officers would too easily call in fire directly atop their position. When the Germans overran their front line it got down to bayonets and bare knuckles, swinging their M-1s like clubs. *I choked one man, stabbed two more, beat another unconscious with my helmet, then smothered him with his own coat. Lucky for me they was all starved weak.* The voice of a ghost. But now Chester understood. So be it, he thought. The old man would not just understand, he would insist. I will not betray her. I will find her. I will bring her home.

"You drop me at the airport, then go on back to Port Arthur."

"That won't do." It was Skillet.

Chester shook his head. "I can't let you—"

"Ain't you to let."

"Skillet . . ."

"You catch your plane." The older man's voice was quiet and cold. "Geno and me, we'll turn on around, head west again. We'll check around San Antonio, see if we can find Lorena. Not, we'll see you in El Paso."

"I can't make it up to you."

"Nobody askin' that."

He slept in the terminal and caught the first flight to El Paso the next morning, touching down noonish, then a cab ride to the rectory of Santa Isabel. The pastor there was Father Declan Foley, but

Chester knew him as Jolt. A boxer once, backwater champion before heading off to seminary.

A cluster of schoolgirls sat in the pews as Father Dec led them in confirmation class. Chester caught that haunting scent, beeswax, candle flame, hand-worn wood, a lingering whiff of incense, almost conjuring belief. Or the want of belief.

The priest glanced up as his visitor ambled forward. The girls followed suit, pigtails spinning. I must look a sight, Chester thought, jaw swollen and bruised, a zigzag cut across his dark-stubbled cheek.

"Father," he said, a nod of respect.

The priest told the girls to open their books, review the difference between actual and sanctifying grace, then led Chester back into the sacristy. He eyed his old friend with solemn disappointment.

"You look, as they say, like hell."

Chester tried to gather himself up, quit halfway. "Feel like I been there."

"You've still got time. What's this about?"

Chester laid it all out, something about being inside the church arousing an instinct toward candor, flipping off the switch to that part of his mind inclined toward deceit and other half measures. It was no small part.

Father Declan heard him out. Then: "The man's a killer."

"I'm with you there. I don't want no more trouble, though. Just Lorena."

"I find it hard to believe he cares about an accordion."

Chester laughed through his nose; it hurt. "Maybe he's planning a new career path."

"My point is, from the sound of things, he means to punish you."

"He's succeeded." Chester felt tired to the bone. This too, he supposed, was the church working on him. "I hope to make that point. If I can find him before he crosses over to Juárez."

"I can ask around."

"I'd be obliged. Old time's sake and all." Chester heard something small in his voice. Begging. "You know the people who know the people and so on."

"Have you bothered praying?"

The question seemed vaguely insulting. Chester tugged at his ear. "Wouldn't say as I have, no."

"Be a good time to start, from all appearances."

"Can't say I feel inclined."

"Try." The priest reached out, his touch surprisingly gentle for such a meaty hand. "Old time's sake and all."

Father Dec gave him an address for a hotel nearby where he could rest while calls were made, then led him out to the front-most pew. Chester knelt. When in Rome, he figured, the deceit sector of his brain flickering back to life.

"By the way," he said, glancing over his shoulder at the school-girls, "just to settle my curiosity, what exactly *is* the difference between actual and sanctifying grace?"

The priest studied him a moment, something in his eye reminding Chester of the brawler he'd known before, glazed with sweat and blood, a smoky light hazing the ring, smell of cigars and saw-dust, all those redneck cheers. "You know about all the women being killed across the border, right? Worst of it's right here, just over the line, Ciudad Juárez."

That didn't seem much of an answer. "Dec—"

"Not just women. Kids. Sooner or later, it's always the kids. They're shooting up rehab clinics too, nobody's sure why. Then there's the kidnap racket. Not just mayors and cops and business-people, now it's teachers, doctors, migrants, anybody. Know what your life's worth? Whatever your family can cobble together. If that. People have stopped praying to God. Why bother? They've turned to Santa Muerte. Saint Death."

The weariness returned. "Not sure what you're getting at exactly, Dec."

"I'm trying to focus your mind."

Chester had to bite back a laugh. Like having your granddad's button box stolen, finding a headless hooker at the back of your bus, and getting punked by somebody's goon squad doesn't focus your mind. "Fair enough."

"Put your problems in perspective."

"All right."

Gradually the priest's stare weakened. Something like a smile appeared. "Sanctifying grace," he said, "comes through the sacraments. Actual grace is a gift, to help in times of temptation."

He returned to the schoolgirls, who shortly resumed their mumbled recitations, a soft droning echo in the cool church. Chester clasped his hands and bowed his head. He tried. But the churchy nostalgia he'd felt before had a weaker signal now. Nothing much came. No gift in his time of temptation.

Father Dec would phone around, every soup kitchen, every clinic, every police station, the holy hotline, calling all sinners. Someone would remember the monkey-faced streetwalker who'd gone off with the Mexican lieutenant known for his deadly sideline. Someone would know where in town the man would sneak back to. He wondered if Father Dec would mention how the woman died, mention who the killer was, playing not on sympathy but on revenge. No, Chester thought, that's my realm, and he thought again of his granddad in the spring of '45, last days of the war, knifing a man, strangling another, smothering a third, whatever it took. And why? He pictured her, the bottomless glow of her wood, the warm tangy smell of her leather straps and bellows, the pearly gleam of her buttons. Remembered the moaning cry she made in his loving hands. No other like her in the world, never. If that wasn't love, what was? Worth suffering for, yes, worth dragging all across Italy to bring back home, worth killing for if it came to that. And it had. He suspected, very shortly, it would again.

He glanced up at the plaster Jesus nailed to the crucifix hung above the altar. If you were half of who they claim, he thought, none of this would be needed. Which pretty much concluded all the praying he could manage.

He rose from his knees, let the weariness rearrange itself in his body, then ambled on out, murmuring "Thank you" to his friend as he passed, smiling at the girls who glanced up at him in giggling puzzlement or mousy fear. Orphans, he guessed, remembering what Jolt had said about the killing, knowing there were thousands of kids like this in every border town, their parents out in the desert somewhere, long dead. Some of the girls were lovely, most trended toward plain, a few were decidedly nun material. One among that last group—he couldn't help himself, just the darkening track of his thoughts—reminded him of the Mexican's tramp girlfriend, La Monita.

He was halfway down the block, thinking supper might be in or-

der, when his cell rang. A San Antonio number. He flipped the
phone open. "Geno?"

A gunshot barked through the static on the line. A muffled keening sob—a gagged man screaming—then grunts, a gasp. Geno
came on the line. "Please, Chester, it's just a box." The voice shaky,
faint, a hiss. "Buy yourself a new one. P-p-please?" Chester could
hear spittle pop against the mouthpiece. The fact that it was Geno
meant Skillet was dead. You don't put the weak one on the line to
make a point with the strong one. You kill the strong one so the
weak one understands.

He slowly closed the phone.

"I'm sorry," he whispered.

He wandered the street for half an hour, dazed one minute,
lit up with fury the next, settling finally into a state of bloodthirsty
calm. In a juke joint off East Paisano he scored a pistol from the
bartender, a Sig Sauer 9mm, stolen from a cop, the man bragged.
In a gun shop nearby he bought two extra magazines and a box
of hollow points, loaded the clips right there in the store, hands
trembling from adrenaline. Feo's gonna walk the border, he told
himself, and the best place to do that is downtown, Stanton Street
bridge. That's where I gotta be.

He walked toward the port of entry, found himself a spot to sit,
lifting a paper from the litter bin for camouflage, spreading it out
in his lap, the gun hidden just beneath. An hour passed, half of
another, night fell, the lights came on. He sat still as a bullfrog,
watchful, eyeing every walker trudging south into Mexico. And as
he did the sense of the thing fell together, like a puzzle assembling itself in midair right before his eyes. If only that helped, he
thought.

A little after eight his cell phone rang again. He considered letting it go but then he checked the display, recognized the rectory
number.

"Jolt," he said.

Silence. "No one calls me that anymore."

"I just did."

"I want you to come back to the church."

"Not happening."

"What you're thinking of doing is wrong."

"All I want's Lorena. There's others want him dead on principle.
That's why he's running."

"He'll be back."

"I suspect that's true."

"Suspect? I know. He's been in touch."

Chester shot up straight. A vein fluttered in his neck. "Feo."

"He wants to work a trade."

"I'm listening."

"No, you don't understand. He can't . . . Not what he's asking. I won't."

"The girl."

Another silence.

"Chester . . ."

"The one I saw in the church today. One who looks just like Rosa Sánchez."

"It's just an accordion, Chester."

The rage blindsided him, a surge in his midriff like coiling fire. "Not to me. Not to my granddad."

"You can't trade a child for a thing."

A *thing*? "Is it still a sin to chew the wafer, Dec? You know, because it really isn't bread anymore. Something's happened."

"Don't talk like a fool."

"Says the man who turns wine into blood."

"Her name is Analinda. The girl, I mean."

Of course, Chester thought, knowing what the priest was up to. Give her a name, she turns precious. She's alive. Like Lorena. "She's his daughter."

"She's *her* daughter."

"Point is, the girl's what he wants, has been all along. Why? I have no clue. Killers are vain, kids are for show. It's an itch, the daddy thing, comes and goes, maybe he felt a sudden need to scratch. The mother gave her away, spare her all that. So he paid me to write her a song, impress her, get her to ease up, forgive him, introduce him to his daughter. Then I went and screwed the pooch on that front, so—"

"He has no right."

"Who are you to say?"

"He'll sell her."

"So offer him a price."

"You said it yourself, he's a killer."

"He's not alone in that. My granddad was a killer. Killed for you. Killed for me."

"Chester . . ."

"God's a killer. Put some heat under that one."

The priest, incredulous: "You want to argue theodicy?"

"Not really." He felt strangely detached all of a sudden, preter-naturally so, tracking the walkers bobbing past. It was no longer in his hands. "I'm just passing the time, Jolt."

"I want you to come back to the church."

"And what exactly does that mean—argue the odyssey?"

"Not the odyssey. Theodicy."

"I know," he said. "Just messing with you."

He spotted it then, the hardshell case he knew so well, nicked and battered from the Italian campaign, a long whitish crease like a scar across the felt, left by the bullet from a Mauser 98 at Galli-cano. The man carrying it walked hurriedly, face obscured by the hood of his sweatshirt. Chester felt no doubt. He flipped his phone closed, rose to his feet, and let the newspaper flutter down, tucking the pistol beneath his shirt. You've taken what belongs to me, he thought, what belongs to my family, the most precious thing we've ever owned. Two good men are dead because of you, not to men-tion the woman, the one you crowed over, said you loved. You de-serve what's coming. Deserve worse. I'm doing your daughter a fa-vor. I'm bringing Lorena home.

He chose his angle of intercept and started walking, not so fast as to draw attention but quick enough to get there, easing through some of the other walkers. From across the street, a second man appeared. Chester recognized him too, the shoulders, the bulldog face, that distinctive jarhead fade.

Let it happen, he told himself, and it did.

Feo caught sight of the ex-Marine, began to run but the accor-dion slowed him down. *Drop it,* Chester wanted to shout, but the Mexican wouldn't let go and then the gunman was on him and the pistol was raised and two quick pops, killshots to the skull. Feo crumpled, people scattered. The killer fled.

Blinking, Chester tucked the Sig in his pants, pulled his shirt over, moving the whole time, slow at first, cautious, then a jog, breaking into a run, till he was there at the edge of the pool-ing blood, the Mexican, the poacher, the Ugly One, lying still, just nerve flutters in the hands, the legs. Strange justice, Chester thought. The sickness at the bottom of the mind.

He pried the case from the dead man's fingers, gripped the handle, and began to run back toward downtown. Something wasn't right. The weight was off-balance, wobbly, wrong. He stopped, knelt, tore at the clasps, lifted the lid. Staring back at him from a bed of sheet music, the eyes shiny like polished bone, was the severed head of Rosa Sánchez.

Sometime later—hours? days?—he found himself propped on a cantina barstool, a shot of mescal in his fist, a dozen empties scattered before him, splashes of overfill dampening the bar's pitted wood, a crowd of nameless men his newfound friends, all of them listening with that singular Mexican lust for heartbreak as he recited the tale of La Monita and Feo, told them of Geno and Skillet, confessed in a whisper his unholy love for Lorena. Time blurred into nothingness, he felt himself blurring as well, just another teardrop in the river of dreams, and he wondered what strange genius had possessed him, guiding him to this place, over the bridge from El Paso to Ciudad Juárez, the murder capital of the planet. Nor would he recall how or when he crossed that other bridge, the one between lonely and alone, but it would carry him farther than the other, days drifting into weeks, weeks dissolving into months, then years, more cantinas, more mezcal, till life as he'd known it became a whisper in the back of his mind and the man named Chester Richard drifted away like a tuneless song.

The ghost in the mirror of the bus terminal washroom, rinsing out his armpits, brushing his teeth with a finger, hair wild as an outcrop of desert scrub, sooner or later shambled off to the next string of lights across a doorway, entered and plopped himself down, crooning his garbled tales of love and murder and music, then begging a drink, told to get out by the owner, indulged by the angry man's wife, exiled to a corner with a glass of tejuino—no mezcal for a gorrón—and he'd wait for the musicians to appear, assembling themselves on the tiny bandstand like clowns in a skit, until once, in that endless maze of nights, a boy of ten shouldered on his accordion in the smoky dimness, and the nameless drunk criollo glanced up from his corner to see the seasoned mahogany dark as cane syrup, the pearl inlays, the purple heart accents, the buttons of polished bone, and with the first sigh of the kidskin bellows came that deep unmistakable throbbing tremolo, and he felt his heart crack open like an egg, knowing at last he was free.

BRENDAN DuBOIS

Ride-Along

FROM *Strand Magazine*

THE NIGHT I WENT to work, I gathered up my reporter's note-book and heavy purse and then went to check on my husband, Pe-ter. My sweetie-pie was sitting up in bed, his left leg in a cast. The bruises about his eyes were beginning to fade, though they still had a sickish green-yellow aura. The television was on and a cell phone was clasped in his right hand.

"You doing okay?" I asked.

He grinned, his teeth showing nicely through his puffy lips. "Like I've been saying, as well as could be expected."

I kissed his forehead. "You okay moving around by yourself?"

"Of course."

"Good," I said. "But you be careful. You go and break your other leg, that means you're stuck in bed. And I don't think this whole 'in sickness and in health' covers bedpan duty."

He moved up against the pillows, winced. "You could have warned me earlier."

"But you wouldn't have listened."

"And why's that?"

"Because you're madly, hopelessly, and dopily in love with me, that's why."

As I headed out Peter said, "Erica? Be careful."

I hoisted my heavy purse on my shoulder. "Don't worry, I will."

And then his face darkened. "One more thing. Sorry I got dinged up."

I shook my head. "No time to talk about that."

I blew him a kiss, which he pretended to catch and slap against his heart with his free hand.

My sweetie.

Cooper, Massachusetts, is one of the largest and poorest communities in the commonwealth, and I drove this warm May evening to one of its three police precinct stations. In the station's lobby the hard orange plastic chairs were filled with residents—most didn't speak English, yet they were busily arguing with each other or with the suffering on-duty officer behind a thick glass window. When it was my turn I said, "Erica Kramer, I have an appointment to see Captain Miller."

The harried officer looked happy to confront an easy issue, and in a manner of minutes I was taken to the rear of the precinct station. Captain Terrence Miller sat me down at his desk and passed over a clipboard with a sheet of paper.

"Look that over, sign at the bottom, and you'll be on your way," he said. Miller looked to be on the upside of fifty, with an old-fashioned buzz cut and a scarlet face.

The paper was a release form stating that one ERICA KRAMER was going to accompany OFFICER ROLAND PIPER as part of a civilian ride-along program, and that by signing said release form, myself and my heirs promised never, ever to sue the city of Cooper if I was shot, knifed, killed, mutilated, or dismembered. I scrawled my signature on the bottom and passed it back.

He checked the form and then he checked me. I knew the look. I had on black nylons, heels, a short denim skirt, and a one-size-too-tight yellow top. He seemed to consider what he was doing, and said, "Well, I guess I'll bring you over to Roland."

"Thanks," I said, grabbing my purse.

Officer Roland Piper was even older than his captain, and in his crinkly eyes and worn face I saw a cop satisfied with being a cop, who didn't want the burden of command and was happy with his own niche. In the tiny roll-call room Roland looked me up and down and said, "All right, then, come along."

We went out to the rear of the station, where a high fence surrounded the parking area for the police cruisers. I followed Roland, he carrying a soft leather carrying case in one hand and a metal clipboard in the other. He was whistling some tune I couldn't recognize and he unlocked the trunk of a cruiser. There were flares in there, chains, a wooden box, and a fire extinguisher, and Roland dropped his leather case in and slammed the trunk down. Then he went to the near rear door, opened it up, and lifted the rear seat cushion, looking carefully in the space behind the seat. He pushed the seat cushion down and closed the door.

He looked over at me. "If you're ready, get aboard."

I went around to the side and got in.

Roland ignored me as he opened up his clipboard and took some notes. Then he turned on the ignition, flipped on the headlights, tested the strobe bar over the roof of the cruiser—the lights reflecting on the rear brick wall of the police station—and flipped on the siren, cycling through four different siren sounds.

"Everything looks good, sounds good," he said, backing up the cruiser. "Thing is, you test this stuff every night. Don't want to find out the sirens or lights don't work when you need them."

I opened up my notebook, scribbled a few lines. "Why did you open up the rear seat?"

He nudged the cruiser out into traffic. "Checking things over. Sometimes perps, they get arrested, even with their hands cuffed, they can dump stuff back there. I don't like stuff dumped in my cruiser. Don't like surprises."

We were now out in traffic. He picked up the radio mic, keyed it, brought it up to his mouth, and said, "Dispatch, Unit 19 out and available."

He looked over to me. "Got that? I don't like surprises."

I made another note.

"I got that," I said.

I looked at the dashboard clock. It was 8:02 P.M.

We went through about a half-dozen blocks before he spoke up. "All right. Why me?"

"Excuse me?"

He made a right-hand turn, past a row of old three-decker homes—the last one on the end a burned-out shell. "You heard me. There's about sixty or so cops in the department. Why me?"

"Because you've been here the longest," I said. "With a half-dozen citations for bravery and excellent police work. I thought you'd be an interesting human feature story."

"You writing for the *Cooper Chronicle,* then?"

"No," I said. "I'm freelance. I've done articles before for other papers in the valley, but I thought maybe I could interest *Boston* magazine, or even the *Sunday Globe,* in your story."

"Hah," he said. "That'll be the day."

We went on for another couple of blocks. He said, "You want to know the deal?"

"Sure," I said. "What kind of deal is that?"

"Deal is, I didn't have to have you with me tonight. Captain couldn't force me. And if he did, I could tell you nothing at all. But you see, the department's getting a new allotment of cruisers next month. I made the deal with the captain. I put up with you and your dumb questions, I get the best cruiser. No more riding along in this six-year-old deathtrap."

"I don't do dumb questions," I said, my hands clasping the notebook tight.

"Huh? What's that?"

Now it was my turn. I said sweetly, "Officer, you heard me the first time. I don't do dumb questions. You're good at what you do, and I'm good at what I do."

He looked at me, scanned my legs, and offered me a thin smile. "All right. Point taken. Just so there's no misunderstandings, there's two rules."

"Go ahead."

We stopped at a traffic light. A group of kids in Red Sox jerseys were on the street corner. When they spotted the cruiser, they faded into the shadows.

"Rule one: you don't get in my way. You stay behind me, and if I tell you to stay in the cruiser, by God, you stay in the cruiser. Rule two: no questions about my personal life. I owe you and the taxpayers of Cooper eight hours a shift, forty hours a week. What I do on my own time, what hobbies I got, hell, who or what I like to date, none of your damn business. Got that?"

"Sure," I said. "Got them both."

The light changed and we moved ahead. And he looked at my legs one more time and said, "You really thought dressing up like that was a good thing for a night like this?"

I flipped a page of my notebook. "Here's a rule for you, officer. No comments on how I'm dressed. You got that?"

Another thin smile. "Gotten."

We rode around Cooper for a while, in an aimless pattern that I was sure was anything but. The radio crackled with different calls for other units, and I said, "Why have you always been a patrolman? Why not try for a promotion?"

He waited a few seconds and said, "Why put up with the aggravation? Same streets, same crime. You're a patrolman, you're responsible for yourself. You become a sergeant or a detective, then you got to manage people. Ugh. I have enough problems keeping myself in line. Hate to think of doing that with other people."

"Then why this part of town?" I asked. "There are three precincts in Cooper—Hillside, Tremont Avenue, and here, the Canal Zone. Why are you here?"

I noticed that while he drove, his eyes were rarely on the road. They were always scanning the sidewalks and the intersections, like a hunter, searching for the ever-elusive prey.

"Describe them for me," he said. "The precincts."

"Hillside . . . well, that's a bunch of nice neighborhoods and the outer suburbs. And Tremont Avenue covers the business district. And the Canal Zone . . . everything else, I guess."

Roland raised a worn hand to the old brick mill buildings built along the banks of the Micmac River. He said, "That's what powered central Massachusetts, last century. These mills, making shoes, making leather, making woolens, shipping them out on the canals. And in the space of a decade it was all gone."

Most of the tall brick buildings were empty of light, empty of life. I shivered. "There's squatters over there, drug dealers, pimps, all sorts of action," he went on. "Oh, some of the mill buildings have been rehabbed with businesses, but it's slow going. And this is where the action is, Erica. And that's what I like. Action means the time passes quick, means I get home in a good mood."

I made a point of taking some notes in my fresh reporter's notebook. I looked at the dashboard clock. It was now 9:05 P.M.

Something chattered on the police radio, and Roland braked, made a U-turn on an empty street, and flicked on the overhead lights.

Our first call of the night.

We sped for several blocks and came up behind another police cruiser, parked right up against a polished black pickup truck with oversize tires. Roland put the cruiser in park and with one smooth motion grabbed the radio microphone. "Unit 19 off at Tucker and Broadway." He put the microphone back into the cradle and said, "You can come out, but stay behind me, all right?"

"Sure," I said, and I stepped out with him.

We walked up to the truck and there were two young men, wearing baggy clothes and backward baseball caps, standing with their hands on the hood. A young female officer looked relieved to see Roland. He talked to her, then she watched as he went through the men's pockets. Coins, cigarette lighters, and then plastic baggies full of white powder were distributed on the hood. Within moments the men were handcuffed and placed in the rear of the first cruiser.

More chitchat with the younger officer, then Roland laughed and got back into the cruiser and I followed.

He put us out on the street, and with microphone in hand he said, "Unit 19 clear."

"What was that about?"

"Just a traffic stop, that's all. Clown driving that pickup truck blew through a stop sign and Officer Perkins there pulled him over. She sensed something screwy was going on and asked for backup."

I said, "I read somewhere that some cops, they don't like women cops out there on the streets. Think they're too weak, they're—"

He said, "That's a load of crap. They're tough when they have to be, and they're great to be at your side during a domestic dispute. Man, I hate domestics. And anyone who can help me out here on the streets, I don't care if they're male, female, or any combination thereof."

A few more notes made in my notebook. Roland said, "You surprised me with that question. I thought you'd stick up for your fellow sisters on the force, something like that."

I smiled. "Guess I'm full of surprises."

The dashboard clock said it was 10:12 in the evening.

The rest of the night went on with more aimless cruising, and I eventually learned that Roland was ex-army military police, had received an honorable discharge, and had started working on the

Cooper force. As for his citations for bravery, he shrugged them off. "Most of that stuff was just being in the wrong place at the right time, and having the chief wanting to make a big deal out of it 'cause it made for good newspaper headlines around budget time."

We also made two traffic stops—one coffee-and-doughnut stop ("And if this gets in the paper, make sure you write that I got a bran muffin, okay? No doughnuts for me," Roland had said), and a fight outside the Sloppy Cow Pub & Grub that resulted in one woman being arrested, two men being put into ambulances, and a good half-hour of paperwork and note-taking on Roland's behalf.

"You having fun?" he asked after we left the Sloppy Cow Pub & Grub, where the owner was taking a hose to wash off the bloodstains on the sidewalk.

"Oh yeah," I said. "A real blast."

Now it was the start of a new day, and my legs were getting cold. I watched the light-blue numerals of the dashboard clock flip, and with each change of the number, it seemed like the air in the cruiser was getting thicker and harder to breath.

Then it clicked over to one in the morning. I yawned. Roland said, "You want to go back to the precinct, head on home?"

"No, I'm okay," I said.

"Whatever," Roland said. We were driving past another burned-out collection of tenements and he said, "There's a story for you. Someone should trace the deeds of those properties, see who owns what. Bet if you dig enough, you'll find that somebody's making a lot of money off those arsons—"

The radio crackled to life. "Unit 19."

Roland picked up the handset. "Unit 19, go."

"Unit 19, 14 Venice Avenue, the Gold Club. Robbery in progress. Other units responding. Caller said robbers appear to be armed."

Roland said, "Unit 19, responding."

He replaced the hand mic, brought the cruiser to a shuddering halt, and then made a U-turn and flipped on the overhead lights. He punched the accelerator and I felt myself thrust back against the seat as we roared down the center of Market Street.

"What's the Gold Club?"

"Jewelry store. Only one in this area. I know them . . . got a large inventory."

"No siren?" I said.

"Nope," he said. "Sirens just let them know we're coming."

Roland braked again and we slewed into a turn, and he said quickly, "Deal is, you stay in the cruiser. All right? Other backups will be here in a bit."

I clenched my purse and notebook tight in my hands. "Right. I'll stay behind. No problem."

The cruiser roared down a deserted stretch of roadway, flanked on either side by empty brick mill buildings and the still water of the canals, and with a slap of his hand Roland switched off the overhead lights. He slowed and then dimmed the headlights.

My voice shook. "Do . . . do you know what you're doing?"

"Yeah," he said. "Alleyway up here will put us right across the street from the Gold Club. You just stay put."

Another turn and Roland eased his way up a narrow alleyway, then switched off the headlights. He slowly inched forward. Up ahead was an overflowing Dumpster, and he parked the cruiser. The handset was in his hand. "Unit 19, off at the scene."

"Ten-four, Unit 19. Be advised, other units about ten minutes inbound."

The handset went back, and with a rattle of keys he unlocked the pump-action shotgun and got it out. My heart was racing right along, and I knew my face was pale and my eyes were wide.

Roland opened the cruiser door and said, "Erica . . ."

"I'm not moving. You just be careful."

"Just my job, that's all." And he got out and closed the door behind him.

I saw his shadow move in front of the cruiser, to the side of the Dumpster. I watched for a minute or two and then, with shaking hands, reached down and took off my shoes.

I picked up my purse and then got out of the cruiser.

The pavement was cold on my bare feet, and I prayed for no broken glass or discarded syringes to be in my way. I reached into my purse and found a comforting object, which I withdrew and then extended. A collapsable police baton. The definition of irony, I guess one could say.

I whispered my way up to Roland, kneeling on one knee, shotgun in hand, looking out across Venice Avenue and the shuttered

doors of the Gold Club and some construction supplies and the
footbridges that went over one of the canals. I raised up the collapsable baton and brought it down hard against the base of his
neck.

Three hours later I was home, tired, thirsty. The light was on in the
bedroom and I walked in, and my sweetie-pie was sitting there, face
expectant, looking up at me.

"Well?"

I pulled a few strands of hair away from my face. "Gee, I missed
you too, honey. Did it go all right? How are you feeling? What happened?"

His face flushed. "Sorry, Erica." He moved about on the bed
some. "I missed you. Didn't sleep a wink. Did it go all right? How
are you feeling? What happened?"

I dropped my heavy purse on the floor. "It went just fine."

"So. Where have you been?"

I gave him the dear-why-didn't-you-empty-the-trash-like-you-said
look. "Where do you think?"

He tossed the cell phone over to me. "Talk to me, then."

So an hour earlier I was in an interrogation room of the Cooper
Police Department, facing an unhappy Captain Miller and a blank-
faced detective named Stephens. The interrogation room was
stuffy and I was twisting and retwisting a paper napkin in my hands,
which I used sometimes to dab at my eyes.

Captain Miller looked to me and then Detective Stephens, a
young hard-faced man with close-cropped black hair going to gray.
"Any more questions?" he asked the detective.

The detective stared right at me, as if he was trying to look
through me and beyond. He had a cheap pen that he fluttered
through his fingers like a magician.

"No," the detective said slowly. "No questions . . . Just want to
make sure we have it straight, what happened. Do you mind?"

"No," I said. "Of course not."

He looked down at his legal pad, read from his notes. "So when
you got to the scene, you said Officer Piper told you to stay in the
cruiser, correct?"

"Yes."

"And after he left—what happened then?"

"What I told you. I saw him go up the alleyway to a Dumpster. I saw him crouching . . . and then . . . I got scared."

Detective Stephens said, "And what happened when you said you were scared?"

"I . . . I scrunched down in the front seat. I didn't want anybody to see me. And then . . ."

I wiped my eyes again with the paper napkin. "It was so quick. A man ran by, carrying something in his hands. He . . . he hit Officer Piper on the back of his head, and then ran around the corner. I panicked. I got on the floor of the cruiser."

"You didn't get out to see what was going on? You must have heard the gunshots." Detective Stephens asked.

Snot was running down my nose. "I was so scared . . . I scrunched down further and waited for the other policemen . . ."

"Mmm," Detective Stephens said. "But then you had the presence of mind to grab the radio and call for help."

"Yes," I said, my voice soft. "I . . . I knew I had to do something, and I pulled the microphone off the radio and called it in. Officer down."

Both Miller and Stephens were quiet, and I said, "What . . . what happened, at the Gold Club?"

Stephens looked to Miller. "It's still under investigation. Looks like a burglary. The two guys are dead and the loot's gone . . . must be one or two others out there somewhere. Sorry I can't tell you any more at the moment. Later today . . . if you wish to check in again, we can probably tell you more."

I nodded, wiped at my eyes. "And . . . Officer Piper. How's he doing?"

"He's at Cooper General Hospital," Miller said.

"Will he be okay?"

Miller smiled for the first time. "That guy's got a thick head. He'll be just fine."

So about twelve hours after I got home from my ride-along, my sweetie, Peter, was in the passenger's side of our Toyota Camry, bags packed, the disposable cell phone having been disposed of, and I was heading over to the driver's side when a black Ford F-150 pickup truck came into the short driveway, blocking us. The door opened up and Roland Piper gingerly stepped out, dressed in jeans and a long-sleeved black denim shirt.

I opened the door and said to my sweetie, "I'll be just a minute."

"You going to be all right?"

"Trust me." I smiled. "I'll be just fine."

I went over to the truck and said, "Officer Piper."

"Erica."

"How are you feeling?"

He turned so I could see a bulky bandage around the base of his head, and then turned back. "Not bad. Out for a week, and docs said I should be ready to go back on duty then."

"Good."

We stood there for a moment, waiting. Then he made the first move, for which I was thankful.

"I'm just a cop with seniority but no command," he said, "but you didn't question me or insult me last night about being just a cop. So don't start insulting me now. All right?"

I folded my arms. "Fine. I won't start by insulting you now."

He leaned against the fender of his pickup truck. "After I was attacked and taken to the hospital, I got to thinking. And questioning. And I decided to do some quick digging. You're not much of a writer, Erica. Three articles in the space of eight years."

"Good writing takes time," I said.

"I'm sure," Roland said. "And your husband . . . he's a ghost. Not much of a payroll record, not much of anything. And the two of you—no criminal record at all. Which means the two of you are either simple and dumb or complicated and very smart. And since you've had a rental agreement on this apartment for just a month, I'm not thinking simple and dumb."

I said nothing, waited. He cocked his head and said, "It was no coincidence you were with me last night. You wanted to be on that ride-along because you knew something was going to happen at the Gold Club. Not a bad setup. Me being knocked out, leaving the scene deserted. Available for whatever. So you'd think . . . not a bad deal."

"A deal," I said.

"So," he said. "Here's my deal. A cut of whatever was taken there and I go away, and you go away, and nothing more is said."

I kept silent and he said, "Erica, no insults now. It's a good deal. I won't even ask you how those two guys got shot up."

I still kept silent, and then he added, "If I got all of that in just a few hours, imagine what the detectives can do in a few days."

I nodded. "How much?"

"I'll trust your judgment. Just know you should be fair, or I'll be insulted, and—"

I jangled the keys in my hand, went to the trunk of the Camry, and Roland moved around and said politely, "Just so there's no misunderstanding. Just want to see your hands. Professional courtesy, wouldn't you say?"

"Absolutely," I said.

I snapped open the trunk, went into a side pocket of a knapsack, unzipped it, and pulled out a plain-brown-paper-wrapped package. Tossed it to Roland, who caught it easily.

"Quick question?" I asked.

"Sure."

"What tipped it for you?"

He hefted the package in his hand. "You said you were doing a profile on me, you asked me all these questions, and after I get whacked on the back of the head—according to the detectives, most likely by one of the gang serving as a lookout—you didn't come to see me at the hospital. That would make your story even better, if you were planning on writing a story. But you weren't."

I closed the trunk of the Camry. "So what are you planning now?"

He smiled. "Early retirement."

"To do what?"

He went back to his truck. "You seem to like stories. So here's two stories for your consideration. Story one: a grumpy, embittered cop, working long hours, little pay, no advancement, sees his chance to score and leave for sunnier places."

"And the second story?"

"A cop with a wife in home health care with a long-term degenerative nerve disease, who needs lots of money, and who realized long ago that if he just stays as a cop and works lots of overtime, he can barely make it . . . and then sees his chance to score and be settled for a long time."

He got into the truck, rolled down the window. I called out to him. "So which story is true?"

"None, both," he said. "You're the writer. You figure it out. And Erica . . . go far and don't come back. The detectives still have a lot of questions about what happened last night. Don't be around. You're a cold one, and you might get by, but don't tempt it."

I started walking to the driver's side of the Camry. "We won't."

Inside the Camry I started up the car. Peter put his hand on my arm. "Had to make a payoff?"

"Yep."

"Things okay?"

"So far, so good."

I backed us out onto the street, thinking, Less than a week. We'll be in California in less than a week.

And I thought again about last night.

So about fifteen hours earlier, after Officer Roland Piper fell to the ground with a moan, I put my shoes back on and continued to work. I slid the collapsed police baton back into my purse and then sprinted across the street to the entrance of the Gold Club. I ducked in a brick alcove near some construction supplies, knowing what was going to happen in a few seconds.

There was a creaking sound.

The door to the Gold Club opened up.

A head poked out. Took a quick scan. Missed me. Ducked back inside.

Hurry up, I thought, hurry up. The cops are coming.

The head poked out again. A whisper.

My unzipped purse was in my hand. I put my free hand inside, curved it around a familiar and comfortable object.

Movement. Two men ducked out, carrying small black knapsacks in their hands, and they started sprinting up the sidewalk, away from me, and—

I stepped out, dropped the purse, hands now cradling a Smith & Wesson 9 mm pistol, and I shot them both in the back.

They dropped to the ground, the knapsacks tumbling next to them, and I stepped up and fired again, finishing the one on the left. The one on the right was moaning, curled over on his side, and I kicked him over onto his back so that he was looking up at me.

"Tsk, tsk, Tommy. Did you think I'd let this go? After my hubby planned it, scoped it, and brought you and your brother in? It would have been fine—but you were too greedy, you twit."

He grimaced. "Sonny . . . should have listened to Sonny . . . he wanted to whack your Peter . . . and I just wanted him out . . . by tuning him up . . ."

"Yes, Tommy, you should have listened to your brother." And then I shot him again, finishing him off.

I looked around. Still no sign of the police. No wonder crime was rampant in this part of town. I picked up both knapsacks and ran back to the cruiser, emptied the contents into my large purse and threw the purse onto the passenger seat and dumped the empty knapsacks into the nearby Dumpster. Went back to the construction gear, pulled out some prepositioned cinder blocks, and in a few minutes, my baton and pistol were dumped into the canal.

Then I ran back to the cruiser, made a desperate radio call, and waited, shivering on the cruiser's floor, doing my best to ignore the still figure of Officer Roland Piper on the ground.

As I drove Peter rubbed my leg and said, "Perfect. You were perfect."

I shook my head and my sweet hubby said, "What's wrong?"

"Something's not right," I said.

"What's that?"

I stopped at a traffic light, noted the exit sign for the interstate just a block ahead.

"Officer Piper, he said I was cold. Can you believe that? He said I was cold."

"Wow."

I turned to Peter. "You don't think I'm cold, do you?"

He laughed. "Erica . . . no way. Not cold at all."

I smiled. "Thanks, hon. I appreciate that."

My hubby laughed again. "Of course, if I said anything else, you'd probably kill me."

I turned, smiled sweetly, and blew him a kiss.

LOREN D. ESTLEMAN

Sometimes a Hyena

FROM *Amos Walker: The Complete Story Collection*

WHY I TOLD THE JOKE AT ALL I can't say. It wasn't that good, but then neither was the bar I told it in nor the bartender I told it to. I was drenched through with the sweat of a long day, with nothing else to show for it but the thought of an unpleasant telephone conversation with the client the next morning. Sometimes you stick with the subject like his own bad taste in aftershave, sometimes he drops you like a weak signal; but the guy paying your freight is never a philosopher.

I'd driven past the place a hundred times without noticing. I hadn't been thirsty the first hundred times. A long way back it had been someone's idea of home, a square frame eight-hundred-square-foot house with a shingle roof and tile siding that reminded you you'd missed three appointments to have your teeth cleaned. It didn't identify itself: the owner had just bought an orange LED sign that said OPEN and stuck it in the front window. But in that neighborhood a bar was all it could be. I still think of it, when I think of it at all, as the Open.

Inside was permanent dusk, two piles of protoplasm dumped on stools at the end of the bar, and a tabletop shuffleboard game whose pine boards had been slapped with a varnish that went tacky in high humidity so that one of the shuttles had stopped halfway down its length one day and decided that was where it would stay. A paint-can opener would be needed to pry it loose.

I don't remember what the bartender looked like. He would be a middle-aged guy running to flab who had seen *Cocktail* once, pictured himself in some swanky joint juggling shakers and stem glasses, and like the shuttle had come to everlasting rest in that spot. Normally I wouldn't have spoken to him beyond ordering a double scotch, but while he was siphoning it out my gaze lit upon a sepia picture in a frame on the wall above the beer taps. Someone had cut a photo of zebras grazing in the veldt from *National Geographic* and put it behind glass to make the place seem exotic.

"Guy walks into a bar," I said.

"Guys do, pleased to say." He slapped a paper napkin in front of me and set my drink on it. "This a joke?"

"That's the punch line from another 'Guy walks into a bar' joke; but you tell me. There's a kangaroo mixing the drinks. Kangaroo looks at the guy and says, 'I see you're surprised to find a kangaroo behind the bar.' Guy says, 'I'll say. Did the zebra sell the place?'"

He grunted, which told me all I needed to know about how he'd wound up in a dump like the Open. A really first-class barman laughs when the joke isn't funny and shakes his head when the story isn't that sad. Now that I think of it, his face belonged on the other side of the bar, tie-dyed with red gin blossoms and yellowed lost opportunities. But then that might just have been my face in the peel-and-stick mirrors in back of the bottles with recycled premium labels. An unexpected glimpse of one's reflection on that sort of day is no treat.

I'd thought of leaving him change from my ten, but I put it away. His kid could scrub pots and pans for his tuition, just like all the other self-made millionaires. I was in what the poets call a dark humor. I looked around for someone to kick sand in my face.

"Fucking cops," the bartender said.

He'd flicked on the TV on the corner shelf under the ceiling, in case my opening routine might lead to a set.

I wasn't the least bit curious. That state of mind is the first off-duty casualty in the life of a detective. I couldn't care less about what the cops were up to that put him out of his sunny mood. So of course I looked up at the screen.

A female reporter stood on a street crosshatched with yellow caution tape, pretending to read from a notepad while red and blue strobes pulsed in the background. An Early Response Team — downtown Detroit jargon for SWAT — had charged a house on the northwest side where an armed man was said to be barricaded with his wife. The husband was in custody, but the wife was dead with a slug in her heart. An unidentified source swore that no firearms were found in the house. An investigation was under way to determine whether a stray police round had killed the woman.

The bartender backhanded his remote at the TV and the screen went black. "They'll sweep that one under the rug toot-sweet. State should make them buy a hunting license."

"I guess you've never been in on a bust."

"I been on the receiving end. Cops think they own the town."

"Anything can happen when the adrenaline kicks in and the guns come out. A little girl got killed the same way last spring. That time they were looking for an armed robber."

"I remember it. Seems to me a cop got an unpaid vacation. He's back on the job and the girl's still dead. You a cop?"

"If I said I was, would you spit in my drink?"

He grinned sourly. "For starters."

The story metastasized over the next few days. A DPD spokesman confirmed the report that no gun was recovered from the house and the bullet, which had shattered when it penetrated the woman's sternum, was a soft-nose .38, a common police weapon. The lab rats in Ballistics were working to reassemble the fragments in order to match them to the gun. So far none of the officers on the scene had admitted to discharging a sidearm. The spokesman refused to say whether their guns were being examined, but that would be SOP.

Another press conference was called by Philip Justice, who announced he'd been retained by the husband to sue the police department for excessive use of deadly force and false arrest. Justice — it was his real name, and maybe the inspiration for his choice of occupations — was a pit viper who specialized in representing ordinary citizens against authority. His strategy never changed. He went in fast and hard, shrill with outrage, blindsiding the opposition before it could get a toehold and wresting pricey settlements with his teeth.

I admired his performance over my morning coffee. He removed his hand from his recently released client's shoulder only to stab a finger at the camera and paraphrase the First Book of Samuel; he'd know the passages on David and Goliath by heart, but he needed the sympathy of atheists too.

It was live coverage. I'd just turned off the set when my telephone rang. It was Justice.

I'd worked for him a couple of times, so I wasn't shocked that he'd tag me to investigate, but the timing was a surprise. I thought he'd be on the line with a judge or the *New York Times,* or anyway someone higher up on the food chain so quickly after going public. I said I wasn't working hard and agreed to meet him in his office in twenty minutes.

He operated high up in the American Building in Southfield, a glass-and-steel arrangement that towered over the horizontal suburb like a birthday candle on a cupcake. The suite was medium gray and pale yellow, and his desk was a glass wafer on composition legs. He got up from behind it, and as usual his six feet six was a shock to the system; sitting down he looked built to ordinary scale. His hair grew straight back and close to the scalp like an otter's and he blinked a lot—I guess from all those TV lights and flash attachments he lived among. He took my hand in a swift, firm grip and gave it back. "Amos Walker, Claud Vale."

I remembered his client spelled his first name without an *e.* He rose from a yellow leather chair, shrinking in on himself unlike Justice as he did so, and lowered and raised his chin in greeting while letting his hands hang at his sides. He was fifty but looked older, with once-red hair like rusted iron and muddy eyes wallowing in bags behind bifocals. A blue blazer hung from thin shoulders, showing four white stitches on one cuff where the manufacturer's label had been removed, a nice lawyerly touch that said the man was unaccustomed to dressing up but had made the purchase to appear presentable in court. The black silk armband was unobtrusive but impossible not to notice.

When we were all seated, me in gray leather, Justice in the ergonomic item behind the desk, he said, "Mr. Vale neither said nor hinted that he was armed. When he refused to open the door to police answering a domestic disturbance complaint by neighbors, the officers assumed the worst and the situation escalated from there."

"Ernestine was divorcing me," Vale said, in a voice like a cassette tape dragging over tired spools. "When GM laid me off and I couldn't find nothing, she said she'd be better off getting a job and looking after herself and nobody else. That's what we fought about. I never laid a hand on her, not in seventeen years. I sure didn't want her dead." He dug out a handkerchief, blew his nose, and lifted his glasses to wipe his eyes.

"We know a shot was fired," said Justice. "We know from which gun. An ERT sergeant admitted it after Ballistics examined his weapon. He claims it went off when Mr. Vale grabbed his arm."

"That's a lie!"

"Of course it is, Claud. Try to calm down. The bullet recovered from Mrs. Vale's body was too fragmented to match conclusively to a weapon, but with only one shot fired and one slug found, we don't need it to build our case."

I crossed my legs. "All I know is what I saw on TV. The cops who answered the domestic complaint swore he shouted through the door he'd shoot if they tried to come inside."

"I never did."

"Claud, please. You're among friends. Even if that were so, it would only have given the department probable cause to enter the house. I'm not debating that, although I believe they mistook what they heard. The fact that no gun was found in the house or within throwing range of any of the doors or windows emphatically demonstrates that the authorities failed to exercise due diligence. We're asking for ten million."

"This is all starting to sound familiar," I said.

"The circumstances are almost identical to those involving the death of a little girl six months ago on the East Side: an Early Response Team officer investigating a felony-harboring situation said the grandmother on the scene struggled with him and his gun went off, killing the child. I wasn't the attorney of record in the suit that followed, but the officer was dismissed and the judge awarded the family five million. I believe double that amount is justified by the fact that the department failed to learn from its earlier mistake."

"You've got it all figured out. So what's my end?"

"I want to swat that mosquito about whether Mr. Vale threatened to shoot the first responders. If one of them doesn't recant I can still make the case, but if there's no truth in it, the city will settle and this never goes to court."

I got out a cigarette, to play with, not to smoke; state law says you can buy them but don't light up. "In other words I ask a couple of cops if they're liars."

"You've got the best lawyer in town, if that's what you're worried about."

"It's not. My insurance carrier might consider stupidity a pre-existing condition." But I proved the point and took the job.

I met Officer Bender in a booth in the Thermopolis, a cop bar in Greektown, in the shadow of 1300, the ornate crumbling head-quarters of the Detroit Police Department. It was early, and the staff was clearing away the debris of the morning rush and laying tables for the noon crowd. We had the place to ourselves apart from them and a couple of tired-looking plainclothesmen from Major Crimes drinking coffee at the bar over baklava and waiting out the end of their shift.

Bender was the junior half of the two-man team that had re-sponded to the domestic disturbance complaint at Claud Vale's house. He was built like a college basketball player, tall and sinewy in his autumn uniform, and during the brief small talk I learned he'd been offered a full-ride scholarship at the University of Michi-gan but had gotten tired of the hoops and dropped out to join the twelve-week police training course in Detroit. He was a good-looking light-skinned black who liked plenty of cream and sugar in his strong Greek coffee.

He finished looking at my credentials and handed them back. "'I'll shoot the first man through the door,' that's what I heard. Book says that implies probability of a weapon. What's it say in yours?"

"It says step off and call for backup," I said. "Only I don't have backup, so I'd just step off. How do you and Wallace get along?" Sergeant Wallace was his partner, a fifteen-year man with the Uni-form Division; three letters of commendation in his jacket and two months' unpaid suspension over a home-invasion suspect who'd died of asphyxiation in the course of a bust.

"He's my partner. I trust him with my life."

"That's what the book says. I'm not taking notes."

"I don't think he'd give me his sister's hand if I asked, but we got plenty of that in the department. He's a good cop. That thing two years ago could've happened to anyone. Guy had a glass throat."

I let that one eddy with the current. "This thing goes the way it went on the East Side last spring, a lot of good cops'll wind up in private security. That goes from the bottom up and never reaches the brass."

He added still more sugar to his cup and stirred it; a weaker man would've had to use two hands. "Call me a liar again, I'll cuff you for whatever I can dream up between here and down the street. Just as soon as I finish my coffee."

That was it for the interview. I thought of paying his tab along with mine, but the bribery charge might be too much temptation.

Cops, even young ones, are rarely so thin-skinned. I'd taken a wild shot and drawn blood.

Sergeant Wallace was temporarily unavailable. He'd taken a personal day and the woman who answered at his home — I assumed it was his wife — said he'd gone bow hunting in Washtenaw County. She didn't expect him back before nightfall.

I couldn't get within a mile of the ERT sergeant who'd fired the round that had reportedly killed Ernestine Vale. He was on paid administrative leave pending the outcome of the internal investigation, and not even Philip Justice could get a contact number for him outside of 1300. But I couldn't think of anything to ask him that the shoot team wouldn't, so I didn't waste time pumping my unofficial sources, who are all more or less legitimately employed and keep jacking up their rates according to the risk of selling confidential information: Homeland Security had become involved, and Justice's pockets aren't that deep. No one's are.

Just to kill time while waiting to corner young Officer Bender's partner, I got a pass through Justice to walk through the scene of the shooting. The cop at the door looked at the pass, confirmed it on the Star Trek radio clipped to his shoulder strap, and stood aside to let me open the door and duck under the yellow tape.

It was a building of historical interest, which locally is as good as an order of condemnation; ninety years ago Henry Ford built dozens and dozens of narrow frame houses with steeply pitched roofs to shelter laborers who had streamed in from the Deep South and eastern Europe to earn five dollars a day assembling Model Ts in

Dearborn. This was one of the few left, and despite intermittent remodeling preserved the shape and character of the original better than most of the rest.

I climbed the nearly vertical staircase and looked at the bedroom purely out of cultural curiosity. All the action had taken place on the ground floor, where according to her husband Mrs. Vale was down with the flu on the living room sofa when the bullet entered her heart at an oblique angle, the coroner said, which corresponded with Vale's version of the event. She'd moved to the sofa anyway preliminary to cutting herself loose from her husband permanently. The sheets had been removed for evidence, but the cushions were stained dark where she'd bled.

On the way out I nodded to the gatekeeper and tried the house next door, a shotgun-style ranch built on the site of what would have been another Ford construction; he created whole neighborhoods from barren fields and reclaimed swamp. The woman who cracked the door two inches at my knock had thick fingers, a suspicious blue eye, and a Ukrainian accent. The eye studied my credentials from top to bottom, but the door didn't budge. "I tell the police everything," she said.

"I won't walk you all the way back through it. What did you hear?"

"I hear bang when the police are there. I think it must be a shot."

"Any sound of struggling?"

"No, just bang. Without police I would think it is a door slamming. Doors are slamming there all the time, yelling, like that day. The people, they don't get along so good."

"Are you the one who complained to the police about the domestic disturbance?"

"I don't want to get into no trouble."

"You won't."

She said it again. I moved on. I was sure now it was her, not that it mattered who'd called. "What about when just the two policemen were there? Did you hear Mr. Vale shouting?"

"I hear shouting. I don't know who or what. Then the two go away. Later more come. One comes to this door and says don't go out, stay away from the windows. I tell him, today is no different from all the rest. I might have stayed in Kiev."

I thanked her. She pressed the door in my face and was still snapping locks when I stepped off the porch.

"I had a sweet shot, a heart shot," Sergeant Wallace said. "This little-bitty birch you couldn't even see deflected the arrow and the best rack I've seen in years went sailing off over a barbed-wire fence."

Veteran cops are masters at dividing their work and home lives. I was there to ask about his part in an affair that had left a woman dead with a slug in her heart and he was telling me about the deer heart he'd missed that afternoon in rural Michigan; no irony in his voice or expression.

We were sitting in his small kitchen in Redford Township, with a group of mismatched appliances that had been replaced as needed and no two at the same time. The pattern was worn almost completely off the linoleum and the table we sat at was sheet metal over pine. He had a squat brown beer bottle in his squat right fist and I could have connected the broken blood vessels in his broad fleshy face like dots. Mrs. Wallace, a small, wrenlike creature who gave the impression of a nervous type until you noticed the steel wire underneath, was in the laundry washing spray-on doe hormones from her husband's camo suit. He wore loose-fitting old suit pants and his back hair curled like tropical undergrowth over the shoulder straps of his BVD undershirt.

I said, "I won't take up much time. What did Claud Vale say when you showed up at his house?"

"'Go away or I'll shoot right through this door.'"

"Those words exactly?"

"They're in my report."

I looked at my notebook. "Your partner said it was, 'I'll shoot the first man through the door.'"

"What's the difference?"

"The second version threatened your lives. The first threatened his door."

He swigged beer and thunked down the bottle. "You work for a lawyer, all right. You know same as me he meant only one thing either way."

"The lawyer I work for would go to town on the difference in phrasing. He'd make it sound like one of you lied and the other backed him up, as partners do, only he got the words wrong. He'd say it was your idea, being the senior man; but anyway he'll play it so both your testimonies wind up in the ashcan."

His face got so dark I couldn't pick out the burst vessels.

I said, "I'm just the messenger. If that's how it went down, fine: tell it on the stand and let Justice do what he can with it. Just don't lose it there the way you're losing it here in your own kitchen. I wouldn't be talking this way if Bender didn't lash out like a snake when I told him his career might depend on what he said in court. He's got a guilty conscience."

"Finished?" He pointed at the beer he'd given me. I hadn't touched it, but I put away my notebook and got up. At the front door I heard the hollow snap and whoosh of a fresh bottle being opened.

Philip Justice subsided into the cushions of his desk chair, closing his eyes and folding his hands across his spare middle as if he'd just finished a feast. "Damn fine work. I had Wallace figured as the weak link, based on that blot on his record. But Bender's our pigeon. I may not even have to call his partner to the stand."

"Thing is," I said, "I think Wallace is telling the truth. I believe Vale made a threat of some kind. Bender didn't hear it—making out emotional words through a thick door comes with experience. Bender decided to back him up after they compared notes. You need a good reason for calling for reinforcements when you write your report, especially after what went down."

"Made a threat with what? He didn't have a gun."

"Not when a search was made. The next-door neighbor heard doors slamming earlier. A handgun report heard through two walls can be mistaken for a door slamming."

He opened his eyes and came forward. The feast had turned into indigestion. "She heard yelling too."

"I can go back and find out if any of that yelling sounded like Ernestine Vale's voice."

"I didn't hire you to make a case for the police. God, you make him sound like a criminal mastermind. You're saying he shot his wife, then staged a fight to bring the cops to his door and set up the Detroit Police Department for her murder."

"It wouldn't be the first time someone tried to get tricky. If he shot her long enough before the complaint went through, he'd have plenty of opportunity to sneak out of the house, dump the gun in a storm drain a dozen blocks away, and sneak back in and fake a fight."

"There'd be a record of a firearm purchase. He's clean. Don't you think I had that checked out? You're not the only PI in town."

"You're right. Where would anyone go in Detroit to get a gun without leaving a paper trail?"

"He's an unemployed auto worker, not a penny-ante hit man. He wouldn't know where to look."

I played with a cigarette. "All I'm saying is I'd like to run it out. You don't want this blowing up in your face in public."

"What do you want from me?" Now he sounded like a successful man being put upon by a poor relation.

"Two things. First, when did his wife file for divorce?"

He fired up the computer on his desk. "April eleventh."

"This is part of the first thing. When did the cops screw up and kill that little girl on the East Side?"

"You can't think those two things are connected. The circumstances—"

"—are almost identical. Your words. When?"

Keys got tickled. He frowned at the screen, showing the kind of reaction he never showed in court. "April fourteenth."

I wrote both dates in my notebook, not that I'd forget. "Second thing: Which plant did Vale work for before he was laid off?"

I found Dix Sommerfield working the employee parking lot at the GM assembly plant in Warren. He was a third-generation member of a Kentucky family that had come north in a body to build tanks for the automobile-factories-turned-defense plants during World War II. He could usually be found, a potbellied presence in a reverse ball cap, selling unlicensed bottles of whiskey and cartons of cigarettes and certain other contraband from the trunk of his wired-together Chevy Nova during shift changes. Tuesdays and Thursdays found him at Chrysler, Mondays at River Rouge, where he spent a lot of time looking over his shoulder for Ford's private police force. The other days of the week you could depend on his being in Warren, his sentimental favorite; his father and grandfather had been loyal to General Motors ahead of Uncle Sam and the Southern Baptist Church.

"I'm looking for a thirty-eight revolver," I said, after we'd exchanged greetings. I'd bought information from him in the past, cash on the barrelhead, and no backlash from the authorities.

Not that he wasn't cagey; the balance had shifted after 9/11, and you never knew when interference from the amateurs in Washington might louse up a smooth system. "I don't deal in that stuff no more," he said, moving the toothpick that lived in his mouth from one corner to the other. "You want a piece, go to Dick's Sporting Goods."

"I want to know about one you sold. Dix, do I have to pull that spare tire out from under all those boxes of Marlboros and look into the well? It was a soft-nose slug, so it couldn't have come from an automatic."

"Wearing a wire?"

I unbuttoned my shirt and spread it.

"That ain't nothing. Drop your pants."

I kicked him in the shin, and when he bent to cradle it gave him a chop with the side of my hand on his elbow. Forget the groin: if you really want to make a painful point, go for the little knobs of bone that stick out from the joints. When the tears stopped flowing I took out a *Free Press* clipping with Claud Vale's picture and stuck it under his nose.

He wiped his eyes with his sleeve and squinted. "Jeez. I been praying for days that one wouldn't come back and bite me in the ass."

"God answered. He said stick to cigarettes and booze. You can't go wrong with the basics."

One week after the story broke, Philip Justice announced he was dropping his suit and that he'd resigned as Claud Vale's attorney. The cops, knowing what that meant, rearrested his former client and went to work on him; no physical abuse, no coercion other than the reliable aggressive questioning in Supreme Court–mandated increments with periods of rest in between, tying the suspect up in his own lies until telling the truth was the only path to sanity. He confessed to murdering his wife, threatening the first responders so that backup was required from 1300, and grabbing the arm of the first cop through the door, forcing his gun to go off, as guns will in that situation. A more thorough search of the crime scene turned up the ERT sergeant's slug in a place where two baseboards met unevenly in a corner. That had been a break for Vale, who hadn't considered what would happen if it were recovered anywhere but in Ernestine Vale's heart. He'd had the foresight to score an *X* in the nose of the slug he'd used before firing it, making it burst apart on entry so that it couldn't be traced to the gun he'd used; the rest was beginner's luck.

The gun itself was never found, but it was no longer required for evidence. I didn't have to go to jail for keeping Dix Sommerfield's name out of the record.

Philip Justice bought me a drink at the Caucus Club downtown. He was still bothered by the loss of what looked like a big settlement and more crusading glory to his name, but he was grateful not to have been made a clown on the evening news. He sipped at his twelve-year-old cognac. "So you got all this on what a couple of cops told you?"

"Some of it." I stirred the ice in my scotch and tossed the swizzle. "The timing cinched it. Vale was brooding about the divorce, losing half of what little he had in the outcome, when that little girl died. He saw a way to get clear and be rich besides."

"That was an armed-robbery investigation, not murder."

"It was enough the same as what he had in mind. When I first heard of Vale I was in a bar."

"Imagine that."

"I'll ignore the implication. I'd told the bartender a joke. I got the idea from a picture of zebras he had on the wall." I told it.

He didn't laugh. "I heard that one. Seems to me a different animal was involved."

"Sometimes it's a hyena sold the place. It's always a kangaroo behind the bar, for some reason. Who knows what makes these things work?"

BETH ANN FENNELLY AND
TOM FRANKLIN

What His Hands Had Been Waiting For

FROM *Delta Blues*

July, 1927

THEY LEFT THE DEAD LOOTERS in the house and were striding toward their horses, Ham Johnson reloading his .30-.30, when they heard what sounded like a cat.

"Ain't no cat," said Ingersoll.

"Naw." Ham clicked a cartridge into the port of his rifle. He clicked in another.

They followed the squawling past the house's slanted silhouette—the owners smart enough to leave the doors and windows open, which had let the floodwaters swirl through. Behind the house, a shade tree, now like something dipped in batter halfway up. Snagged in the top branches, a coop filled with dead chickens.

Anyway, Ingersoll was right about it not being a cat. It was a baby.

The men stared. A bushel basket on a low branch held the red-faced thing. In the mud, beneath the basket, a shred of blanket it'd kicked away.

"Mother of God," Ingersoll said.

"Wasn't nothing of God about this one's mother," Ham said. He raised his right arm, aiming his shotgun at the door of the house, and closed one eye. "She was the one. Got damn it. When she heard us coming she must've up and left this one here and hid herself in the house."

Ingersoll considered the baby. It wore a gnarl of diaper and was impossible to name boy or girl. It was bald. Red from crying and he realized they'd been yelling above its noise.

"You better off," Ham told it. "Take a chance with the current elements. Maybe a gang of coyote'll take you in. Isn't that what happened to you, Ingersoll? Band of coyotes found you in the tundra and raised you as their own?"

Ham shoved the silver tray they'd taken from the looters into his saddlebag. A white man just over six feet tall with a red face and bright red hair he kept cut short, Ham wore muttonchops (also red) he called burnsides, and a belly nutria derby that he was slightly vain about and endeavored to keep clean. Ingersoll's hat was bigger and more practical, a black Stetson Dakota.

"Ain't no coyotes this far south," he said.

"Is too," Ham said. He kicked his leg to flap his boot sole down—the leather wet so long it'd rotted—and fitted his boot into his stirrup and swung onto his saddle.

"It's wild dogs a-plenty, Ham. But it ain't no coyotes."

Ingersoll was looking beyond the house, studying the inland sea of dried and drying mud where cotton plants had once been, the horizon unrelenting brown, flat and cracking like so much poorly thrown pottery. Twice he had seen arms of the dead reaching out of it.

The levees had ruptured back in April, and even here, twenty-five miles southeast of the Mounds Landing crevasse, the waves had surged six feet. Thunderous breakers of coffee-colored froth had flattened near every tree and building, then just wiped them all away, like something out of Revelation. Ingersoll recalled the buried road to Yazoo City, a bloated mare and in front of its muzzle a bloated Bible as if the horse were verifying the events of the end time when they befell him.

"Tell Junior goodbye," Ham said.

"What you mean?"

"I mean it's somebody'll come along sooner or later and get this damn baby's what I mean. We got to skedaddle." He looked over his shoulder at the basket, now swaying in the breeze. "What's that lullaby? 'When the bow breaks, the cradle will fall, and down will come baby, cradle and all.'"

"Ham—"

"C'mon," Ham said. "Let's get to New Orleans, spend some of

this looter loot. I got me a mind for a foreign girl. Russian if we can find one. Get a steak and lay some pipe. Then buy me a new pair of boots."

"I can't leave no baby, Ham."

"Well we ain't bringing it, Ing."

The foul wind from the east moaned through the leaning mule barn.

"Adios, Junior," Ham said, and gigged his sorrel with his heels. *"Vaya con dios."*

Ingersoll stared down at the kicking baby like maybe he'd had a baby himself long ago. And a wife.

But he hadn't. He was twenty-seven years old. He had no living family anywhere. He'd never even touched a baby.

"Ah, hell," he said and looked at the pewter sky, which gave a chuckle of thunder.

Wild dogs following. Or coyotes if you asked Ham. Ingersoll rode a quarter mile behind his partner and figured the big man wouldn't hear the thing fussing in his arms. It smelled like piss and flung its fists out and kicked. As he rode it was the beating and kicking that impressed Ingersoll. Little dickens had some fight.

In an hour the baby had lulled to a hiccupping sleep and Ingersoll let the horse follow the deeply etched tracks Ham's sorrel was carving. Ingersoll had learned to trust Ham's lead after Ham had spotted and dispatched two of the saboteurs back in Marked Tree, Arkansas. Their next orders, sent via telegram by Coolidge's men, had brought them to the Old Moore plantation near Greenville, Mississippi, where they were told to monitor local Negroes, some growing seditious, planning to head north, put the lapping Mississippi far behind them. But the landowners—and the officials the landowners elected—couldn't allow the Negroes to leave. Who would pick the cotton then?

But the cotton hadn't mattered. They were perhaps a dozen miles from Mounds Landing, searching for runaway Negroes, when that levee had burst. As if from the sky they heard it, heard the terrible roar, like a twister first but then an earthquake, it seemed, coming from beneath the horses. "Go," Ham had yelled. They spurred their mounts to a gallop and within minutes the floodtide was upon them, washing trees and bodies past, brown water splashing over the horses' hooves first, then quickly over their withers to the riders' legs and then the horses were careening and swimming and the men fighting to stay on, the land gone behind them, there passing in the current a church steeple, there a wagon still hitched to a pair of kicking mules, there a schoolhouse desk.

Now Ingersoll's horse gave a lurch. He grasped the baby, which startled it awake, its arms flying outward, and set it to crying. The horse's back legs had sunk, stuck again. Ingersoll would have to dismount and wrench its hooves free. But what to do with the baby?

"Ham?"

He heard a horseshoe clip a rock behind him and lowered his head and shook it.

"I told you about that damn baby," Ham Johnson shouted at his back. "Look where your instincts are."

"It's my decision," Ingersoll called over his shoulder. "I'll ditch it first people we find."

Ham skidded to a stop beside Ingersoll's horse, wiggling its rump and straining its neck and rolling its eyes in panic. Ingersoll slid off, clutching the squalling baby. It was horribly red in the face and its tears left tracks in its coat of dust.

"I think it's hungry," Ingersoll said.

Ham leaned and spat. "So am I." He spurred his horse, which threw beads of mud on Ingersoll's neck as it trotted away.

Ingersoll looked before him, behind. His own feet were heavy with mud and he saw nothing to do but set his upended Stetson in the mud and place the wailing baby ass-first in its crown. When he saw it wouldn't topple out he stood behind the horse, talking to it, and grounded his feet and squatted and with both hands around the horse's fetlock yanked it free, the mud yielding with an anguished and greedy slurp.

It was a long afternoon that they traveled south across the birdless crackled brown mudscape without ever arriving at its edge. At four it rained and woke the baby but they kept riding. They passed through the rain and through a spell of cool, the air dotted with mosquitoes, before it got hot again. Twice Ingersoll's horse jumped the bloated bodies of goats, his mount so weary and jaded it hardly broke stride. They crossed a patch where strange arcs and teeth of stone pressed through the mud that Ham said must have been a cemetery. As they rode, Ingersoll switched the baby from sore arm crook to sore arm crook, grateful that his horse had fidelity, hardly needed guiding at all.

As they pushed south, Ingersoll held his drinking pouch — he'd mixed sugar and water — for the baby to suck on. He'd also peered in its swaddle and seen its tiny knob, cleaned its backside with a rag dipped in puddle water, and rigged his kerchief to make a new diaper.

They dismounted at the top of a small hill with a swift swollen creek below, a butter churn bobbing against speckled rocks. Ham hobbled the horses, keeping them close and saddled. Ingersoll took off his Stetson and frowned at the rotten smudges on his fingers but lowered the baby in it anyway, extending its arms along the brim. Ham had arranged a few twigs and branches and soon had a fire sputtering, its pops and sparks and orbiting moths a fascination for the baby, who pointed a crooked finger.

They chewed beef jerky and drank water from their canteens and rolled out their bedrolls. Ham unstoppered his pouch of mescal and pushed out his feet like he did when he was fixing to elaborate. His boots, caked in mud, were twice their regular size. Ingersoll reached into his saddlebag and lifted out his taterbug mandolin, a bowl-backed beauty of maple and mahogany, now warped a few degrees because of the rain. They'd found it washed ashore in a hussar trunk that Ham opened by shooting off the lock. Ingersoll, by tuning it a step and a half below standard, could play all the blues keys on it.

He laid down a few licks and the baby turned its attention to watch Ingersoll with its bright blue eyes. Ingersoll began to pick out a little ballad he'd made up.

"Tell this youngun your real name, Ham."

His partner swigged from his pouch. "Nobody knows it, living ner dead."

Ingersoll always enjoyed the next question for the contradictory answers it provoked. "And tell him how you come to be called Ham."

Ham took another pull. "You know how babies have that good smell, that sweet smell to their heads? Well, when I was a baby, my head gave off the perfume of ham."

"Oh, yeah?" Ingersoll played two bar fills and saw that the baby's eyelids were heavy, its head bobbing toward sleep.

"Yeah. Smelled like ham, like real good roast ham. People around me always getting hungry. It was my breath, something from inside. Over the years"—he took another swig, and Ingersoll laid down a blues lick—"over the years, I learned to stand downwind of folks. Naturally, as I grew I lost that sweet ham smell some, but it's still there if you get close, whore-close. In fact, had there been this flood back then, I'd likely have been the first one cannibalized. 'Ham Johnson,' they'd say, shaking their heads. 'Damn but he made a fine breakfast.'" Ham leaned to pass the mescal. "Nobody would of ever thought he'd a been a genuine war hero and confiscated by the military government itself to pursue saboteurs of levees—"

"Dynamite-wielding saboteurs," Ingersoll added, taking a drink.

"Dynamite-wielding saboteurs of such a low stripe," Ham said, "that they're willing to set their charges wherever the highest bidder says." He started talking about how one group of saboteurs, posing as government engineers, had taken money from a village on the east side of the river and then blown the west side, flooding a village over there in order to keep theirs dry.

Ingersoll handed the tequila back and laid down a turnaround in E, just showing off now. He'd gotten his first guitar at ten, and holding it felt like somebody had attached a missing piece to his body. By fourteen he was making a living, a little gambling on the side, playing blues up in Clarksdale. But in 1916 he left for the Great War, put down his guitar for a U.S. government–issue Mossberg .50-caliber rifle. He'd taken to it the same way, either-handed and cool-headed and pitch-perfect and fingers as nimble as air.

Finally Ham belched and tapped his chest and aimed the neck of his pouch at the baby in the Stetson.

"Sleeping like a got-damn baby," he said.

Ingersoll went to his saddlebag, put his taterbug back, and removed his spare dungaree shirt. He tucked it around the baby, whose breathing seemed shallow. "We need to get some milk fore long. Tomorrow."

Ham sighed. He pulled his legs in and stood. "You want first watch?"

Ingersoll slipped his thumb into the baby's hand and felt his fin-

gers close around it. He waggled his thumb and admired the baby's
fierce grip. "Yeah."

"Well, I'll turn in."

"All right."

Soon he was asleep and Ingersoll sat holding the hatful of baby
in his lap. When the fire cracked out an ember that lay fizzing in
the mud, the baby opened its eyes. It began to fuss and so he lifted
it out and held it against his shoulder and started rocking, singing
the one about the Corps men sandbagging the levee: "I works on
the levee, mama, both night and day. I works so hard to keep the
water away," he sang. "It's a mean old levee, cause me to weep and
moan. Gonna leave my baby, and my happy home."

The first homestead they came to the next morning was deserted—aback their horses, through the busted door, they saw
standing water and a rat swimming in a lazy circle. Ingersoll was
anxious. During the night he'd dreamed about riding up a grassy
hill crowned with a sweet olive tree and finding tethered to it a
massively uddered milk cow, and he admitted now to himself that
he didn't give a damn about finding the saboteurs unless they were
running a dairy. The baby had been feasted upon in the night by
mosquitoes and bore the bites stoically. It didn't cry and felt hot.
Riding, Ingersoll kept touching its head.

The next place they came upon seemed as deserted as the first.
It was a stone building with slotted windows. Essentially a small fort,
bearded along its bottom in green mold. Nothing moved.

But Ham said, "Wait."

Ingersoll shifted the baby behind him and raised his sixteen-
gauge toward the windows.

Ham was already off his horse and standing against the wall with
rifle ready. He spun and kicked in the log door. Ingersoll was on
the ground using his horse for cover. He'd put the baby behind
him and it was starting to fuss.

"Come on in," Ham called to him.

Ingersoll blocked the baby with his body as he sidewindered up.
He trailed his single-barrel in the room and followed his partner's
gaze to four people crouched in the corner. They were thin, white,
dressed in rags. Three were men and one, behind them, a stringy-
haired woman. The room smelled like piss. There wasn't a stick of

furniture. Only a big washpot and the remains of a fire in a dugout fireplace. They weren't saboteurs, or even looters, but Ham eyed them warily. The baby was crying in a raspy way.

Then the girl stepped forward. "Can I hold it?"

She was skinny but her breasts were enormous under her tattered housedress. They were wet at the nipples.

"What the hell?" Ham glanced at Ingersoll.

"Here." Ingersoll offered her the baby.

She took it and turned her back to them and the baby's squall muffled for a second and then ceased, replaced by wet sucking sounds. She stood, rocking from side to side.

"Oh." Ham grinned and lowered his weapon.

"You can put yours away too, son," one of the men said to Ingersoll. "We ain't got no guns. All we got is sticks."

Another of the men raised his, a pathetic cane.

Ingersoll slid his shotgun into his boot holster.

"What's your all's story?" Ham asked the oldest-looking of the men, though in truth you couldn't tell how old (or how young) any of them were.

"Our story?" The man looked around. He flung out his arms. "Here it is. Me." He pointed. "Him. Him. Her. This place that used to be a farm. Forty days and nights of rain, no goddamn ark. Near six days spent on the roof with a bellowing coon dog till we ate it. Then suddenly appear a baby and two maniacs with guns. That's our story."

"What happened to her youngun?" Ingersoll asked, nodding to the girl.

She stiffened and looked at him over her shoulder.

"It died," one of the men said.

"How?"

He looked down.

"The way babies die," the oldest man said. "In the middle of the night."

"Y'all been sucking her milk?" Ham asked.

The old man met his gaze. "It's worse sins than that when you're starving."

Ingersoll and Ham exchanged a glance.

"I expect it is," Ham said.

Ingersoll looked at the girl. She just rocked with her eyes closed as the baby's hand climbed her neck and hooked a finger in her lip.

"Who're y'all?" another of the men asked.

"We ain't nobody you need to worry about," Ham said.

"Is anybody coming to help us down here? Is anybody sending food?"

Ingersoll shook his head. "Just to the camps in Greenville. Y'all should head over there. They're giving tents and food and seventy-five cents a day to levee repairers."

"We ain't leaving," the old man said.

"Suit yourself," Ham told him. "But the next party through might not be so kind as we are."

It was decided they'd leave the baby with the girl. They also left matches, sugar, lard, and jerked beef, which the men fell upon instantly.

"Don't eat too fast," Ham said. "You'll produce it right back."

The girl didn't want any. Ingersoll studied her and she smiled and revealed a row of small, even teeth.

"What's your name?" he asked.

"Dixie Clay."

"You okay, Dixie Clay?"

She didn't answer.

"She's fine," the younger man said.

"Let's skedaddle," Ham said to Ingersoll. He touched the brim of his derby with his rifle barrel and turned for the door.

Ingersoll watched the girl. For a moment she seemed to lean in his direction, her eyes intensified at him, until the young man stepped in front of her.

"Thank you for your kindness," he said.

"I'll be back," Ingersoll said. "To check on that baby."

He was quiet as they walked their horses side by side, though Ham kept trying to provoke him.

"I read water poured through the Mounds Landing crevasse harder than Niagara. Did you know that?"

"No."

"True. Three-quarters-mile crevasse, and near three hundred levee workers swept clean away right then and there. Unless newspapers lie."

"Some do."

"Could be our saboteurs made that breach," Ham said.

Ingersoll didn't answer. He kept seeing the girl's eyes and how tightly she held the baby to her chest.

It was growing dark and Ham said this looked like a good spot to camp, didn't it, pretty dry. They dismounted and Ham sat on his roll and tugged at his boots, which slurped free. He peeled down his socks and sat looking at his toes, wrinkled and mushroomed.

Ingersoll took off his hat and set it on the ground beside him. How empty it seemed. Ham produced two cans of beans and his opener as Ingersoll turned the pegs, played a lick, tuned it again.

Then he put it down and looked up into the night. "I'm tired of never seeing no stars," he said.

"Just be glad it ain't raining. You gone play?"

"Not right now."

Ham set the cans of beans in the fire to warm and they'd just begun to bubble at the top when he sat alert and laid his hand on his .30-.30. Ingersoll had heard it too, dried mud crunching, and they rolled away from the fire on their bellies, aiming into the dark.

"Don't shoot. I got the baby."

"Oh for Christ sake." Ham spat into the dark.

Dixie Clay stepped forward into the firelight. She was clutching the baby, and she was bleeding across the forehead some.

"We nearly blew your fool head off," Ham said, pushing to his feet. "And for making me spill my mescal, you'd a deserved it."

Dixie Clay looked at Ingersoll, rising himself.

"You okay?" he asked.

"Yeah."

"They following you?"

"No. I don't think so."

"They will," Ham said.

"The baby," she said, "the baby wasn't safe there. With them."

Ingersoll looked at Ham, who didn't meet his eyes and sat down before the fire. He commenced to scraping mud from his boot with a stick.

Ingersoll waited for her to say more, but she didn't. "They eat your baby?" he asked at last.

She lowered her head.

"Girl? I asked you a question. If you don't answer I'm gone send you right back to 'em."

"Yeah."

"Yeah?"

"Yeah. They eat her. She was dead already and they said we had to or they'd starve."

"But they won't eat this one," Ham said. "They got food now. We gave 'em some."

She hugged the baby higher on her chest. It was still wrapped in Ingersoll's shirt.

"Well?" Ham demanded.

She was looking at Ingersoll. "Something's wrong with them. Something went wrong."

Ham resumed scraping mud from his boot heel.

"Sit down," Ingersoll said to the girl, and pointed to his roll. She sank onto it, still holding the baby. It gave an enormous yawn. Its color was better.

He opened his pack and offered her an apple.

"No, thank you."

But he tossed it anyway and she caught it with one hand without disturbing the baby.

"Eat it, girl. Otherwise you and this little one both gonna die and all for nothing."

She took a bite and chewed and looked at the baby in her arms and looked back up. "What's gonna happen to us?"

Ingersoll wondered the same thing.

When Ingersoll woke the next morning, Ham had already put coffee on and was pissing into a mud puddle fifty yards off. Ingersoll looked across the ashen coals where he'd laid out his bedding for the girl. She'd slept with the baby nestled against her, and in the dawn light he saw where some of her blood had crusted on the baby's cheek. For the first time he wondered what its name was.

Ingersoll rose quietly and stretched and filled their tin cups with coffee and went to where Ham was loading the saddlebag.

"Obliged," Ham said.

They stood together facing the lip of sun pushing itself over the flat brown world, glazing the mud puddles like copper ingots.

Ham sipped his coffee and studied his partner. "What the hell are you about to do?"

"I don't know."

"Yes you do."

"I can't leave 'em."

"Yes you can."

"No I can't, Ham."

"You've connected 'em and saved that damn baby's life. At some point you just have to do your job. Our job."

Ingersoll stood silent, watching the sunrise.

"Shit," Ham said. He flung his coffee into the mud.

"Just tell 'em I'm dead. When you get back."

Ham sighed. "That won't even be no lie," he said. "It's what you call a self-fulfilling prophecy. If the looters don't get you, or the saboteurs, ole Coolidge will. You done seen too much."

"Just do what you have to."

"I will, Ing. Got damn it."

They shook hands and looked for a long moment into one another's eyes. Ingersoll couldn't see a thing in Ham's and wondered what Ham saw in his own. For the first time it occurred to Ingersoll that if Ham killed him now he'd merely be doing his job. But instead Ham nodded and turned away and Ingersoll turned too with his coffee and went to nudge the coals.

The girl's face had relaxed from its fear and he watched her sleep. She was pretty under the dirt and the blood, freckles on her upturned nose and brown hair that she could probably fix nice if she wanted. The baby was sleeping too, its mouth slack around her nipple, a trace of watery milk on its tongue. He stood and turned to gaze across the cracked leather earth to where Ham was cinching the girth on his horse.

"Last chance," Ham called. He kicked the flap of his boot sole down and swung into the saddle, grinning. "Russian girls can smoke cigarette with they virginias. They let you do 'em up the chute if you pay 'em five more dollars."

"Naw," Ingersoll said, grinning too, and raised his hand, and Ham raised his back and then turned and rode away, the sorrel kicking up arcs of mud behind him.

When Dixie Clay woke he doctored her head a little while she licked her thumb and rubbed some of the dirt and dried blood from the baby's cheeks. He told her about Ham leaving and then turned his attention to heating another can of beans so she could nurse. He sang as he stirred, a tune of nonsense, swimming with bowlegged women, the words not making sense but neither were his feelings.

They were aback his horse, the girl before him on the saddle, holding the baby, and they were headed west. The sun was out and the earth drier, trees on the horizon. Dixie Clay said she was two months shy of eighteen. One of them back there had been her husband.

"Which one?"

"The one with the different-colored eyes."

"What was his name?"

She paused. "I'll say it just this one more time. But don't never ask me again, okay?"

"Okay."

"Jesse Swan Holliver." She brushed away a mosquito from the baby's forehead. Then she turned her head to look up at him. "I'm better off now."

A little while later, facing forward in the saddle, she said it again. "I'm better off now."

He rode on, thinking, as she slept within the cage his arms made. He remembered killing the looters in the house in Leland. Killing the baby's mother. She'd had a gold-plated .45-caliber pistol and she was fixing to shoot him. Instead he shot her. Now in his imagination he shot her again. He shot her and then the man she'd been with and the one before him and the saboteurs in Marked Tree and the Krauts on the Flemish Coast and all the way back through his life of murder and mandolining. He probably should have shot Dixie Clay's husband and the other two, and might come to regret not doing so. But it was not yet noon and already he'd carried them fifteen miles farther west from the river and closer to land where you could see some stars. Even the horse seemed spry, its head high and pace quickening despite the heavier load.

The girl nodded in the saddle as she slept. He thought about the Memphis Minnie song, "Gotta leave my baby, and my happy home." He sang it softly to himself and Dixie Clay opened her eyes.

"You gone leave me?" She sat up and turned to look into his face.

He could smell her sour sleep breath, his chest warm from where her back had rested.

"It don't look like it," he said.

She reached to where his hand lay over the pommel and wove her fingers through his. He wondered if she noticed how callused he was. He wondered was it too late to unlearn being good at certain things with your hands. He wondered about the tiny half-moon scar on her lip that shone white when she smiled as she was doing now. He had time to find out.

He looked into her lap where she held the baby, his eyelids jerking in sleep, but his breath was easy, his lungs puffing, and Ingersoll knew they were tiny bellows that would play the rest of his days.

"He's dreaming," she said.

"Yeah," he said, "he must be."

ERNEST J. FINNEY

A Crime of Opportunity

FROM *Sewanee Review*

NO MATTER HOW FAST or how far she ran, she was never going to outrun herself. That was the sorry truth, Delilah thought.
She was still here. She slowed on the last stretch through Golden
Gate Park and found Mrs. Stowe—no, she had to remember,
Renée—waiting where she said she'd be, by the windmill. They
crossed the highway to the sidewalk along the seawall that paralleled the dunes. It was already dark at six, a November dark, a West
Coast dark, nothing like New York in November, where you always
seemed to be in the shadow of the buildings. And not as cold here,
as if the wispy fog were insulation against the wind.

Where were they now? Even after five months in San Francisco
she still got lost, running, day or night. She wasn't sure what direction they were going now—north, south?—though she could
hear the waves slap against the sandy beach. She didn't want to
seem anxious; Renée would say, "Okay, Delilah, what is it?" with
that hint of impatience in her voice. Once she'd told Renée, "Prepare for the worst and it will never happen," and Renée had come
back with, "Preparation inhibits spontaneity. Forget those maxims,
Delilah. You're no longer in the Girl Scouts."

She hadn't taken her cell phone or her pager. Renée never com-
mented, though, if she got a call from her office; Renée knew her
job involved instant decisions at all hours. The plan tonight was
that they would walk for a while and end up in a small neighborhood restaurant Renée knew about. She could phone in to the office from there, Delilah thought, to get the new euro high against
the dollar.

Renée was in her storytelling mode, this time about her paleon-tologist husband's first discovery in Patagonia. "We lived in one of those white canvas pyramid tents: I remember how the dozen or so guy lines would sing in the night wind. The place where Sonny had chosen to dig was a treasure trove of Pliocene-era fossils. The armadillo, by the way, has hardly changed at all in forty-five million years: it has stayed the same since the Eocene period, a living fossil. We had twenty of the local Indians to work the site. Wonderfully conscientious men and women."

Striding along in her British outfit, long tartan skirt, turtleneck sweater, and camel-hair blazer, heavy brogans, her gray hair topped by a beret, Renée was becoming more English with each sentence. Her husband had been born in London. Clothes seemed made for her: she was tall, narrow, long-waisted like the models you saw in magazines. Extremely trim, though she ate like a horse. She was swinging her cane—her English shooting stick, she called it—which turned into a kind of stool when you stuck the metal spike at the end into the ground and opened the handle.

"Let's stop for a minute so I can stretch." She interrupted Renée's story to steer them to a cement bench under a streetlight. She was warm in her sweats and twisted her fanny pack around so it didn't stick into her side before she started her stretches. Renée paced in the square of light; she couldn't sit still either. What was amazing was that Renée looked no more than forty, say, maybe fifty. But she had to be nearly eighty. One of her stories took place in 1939. Her face was almost unlined, though there was no sign of surgery. She had young breasts; she'd seen them when Renée was trying on a dress at Nordstrom's. There were no liver spots on the back of her hands.

There had been occasional passersby, a woman walking a dog, but now two men stopped. "Lovely evening," one said. Renée stopped pacing but didn't pause in her tale about discovering that she'd been sitting upon four vertebrae of a species never before found in South America. "Why don't you two ladies hand over your purses and start taking off your clothes." The one who spoke was wearing a leather jacket like an undercover cop in a TV series. Then he yelled, "You heard me—strip."

That got Renée's attention. "I beg your pardon. Are you speak-ing to us?"

In response, the other one, like a conjuring trick, slowly drew a machete from the sleeve of his raincoat. Renée laughed out loud like she had seen something funny.

It all happened so fast there was no time to be scared. "Run," Delilah yelled, grabbing for Renée's hand. But Renée had stepped aside and had raised her shooting stick one-handed, as if she was going to twirl it like a baton: a blade of grass was dangling from the point of the stick. Cell phone, Delilah thought; pretend you've got it, and she reached into her pocket and yelled "I'm calling 911" the same instant she saw the blade of the machete catch the light as it came down toward Renée's head. It was too fast for her to see exactly what happened, but one man screamed, the other fled, and the machete fell with a clang to the sidewalk. She caught Renée's hand this time, and they ran too.

After a block and a half they couldn't hear the screams anymore. Renée slowed a little, still walking so fast Delilah had to jog to keep up. "Renée, shouldn't we get the police?"

"No, no; I don't think so. I just administered a life lesson to that young man. The police would only confuse the issue. Remember now, it's not the groin or the kneecap you kick. The whole business with karate and jujitsu and the rest is overrated. Too physical. You have to go for the eyes in a situation like that. Car keys are very good. Your thumb will do too."

By the end of the block Renée had resumed her Patagonia story in Argentina. But the image of the point of the walking stick spearing the man's eyeball made Delilah feel dizzy, made her own eyes water. It was the second time she'd heard Renée say *life lesson*. The first had been on the day they'd met.

She could admit it now; she was a mess then. Bewildered, was that it? By the move to San Francisco from New York. It was before noon; the restaurant was already packed; they'd lost her reservation. It shouldn't have thrown her, but it did. Just going to lunch could throw her into confusion. She didn't like eating alone anyhow, wasn't used to it yet, especially in a place like this, locally famous. She was ready to flee, and then the maître d' asked if she'd mind sharing a table. She followed the waitress across the the dining room to a table by the window next to the street, and the woman seated there stood up and introduced herself, Renée

Stowe. From the beginning the woman made her feel comfortable, relaxed, talkative. They decided to split a bottle of wine. After they ordered dessert, Delilah heard herself let go, recite line by line her secret, private résumé she didn't dare go over very often, even to herself. Falling in love that first time in college, graduating, marrying, getting her law degree. Thinking her life would be like her parents' life, two happy people who loved each other. Was it playing house? Was she fantasizing? Did having sex with the lights on mean you'd love someone forever? People fell in love: how was it they fell out of love?

And the law: she'd been wrong about that too. The third member of her immediate family to become a lawyer. How could she have thought that being a defense lawyer for the city of Pittsburgh could mean that any of the defendants would be innocent? That she could get them off by her very brilliance after they'd committed and already confessed to some terrible crime? Let them back into society to continue those desperate acts? As part of a team or on her own, she'd lost some twenty-one cases, four capital, in the fourteen months before she quit. Felons at the city jail called her the funeral director. Defendants insisted on another attorney the minute they saw her walk through the door. As her father had always said, there was no correspondence between the law and justice.

And divorce didn't end a marriage, she found out. You still heard from your mother-in-law, his favorite niece, the former spouse himself, who wanted to have dinner. To try again. What happened to us? he asked. There were no words to answer that. It was all so sad, like five years of her life had been erased. She fled to New York City. Left litigation, got a job as legal counsel for the Zoological Society; her father had known someone. That was where she'd met her second husband, who was on the board. He was in finance.

Charming? Intelligent? Witty? Mysterious? Wayne was unaware he was all those things. He'd lived abroad most of his life, much of it in Asia, where his Quaker father, an MD, had developed a number of rural clinics. Hand-to-mouth existence. Not much school, no real formal education. He spoke five languages and two Chinese dialects. Often stopped at the medical school to sit in on a lecture. Took her to a conference in Montreal to look over innovations in emergency-room technology. She introduced him to marathons.

At the time she'd thought rather highly of herself. Her divorce had improved her image, hadn't diminished her but made her more experienced, a woman of the world. She didn't see it as a failure. And she hadn't seen Wayne as a challenge. He pursued her.

At this point she embarrassed herself and Renée too. She hadn't realized she was weeping, but big tears were falling into her water glass with a splash that wet her knuckles. The idea that she would never see Wayne again finished her, melted all her resolve. She must have sobbed out loud next because Renée placed her hand on her wrist and said calmly, "There is no life lesson to prepare us for loss and grief. Get a grip, dear." Handing her a handkerchief, Renée took over the conversation, chatting away, then excused herself after a comfortable interval to go to an appointment. When Delilah motioned to the waitress for the check, she was told Mrs. Stowe had already taken care of it. A couple of days later—they had exchanged cards at some point—she received a note from Renée: "Delightful time. I lunch at that restaurant at eleven each Wednesday; hope we meet there again."

Work was chaotic: the dollar was plummeting; all currencies were careening. Her company, an intermediary between international banks, handled money transfers. Trying to keep ahead of the exchange rates—yen and yuan, pound and peso—was the best part of her job, like trying to count the angels dancing on top of a dozen pins. You had to be fast and right when so much money was involved.

Wayne had recommended her for the position at his firm; he was the comptroller. She had wanted a change, some excitement. And she turned out to be good. Better than good; within a year she had her own office and secretary. She and Wayne were serious by then, living together. It wasn't like her first marriage, following the prescriptions for happiness: communicate, compromise, share experiences, always be a generous lover. Flowers and candlelight. Wayne ignored those rules, or better, he wasn't aware of them. He believed in fidelity, but that was all. Insisted they live in his little apartment in Queens. He couldn't drive, had never owned a car, used public transportation, sometimes made terrible mistakes, mispronouncing common English words. She loved him all the more for it.

Her mother had told her when she was a girl that she was going to be beautiful someday. She'd always thought it just was something mothers said to ordinary-looking daughters. But one day when she was twenty-seven, applying lipstick, she noticed something different. It looked like her nose and chin had somehow decided to join her mouth and eyes and become a whole that was almost striking. Was she seeing things? That's when she met Wayne. He was the one who put it into words. He was tracing the outline of her lips with his forefinger as they sat at a table in the New York Public Library. "You are beautiful," he said. And she believed him.

He'd taken her to a hundred Chinese restaurants so she could learn the regional foods. They had dinner so often at a Hunan place near their Queens apartment that the owners called them by their first names. She'd proofread the daughter's eighth-grade essays there. One night, when the long table in the center of the room was filled with a large family, Wayne leaned over and said something in Chinese to an old lady at the table, and they traded stories back and forth throughout dinner. Wayne knew the small city the woman was from, and he laughed and laughed at one yarn, which he translated for Delilah. "In a country full of national heroes, from emperors to Mao, we have erected only one statue in my city. Many years ago a tributary of the Yellow River overflowed and left a deep pond in the neighborhood. Two sisters were playing nearby and one fell into the pond and was going under for the third time. A duck that had been living on the pond for years swam over to her, and the girl was able to hold on to the duck and make it to shore. In appreciation the grateful city raised the money for a bronze statue of the duck to be placed by the pond."

"Is it a parable? Is there more?" she'd asked him. "I don't get it."

He'd smiled at her then. "Think about it," he'd said.

She'd get glimpses of Wayne sometimes in San Francisco, think she saw him crossing Union Square or waiting for a bus as she walked by. She'd stop and go back. It was never he. She never saw him while she ran, though. He never appeared as she sprinted up some famous San Francisco hill, gasping for air. She was running twice a day now.

In addition to lunch on Wednesday, Delilah and Renée were eating dinner twice a week at an Argentine restaurant Renée had discovered. Unbelievable grilled steaks. No chemicals, no feedlots; the steers were free-range. According to Renée, the owner had a foot-hill ranch in the wilds of the San Joaquin Valley. Delilah smiled as Renée ladled more chimichurri onto their steaks. She was working on being cheerful. She often felt that Renée had to restrain herself from reaching across the table and shaking the spit out of her, yelling, "Quit dwelling on your open wounds."

She'd almost stopped being morose. She liked hearing herself laugh again. They'd even double-dated: Renée's nephew and a gentleman from an escort service for Renée. The ersatz nephew was paid too, Delilah was almost sure. It had been hilarious. "Men are such good actors," she'd told Renée when they were being driven home in the limo. "Don't go there, dear," Renée had said, more sharply than usual. By that time she'd told Renée the rest of the story. Wayne's disappearance. Scandal. Over $700 million missing. The enormous reward offered. Gone without a trace, both the money and her second husband—the one she thought she couldn't live without.

She'd gone home to Philadelphia for comfort, once it was clear what had happened. "It's not the end of the world," her mother and father told her. But it was. You could only fall in love like this once, she understood then. It was too hard on you; you'd never survive another loss. The firm had treated her like she had been suddenly widowed, as if Wayne had died tragically. They never so much as suggested she might know where Wayne had gone. She would have told them if she'd had any idea at all, just to see him again. It was too hard to stay in Queens without Wayne. When she asked to be transferred to the West Coast, it was arranged immediately; the firm paid her moving expenses. They trusted her: she'd been told that several times by various executives.

Sometimes she thought back to the times she and Wayne had gone to Quaker services—meeting for worship, they called it. It had seemed so incongruous, the silence, listening for some transcendent voice in a meeting house in Brooklyn. Was this how it had been in China when he was a boy, these hours of silence, waiting to hear from God? It was so un-Episcopalian: that had been more like playing dress-up every Sunday. She found a Friends meeting listed in the San Francisco phone book and went to it a couple of times on the sly so she wouldn't have to explain to Renée. In the silence

she thought about Wayne. Tried to imagine what Wayne would
have been thinking about in those Quaker meetings on Schermer-
horn Street.

Renée promised to show her the state of California. She drove
like a truck driver in her Mercedes, straight down the middle of the
freeways as fast as she could get away with. Delilah had expected
they'd see a lot of museums, but they never went close to one except once, when they got lost and ended up in L.A. by the La Brea
Tar Pits next to the Los Angles County Museum. No operas, no
concerts. And the international wonders — the giant sequoias and
the coast at Big Sur — were never on the agenda. They did drive to
Yosemite Valley one Saturday, parked near an old apple orchard by
a campground. Delilah started to get out to look for the waterfalls.
"Don't," Renée said, looking at her watch, "you'll ruin it," and they
headed back to S.F. after five minutes.

It was the freeways Renée loved: the physical act of driving up
and down the state on black macadam was her idea of exploring.
They'd shoot up 5 heading who knew where. Delilah stopped asking, because all Renée said was, "You'll see." Renée could keep
on driving for seven or eight hours. They'd reach some destination — Yreka, say — and spend the night. If there was a good restaurant in the town, Renée would find it. They'd barhop or walk somewhere. Renée could strike up a conversation with anyone. They got
invited to a potato farmer's home for tea. Joined an Audubon Society tour of a sewage treatment plant at which forty-three different
species of birds had been counted. They rented bikes in Clover-
dale and rode them all afternoon. They rode up 101 and switched
to 1 to see Fort Ross and Gualala.

She had been feeling so much better lately — focused. Being
around Renée was like taking a tonic that made you stronger.
Renée was not only smart; she kept current: she didn't own a TV or
computer, but newspapers and magazines were stacked all over her
place in Sea Cliff. She was never patronizing when they talked politics, never used her longevity as a lever. Thanks to Renée, Delilah
was clear finally on the difference between communism and social-
ism: one collapsed; the other was thriving in Scandinavia and Canada. Renée said that while most wealthy people were Republicans
because they benefited most from the party's policies, there was no

rational explanation why anyone making less than fifty K would ever vote for that party, but she was no limousine liberal: when pressed, she denounced all parties, and when pressed further, said she was an anarchist. "Laws are like broken stoplights; you have to drive through them," she said.

They were in the dining car of the Coast Starlight from San Luis Obispo to L.A. when Renée said that. And when Renée continued by saying, "The Pacific Rim. The West Coast, dear, is where the future lies," Delilah sat back for the lecture that was sure to follow.

"The East Coast is still dominated by Western Europe. We may be the sole superpower now, but it's not only because we are being led by a twit that we get all this disrespect from Europeans about the Mideast. We'll always be a stepchild there. The Russians are in the same boat. It'll take another two hundred fifty years before we can stop revering European culture and think for ourselves. The West Coast, however, shares nothing with the Far East but capitalist greed. Look at Japan today. Look at China. We will never understand Asia, but that's a strength. We'll use each other forever. And that assures the future. If it's true that New York City is the capital of the world, California is the first nation-state of that same world. The place is its own mythmaking machine, and the whole world wants to be part of that myth, wants to come here. Who wants to live in New York? Just people from Indiana and Minnesota."

"Since I get to benefit from your wisdom, I get to pay for dinner," Delilah said. Renée was a check-grabber. The food was so-so; they ordered another bottle of wine. Renée was talking about a paper by her late husband, the paleontologist Sonny. Would she ever be able to say Wayne's name so easily? She understood she had loved Wayne too much. That's why she couldn't let go. When Renée talked about Sonny, it was never in detail. He never came alive.

She'd been telling Renée work stories, and when she brought home a CD with evaluations of Singapore's current financial position relative to South Asia, Renée wanted to see what it looked like. When it came up on the screen it had to be incomprehensible to a layman, but Renée still watched the screen as if she understood what she was seeing. "This reminds me, I'd like to visit your office sometime, Delilah," Renée said. "I'd like to loan you a painting, a

Ray Strong landscape I bought a few years ago, but I want to see how it will fit there."

"It wouldn't be possible, Renée. No visitors. It's the most security-conscious place in the city. It takes an employee ten minutes to go through all the controls." She hated to see that look on Renée's face, but there was nothing for it.

Then, the next day at her desk, it came to her: she could take Renée to the firm's Christmas party. Pass her off as her grand-mother. Renée would be insulted: she liked to say they were like sisters and seemed not to be kidding; she was so vain she wouldn't allow herself to be photographed. But she'd like the fact that they were breaking the rules. The photo was a problem, though. She'd never get Renée near the place without a company ID tag with photo.

She was patient, and a couple of days later she snapped a photo from across the street as Renée stepped out of her hair salon. It caught her in a half-smile, her storytelling face. Delilah hoped she'd look half so good herself at Renée's age.

Renée was full of surprises. She phoned on Friday night to say, "I have an outing planned, dear. Wear warm clothing. I'll pick you up at four A.M." Delilah had schooled herself not to show surprise, but it was hard not to when they drove down to the wharf and boarded a party boat and went out trawling for salmon under the Golden Gate Bridge toward the Farallon Islands. Typical Renée outing. Pic-nic lunch. Bubbly, good Napa champagne. Everyone calling each other by their first names. Renée won the boat pool for biggest fish with her thirty-four-pound salmon.

They made a day of it, met for dinner that night at the Argentine restaurant. Went to a couple of neighborhood bars with names like Tiny's and neon outlines of martini glasses. Delilah drank too much. But she knew she could relax around Renée, be herself. At two A.M. they ended up in a Chinese restaurant on Clement Street. They ordered General Tso's chicken. Hunks of deep-fried chicken with sweet-and-sour sauce. She had to concentrate with her chop-sticks if she wanted to get any food close to her mouth.

She started talking about Wayne. Not maudlin or full of sorry-I-didn't-do-this-or-that. When Renée, who she hadn't thought was listening, asked, "Delilah, where is Wayne?" the question didn't catch her by surprise. She wanted to explain to her friend that she didn't know. But she heard herself say, "Somewhere in Asia, maybe." He'd been all over China and Mongolia as a boy; his father took him by horseback to clinics way up in the mountains. Had actually ridden a camel on the Silk Road. Had a story about the old Orient Express that left Moscow and ended up at the Sea of Japan. He'd bring out maps sometimes to show her where he'd been, saying the names of places in Chinese and then in English. "Here"—they were lying on the rug on their stomachs in front of the fire—"is the most interesting place in the world. A Shangri-la. It doesn't have a name. But it's not far from the city with the statue of the lifesaving duck." They had met the old woman again at the Hunan restaurant the night he said that.

"But why take all that money just to live in some primitive place like Outer Mongolia?" Renée wanted to know.

She had to think about that. She must chew the food in her mouth first. She didn't know. She shrugged her shoulders.

"Surely he gave some hint where he planned to go. He spoke Portuguese. Brazil? Mozambique?"

She had thought about it, of course, going over every word he'd ever said. He had no family that she knew of. His parents were dead. She slowly moved her head back and forth.

The more she considered it, she thought later in her flat, brushing her teeth, the more she realized Wayne had loved her. She was sure of that part. I'll never let you go, he told her once. He hadn't used her; he could have taken even more money if he had asked her to help. Was he waiting for things to cool down and then he'd send for her? She'd go in a minute. That was wishful thinking on her part. A pretty picture, Renée would say. They were only together eleven months: how well can you know someone in that time? The General's chicken had been one of Wayne's favorite dishes.

Delilah was at work in her office when two uniformed armed guards came through the door, followed by her supervisor and the senior vice president. "Ms. Winslow, we'd like you to come with us." She tried not to look surprised. When she stood up too quickly, one of the guards rested his hand on his pistol.

For the next five hours she sat in a comfortable chair and answered hundreds of questions put to her by the head of security. They gave her coffee and bathroom breaks and lunch. She signed a waiver that both her office and apartment could be searched and her finances audited. She cooperated completely until they asked if she'd submit to a lie-detector test and a body search. Then she exploded. "Hey, wait a minute; explain to me what I'm supposed to have done." Someone standing behind her said, "Ms. Winslow, you're in a heap of trouble." A screen came down the wall like a shade and the lights went out. A police photo of Renée came on the screen, with numbers on the bottom. "This is an Interpol mug shot, after she did Lloyds of London out of forty-three million pounds. Insufficient evidence. She's been thieving for over forty years."

"You don't think . . . ?"

"We don't know what to think. You were passing her off as a relative to breach security. You tell us."

"I was just trying get her into our Christmas party. That's all." Be careful, she told herself. This is serious. Serious. Serious. "Let me remind you, in case you have forgotten," she said as loud as she could, "I'm a lawyer. If you don't intend to charge me, I'm going home." Still no one spoke. She stood up. The light went on. Her eyes adjusted to the light, but Renée's photo stayed on the screen like a ghost passing through the room.

"Do you want to continue working here?" the senior vice president asked.

"After this, why would I want to? Unlike yourself, I'm capable of other things."

"We are going to require your help, Ms. Winslow."

"I'll be in my office at seven A.M. as usual. We can discuss it then."

Once she got to her flat she found herself going over everything that had transpired since she'd met Renée. Had she been duped again? Or had she duped herself both times? Believed what she wanted to believe? She had to think this out. If Renée was wanted by Interpol, why hadn't they picked her up? And her job, why had she felt devastated at her first thought: please, don't fire me. It might have its moments, but it was an awful place to work: a bunch of moneychangers. Bottom feeders.

She was up at her usual time, five A.M. Went for her run. The dark streets were full of people doing the same thing, getting some exercise before sitting down indoors all day. It might have been her imagination, but a woman across the street had seemed to turn the same corners she did. Imagination. Once she got to work, it was as if nothing had ever happened. She spent the morning in her office. No one appeared. Had lunch at her desk. The firm didn't forget things like this. Something would happen. But nothing did, not by five o'clock anyway. She went home. No messages from Renée, which was not so unusual. Tomorrow was Wednesday; they'd meet for lunch. She'd wait.

Nothing happened at the office Wednesday morning either. She thought of what Wayne had said to her once: "People pretty much do what other people expect them to do." That couldn't be true. Was that true?

Nothing from security: she should stop worrying about it. Concentrate on what she was going to say to Renée. What was there to say but goodbye? How could Renée have made up all those elaborate stories? But wasn't that what Wayne had done too? Maybe it was all fantasy about his life in China. Had any of that been true? For some reason she felt confident, as though she was going to make the right decisions now. She had changed—thanks to Renée, she had to admit to herself. It was almost physical, as if she'd developed a third eye and could see better.

Renée wasn't at the restaurant. She sat at their table half an hour before ordering. Ate her lunch and decided against dessert. Draining the last of the water from her glass, she saw through its thick base a distorted image of Renée approaching the table. She was so surprised she kept the glass to her mouth, watching, until Renée was seated at her place. She dreaded this part, she realized. "I didn't expect to see you," she said. "I thought you were going to miss this time."

The waitress came to take Renée's order. She was taking her time over the menu. Watching her, Delilah didn't feel angry so much as puzzled. "Here," Renée said, handing her a jewelry box. "This is for you." Inside was an old-fashioned silver brooch with a stone she couldn't identify. Renée had never given her anything before.

"It's beautiful," she said. "Thank you."

"It's a gift. Humorous, I hope. It's from one of the first specimens I was taught to identify in the field. Mineralized dinosaur droppings. I found it going through some things in an old trunk. I like the medieval name for these, *fumets*. The specks of blue are fossilized plants, probably—"

She interrupted. "Were you ever in South America, Renée?"

The woman didn't change expression, stirred her coffee, one, two, three times around. "In fact, I was. It was my father who was the paleontologist, and I spent one summer with him in Patagonia. It was my first life lesson. That was while my mother was traveling by ocean liner back and forth to Europe, fleecing unwary wealthy travelers. Marrying some of them. She was a bigamist many times over. I inherited my propensity for larceny from her. I loved my mother more than I could say." Renée was getting that dreamy look; she could go on for hours.

"Why should I believe anything you say? I've heard too many inventions. You were going to use me, Renée." She'd said it too loud. People were looking their way.

"Let me remind you, my motives may not have been pure, but where would you be without me, Delilah?"

"I wouldn't be a suspect in a scheme to rob my firm."

"They won't do anything. Stand up for yourself."

"What I don't understand is why, at your age, are you still doing this? You must have more money than you will ever need."

"At my age? You're missing the point, dear. There's no better buzz than making a law or breaking the law. Ask any politician. Or lawyer, for that matter. Judge. Priest. Thief. I'm not trying to justify stealing in a moral sense. But at my level it's an art form. The movement of a decimal point. The timing of a bank transfer. Insider information. Corporations do it every day."

"You must spend all your life looking over your shoulder. What a burden."

"I've never found it so. You're not grasping the fact that some people don't mind that. Thrive on it, in fact. Come on, Delilah. It's not as if you've never known another person of my sort."

She didn't catch the last bit, went on with what she wanted to say: "So being a thief is more rewarding than living a normal life?"

"Oh my, have I failed completely, dear? Did I waste all that time on you?"

Then it registered. The other person was Wayne. There was

something wrong with this. Renée was acting the same as always, but this was a conversation within a conversation. She needed to listen more carefully. She looked for an opening. "They are going to lock you up, Renée."

"Don't believe everything they tell you, dear. That's law enforcement's great secret: rarely do they ever catch anyone unless they get an accomplice to turn snitch. Or trick someone into confessing. Those old charges they have against me: worthless. You don't think I know what they know? I have never spent a night away from my own bed."

The waitress brought Renée her lunch. This was not going the way Delilah had anticipated. Renée was too clever for her. "What would you have done if I'd cooperated?"

Renée looked unsurprised. "Did they talk you into wearing a wire, dear?"

For some reason the idea of a tape recorder was so preposterous, so funny, that Delilah started laughing out loud. Renée stopped eating and examined her face as if looking in a mirror, then dropped her left eyelid in a slow wink. Delilah understood who was wired then.

"It would have been a small fiddle, Delilah. Maybe ten, no more than twelve million. Petty cash for them. Nickel and dime. Some foreknowledge from you, and I take it from there. Your end is, say, eight or nine percent. Euros, of course. Nothing like what your husband got away with."

"Husband?

"You've never divorced him, have you? You still use his last name. Now that man should have his picture in the dictionary at the word *thief*. He could give me lessons. He disappears, no trace, not a photo or a fingerprint left behind. The perfect crime. Except he left you behind, his true love. It's a real mystery."

The customers in the restaurant had thinned out; it was almost two. "How will Wayne contact you, Delilah? A man who works for the firm for nine years before he makes his move, phenomenal planning, timing, waiting for the perfect moment. Just between us. It's been sixteen months. He must be getting lonely, wouldn't you say?"

She finally understood. It takes a thief to catch a thief. The firm had come up with all this to get their money back? What was Renée really, a retired high school teacher, an amateur actress? Or maybe she'd always worked in law enforcement. Whatever she was, Renée was lobbing a ball over the plate for her to hit.

She spoke slowly, so every word would be recorded. "Renée, you surprise me. To even consider I could betray the people I work for . . ." She tried to sound sincere. She couldn't read Renée's expression. "And as for Wayne, if he were ever to contact me, I'd turn him in in a second. Refuse the reward, of course, but I'd have to turn him in. It's a basic life lesson: you always try to do the right thing." She stood up to leave, and Renée reached across the table and squeezed her shoulder. She was going to miss Renée.

The vice president came into her office at four P.M. with the director, who did all the talking. "We have a complete severance package we want you to look over. A year's salary, medical, generous lump sum. But if you accept, we want you out of here by five."

She just glanced at the four pages. She had expected something like this after her lunch with Renée. A mentor to the end. Maybe. She tore the pages down the middle; Renée would not approve of such melodrama. "I don't need anything from you." She picked up her purse and walked out. She was free; they'd given up on her as a way to find Wayne. Probably. Maybe.

On the way back to her flat she thought again about the duck tale. What she had never been able to compute was the image of a duck saving a child. She was too literal-minded or something. "A big dog, yes, but a fowl?" she had asked Wayne. "It's the woman's story," he'd said. "You have to trust her version. I do." Maybe it was a very large duck. Swan-sized.

What was she going to do now? She looked at herself in the bathroom mirror. Renée's brooch was on her lapel; she must have pinned it on at some point during lunch. A dinosaur dropping. It seemed fitting, somehow. She'd wear it on her journey. A long one, cautious, circuitous. Looking for a statue of a duck.

ED GORMAN

Flying Solo

FROM *Noir 13*

"YOU SMOKING AGAIN?"

"Yeah." Ralph's sly smile. "You afraid these'll give me cancer?"

"You mind rolling down the window then?"

"I bought a pack today. It felt good. I've been wanting a cigarette for twenty-six years. That's how long ago I gave them up. I was still walking a beat back then. I figure what the hell, you know. I mean, the way things are. I been debating this a long time. I don't know why I picked today to start again. I just did." He rolled the window down. The soft summer night came in like a sweet angel of mercy. "I've smoked four of them but this is the only one I've really enjoyed."

"Why this one?"

"Because I got to see your face."

"The Catholic thing?"

"That's right, kid. The Catholic thing. They've got you so tight inside you need an enema. No cheating on the wife, no cheating on the taxes, no cheating on the church. And somebody bends the rules a little, your panties get all bunched up."

"You're pretty eloquent for an ex-cop. That enema remark. And also, by the way, whenever you call me 'kid' people look at you funny. I mean, I'm sixty-six and you're sixty-eight."

Ralph always portrayed himself as a swashbuckler; the day he left the force he did so with seventeen citizen complaints on his record. He took a long, deep drag on his Winston. "We're upping the ante tonight, Tom. That's why I'm a little prickish. I know you hate being called 'kid.' It's just nerves."

I was surprised he admitted something like that. He enjoyed playing fearless.

"That waitress didn't have it coming, Ralph."

"How many times you gonna bring that up? And for the record, I did ask for a cheeseburger if you'll remember, and I did leave her a frigging ten-dollar tip after I apologized to her twice. See how uptight you are?"

"She probably makes six bucks an hour and has a kid at home."

"You're just a little bit nervous the way I am. That's why you're runnin' your mouth so hard."

He was probably right. "So we're really going to do it, huh?"

"Yeah, Tom, we're really going to do it."

"What time is it?"

I checked my Timex, the one I got when I retired from teaching high school for thirty years. English and creative writing. The other gift I got was not being assaulted by any of my students. A couple of my friends on the staff had been beaten, one of them still limping years after. "Nine minutes later than when you asked me last time."

"By rights I should go back of that tree over there and take a piss. In fact I think I will."

"That's just when he'll pull in."

"The hell with it. I wouldn't be any good with a full bladder."

"You won't be any good if he sees us."

"He'll be so drunk he won't notice." The grin made him thirty. "You worry too much."

The moon told its usual lies. Made this ugly two-story flat-roofed cube of a house if not beautiful at least tolerable to the quick and forgiving eye. The steep sagging stairs running at a forty-five-degree angle up the side of the place were all that interested me. That and the isolation here on the edge of town. A farmhouse at one time, a tumbledown barn behind it, the farmland back to seed, no one here except our couple living in the upstairs. Ken and Callie Neely. Ken being the one we were after.

We were parked behind a stretch of oaks. Easy to watch him pull in and start up those stairs. I kept the radio low. Springsteen.

When Ralph got back in I handed him my pocket-sized hand sanitizer.

"You should a been a den mother."

"You take a piss, you wash your hands."

"Yes, Mom."

And then we heard him. He drove his sleek red Chevy pickup truck so fast he sounded as if he was going to shoot right on by. I wondered what the night birds silver-limned in the broken moonlight of the trees made of the country-western song bellowing from the truck. A breeze swooped in the open windows of my Volvo and brought the scents of long-dead summers. An image of a seventeen-year-old girl pulling her T-shirt over her head and the immortal perfection of her pink-tipped breasts.

"You know what this is going to make us, don't you? I mean, after we've done it."

"Yeah, I do, Tom. It's gonna make us happy. That's what it's gonna make us. Now let's go get him."

I met Ralph Francis McKenna in the chemo room of Oncology Partners. His was prostate, mine was colon. They gave him a year, me eighteen months, no guarantees either of us would make it. We had one other thing in common. We were both widowers. Our kids lived way across the country and could visit only occasionally. Natural enough we'd become friends. Of a kind, anyway.

We always arranged to have our chemo on the same day, same time. After the chemo was over we both had to take monthly IVs of other, less powerful drugs.

Ralph said he'd had the same reaction when he'd first walked into the huge room where thirty-eight patients sat in comfortable recliners getting various kinds of IV drips. So many people smiling and laughing. Another thing being how friendly everybody was to everybody else. People in thousand-dollar coats and jackets talking to threadbare folks in cheap discount clothes. Black people yukking it up with white people. And swift efficient nurses Ralph Francis McKenna, a skilled flirt, knew how to draw in.

Once in a while somebody would have a reaction to the chemo. One woman must have set some kind of record for puking. She was so sick the three nurses hovering over her didn't even have time to get her to one of the johns. All they could do was keep shoving clean pans under her chin.

During our third session Ralph said, "So how do you like flying solo?"

"What's 'flying solo'?"

"You know. Being alone. Without a wife."

"I hate it. My wife knew how to enjoy life. She really loved it. I get depressed a lot. I should've gone first. She appreciated being alive."

"I still talk to my wife, you know that? I walk around the house and talk to her like we're just having a conversation."

"I do pretty much the same thing. One night I dreamed I was talking to her on the phone and when I woke up I was sitting on the side of the bed with the receiver in my hand."

Flying solo. I liked that phrase.

You could read, use one of their DVD players, or listen to music on headsets. Or visit with friends and relatives who came to pass the time. Or in Ralph's case, flirt.

The nurses liked him. His good looks and cop self-confidence put them at ease. I'm sure a couple of the single ones in their forties would probably have considered going to bed with him if he'd been capable of it. He joked to me once, shame shining in his eyes, "They took my pecker, Tom, and they won't give it back." Not that a few of the older nurses didn't like me. There was Nora, who reminded me of my wife in her younger years. A few times I started to ask her out but then got too scared. The last woman I'd asked out on a first date had been my wife, forty-three years ago.

The DVD players were small and you could set them up on a wheeled table right in front of your recliner while you were getting the juice. One day I brought season two of *The Rockford Files,* with James Garner. When I got about two minutes into the episode I heard Ralph sort of snicker.

"What's so funny?"

"You. I should've figured you for a Garner type of guy."

"What's wrong with Garner?"

"He's a wuss. Sort of femmy."

"James Garner is sort of femmy?"

"Yeah. He's always whining and bitching. You know, like a woman. I'm more of a Clint Eastwood fan myself."

"I should've figured on that."

"You don't like Eastwood?"

"Maybe I would if he knew how to act."

"He's all man."

"He's all something all right."

"You never hear him whine."

"That's because he doesn't know how. It's too complicated for him."

"'Make my day.'"

"Kiss my ass."

Ralph laughed so hard several of the nurses down the line looked at us and smiled. Then they tried to explain us to their patients.

A nurse named Heather Moore was the first one. She always called us her "Trouble Boys" because we kidded her so much about her somewhat earnest, naive worldview. Over a couple of months, we learned that her ex-husband had wiped out their tiny bank account and run off with the secretary at the muffler shop where he'd been manager. She always said, "All my girlfriends say I should be a whole lot madder at him, but you know, when I'm honest with myself I probably wasn't that good of a wife. You know? His mom always fixed these big suppers for the family. And she's a very pretty woman. But by the time I put in eight hours here and pick up Bobby at daycare, I just don't have much energy. We ate a lot of frozen stuff. And I put on about ten pounds extra. I guess you can't blame him for looking around."

Couple times after she started sharing her stories with us, Ralph made some phone calls. He talked to three people who'd known her husband. A chaser who'd started running around on Heather soon after their wedding day. A slacker at work and a husband who betrayed his wife in maybe the worst way of all—making constant jokes about her to his coworkers. And she blamed herself for not being good enough for him.

Then came the day when she told us about the duplex where she lived. The toilets wouldn't flush properly, the garbage disposal didn't work, both front and back concrete steps were dangerously shattered, and the back door wouldn't lock. Some of her neighbors had been robbed recently.

The landlord was a jerk—lawyer, of course—named David Muldoon. Despite the comic-book surname he was anything but comic.

Ralph checked him out. A neo-yuppie who owned several income properties in the city, he was apparently working his way up the slumlord ladder. Heather complained to the city and the city did what it did best: nothing. She'd called Muldoon's business office several times and been promised that her complaints would soon be taken care of. They weren't. And even baby lawyers fresh from the diploma mills wanted more than she could afford to take Muldoon on.

We always asked her how it was going with Muldoon. The day she told us that the roof was leaking and nobody from his office had returned her call in four days, Ralph told her, "You don't worry about it anymore, Heather."

"How come?"

"I just have a feeling."

Heather wasn't the only one wondering what the hell he was talking about. So was I. He said, "You got the usual big night planned?"

"If you mean frozen dinner, some TV, maybe calling one of my kids who'll be too busy to talk very long, and then going to bed, yes."

"Maybe watch a little James Garner."

"Yeah, or put on Clint Eastwood and fall asleep early."

"Glad you don't have plans, because we're going on a stakeout."

"I go to bed at nine."

"Not tonight. Unless we get lucky. Maybe he'll get laid and get home before then."

"Who?"

"Muldoon, that's who."

"You know for a fact that he's got something going on the side?"

"No. But I always listen to my gut."

I smiled.

"I say something funny?" Sort of pissed the way he said it.

"Do all you guys watch bad cop shows before you graduate? Your 'gut'?"

"Most of these assholes cheat."

I thought about it. "Maybe you're right."

"Kid, I'm always right." Grin this time.

Turned out it was the secretary in the law firm on the floor below Muldoon's. Not even all that attractive. He was just out for strange in the nighttime.

We waited leaning against his new black Cadillac.

"Who the fuck are you two supposed to be?"

"We're supposed to be the two guys you least want to hear from." I was happy to let Ralph do the talking.

"Yeah?" All swagger.

"Yeah. You're taking advantage of a friend of ours."

"Get the fuck out of my way. I'm going home."

"It's a bitch getting rid of that pussy smell on your clothes, isn't it? Wives like to pretend they can't smell it."

Dug out his cell phone. Waggled it for us. "I don't know who you two assholes are, but I'll bet the police won't have any trouble finding out."

"And your wife won't have any trouble finding out about the snatch in that apartment house behind us either."

I didn't realize what had happened until I saw the counselor bend in half and heard him try to swear while his lungs were collapsing. He fell to his knees. Ralph hit him so hard on the side of the head Muldoon toppled over. "Her name's Heather Moore. She's one of your tenants. She doesn't know anything about this, so don't bother trying to shake her down for any information. You've got two days to fix everything wrong in her apartment. Two days or I call your wife. And if you come after us or send anybody after us, then I not only call your wife, I start looking for any other bimbos you've been with in the past. I'm a retired homicide detective, so I know how to do this shit. You got me?"

Muldoon still couldn't talk. Just kept rolling back and forth on the sandy concrete. He grunted something.

That was how it started. Heather asked us about it once, but we said we didn't know anything about it. Heather obviously didn't believe us, because two weeks later a nurse named Sally Coates, one neither of us knew very well, came and sat down on a chair next to the IV stand and told us about her husband and this used-car salesman who'd sold them a lemon and wouldn't make it right. They were out seven grand they hadn't been able to afford in the first place, but they had to have a car so her husband could get to the VA hospital, where he was learning to walk again after losing his right leg in Afghanistan. The kind of story you watch on TV and want to start killing people.

All innocence, Ralph said, "Gosh, Sally, I wish we could help you, but I don't see what we could do. There isn't any reason he'd listen to us."

"I can't believe it," Sally said the next time we saw her. "Bob got a call the day after I told you about this salesman. The guy said to bring the car in and they'd get it fixed up right so we wouldn't be having any trouble with it. And there wouldn't be any charge."

"I'll bet you did a lot of praying about it, didn't you, Sally?"

"Of course. We have two little ones to feed. Keeping that car running was breaking us."

"Well, it was the prayers that did it, Sally."

"And you didn't have anything to do with it?"

"Ask him."

I shook my head. "What could we have done, Sally? We're just two old guys."

After she left, Ralph leaned over from his leather recliner and said, "The only good thing about dying this way is we don't have to give a shit about anything. What're they gonna do to us?" That grin of his. "We're already dead."

I developed a uniform. A Cubs cap, dark aviator glasses, and a Louisville Slugger. According to Ralph I was "the backup hood. They're scared enough of me. Then they see this guy with the ball bat and the shades—they'll do anything to cooperate." He didn't mention how old we were.

The nurses kept coming. Four in the next three months. A nurse who was trying to get a collection of family photographs back from an ex-boyfriend she'd broken up with after he'd given her the clap, spurned boyfriend stealing the collection and keeping it for her breaking up with him; the nurse whose daughter's boyfriend was afraid to visit because two bully brothers down the block always picked on him when he pulled up; and the nurse who liked to sit in on poker games with five guys who worked at an electronics discount house and thought it was pretty damned funny to cheat her out of forty to sixty dollars every time she sat down. It took her four months of playing twice a month to figure it out.

No heavy lifting, as they say; no, that came with a tiny, delicate young nurse named Callie. We noticed the bruises on her arms first, then the bruises on her throat, despite the scarf she wore with her uniform. Then came the two broken fingers and the way she limped for a couple of weeks and finally the faint but unmistakable black eye. A few of the other nurses whispered about it among themselves. One of them told us that the head nurse had asked Callie about it. Callie had smiled and said that "my whole family is clumsy."

It was during this time that both Ralph and I realized that we probably wouldn't be beating the prognoses we'd been given. With me it was a small but certain track of new cancer suddenly appearing on my right thigh; with Ralph it was the return of heart problems he'd had off and on for two decades.

We didn't talk about it much to each other. There isn't much to say when you get to this point. You just hope for as much decent time as you can get, and if you've been helping people here and there you go right on helping them as long as you can.

We followed Callie home one night, found out that she lived in a tumbledown farmhouse as isolated as a lighthouse. The next night we followed her home, and when she stopped off at a shopping center we waited for her by her car.

She smiled. "My two favorite patients. I guess you don't get to see me enough in chemo, huh?" The cat-green eyes were suspicious despite her greeting. She'd developed another one of those mysterious limps.

"That's right. Tom here wants to ask you to marry him."

"Well," the smile never wavering, "maybe I should talk that over with my husband first. You think?"

"That's what we want to talk to you about, Callie," I said. "Your husband."

The smile went and so did she. Or at least she tried. I stood in front of the car door. Ralph took her arm and walked her about four feet away.

He said something to her I couldn't hear, but her I heard clearly: "My personal life is none of your damn business! And I'm going to tell my husband about this."

"He going to beat us up the way he beats you up?"

"Who said he beats me up?"

"I was a cop, remember? I've seen dozens of cases like yours. They run to a pattern."

"Well, then you weren't a very *good* cop, because my husband has never laid a hand on me."

"Three restraining orders in five years; six 911 calls; the same ER doctor who said he's dealt with you twice for concussions; and a women's shelter that told me you came there twice for three-night stays."

The city roared with life — traffic, stray rap music, shouts, laughter, squealing tires — but right here a little death was being died as she was forced to confront not just us but herself. The small package she'd been carrying slipped from her hands to the concrete and she slumped against her car. She seemed to rip the sobs from herself in tiny increments, like somebody in the early stages of a seizure.

"I've tried to get away. Five or six times. One night I took the kids and got all the way to St. Joe. Missouri, I mean. We stayed in a motel there for two weeks. Took every dime I had. The kids didn't mind. They're as scared of him as I am. But he found us. He never told me how. And you know what he did? He was waiting for us when we got back from going to a movie the kids wanted to see. He was in our room. I opened the door and there he was. He looked down at Luke — he's eight now; he was only four then — and he said, 'You take care of your little sister, Luke. You two go sit in my truck now.' 'You better not hurt her, Dad.' Can you imagine that — a four-year-old talking like that? A four-year-old? Anyway, then he looked at me and said, 'Get in here, whore.' He waited until I closed the door behind me and then he hit me so hard in the face he broke my nose. And my glasses. He forced the kids to ride back with him. That way he knew I'd come back too."

This was in the food court of the mall where we'd convinced her to come and have some coffee with us. You could reach up and grab a handful of grease from the air. I'm told in Texas they deep-fry quarter sticks of butter. If it ever comes up here, this mall will sell it for sure.

"But you always come back."

"I love him, Ralph. I can't explain it. It's like a sickness."

"It's not like a sickness, Callie. It *is* a sickness."

"Maybe if I knew I could get away and he'd never find me. To him those restraining orders are a joke." Then: "I have to admit there're sometimes — more and more these days, I guess — when I think maybe it'd be best if he'd just get killed driving that damned truck of his. You know, an accident where he's the only one killed.

I wouldn't want to do that to anybody else." Then: "Isn't that awful?"

"It is if you love him."

"I say that, Tom. I *always* say that. But the woman at the shelter had me see a counselor and the counselor explained to me what she called the 'dynamics' of how I really feel about him. We had to take two semesters of psych to get our nursing degrees, so I'd always considered myself pretty smart on the subject. But she led me into thinking a lot of things that had never occurred to me before. And so even though I say that, I'm not sure I mean it." Then, shy: "Sorry for all the carrying-on in the parking lot. I attracted quite a crowd."

"I collected admission from every one of them."

She sat back in her curved red plastic chair and smiled. "You guys—you're really my friends. I was so depressed all day. Even with the kids there I just didn't want to drag myself home tonight. I know I was being selfish to even think such a thing. But I just couldn't take being hit or kicked anymore. I knew he'd be mad that I stopped at the mall. Straight home or I'd better have a damned good excuse. Or I'll be sorry. It's no way to live."

"No," I said, "it sure isn't."

"Now let's go get him."

Callie had mentioned she was taking the kids for a long weekend stay at a theme park, which was why we'd decided on tonight.

Neely didn't hear us coming. We walked through patches of shadow then moonlight, shadow then moonlight, while he tried to get out of his truck. I say tried because he was so drunk he almost came out headfirst and would have if he hadn't grabbed the edge of the truck door in time. Then he sat turned around on the edge of the seat and puked straight down. He went three times and he made me almost as sick as he was. Then of course, being as drunk as he was, he stepped down with his cowboy boots into the puddle of puke he'd made. He kept wiping the back of his right hand across his mouth. He started sloshing through the puke, then stopped and went back to the truck. He opened the door and grabbed something. In the moonlight I could see it was a pint of whiskey. He gunned a long drink, then took six steps and puked it all right back up. He stepped into this puke as well and headed more or less in the direction of the stairs that would take him to his apartment. All of this was setting things up perfectly. Nobody was going to question the fact that Neely had been so drunk it was no surprise that he'd fallen off those stairs and died.

We moved fast. I took the position behind him with my ball cap, shades, and ball bat, and Ralph got in front of him with his Glock.

Neely must've been toting a 2.8 level of alcohol because he didn't seem to be aware of Ralph until he ran straight into him. And straight into the Glock. Even then all he could say was, "Huh? I jush wan' sleep."

"Good evening, Mr. Neely. You shouldn't drink so much. You need to be alert when you're beating the shit out of women half your size. You never know when they're going to hit back, do you?"

"Hey, dude, ish tha' a gun?"

"Sure looks like it, doesn't it?"

He reeled back on the heels of his cowboy boots. I poked the bat into his back. I was careful. When he went down the stairs it had to look accidental. We couldn't bruise him or use any more force than it took to give him a slight shove. If he didn't die the first time down he would the second time we shoved him.

"Hey."

"You need some sleep, Neely."

"—need no fuckin' sleep. 'n don't try'n make me. Hey, an' you got a fuckin' gun."

"What if I told you that I've got a pizza in the car?"

"Pizza?"

"Yeah. Pizza."

"How come pizza?"

"So we can sit down in your apartment and talk things over."

"Huh?"

"How—does—pizza—sound?"

Ralph was enunciating because Neely was about two minutes away from unconsciousness. We had to get him up those stairs without leaving any marks on him.

"Pizza, Neely. Sausage and beef and pepperoni."

I allowed myself the pleasure of taking in the summer night. The first time I'd ever made love to Karen had been on a night like this near a boat dock. Summer of our senior year in college. We went back to that spot many times over the years. Not long before she died we went there too. I almost believed in ghosts; I thought I saw our younger selves out on the night river in one of those old rented aluminum canoes, our lives all ahead of us, so young and exuberant and naive. I wanted to get in one of those old canoes and take my wife downriver so she could die in my arms and maybe I'd be lucky and die in hers as well. But it hadn't worked out that way. All too soon I'd been flying solo.

Neely started puking again. This time it was a lot more dramatic, because after he finished he fell facedown in it.

"This fucking asshole. When he's done you take one arm and I'll take the other one."

"I thought we weren't going to touch him."

"That's why you shoved those latex gloves in your back pocket same as I did. You gotta plan for contingencies. That's why cops carry guns they can plant on perps. Otherwise we'll be here all night. Clint Eastwood would know about that."

"Yes, planting guns on people. Another admirable Eastwood quality."

"Right. I forgot. Tender ears. You don't want to hear about real life. You just want to bitch and moan like Garner. Now let's pick up this vile piece of shit and get it over with."

He'd worked up a pretty good sweat with all his puking. It was a hot and humid night. His body was soggy like something that would soon mildew. Once I pulled him out of his puke I held my breath.

"We don't want to drag him. They'll look at his boots. Stand him upright and we'll sort of escort him to the steps."

"I just hope he doesn't start puking again."

"I saw a black perp puke like this once. I wish I had it on tape."

"Yeah, be fun for the grandkids to watch at Christmastime."

"I like that, Tom. Smart-ass remarks in the course of committing murder one. Shows you're getting a lot tougher."

We took our time. He didn't puke again, but from the tangy odor I think he did piss his pants.

When we were close to the bottom step, he broke. I guess both of us had assumed he was unconscious and therefore wouldn't be any problem. But he broke and he got a three- or four-second lead while we just stood there and watched him scramble up those stairs like a wild animal that had just escaped its cage. He was five steps ahead of us before Ralph started after him. I pounded up the steps right behind him. Ralph was shouting. I'm sure he had to restrain himself from just shooting Neely and getting it over with.

Neely was conscious enough to run but not conscious enough to think clearly, because when he got to the top of the stairs he stopped and dug a set of keys from his pocket. As he leaned in to try and find the lock, his head jerked up suddenly and he stared at us as if he was seeing us for the very first time. Confusion turned to terror in his eyes and he started backing away from us. "Hey, who the hell're you?"

"Who do you think we are, Neely?"

"I don' like thish."

"Yeah, well, we don't like it either."

"He got a ball bat." He nodded in my direction. He weaved wide as he did so, so wide I thought he was going to tip over sideways. Then his hand searched the right pocket of his Levi's. It looked like he'd trapped an angry ferret in there.

Ralph materialized Neely's nine-inch switchblade. "This what you're looking for?"

"Hey," Neely said. And when he went to grab for it he started falling to the floor. Ralph grabbed him in time. Stood him straight up.

But Neely wasn't done yet. And he was able to move faster than I would have given him credit for. Ralph glanced back at me, nodded for me to come forward. And in that second Neely made his sloppy, drunken move. He grabbed the switchblade from Ralph's hand and immediately went into a crouch.

He would have been more impressive if he hadn't swayed side to side so often. And if he hadn't tried to sound tough. "Who'sh gotta knife now, huh?"

"You gonna cut us up, are you, Neely?"

All the time advancing on Neely, backing him up. "C'mon, Neely. Cut me. Right here." Ralph held his arm out. "Right there, Neely. You can't miss it."

Neely swaying, half stumbling backward as Ralph moved closer, closer. "You're pretty pathetic, you know that, Neely? You beat up your wife all the time, and even when you've got the knife you're still scared of me. You're not much of a man, but then you know that, don't you? You look in the mirror every morning and you see yourself for what you really are, don't you?"

I doubt Neely understood what Ralph was saying to him. This was complex stuff to comprehend when you were as wasted as Neely was. All he seemed to understand was that Ralph meant to do him harm. And if Ralph didn't do it, there was always the guy in the ball cap and the shades. You know, with the bat.

Neely stumbled backward, his arms circling in a desperate attempt to keep himself upright. He hit the two-by-four that was the upper part of the porch enclosure just at the lower part of his back and he went right over, the two-by-four splintering as he did so. He didn't scream. My guess is he was still confused about what was happening. By the time he hit the ground I was standing next to Ralph, looking down into the shadows beneath us.

There was silence. Ralph got his flashlight going and we got our first look at him. If he wasn't dead, he was pretty good at faking it. He didn't land in any of those positions we associate with people who die crashing from great heights. He was flat on his back with his arms flung wide. His right leg was twisted inward a few inches, but nothing dramatic. The eyes were open and looked straight up. No expression of horror, something else we've picked up from books and movies. And as we watched the blood started pooling from the back of his head.

"Let's go make sure," Ralph said.

It was like somebody had turned on the soundtrack. In the moments it had taken Neely to fall all other sound had disappeared. But now the night was back and turned up high. Night birds, dogs, horses and cows bedded down for the evening, distant trucks and trains, all turned so high I wanted to clap my hands to my ears.

"You all right, Tom?"

"Why wouldn't I be all right?"

"See. I knew you weren't all right."

"But you're all right, I suppose. I mean, we just killed a guy."

"You want me to get all touchy-feely and say I regret it?"

"Fuck yourself."

"He was a piece of shit and one of these nights he was gonna kill a friend of ours. Maybe he wouldn't even have done it on purpose. He'd just be beating on her some night and he'd do it by accident.

But one way or another he'd kill her. And we'd have to admit to ourselves that we could've stopped it."

I walked away from the edge of the porch and started down the stairs.

"You doin' better now?" Ralph called.

"Yeah—yeah, I guess I am."

"Clint Eastwood, I tell ya. Clint Eastwood every time."

Turned out Neely wasn't dead after all. We had to stand there for quite a while watching him bleed to death.

I was visiting my oldest son in Phoenix (way too hot for me) when I learned Ralph had died. I'd logged on to the hometown paper website and there was his name at the top of the obituaries. The photo must have been taken when he was in his early twenties. I barely recognized him. Heart attack. He'd been dead for a day before a neighbor of his got suspicious and asked the apartment house manager to open Ralph's door. I thought of what he'd said about flying solo that time.

Ralph had experienced the ultimate in flying solo: death. I hoped that whatever he thought was on the other side came true for him. I still hadn't figured out what I hoped would be there. If anything would be there at all.

The doc told me they'd be putting me back on chemo again. The lab reports were getting bad fast. The nurses in chemo commiserated with me as if Ralph had been a family member. There'd been a number of things I hadn't liked about him and he hadn't liked about me. Those things never got resolved and maybe they didn't need to. Maybe flying solo was all we needed for a bond. One thing for sure. The chemo room hours seemed a lot longer with him gone. I even got sentimental once and put a Clint Eastwood DVD in the machine, film called *Tightrope*. Surprised myself by liking it more than not liking it.

I was sitting in my recliner one day when one of the newer nurses sat down and started talking in a very low voice. "There's this guy we each gave five hundred dollars to. You know, a down payment. He said he was setting up this group trip to the Grand Canyon. You know, through this group therapy thing I go to. Then we found out that he scams a lot of people this way. Groups, I mean. We called the Better Business Bureau and the police. But I guess he covers his tracks pretty well. Actually takes some of the groups on the trips. Five hundred is a lot of money if you're a single mother."

The chemo was taking its toll. But I figured I owed it to Ralph to help her out. And besides, I wanted to see how I did on my own.

So here I am tonight. I've followed him from his small house to his round of singles bars and finally to the apartment complex where the woman lives. The one he picked up in the last bar. He's got to come out sometime.

I've got the Louisville Slugger laid across my lap and the Cubs cap cinched in place. I won't put the shades on till I see him. No sense straining my eyes. Not at my age.

I miss Ralph. About now he'd be working himself up doing his best Clint Eastwood and trying to dazzle me with all his bad cop stories.

I'm pretty sure I can handle this, but even if it works out all right, it's still flying solo. And let me tell you, flying solo can get to be pretty damned lonely.

JAMES GRADY

Destiny City

FROM *Agents of Treachery*

FOUR MEN WALKED through the December night along tracks for Washington, D.C.'s subway and Amtrak trains that rumble through America. Their shoes crunched gravel. *Musica ranchera* drifted from a nearby industrial park where Sami, who drove a taxi, remembered signs for a Latino ballroom.

"When?" Maher was a California blond born with the name Michael.

"Soon," said Ivan, their Ameer.

Zlatko said, "Ameer, I have money for my last buys tomorrow."

"Brother, I can ride you with my taxi," said Sami.

"No," said Ivan. "Work alone. Let no one see us as fingers of a fist."

"A fist is five," said Maher. "I thought there were only us four."

"Jihad is the thumb that shapes us," proclaimed their Ameer.

Sami said, "Someone's coming."

A trio of hombres swaggered toward them through the darkness.

"Hola, amigos," said that trio's jefe. "What you doing here, eh?"

"Leaving," said Sami.

"Don' thin' so." Jefe soured the night with his beer-and-tequila breath. "You gringos got lots of nowhere to run."

His tallest compañero frowned. "Not gringos. Only the blond *guero.*"

"Who cares?" Jefe drew a black pistol. "Tool up, Juan."

The third Hispanic fumbled inside his coat's back collar.

Maher jumped Juan as he unsheathed a machete.

Jefe blinked—and Sami ripped the pistol from him with a move taught in Al-Qaeda's Afghan camps, while Zlatko and Maher wrestled the machete from Juan.

Ivan relieved Sami of the gun. "See what they have."

"Amigos!" said Jefe as Sami searched the three thugs, made them kneel on the gravel. "We all just joking, sí?"

Maher said, "Shut up, motherfucker!"

Sami gave confiscated cell phones, cash, and IDs to Ivan. Zlatko threw away the machete.

"Let's go," whispered Sami. "They can't tell anybody anything."

"Whach you sayin'?" called out the kneeling jefe.

Ivan whispered, "They are *kuffars*. Unbelievers."

"That is not enough." Zlatko shrugged. "But they saw we don't belong—especially with Maher."

"They can't tell police or FBI or CIA," said Sami. "They don't dare."

"You talkin' FBI? *La migra?* Don' fuck with us! We MS-13!"

Ivan said, "Loose ends. They'll tell someone. And America is full of ears."

He put the pistol in Maher's hands. The blond kid stared at it. Stared at three men kneeling before him. The night floated their clouds of breath.

Ivan told him, "You asked *when*. Allah granted you the answer."

Maher fired three flash-cracking shots. The thugs crumpled into the gravel.

Ameer Ivan led his followers away from the trackside executions. He gave Zlatko the gun. Distributed the dead men's cash to all of his soldiers. Sami saw Zlatko tuck his bills inside an envelope he returned to his jacket's outside right pocket.

The Ameer tossed the thugs' cell phones. Plastic clattered on unseen rocks.

Maher staggered away from his comrades. Vomited.

"Be proud, Maher." The Ameer wrapped an arm around the youngest man's shoulders. "Diverting the enemy with the gun let us attack."

Maher mumbled, "I went wild in my mind."

"And learned a key lesson," said the Ameer. "Timing. *When* is *now*, and if all goes well with Zlatko's work . . . three days."

"*Three days?*" said Sami. "Are you sure, Ameer?"

"Yes." They neared the gap in the chain-link fence. "And only we four know."

"And Allah," said Zlatko.

"Sami," said the Ameer. "Keep that *vaquera* in your control."

"She is no problem," said Sami.

They left the tracks for a street that was once a route from the capital to a rural town. Now city sprawled from Congress's white dome to far beyond D.C.'s Beltway.

Ivan stood alone by a roadside white pole, an ordinary, fortyish man waiting for the bus that took him to his gold SUV stashed among a multiplex's moviegoer machines.

When the bus rolled out of sight, his three warriors walked from the shadows to a Metro subway station. Sami made Maher stand alone on the platform. Zlatko's nod approved such tradecraft for the cameras mounted on the platform's ceiling.

A silver subway train snaked to a stop. Maher carelessly drifted onto the same car as Zlatko and Sami. Words bounced in his eyes. Sami's glare welded the young man's jaws shut.

The subway slid out of the station. Zlatko sat between Sami and the window. They memorized their fellow passengers: A black guy bopping to earphone music. Two Spanish-babbling women dressed like office cleaners. A white-haired security guard.

Zlatko whispered, "Brother Maher did well, though not like our karate school teaches. But he would not last fifteen minutes in interrogation. He needs to tell. Get fame so he can be real. I worry that he'll always be a born American."

"Our Ameer must know what he's doing, choosing Maher."

"The smallest cog turns the whole assembly." His engineer past haunted Zlatko's words. "But, brother, that is not what troubles me most."

Brake squeals killed Sami's question. The train stopped. Zlatko and Maher stood to leave the train for wherever they would spend that night, facts the jihad brothers did not share among themselves.

Sami stood to let Zlatko pass. Pickpocketed the money envelope.

Zlatko stepped onto the platform.

The train slid away.

Sami rode to a neighborhood known for vegetarians, PEACE

lawn signs, and citizens who thought the 1960s meant something holy. A bus took him to twin high-rises on a smog-soaked hill.

A high-rise elevator clunked him to its ninth floor. He entered his one-room apartment and closed the door with a *thunk* for any eavesdropper. Fought for breath. *You're clear! Clear!* He eased back into the hall. Glided down the stairwell like a shadow.

In the basement, Sami dialed open the combination lock on an electric breaker box. Left the Glock pistol on the box shelf. Turned on the shelf's cell phone, texted a four-word message. Grabbed keys for a stashed car, drove toward the white dome center of town, and parked by a brick building with a peeling sign for Belfield Casket Company. The coffin factory's door flew open.

Harry Mizell—who looked like a bear—waved Sami inside.

Harry and boyish FBI agent Ted escorted Sami through the beehive of cubicles where men and women monitored computers and whispered into phones.

They sat Sami at a conference table in a windowless room. Video cameras clung to the walls. Sami imagined the scene transmitting to the aging H-shaped CIA headquarters, to Homeland Security's new complex in a powerful congressman's district, to the FBI. Maybe even to the White House.

Sami wondered if the private contractor Argus, whose ID dangled from Harry's neck, got a direct feed.

As COOK—Case Officer/Operation Control—Harry debriefed. Ted, who wore the FBI ID Harry had forsaken, sat mute at the table.

Sami told Harry, Ted, and the cameras about the murders. About *when.* Put the pickpocketed envelope on the table. Told Harry, Ted, and the cameras what they had to do *now, right now.*

Harry said, "When you texted 'Crash Exfilt Base Soonest,' we cocked to rock. *Now* . . . Now you sit tight. Relax."

Harry left the room. Left the FBI agent in charge of their spy. The glass eye of a video camera captured Sami's slump.

Ted cleared his throat. "Do you want a soft drink?"

"A soft drink?"

The FBI agent nodded yes.

"No, Ted. I don't want a soft drink."

Hmmm. The room's CTSU—Covert Transmission Suppression Unit.

"Sami," said Ted, "I pray for you every day."

"You don't know how much that means to me."

The FBI agent nodded. "God's work."

"So they tell me."

Ted let Sami go to the bathroom alone. The fluorescent retreat smelled of ammonia and angst. Sami washed his hands, face. Stared into the sink's mirror. Was there a camera behind that glass?

An hour later, Harry returned. "Bottom line, our op is still running."

"*What?*" Sami whirled to the video cameras. "We've got them *right now* on triple murder charges! Scoop them up!"

"Bosses say we need to find who's behind the cell, Al-Qaeda or—"

"There is no mastermind link! No organizational chart like we've got. That's mirror reasoning. These guys are homegrown! Self-contained."

"So you say, and I'm inclined to agree, but . . ." Harry got up from the table, disconnected the visible cameras. "Ted, leave us alone."

"I'm the FBI liaison and thus the official presence for—"

"Ted, Homeland Security outsourced Argus Inc. to run this op. I'm Argus's archangel. Go write a cover-your-ass e-mail about how I kicked you out."

The door closed on Ted's exit.

"Realize what we've got here," said Harry.

"You were CIA special ops in JAWBREAKER hunting Al-Qaeda in A-stan. CIA used your real Beirut life, snuck you in with captured Taliban guys our Paki allies freed. For years you've worked your terrorist bona fides all over the globe.

"Just like your buddy Zlatko. After Bosnia, he pops up looking for phony papers in Rose's outlaw gig. She's righteous enough to call her ex-FBI buddy, *moi*. My clout jerks you from CIA to Homeland Security. We put you next to Zlatko at Rose's. He brings you to Ivan, a Chechen physician who found Zlatko at the night school English class where Ivan teaches *and* fishes. Ivan had already hooked that goofy suburban kid who showed up at a mosque before they shoved Ivan out as a false Muslim.

"And presto," said Harry, "we've penetrated a terrorist cell. A cell that's going to attack in three days. And with ninety-three Islamic terrorist groups on our radar, our bosses are convinced this cell has got to be somebody's baby. Those sponsors are who we want."

"Three people got murdered *tonight*. That's enough!"

"Those thugs don't count right now."

"So we won't tell the local cops? What about those men's families? Hell, if they are MS-13, those murders could spark a street war!"

"Terrorists are America's number-one priority. Ivan compartmentalizes. He might have other soldiers. Something even the hard boys can't sweat out of him."

"They're going to hit on Christmas Eve!"

"Is it coordinated? What's their target? Their method?"

"Take them down, Harry. Get me out."

"We all want out. But we are where we are. This op—"

"No, not this op. *Everything*. I want all the way out. Now."

"Oh." Harry leaned back. "I can't make you spy. But bottom line, our gov bosses are going to let the cell run to get what they want whether it's there or not. Without you on the bricks, without me as COOK, will guys like Ted do it right?"

"Not my problem."

"My company and I get paid big bucks however this breaks. But I want to nail this job. I'm no walk-away guy. What kinda guy are you?"

That image sat at the conference table like a giant question mark.

Sami blinked. "Three days—and *before* they pull a trigger."

"Damn straight. So what are you going to do?"

Sami stood to leave, took the pickpocketed cash. Told Harry, "I'm going to fuck with them."

The next morning Sami worked his cab between Capitol Hill and glistening downtown. Such fares made him remember his high school senior class trip to "our nation's capital," how "the Hill" had been open driveways looping past the vanilla ice cream Capitol. White-shirted congressional cops looked like marshmallow men.

That post-9/11 routine December morning, concrete barricades blocked all vehicle approaches to the white marble heart of Congress. Steel barriers funneled pedestrians past barbell-muscled, black-jumpsuited, mirror-sunglassed sentinels with M-4 assault rifles or shotguns strapped across their armored chests.

But it's not Beirut, he thought. Not yet. I can stop that clock.

At 10:07 he flipped down the ON CALL visor sign. Drove to an Asian fusion restaurant where lunch for one cost enough to feed a shantytown Malaysian family. Parked in the alley so he faced the restaurant's service door.

10:11: Two cooks walked past his cab and into the restaurant. 10:13: A sixtyish Vietnamese man in busboy's black shirt and pants took a Saigon second to scan the vehicle crouched near his destination. 10:14: Zlatko strolled into the alley carrying a dishwasher's white apron and a flat expression. Used the restaurant's back door. 10:21: Zlatko appeared in the cab's mirrors, arms by his side, coming toward the blue taxi on a circular route justified, Sami guessed, by the bummed cigarette tucked above nonsmoker Zlatko's right ear.

Zlatko got in the back of the cab.

Right behind me! Can't see his hands!

Sami said, *"As-salaam alaykum."*

"Why are you here?" Zlatko's eyes burned in the rearview mirror.

"On the subway, you said you are troubled. We are brothers. I came to help."

"And that is all? No confession?"

"What do either of us have to confess?"

Zlatko shrank in the backseat.

"On the train, I was worried our Ameer has confusion about what is righteous and *halal*. What is *haram* and not permitted. How the Koran forbids killing innocents, women, and children, so the planes that hit the towers, the one crashed in that green field, they must be *haram*. The Pentagon plane, against soldiers, yes, *halal,* and civilians there who served the soldiers, unavoidable. Loose ends or contingency casualties. But instead of worrying about our Ameer, I should have paid attention to my own duties."

Zlatko shook his head. "Last night I lost our money envelope."

"Wait—you thought *I* stole it?"

"Ours is a wicked world. I saw the bodies of my wife, two daughters, son. Saw what my neighbors had done to us Muslims in our Bosnian town while I was out riding my bicycle thinking about the

Olympics . . . Forgive me: I feared this *kuffar* world around us had swallowed your soul. But it is I who lost the money. Have endangered our mission."

"You are not to blame for accidents." Sami let his mercy sink in, then threw out a hook. "Have you told our Ameer?"

"Not yet."

"How much money do you need?"

"All of my end should cost around nine hundred and fifty dollars. I've spent about six hundred. All the rest plus the extra from last night was in the lost envelope."

"I have a hundred and forty-seven dollars. If I hustle now, my taxi can make the rest."

"You are a true brother! I will be waiting down the block in that grocery store parking lot at two-oh-five."

As Zlatko left the cab, out of his sleeve popped a restaurant butcher knife.

That's why he sat behind me.

He let Zlatko sweat until 2:19, raced the taxi into the grocery store lot. Zlatko told him: "Radio Shack on Georgia Avenue."

There Zlatko made Sami wait in the parked taxi. Sami kept a window open to hear the street. An instrumental "Jingle Bells" from a store competed with a man ringing a handheld bell by a red bucket.

Cari Jones defied her dark hair with blond highlights, wore a black leather trench coat, marched past the taxi telling her cell phone, "Soon as I get there, Mom'll say it's great I have a career, but my baby clock . . ."

Zlatko put packages in the taxi's back seat. Climbed in front with one Radio Shack sack, told Sami to drop him off on a corner different from any the Homeland Security/FBI/outsourced street dogs had trailed him to before they broke off surveillance to avoid spooking the streetwise warrior.

Zlatko pulled two prepaid cell phones from the sack, fished out the manual, saying, "*Yes,* call waiting, call conferencing, call blocking . . ."

He looked at Sami. "In Baghdad, we learned you don't want to be holding the right cell phone when someone dials a wrong number."

After he left Zlatko, Sami drove eleven blocks to find a pay phone. Twenty minutes later, as he cruised up North Capital Street, Sami drove past a waving ebony-skinned lawyer in an Italian suit to pick up a white man who looked like a rumpled bear.

"I wish your Ameer let you guys carry cell phones," said Harry as he settled in the back of Sami's taxi.

"No cell phones. Coded messages on Facebook from computers at libraries, Staples, and Internet cafés."

"But Zlatko just bought two phones. 'Course, it's in the rule book that every black ops honcho, spy runner, and Ameer lies to his button boys."

"Every case officer lies? Even you?"

"I play by my rules." Harry winked. "We've got our geniuses reverse-engineering Zlatko's latest buys from that Radio Shack."

The rearview mirror showed Sami a tan sedan.

"It's Ted," said Harry. "Don't shake him, okay? He's learning. He's got to. FBI, CIA, Uncle Sam's top street shooters are turning in their papers, going private, getting outsource-contracted back to do the same job at twice their government paychecks."

"Private armies fight for private profit. Government is about citizens carrying their public weight."

"When did Sami start caring about how Uncle Sam works?"

"I'm almost straight, remember? After your geniuses report, you'll have the who, when, and how. You can take down the cell. I can fly free."

Sami fed the taxi into traffic up Constitution Avenue past Smithsonian museums.

A dead pigeon lay in their traffic lane. Sami saw a sunbaked soldier named John Herne standing on the corner, staring at the fallen bird as if it hid a bomb.

"Look at this town," said Harry. "I remember when this was an AM radio burg where white folks were scared to come out after dark and Nixon had his finger on the Doomsday trigger. 'Top dollar' meant a civil service paycheck. Nobody was from D.C. People came here as cause-humpers. Now, crash or no crash, all the big money has a D.C. cash register."

"Some say we're inevitable. Like Rome, only adjusted for the Internet and Mister Glock .40. I say if we create a Sophia Loren like Rome did, let the D.C. of Washington stand for 'Destiny City.'"

"My jihad brothers say the same thing. So do Ted and his evangelical crusaders."

"What do you say?"

"That real people are trapped in those big ideas."

"Yeah, but what about Sophia Loren?"

The two men laughed.

"D.C. is your story, Sami. *Destiny City.* Born and bred for it. Spy life and street action are all you know. What makes you think you can quit?"

Harry's cell phone rang. He took the call. Listened. Clicked off. Told Sami, "Our geniuses got no idea what Zlatko is building. We're flooding every Radio Shack kinda place with agents and Zlakto's photos to see what he bought before, but it's elbow-to-elbow Christmas rush in those stores."

They rode past a block strung with colored bulbs.

"In this life," said Harry, "you're either doing something or something's getting done to you. What's your deal, Sami?"

Sami let Harry out of the cab, drove to a commercial strip where French and African patois jammed with Spanish. Cruising cars blasted gangsta rap idolized by white Kansas teenagers. Sami parked his cab in the lot of a four-story commercial building.

He checked his watch: 4:29. Ivan usually closed his doctor's office at 5:00 and drove his gold SUV home. Sami scanned ethnic stores, discount furniture barns, a veterinary hospital with a green Dumpster. Told himself he couldn't see flies circling the emerald steel. Wondered where Harry'd set up the surveillance posts. Wondered if they'd called in his presence, if a satellite snapped his picture.

"Understand our new spy biz," Harry had told Sami. "Sure, satellite surveillance of Doc Ivan's office and house is overkill, but it's about buy-in.

"We got something real, but if it's only a Homeland/CIA/FBI-outsourced Argus show, with sixteen major spy shops dancing for the old U.S. of A., we might be weak on bureaucratic muscle. So I partnered my company with a contractor for the National Applications Office to satellite-monitor your Ameer. Now NAO'll line up to make sure we get what we want so they can share our credit."

I'm a taxi driver, thought Sami. I take you where you want to go.

I'm a spy. I take you where you want to go.

At 4:47 a brown medical transport services van parked at the building. The driver in a white uniform got out to lower the electric motored stairs.

They shuffled out of the building. Some were black, some brown. A wispy blond girl on crutches swung toward the van. They were all poor. The bottom line mattered as much as any for two women in black burkas that exposed only their eyes.

Last out of the door came Ivan, a doctor who didn't care about health insurance, charged what patients could afford for what he could do. Sometimes, like now, that meant walking a white-haired old lady to the van.

Sami parked behind the van, pulled on a black Detroit Tigers baseball cap to hide his face as he joined his Ameer and the old lady.

"Taxi," said Sami.

Ivan kept the poise of an emergency room boss. "Here you go, Mrs. Callaghan."

The white-haired old lady wrinkled her brow. "But . . . I didn't order a cab."

"You've got a voucher for today," said her doctor. "Remember?"

"I do?"

"Yes."

The white-uniformed van driver took his cue from Doc Ivan. The stairs' electric motor whined, the doors shut, and away drove the brown van.

Her doctor said, "Emma, did you drop your gloves in the elevator?"

The old lady looked at her trembling bird hands. "I must have."

"I'll wait with the cabbie. Take your time."

She toddled back inside the building.

"Ameer, I must confess," blurted Sami. He told him about breaking the rules to confront a worried Zlatko and replace the lost money.

"But why are you here now?"

"I fear that Zlatko's vision of what is acceptable for our target and the vision you and I share . . . I fear a conflict of faith. I have seen this before."

"In Beirut," said the Ameer, "where holy martyrs blew up the Marines' barracks and Ronald Reagan slunk away. There we learned Americans will back down. Then sex-crazy Clinton ran from one Blackhawk helicopter crash, missed Osama with missiles."

The Ameer put a fatherly hand on Sami's shoulder. "Sometimes it's easiest for a soldier not to know all, so if his heart is challenged, his conscience is clear. Don't worry about Zlatko. He will do what must be done. His part will not pain his soul. All else is sacrifice to contain this disease called America. Americans fear death. Their overreaction to us will force our misguided Muslim brothers to rally to our true path."

"What of my part, Ameer? I have done so little."

"You are whispered about online." The doctor smiled, so Sami knew the legend birthed by the CIA still lived. "Praise Allah that I work in a building where if you make friends, keys are shared. With my colleagues at the medical imaging office. With two *kuffars* who repair computers that are probably stolen."

Dozens of computers! Untraceable! That's how he makes contacts!

"I dared not put you too close to the operation. If your fame attracted attention . . . But in two days, we will both be heroes on the run."

The building's glass doors showed Emma tottering toward them.

The Ameer told Sami what to do that night at the *vaquera's*. Told Sami where to go tomorrow morning.

Emma wiggled her gloved hands. "They were in my pockets!" Sami drove her home, refused a tip of her few silver coins.

He drove to a pay phone. Called Harry, told him about the computers, the Ameer's new orders. Argued for the cell to be rolled up. Got told, "We're gonna let it ride." Drove to 13th Street's hilltop panorama of Destiny City, parked on a block of row houses where a Latino grocery store flanked a green door.

He pushed the doorbell for the green door. Made a loud *ring!*

Invisible feet clunked down unseen stairs. The door's glass peephole darkened as someone looked out. The green door opened. Star-streaked midnight hair curled to her blue sweater. She wore faded jeans. Had a clean jaw, high cheekbones with a puckered scar on her heart side from the punch she'd taken in junior high soccer. The scar gave her lips a perpetual sardonic smile. Those fleshy lips along with her desert tribe Jewish Sephardic tan skin and the *Sinaloensa* Mexican she'd perfected while surfing away the summer before law school fooled people into thinking *Rose* was gringo for *Rosalita*.

"I wasn't expecting anyone," said Rose.

Climbing those stairs behind her rounded blue jean hips, Sami smelled Christmas pine, spices like cumin and chili from the downstairs store, perhaps incense, her musk.

Her apartment's main room held a computer, fax, photocopy machine. An eviction-salvaged sofa. Two chairs separated by a table where Sami had set his tea the morning he'd been officially waiting for a fax from the Taxi Commission but truly waiting for Zlatko to return for credit card applications the *vaquera* had promised him.

Sami's eyes swept through the kitchen to the closed door for a room lined with law books, government manuals. The door to her bedroom — closed. He refused to fear the closed doors. Refused to wonder whether Harry had bugged all of Rose's rooms.

She stood behind Sami. "Are you here for work?"

"Yes."

Shadows filled the apartment. Her walls and fading-gray-light glass windows kept out sounds of the street. Muffled screams.

He lunged with his hands like a Muay Thai strike, caught her face in his prayer grasp, pressed her against the wall as she met his kiss.

Night took the city.

They sat naked in her bed, propped on pillows, covers drawn up. A lamp glowed.

Rose lit a joint. "Do you think Harry figured this would happen?"

"He's practical."

"For your crew, I'm just an inferior woman you seduced to use, but Harry . . . Maybe he figures, What the hell, let them get some happy."

"Maybe," said Sami as he watched her take a hit.

Across town in her Virginia apartment, redheaded Lorna Dumas exhaled burned tobacco, stared at the blue uniform on her bed, thought, I gotta quit smoking.

Upstairs from her green door, Rose asked Sami, "Do you still think of yourself as Muslim?"

"Feels like some God is chasing me."

"Nice dodge." Rose passed him the joint.

Sami took a hit.

She said: "Getting stoned puts you in solid with both your jihad and the FBI."

"I always wanted to be popular. What about you?"

"My mother taught my girlfriends how to give a blowjob," said Rose. "Made me promise not to have sex until I knew what the hell I was doing.

"Who the hell ever knows what they're doing? I fell for the wrong guy over and over again, became a kick-ass federal prosecutor who one day found a certain *political* slant to her job, spent two years as a public defender, realized that helping unconnected people work the system was the only way they were ever going to get a fair shake.

"So now I'm the *vaquera*. Don't speak enough English to fill out an immigration form without fucking yourself? Go to the *vaquera*. Work permits, car registration, insurance, your political asylum application with the photo of you minus your arm that got hacked off in Sierra Leone—hey, America is the fill-in-the-blank society.

"Then came Zlatko. Everybody lies, but he lied like an antiabortion murderer I interviewed when I was a prosecutor. Hard-core eyes. Plus no way was he Albanian. I can't trust badges, but the tingles made me call my old pal Harry."

She hit the joint, held it to him. "Zlatko found me through the people who snuck here with him from Mexico, right?"

Sami waved away another hit—

—*fluttering wing* vision vanished like smoke.

"Right," said Rose. "I'm not supposed to know anything."

"Be glad you've got no idea what it's like out there."

"I stipulate to a certain degree of unreality. But I'm no virgin."

Sami said, "I knew this kid. His virgin mission, he gets handed killing three guys. Said he went 'wild in his mind.' That's what it's like out there. You live *behind* the world others see. All alone out there on a street full of invisible gunmen is *you*."

"You adopt survival mechanisms," she said.

"Fuck survival. You beat the other guy.

"Beirut. I'm thirteen. Men drove into the neighborhoods, gave us kids AK-47s. I never thought to ask who the ammo really *really* came from. Barricades cut up my home blocks. Sandbags, barbed wire, fuel barrels. Fuck what our parents said, we were cool and saving our world. I learned to run fast because I was small, and the fucking snipers' priority was wounding kids because that suckers out rescuers.

"One day, down the block at some other crew's barricade, those guys made an old man step out front, hands in the air. We see he's one of us, a Muslim. They tell him to walk to us. So he does, him and us thinking it's a swap. They let him get 'bout nine feet from our sandbags. Shot him dead.

"We couldn't leave cover to pull his body in, so it lay there. After three days we had to abandon our barricade. The stench. The flies.

"Two weeks, different barricade, same thing—only now it's a teenage Muslim guy just like me, hands up, had taken three steps toward our spot.

"I nailed him. Head shot." Sami paused. "He was dead as soon as he walked my way. I just got to choose his time and place, his meaning."

Night held the city.

"Is that why you left Beirut?" asked Rose.

"PLO guys I idolized took custody of a sniper we captured, set him free. Started me thinking: Whose side is anybody really on? Then my father got a job at the Marine barracks. One of our factions blew it and him up. The Marines took care of my family. Put me in a Detroit high school. Soon as I could, I joined the Corps. *Semper fi.*"

"Me too," she said.

He leaned into a kiss she captured. She kicked off the covers, cupped his hand over her breast. Seven minutes later, he guided her on top of him, straddling him, arcing over him like a quarter moon as he whispered, *"I see you. I see you."*

Afterward, Rose lay across him. "Don't say anything. Neither of us. Not unless we can say it again and again and again."

"Until," he said. *"Until,* not *unless."*

Their flesh goose-bumped. He reached for the sheet and blanket.

"Are you hungry?" she said.

"Not now. Now you have to fall asleep."

"Why?"

"I have to use your computer when you don't know it."

"Oh," she said.

"But I can spend the night."

And he did, his last waking moment echoing a fluttering wing.

A mile away in her go-to-sleep teddy bears bedroom, seven-year-old Amy Lewis whispered to her best friend through a cell phone bought for the adventure: "Gramma says I'll really be going to bed a whole three hours later because the world is round!"

Wake up! Sami bolts upright in Rose's bed. Glides through the dark to her main room, grabs her phone, taps in the panic number, gets routed to a woken bear who hears Sami whisper, "The Ameer! Keys! Medical imaging office! He's got access to—"

"Fuck!" Harry killed their call.

Sami calmed his jackhammering heart. Made himself go back to sleep. Have faith in himself and a bear.

Gray clouds covered the morning sky. Sami drove to where the Ameer had sent Maher. Maher waved. Too friendly for just a cab, but this feral kid's street skills had beaten Harry's tails. Maher climbed in front. Another mistake. Sami thought, Where do you live? How do you get money? Did you come up with using Facebook?

"What's that smell?" said Sami as they drove around the Beltway.

"Sorry, chemicals from the dry cleaners. The Koreans are nice. Took me a month to get the job through that Christian youth hostel."

Maher carried a backpack. "The newspaper calls it the Trackside Slaughter. Ballistics say the gun was also used to shoot a gang-banger from the Clifton Terrace crew. The cops can't figure Latino *and* black bodies."

The future filled Maher's eyes. "We'll be something to write about. Brother," he said, "I know Ameer is worried. But I'm chill. He's so smart! Combining what you've got to do with checking me out while I get the last of my shit, like, how tight is that?"

"Very tight." Sami grinned. "Is that how American kids say it?"

"Yeah." Suburbia flowed past the taxi. "Look out there. Redondo Beach. Akron where my cousins live. Here. It's all the same TV shows. Stupid news about dumb rich girls who do nothing but get their pictures taken. The holy Jesus in the Koran, blessed be his name, what if he were driving with us today, seeing all this meaningless crap? We gotta stop all the ruining. If not us, who?"

"We're in the same car, my brother."

The gun shop sat in a Beltway exit mall. A pine wreath decorated the barred door. The clerk behind the glass counter wore a hol-stered Glock and a red Santa Claus hat.

"Hey, guy!" The clerk smiled at Maher. "Good to see you again."

"Yeah." Maher handed the clerk his California driver's license for routine processing by the law with a five-year backlog.

The clerk filled his eyes with nonblond Sami.

"This is my uncle," explained Maher. "He's Jewish."

"Oh, well *Sha-lum Ha-nooka.*"

"Shalom," said Sami.

Maher rented a 1911 Colt .45 automatic and ear protectors, bought four boxes of ammo and a black silhouette from a target display that featured a pistol-pointing, grizzled Arab in a burnoose and bumper stickers proclaiming that an aging, antiwar movie ac-tress should *still* be bombed back to Hanoi.

The store's shooting range had ten lanes, three occupied. Gun-fire boomed. As Sami shot holes in their target, Maher dumped three boxes of ammo into his backpack.

"The .45s are the biggest bullets," said Maher, taking his turn on the firing line. He showed no post-traumatic stress syndrome from the last time he'd fired a gun.

As they left the gun shop, the clerk said, "Happy New Year!"

At the next mall, the sporting goods store roared with crazed shoppers. Sami gave a clerk the order printed from Rose's com-puter. The clerk said, "You know these bikes are unassembled in boxes, right?"

"Cheaper that way."

"It's for orphans," said Maher.

"God bless you." The clerk took their cash so they could skip the line.

"Um," said Maher. "Do you guys sell steel cup protectors? You know. For . . . for down there. For hockey."

"I think they're all plastic."

As they carried three bike boxes to the taxi, Sami said, *"Hockey?"*

Maher shrugged. "Won't happen tomorrow, but when I become a holy martyr, the virgins waiting for me in paradise will get one too. I wanna be able to have kids."

"You want to have children in paradise?"

"Got to be a better place to raise them than here."

They crammed the bike boxes in the taxi. Drove to a subway

stop. Only then did Maher relay the Ameer's orders for that night, where to be tomorrow, what to do precisely when. Before he vanished into the crowd, Maher said, "I love you, brother."

Thirty-four minutes later, Harry rode in the taxi beside Sami and said, "Before dawn, NEST black-bagged Ivan's building—not the Nuclear Emergency *Search* Teams, their shadows whose *S* stands for *Strike*. They pulled all hazmat out of the medical imaging office, substituted fake material, and broke the machines so nobody will wonder when they don't work. We're still balancing records hacked from the office computers, but it looks like all radioactive material is accounted for. Put that together with your horny teenager looking for a metal cup to shield his balls, and they're probably building a put-together-at-the-last-minute dirty bomb."

"So now it won't be dirty, but it'll still be a bomb."

"Yeah, but even if they augment hydrogen peroxide or chemicals from a dry cleaner with gunpowder from bullets, how big could it be?"

"How many deaths add up to 'big'?"

"We don't think that's the point," said Harry. "We know what Zlatko is building. I posted what we had on A-Space and Intellipedia, the classified sites, set it up like a game. A dozen nerds came up with an Explosive Magnetic Generator of Frequency. The Soviets perfected them. Both Ivan and Zlatko grew up behind the Iron Curtain. A U.S. general challenged some grad students a few years ago, and they designed an EMGF to fit in a pickup truck with a cost of eight hundred dollars—most of it bought from Radio Shack.

"EMGFs are why you turn off your cell phone when you fly. They don't really explode, they beam a sphere of electronic waves that fries unshielded computers, phones, circuit boards for car engines—"

"That's why I'm supposed to turn off my taxi tomorrow at precisely two P.M.!"

"And why you're parking where they told you. That pull-off by the Potomac is across the freeways from the Pentagon. EMGFs are designed to slam the enemy's command and control centers. They're invisible inside any pickup-sized vehicle . . ."

"Like the Ameer's SUV," said Sami.

"Assemble an EMGF with an electric motor into your shielded vehicle, drive it—hell, *park it*—outside the Pentagon's secure perimeter, turn it on, fry systems all over a mile-thick spherical zone. We'd be burned all the way to Baghdad and A-stan."

"What about the bomb they think is dirty?"

Harry said, "We figure it's a Baghdad double tap. They park the EMGF vehicle. The longer the EMGF runs, the more it destroys. When SWAT teams figure out what's going on, blitz the source . . . *boom!* Booby-trapped. Radiation is bonus blood."

"And the cell phones?"

"Maybe one of your crew is gonna be a martyr, stay behind, detonate the booby trap when he sees SWAT closing in. That'd be optimum."

"Frying the Pentagon meets Zlatko's conscience. After they ditch the EMGF vehicle, I'll be the walk-to getaway. If my cab engine gets fried, bikes will still work. Three bikes, four brothers, one stay-behind."

"When do we hit them?" said Sami.

The blue taxi crawled through holiday traffic.

"No!" said Sami.

"After dark, the Pentagon gets ringed by camouflaged snake eaters. Tomorrow when your brothers attack, we got 'em. Odds are, we get two alive for interrogation."

"Take them now!"

"Then we get Ivan, but even you don't know where the other two are. We can't let them run free. And if we take them too soon, we won't find out who they report to."

"They answer to no one but themselves! You said you get that!"

"I do—our bosses don't."

"Get the fuck out of my cab."

On that night before Christmas Eve, Sami assembled three bikes in his apartment. He looked around the mattress-on-the-floor hideaway that his Ameer believed had been made safe from discovery by the *vaquera*'s tricks, told himself, No more lying rooms.

At 9:30 he broke all the rules, used the breaker box phone outside in the night.

Cold kisses wet his skin. He told Rose, "It's starting to snow."

"Too early for holiday clichés. Can't count on the weather."

"Tomorrow starts a whole new season."

"I'm ready," said Rose.

The city went to sleep.

Cari Jones brushed her streaked blond hair, saw her black leather coat hung ready to go, decided to try computer dating when she got back.

John Herne packed three different pill bottles for post-traumatic stress syndrome in his soldier's duffel at Walter Reed Hospital.

Lorna Dumas decided to let her red hair swing free on her blue uniform tomorrow, threw her cigarettes down her building's trash chute.

Amy Lewis chose her bestest brown teddy bear for Gramma's.

Morning woke Sami to a snow-dusted town.

At ten A.M. he grabbed the cell phone and Glock. Loaded three bikes into his taxi. *They gotta see what they're expecting.* Called Harry: "Launching." Drove his taxi into Christmas Eve snowstorm traffic.

"It's a mess out there," said the man on news/traffic radio. "Washingtonians have never figured out how to drive in the snow, and we weren't expecting this storm."

Sami flashed on the Beirut radio announcer who daily reported which commuter streets were ruled by snipers.

He eased the blue taxi over slick streets: *Fender-benders fuck up ops.*

Windshield wipers washed Sami's view as he drove through a whooshing tunnel, popped up on an interstate threaded along the city. Green metal highway signs arrowed routes for I-395 south to Virginia, for exits to the Jefferson Memorial, federal office complexes, the airport, George Washington Parkway, the Pentagon.

Traffic on the bridge over the Potomac parted for the blue taxi obviously headed to the airport, taking that exit—but then unexpectedly pulling off the main road into a tree-lined turnout where the sign read ROACH'S ROOST WATERFOWL SANCTUARY.

Bad day to be a bird. Sami parked the taxi away from the only other vehicle in the bird watchers' roost, a battered car with bumper stickers reading "One Planet, One People" and "Audubon Society." A passenger jet roared overhead. Snowflakes died on the warm blue taxi. A husky man wearing a parka stood at tripod-mounted binoculars aimed at the icy gray river, at the highways that blocked a view of the Pentagon.

Parka Man turned to face the taxi and Sami saw he was a bear.

Harry lumbered to the taxi, got in beside the driver. "Anything—*anything*—from your Ameer, the others?"

"What's wrong?"

"It's nearing noon. Attack time is two P.M. Doc Ivan came to work like always. But his SUV is still in its parking spot. Given the traffic, the weather, the time they'll need to fit in the EMGF and some electric motor—"

"Hit him! Hit him now!"

Harry started to protest—barked orders up his sleeve: "COOK to all units: HRT Alpha: Take down Target One. I say again: Hit Target One now! Go! *Go!*"

The idling taxi grew close. Sami shut off the engine. A passenger jet roared overhead. The bear unzipped his parka. The taxi smelled of bike oil and rubber, fading car heater fumes, salty hope.

Harry's eyes lost focus. He listened to his radio earpiece. Blinked.

"Shit!" Harry radioed, "Core plan! Reset to core plan!"

Told Sami, "All they found in Doc Ivan's office was a scared old lady in an examination robe. She's Muslim, did what the doctor ordered. Ivan walked out of the building right under our eyes inside her full *burka,* rode that charity van to *poof.*

"S'okay," Harry said. "He's just being cagey. Doesn't know we're on him. He'll keep with the plan. We're set if he comes back for his SUV. They'll attack the Pentagon and we'll nail them. Everything's cool, got FBI execs visiting Muslim leaders here to assure them that the busts are legit. It's okay."

Sami said, "I don't know about them having other vehicles!"

"That's the way a cell works. Nobody knows everything."

"Except the guy you let slip away."

"Life is risk. You don't play it that way, you get played." Harry shrugged. "You gotta go with what you know. That's why we have spies."

They sat waiting in the cold until 12:51 — *trigger* (time) *minus 69 minutes.*

A tan sedan pulled into the parking lot. Ted raced to the taxi through sleet. Through the lowered driver's window and the hail of ice pellets he said, "An hour till they're due here. We do this now or I have to pull Sami!"

"What?" said both Sami and Harry.

"You're six months overdue for your mandatory drug test. Has to be cleared immediately, or we pull you off. I got a portable kit in the car, on-site processing will clear you so you can stay on—"

"This is bullshit!" yelled Sami. "We've got a terrorist attack!"

"I've got orders," said Ted. "The Hoover Building says I'm fired if I don't get this done right darn now."

Harry said, "Okay, Ted. He'll be right over."

The FBI liaison ran for the shelter of his tan sedan.

Sami stared at the bear.

"Go do it. Time like this, we all gotta pee."

"If I go . . . I'm gone."

"Ahh." A jetliner roared overhead. Harry smiled. "Fuck them."

The bear used his cell phone.

"Hey, Jenny." He asked Sami for his real name, Social Security number, CIA identifiers. Relayed them to Jenny. Said, *"Crash RIP."*

Hung up. Grinned at Sami. "Congratulations. Ted's off your case, but give him what he wants or he could still fuck this up. You've been Rebooted In Place, RIP. Now work for Argus. Twice the salary, half the BS."

Harry sent the dazed spy to the tan sedan.

"Sorry," said Ted as Sami filled a plastic bottle with his urine.

Don't give this holier-than-thou bureaucrat the time of—

"This is so stupid," said Ted. "So what if Argus wants to cer-tify—"

"This came from Argus? Harry's company?"

"Well . . . sure. This is their show."

Sami left Ted watching liquid change colors in a bottle. Slammed the door when he climbed in the blue taxi. His expression killed the bear's grin.

"Why?" said Sami.

"You're too good to lose."

"I'm quitting! I'm not working for Argus!"

"Sure you are. It'll take a year commitment to get your ass out of the drug-use sling. And yeah, don't worry: I'll protect Rose. Why wouldn't I? One more op. You spy as the holy warrior hero who es-caped from the Christmas Eve D.C. bust."

"Fuck you!"

"Fucking costs. I know what you're thinking," continued Harry. "Going Beirut on me gets you nothing but Uncle Sam's sniper scopes zeroing your back."

The bear said, "I didn't pick any of this war. But I'm not going to lose."

Snowflakes hit the taxi windshield. A jetliner roared overhead.

The bear sighed. *T minus 47 minutes.* The choppy gray river lapped against the riprap of the bird sanctuary. Harry relocated Ted's tan sedan next to the bumper-stickered car. *T minus 17.* Pentagon units reported all clear. A jetliner roared. Ted got out of the tan sedan to look through the tripod binoculars.

Sami yelled, "They're not after the Pentagon!"

"What?"

"The Ameer doesn't give a shit about our 'command and control.' He hates our whole thing. He wants fear. To humiliate us. Make us overreact. Maher's expecting to live today. Ivan wants to be a hero on the run. He implied that Zlatko's mission is solo and won't bother his beliefs. Zlatko'd love to hit a target like the Pentagon, but he's not coming here. So that's not it. Three bikes: Ivan, Maher, me. Here!"

Harry touched his radio earpiece. Said, "That Al-Qaeda media group al-Sahab, 'The Clouds.' NSA just intercepted an e-mail to them via a D.C. server saying that today will be a great day, to watch the skies."

A jetliner roared overhead.

"They know the taxi!" Sami ran toward the tan sedan.

A bear charged his heels.

A Marine sniper popped out of his hide, his rifle hungry for a target.

Harry crammed himself behind the wheel of the tan sedan, Sami dove in the front seat, and Ted jumped in the back, even though he didn't know why. The tan sedan fishtailed out of the bird sanctuary as Harry yelled, "Told you they were linked!"

"Ivan posted bragging rights, not—just drive! Go, go!"

Christmas Eve afternoon on the way to the airport. Falling snow. Cars surging bumper to bumper on a two-lane, one-way road.

"Get around them!" yelled Sami.

Harry whipped the tan sedan onto the shoulder. Horns honked. They ran over a highway reflector pole. Slid past a parked airport police cruiser. Spinning red lights filled their mirrors.

"Call them off!" yelled Sami.

"No unencrypted radios!" Harry yelled into his sleeve at *T minus 13.* "They could have a police band monitor! Cell phone the airport cops!"

Ted yelled, "What are we looking for?"

"We gotta know it when we see it!" said Sami.

The electronic marquee sign mounted over one-way airport traffic read THREAT LEVEL CODE ORANGE. The digital clock revealed *T minus 11*.

Ronald Reagan National Airport sits across the river from the white dome of the Capitol. The "old" terminal is a gray concrete box few airlines use. The air-travel gem is the "new" white stone terminal: one million square feet, three levels, a rectangle shopping mall with three-story windows between thirty-five gates to jetliners. The airport control tower rises from the terminal's far end like a towering rook from chess.

The tan sedan forced its way back into airport traffic.

Harry barked orders up his sleeve.

Wide-eyed Ted braced himself in the backseat.

Ahead, at the old terminal, sweeping into the car-clogged road, airport cop, phone pressed to his ear, hand on his holstered pistol, he—

Halts the chasing cop cruiser.

Autos hunt drop-off parking spots. Travelers drag wheeled suitcases. Snow falls.

"Nothing!" yelled Sami. "I see nothing! Go! Go!"

Driving in bumper-to-bumper traffic to the upper level of the new terminal ate two minutes off the clock. Three lanes of vehicles lined the sidewalk.

"Couldn't evacuate this place now!" Harry's eyes scanned the chaos.

"Gotta be here, gotta." Sami stared through the falling snow. Saw—

"Way down at the end! Close to the control tower!"

Parked near the sidewalk. Flashers blinking. A brown van.

MEDICAL TRANSPORT SERVICES.

"The stairs' electric motor! They'll use that!"

Out! Sami ran crouched alongside moving cars. Fog blurred the van's windows. Exhaust smogged out the tailpipe: engine running. *Driver will be watching side mirrors.*

Sami dove under the van. The shock of ice slush soaked his pants and shirt as he crawled on his elbows. *Hot muffler!* Gas stench, he crawled to the front tire, rolled out—

He rose like a cobra beside the driver's closed window.

Startled stolen-white-uniform-wearing Ivan on the other side of that glass.

A woman rolled a hard-shell pink suitcase past Sami. He grabbed it— *"Hey!"*—swung the suitcase through the air. *Bam!* The driver's window cobwebbed into a thousand shards. *Bam!* The pink suitcase knocked the cobwebbed window into the van.

Driver's seat Ivan whirled toward a control box. Sami grabbed the Ameer's lips, pulled him through the shattered window, slammed him to the slushy pavement. *"Stop! Police!"* Sami kicked the Ameer in the head, drew his Glock, imagined the pull of the trigger, the recoil, the splat of brains on wet pavement. *"Alive, Sami!"* yelled Harry. Strangers screamed. *"Police! Drop your weapon!"*

Ted bellowed above the chaos, "FBI! Everyone freeze!"

"No one's in the van!" Sami glared at the traffic cop who'd helped the medical crew park the brown van at the curb. "Was there another guy?"

"They had a patient pickup! With a wheelchair." The cop pointed to the terminal.

"What did he look like?"

"Like a guy! White guy. Blond hair. White uniform. EMT vest."

Ghosts whispered to Sami, *"Diverting the enemy . . . let us attack. Timing."*

"Harry!" Sami yelled to the man cuffing the unconscious Ameer. "It's Maher!"

"Go!" Harry guarded a brown van with a neutralized EMGF near an airport control tower and people-packed jetliners flying through a snowstorm.

"Ted—you know Maher's face—work down from the other end!"

The FBI agent leaped into the tan sedan. Siren wailing, red light spinning, Ted raced back the way they'd come—straight into on-coming one-way traffic.

Sami ran toward the terminal, told the uniformed cop, "Stay away from me!"

Don't blow my cover. I'm a spy. I'm a spy.

Plunging into a sea of shuffling humanity. Shoulder to shoulder. *Move!* Suitcases rolled like roadblocks. Crowd hubbub. Scents of Christmas pine, lemony floor cleaner, sweat, petroleum luggage fabric. Through the bedlam cut ringing phones.

Sami shoved his way toward the other end of the terminal.

Where is he? White uniform. Blond guy. Vest. Pushing an empty wheel-chair.

Sami didn't exactly know how his brothers packed the wheel-chair's tubular frame with gunpowder and particles they thought were radioactive. Wired an IV bag of liquid to the same detonation device Zlatko engineered for the gunpowder. But Sami *knew.*

A digital clock on the wall told him *T minus 1.*

The diversion bomb timed to cover the EMGF transmission. First responders might mistake the brown medical van for one of their own. Let it run as jetliners tumbled through the snowflakes.

Where are you? Move, out of my way! Sami jumped for a glimpse over the teeming crowd. "Watch it!" Somebody bumped him. *There's the terminal wall, the end, the last/first street exit, there's—*

An IV-bagged wheelchair sat by the wall of windows.

Sami leaped onto a planter—*There!* Fifty feet from the wheel-chair. Nearing the exit: blond, EMT vest over a stolen white uni-form. *Get to him! Con him! Neutralize!*

"Maher!" bellowed Sami.

Quiet filled the moment as if in slow motion. Maher turned. Saw his brother waving at him above the airport crowd. A quizzical look filled the California blond's face. He reached his right hand inside the vest.

Forty-four feet away, known murderer and terrorist Maher's text-book gesture equaled *gun!* FBI Special Agent Ted Harris drew his service weapon, pushed an old man out of the way, acquired his target—fired three booming shots.

Panic exploded. Screaming. People tried to run. Dive. Hide.

"FBI!" yelled Ted. "FBI!"

Shots one and two blasted Maher off his feet.

His third bullet crashed into a metal heating grate above an exit.

Sami fought through the scared, silent mob toward where Ma-her sprawled on his back as combat-shuffling toward him came Ted, his eyes on what the suspect had pulled from his vest, still held in his right hand: only a cell phone.

Maher rose on his elbows, vaguely heard *"Don't move!"* Saw his white shirt reddening. Felt *phone* in his right hand. Saw brother Sami scrambling through the huddled crowd to save him. Maher smiled blood. Saw Sami stumble, crawl closer. Maher's right thumb hit speed-dial as he raised a weakening left thumbs-up.

Sami screamed, *"No!"*

In the city, Zlatko stood outside a green door, left hand pushing a buzzer while his right hand held a pistol tied to four other murders as he terminated a loose end who ran downstairs to the peephole he'd blurred with street slush.

In Ronald Reagan National Airport, soldier John Herne huddled with blondish, black-leather-coated Cari Jones. Beside them was redheaded, blue-uniformed, airline service rep Lorna Dumas pulling Amy Lewis and teddy bear closer to the shelter of an empty wheelchair rigged with a cell phone programmed to block every call. Except one.

They all heard *ring!*

CHRIS F. HOLM

The Hitter

FROM *The Needle: A Magazine of Noir*

THE PLAZA SHIMMERED in the midday heat, flush with handsome brown-skinned people bedecked in the garish red so favored by their nation's ruling party. They awaited the appearance of their newly reelected leader, a paunchy smile-and-haircut of fifty who fancied himself a revolutionary, and whose trademark fatigues always looked as clean and pressed as any banker's suit.

I awaited his appearance too, from my perch four stories above the square—my nerves jangling as they always do before a job, my rifle stock held flush to my shoulder in anticipation of the coming shot.

He was late.

Despite the wait and the oppressive heat, the crowd seemed jovial enough. Not exactly a surprise—everyone for blocks around had been screened six ways from Sunday to ensure a pretense of unity and good cheer. To ensure the cameras caught none of the starving, the torture-scarred, or the dissidents spurred to violence by the widespread reports of election fraud that, though suppressed here, were plastered across every newspaper in the Western world.

Lucky for me, their screening wasn't perfect.

If you want to kill somebody badly enough, no screening ever is.

Some below waved flags of yellow and green. Some held small children atop their shoulders as they jockeyed for position. Most laughed and whooped along to what I could only assume were charming ditties about the triumph of the proletariat, written in a language I didn't speak and blasted through the PA so loud it shook droplets of sweat loose from the tip of my nose. As they fell, they tapped a lazy rhythm on my hotel room's window frame. Reminded me of a radiator cooling, or the ticking of a watch in need of winding.

As if I needed reminding it was past time.

As if my itchy trigger finger wasn't reminder enough.

I trained my gun sight on the PA for a moment, entertained the thought of quieting the fucking thing for good. But then, why prematurely pierce the plaza's good cheer?

No. Best to wait.

And I was very good at waiting.

I'd been staying here a week. In this tiny island nation, in this tiny sweat-lodge room. I watched the election on the rheumy black-and-white bolted to the wall in the corner. Watched UN officials cluck their tongues as, one by one, all challengers conceded. Watched last night's drunken dancing in the square as party loyalists celebrated the only result that ever would have been allowed, all the while wondering if any of them suspected they were standing in the very spot their leader was to die.

I watched it all atop a mattress made lumpy by dint of the M40A3 sniper rifle I'd stashed inside it on my first day here. Sliced it open at one end with a blade taken from one of my own safety razors, stitched it back up with a sewing kit sent up by the front desk. One never knows who might wind up poking around one's room, after all—and in a nation where the courtrooms sit suspiciously empty given the number of executions carried out, one can never be too careful.

For a moment, the PA fell silent. Then the bombastic strains of a victory march blared from its speakers. The crowd hushed in anticipation, and then erupted in cheers as their fearless leader bounded up the stairs to the bunted riser and headed toward the podium, all waves and gleaming teeth.

The music built to a thundering crescendo. The crowd seethed with ecstatic frenzy.

I exhaled a measured breath, willed my drumroll heart to slow.

He reached the podium and stood hands raised, palms out—a mock plea for quiet. The crowd raged on, as he no doubt hoped they would. The victory march continued.

My body still, I sighted my target and squeezed the trigger: three pounds' pressure — no more, no less.

A crack like thunder echoed through the plaza. When Haircut heard the shot, he hit the deck. The man had a survivor's instinct, I'll give him that — he reacted a full second before anyone else in the square. But ultimately, his gesture of self-preservation was futile; by the time you hear the gunshot, the bullet's come and gone.

Lucky for him, he's not who I was aiming for.

When my target's head exploded in a mist of blood and brain, spattering the face of a young girl who sat on her father's shoulders beside him, the crowd contracted. For just a heartbeat, they were one — hunched together, a cornered animal, trying in vain to assess this sudden threat. Then the little girl began to scream, and the crowd's reaction tipped the slope to panic.

They pushed against each other — clawing, scrabbling, anything to get away from the mess of ruined flesh that, seconds ago, had been a man. As if he were contagious. As if they might be next.

Armed security materialized as though from nowhere at the perimeter of the square, their weapons brandished as they locked down the plaza's exits. A couple warning shots to dissuade the charging masses, and the crowd diverted as one like a flock of birds in flight.

More gunfire, a strangled cry — these from the sole guard manning a secondary entrance to the plaza — and the perimeter was breached. The guard disappeared beneath the surging crowd, and his brothers-in-arms responded by turning their rifles on the crowd. A chopper thudded overhead, no doubt to spirit Haircut and his detail away from the melee. Never mind he knew damn well the threat to him had passed; being caught on camera watching helplessly as your citizens rioted before you was bad business for a despot.

And riot they would, until the lot of them were locked up or dead or far away from here. Which is why the soldiers should have said to hell with orders and let them flee the square. But most of them were kids — green, untrained. They didn't know any better. They didn't know some orders were best ignored.

I turned from the window, stretching and rubbing grit from my eyes. I didn't need to see the rest — I'd seen enough of these scenes over the years to know that's how they always play. Pop a leader up onstage and the crowd will scatter, sure, but deep down, they know they're not a target.

You want to see real panic, pop a member of the crowd.

Not that panic was my goal. My goal was to get paid. Panic was merely an inevitable side effect. And that which one can reliably predict can be used to one's advantage — say, for example, in making one's getaway.

I left the gun. I left the room. I left the hotel. I left the country. The details of my egress, I won't bore you with; they're more prosaic than you might expect. After all, no head of state had died that day — just some lowly schlub nobody'd ever miss. Hell, by the time my plane was wheels-up, Haircut had gone before the cameras to calm his panicked nation and commend his security detail for detecting and eradicating so imminent a threat as said schlub posed.

You'd think it'd sting, watching someone else get credit for your kill, but the eight hundred grand in my bank account was salve enough to soothe my wounded ego.

In the days that followed, Haircut and his ministers painted the deceased as a supporter of the far-right fringe, out of touch with the mainstream and spurred to violence by Haircut's landslide victory. When all was said and done, two dozen so-called co-conspirators saw the business end of the firing squad for the part they'd played in the botched assassination.

It was a tidy justification for a bit of housecleaning, but it was bullshit nonetheless. You don't call me if you want to pop an amateur. In fact, you don't call me at all — I call you. And when I do, you'd be well advised to take the call.

See, I hit hitmen.

Which means if you hear from me, someone wants you dead.

That smear of brain matter I left back in the square? Former triggerman for the Varela cartel by the name of Juan Miguel Garcia. Went freelance a few years back. Hired to hit Haircut by a consortium of sugar manufacturers, if you can believe it. Seems under Haircut's tutelage, the state reclaimed a hefty chunk of land that had belonged to them, and they thought perhaps new leadership might be more inclined to negotiate its release.

Not that their reasons matter much to me. Everybody's got a reason to kill. It's the ones who've got the means to that I keep tabs on.

It's the ones who've got the means to that I end up putting in the ground.

Garcia's benefactors set the price on Haircut's head at eighty K. I asked Haircut for ten times that. My biggest payday yet—but then, ten times the hit's my going rate, and it's nonnegotiable. The smart ones pay. The ones who don't aren't around long to regret it. Haircut did some homework, ponied up. Now he lives to subjugate another day, and Garcia gets a dirt retirement. And me and my eight hundred grand live happily ever after.

Or at least, that was the plan. Seems that in my line of work, happily ever after is hard to come by.

Just ask Garcia.

The sun shone blinding orange over my front left fender as I pushed the rented Beemer past seventy, just back from the Garcia job and heading southwest from Dulles into the rolling Virginia countryside. A few miles east of Morgantown, I slowed. I parked the Beemer on the shoulder atop a gentle rise and watched the sun set behind the rambling buttercream farmhouse nestled in the woods across the road.

The lights inside the house were on, and through the French doors that led out to the deck, I could see Evie in the kitchen making dinner. Long and lanky in a tank top and low-slung jeans, with an easy grace and a smile to match, she chopped and diced and measured and stirred, pausing occasionally to brush her hair back from her eyes and chatting all the while with someone just out of sight.

Her husband, no doubt.

The fucking bastard.

Not like I can blame the guy for stealing my wife away from me; by the time Evie met Stuart, she thought me years dead. And my grandma always used to say you meet a girl who looks as good in jeans as Evie does—a girl who can eat a burger with her elbows on the table and look like a lady doing it—you hold on to her forever. I didn't listen.

Guess Stuart was the type to mind his grandma. Well, that, or he worked out that lesson all on his own—and either way, it made him a better man than I'll ever be.

Of course, the fact that he was a mechanic and not a hardened killer didn't hurt in that regard, either.

Still didn't mean I had to like the guy.

Evie held a spoon out for Stuart to taste, and he stepped into sight, first taking the proffered bite, and then wrapping her in his arms and twirling her around. Her peals of laughter carried through the open kitchen window—melodic, beautiful—and took me back to the summer we graduated high school. We were only just engaged—Evie working weekends slinging soft-serve, boot camp still three months off for me—with barely ten bucks between us and not a care in the world, lounging and laughing and making love at my family's camp not three miles from here.

Then I noticed the roundness of her belly in profile as the man who wasn't me swung her round and round, and my nostalgia hardened into something cold and sharp in my chest.

Evie was pregnant.

Which would have been a cause for joy if it were mine.

If Evie didn't think me dead.

If, all those years ago when faced with this path, this job, this empty life, I'd instead chosen to be a better man.

You're probably wondering how it all went wrong. How anyone could go from happy and laughing to watching from the outside as some other guy gets to live his life. How anyone could go from fighting for God and country to killing for money. And truth be told, the progression was simple enough.

Mind you, simple's not the same as easy.

Picture a fresh-faced patriot of eighteen, straight out of basic training. Kid we're talking about's as green as can be—he barely knows which end of his rifle is which.

Picture him pleased as punch at being selected to pull guard duty for a visiting dignitary and his family. Said dignitary comes across as a kindly older gentleman, beaming as he introduces his wife and children to the kid, and thanking him for his protection, for his dedicated service. Looking back, that dignitary probably wasn't a day over forty-five, but as young as this kid was, he may as well have been a hundred.

Now picture how that kid might react if he saw the dignitary and his family slaughtered before his very eyes—taken out not honorably in battle, as a man should be, but instead by cowards operating in darkness.

I don't have to picture it. I see it every time I close my eyes.

I was not that kid.

I'm the guy who killed him.

See, back in boot camp, I was identified as having certain qualities. Qualities the military finds valuable in a covert operative. To this day, I'm not certain what specifically put them onto me, but whatever it was, they weren't wrong. I took to the training like a dog to the hunt, and why wouldn't I? Black ops was my chance to make a difference. To tip the balance. To make the world safe for democracy.

Yeah, I know how it sounds. But I enlisted in the weeks after 9/11. Back then, the Kool-Aid was flowing pretty freely, and that kind of naive, pie-eyed thinking was the norm among us grunts. But don't worry—I didn't think that way for long.

The job itself proved just the antidote.

We were a false-flag unit, operating under orders of the U.S. government but without the safety net of our nation's military backup or diplomatic support. Think back on the giant fucking mess our nation made of Iraq and Afghanistan these past eight years, and on our lapses of judgment and common decency along the way. Now think on the fact that what you know about those conflicts is what our leaders let you know, and you can begin to guess the nature of the missions we were sent on—missions our government worked hard to ensure would never see the light of day.

I don't mean to say we didn't do some good. Many of the threats we neutralized were just that. But some of them weren't. Some of them were just people we killed.

Hell, when it comes right down to it, all of them were just people we killed. Some of them just warranted killing, is all.

I couldn't honestly tell you if that dignitary needed killing or not. I can say we didn't need to kill his wife and kids. Or his entire security detail, who weren't any more a threat to us than the wife and kids had been. Hell, most of them weren't much *older* than his kids. But we did. We killed them all.

Well, my unit did, at least. Me, I froze up after I slit the young guard's throat. He'd kicked the door in to find me standing over his friend the dignitary, knife in hand, and I got to him before he could unsling his rifle from his shoulder. Cut him ear to ear, clean through his windpipe, and listened to his strangled cries as he died. He looked so, I don't know, *surprised,* as if he couldn't square exactly how it had come to this. For that matter, I couldn't square it either—but something tells me that would've been cold comfort to him as he lay dying.

There were other missions after that. Other kills. But that kid was the one who broke me. I don't know—maybe I felt some kinship with him. Maybe I'd just had my fill of taking orders from those who refused to get their hands dirty. Hell, maybe it was the phase of the fucking moon.

Whatever it was, after I killed the kid, I withdrew into myself. I stopped writing Evie. Stopped calling. I didn't figure I was worthy of her love on account of what I'd done. I'm pretty sure I was right on that count.

I wanted to die. To disappear. And when a roadside bomb in Kandahar made chop suey of my unit, I saw my chance to do just that.

Turned out it was easier than I expected. There was no formal inquiry into the bombing, no attempt to recover the dead. And why would there be? They bore no emblem of our government, and officially they didn't even exist. They were simply left to rot in the desert, disavowed in death as they would have been in any other failure.

This gig hitting other hitters started out as retribution, I suppose, or some misplaced sense of justice. I guess I figured once you agree to hit somebody, you deserve whatever's coming to you. That ridding the world of people who kill for a living was some kind of public service.

Yeah, I get the irony of the situation.

But whatever my reasons at the outset, eventually this job became just that—a job to me. Something I did because I was good at it. Too good to walk away.

Something I did because I didn't know how to do anything else.

Or maybe that's bullshit, and I kept at it because I figured one day somebody was going to turn the tables on me and put me in the ground.

God knew I deserved it.

And God knew I wasn't going to do it myself.

From my vantage point across the country road, I watched Evie's house for hours—the house I helped to pay for, funneling Evie blood money through a dummy trust set up to look like a structured settlement for the widows of war dead who fell victim to faulty body armor. Like some half-assed act of charity could make up for what I'd done to her—leaving her a widow at twenty-three.

Like it could help me get to sleep at night.

I watched as darkness descended over the whole of Virginia, and the stars rose cold and bright. I watched as, one by one, the lights went out, and the only illumination was the flicker of the TV screen in the upstairs bedroom window. I watched until even that went dark, and dawn broke across the eastern sky. Then I climbed back into the Beemer and set out on the long drive home.

A Google alert is all it takes to get you dead these days.

Crazy, isn't it? Lucky for you, though, a Google alert is also all it takes for you to get a call from me, and if your check clears, I maybe bag the guy who wants to get you dead.

Technology's a hell of a thing.

Take this particular Google alert, for example: a set of race results from Vernon Downs, a small-time harness track in upstate New York. Big winner of the day was a mare named McGurn's Lament.

Only here's the thing: there's no such horse as McGurn's Lament. And if you were to try and make sense of the day's stats, you'd find that they resist sense-making. That's because those stats aren't stats at all.

They're a book cipher.

The Syndicate's been passing messages this way for years. Got their fingers in a half a dozen race sites so they can spread the bogus results around, avoid raising any hackles. They use made-up horses as code names indicating the nature of the message— Brown Beauty if they're moving smack, Luscious Lady if they're talking whores, and so on—with the pertinent details encrypted in the results that follow. McGurn's Lament signifies a hit. An in joke of sorts, I guess. McGurn was Capone's chief hitman, the guy responsible for the St. Valentine's Day Massacre. He was gunned down himself a few years later, in the middle of a frame of tenpin. You see the name McGurn's Lament, you know the numbers are going to code for a name—and if you're lucky, an address. Even money is whoever that name belongs to isn't long for this world.

It works like this. Say the horse wearing number thirty-eight came in sixth. That means the sixth letter on the thirty-eighth page is the one you want. Big enough block of numbers, you can encode damn near any message you like. Any message like a name and an address. Any message like *Take your time* or *Make it look like an accident* or whatever. And because nearly every letter of the alphabet appears in dozens of places throughout the course of any book, there's none of the pesky repetition that code-breaking programs rely upon to work their mojo. Unless you know what book the code is referencing—and I'm talking the exact edition—there's no way you're going to crack the fucking thing.

Lucky for me, I knew what book they were referencing. Convinced a Syndicate guy I popped a few months back to cough it up in return for doing him quick. Nineteen sixty-nine first edition of *The Godfather.*

Never let it be said that Mob guys don't have a sense of humor.

The target's name was Michael Rigby. From what I could gather, he was like the Chicago Mob's very own IT guy, at least until he took them for a cool twenty-eight mil and then turned stoolie for the feds—decimating their northwest operation in the process. The remainder of the message consisted of a URL, a bounty of twenty-five K, and three short words of instruction: MAKE IT PUBLIC.

The URL led to a piece in the Springfield, Missouri, *News-Leader,* dated yesterday, about a local Radio Shack employee named Mark Reynolds who hit the jackpot playing slots at a Kansas City casino to the tune of over $2 million. Article asked him how he felt. "Lucky," was his reply.

Only Mark Reynolds of Springfield, Missouri, didn't seem so lucky to me. Because Mark Reynolds's stupid mug was smiling back at me from my computer screen, and he looked an awful lot like a stoolie IT guy named Michael Rigby.

Guess WitSec figured stash a guy in a town called Springfield and even if somebody lets it slip, you've got to search the country over before you find the right one.

Then again, maybe Rigby *was* lucky. After all, between what he stole from the Mob and what he won playing the slots, he had enough money to cover my fee sixty times over.

Which meant maybe he'd live long enough to spend the rest.

"Morning, Michael."

It wasn't morning. Hadn't been for hours. But given the rumpled state of Rigby's slept-in clothes and his gravity-defying hair, it may as well have been. Though where he was going with bedhead at three in the afternoon was beyond me.

I'd been hiding in his garage since six A.M., waiting for him to show. The way he leaped for the gun stashed under his workbench when he saw me, I'd say he'd been waiting for someone like me a while too.

"Don't bother," I said.

He bothered. *Click click click click click.* When he caught on his piece was empty, he threw the fucking thing at me. It bounced off the wall to my right and clattered to the concrete floor. I tried not to take it personally.

"Relax—I'm not here to kill you."

But Rigby wasn't listening—he was too busy doing his best Gene Krupa impression on the wall-mounted button that opened the garage door. I'd disabled that too, of course. This wasn't my first day on the job.

He peered at me a moment with manic Muppet eyes over the top of his tan mid-nineties Skylark, and then bolted for the driver's side door. Damn near got inside, too, but he froze once I told him the score.

"Or rather, what I should have said is, *I'm* not here to kill you, Michael, but there are others close behind who mean to. And if you leave, you're on your own—I won't be able to protect you."

He paused halfway through the Buick's open door, digesting what I'd said.

"You with WitSec?"

"No," I replied. "I'm not with WitSec."

Rigby laughed, black and bitter as old coffee. "'Course you're not. Figured maybe they saw my picture in the paper, sent you out to keep an eye on me, but I shoulda known those asshats don't give a damn about me—not anymore."

"Wait a minute—you're telling me you're no longer in the program?"

"Nope. I told those fuckers to take a hike about a year back. Always keeping tabs. Checking up on me. Poking round my business. Couldn't get at a dime of the dough I'd stashed, them looking over my shoulder all the time. So I dropped out. Told 'em I was fine. And I woulda been, too, if it wasn't for that fucking picture. That is what brought you here, isn't it?"

"Yeah. That's what brought me here. And I'm not the only one who's seen it."

Rigby cocked his head, like I was some kind of math problem he could maybe figure out. "So if you ain't with WitSec, who the hell are you?"

"Who I am isn't important. What's important's who I work for."

"Okay then—who do you work for?"

"You, actually. Or rather, I will, for the bargain-basement rate of a quarter million dollars."

"A quarter million dollars."

"That's right."

"Which gets me what, exactly?"

"You know those guys coming to kill you?"

"Yeah?"

"I kill them first."

Another barking laugh. "Shit—you're like some kind of hitman entrepreneur? Now I've fucking heard everything. But seriously, dude, don't you think a quarter mil's a little steep?"

I showed him my palms. "Hey, that's your call to make. But I would've thought a guy with thirty million in the bank would have no trouble forking over a paltry quarter mil to avoid his own grisly murder."

"Look around, pal—I look like I got thirty mil?"

I looked around. He had a point. I told him so.

"Damn right I got a point. See, the Marshals Service took it personal when I kicked 'em to the curb. Guess once I did they figured out I wasn't square with them when I told 'em I didn't know shit 'bout all the money that went missing. Next thing I know, I got a federal prosecutor sniffing around, asking all kinds of pointed questions about unreported income and wondering if maybe I had any back taxes needed filing. Ain't been near my stash since, for fear they'd bust my ass. Don't have to tell you if they locked me up, I'd be shanked within the week, and ain't no pile of money worth that. So instead I figured fuck it—easy come, easy go. Time to seek out other sources of income. Hence my little trip to the casino."

"A two mil payout goes a long way toward putting you back in the upper class," I said. "Picture aside, that was quite a stroke of luck."

"Luck? You think that shit was luck? Took me eight months to write a patch that could get through the casino's firewall and hack those slots. I earned every fucking dime of that money."

"And now that you have it, you'll have no trouble paying me."

"Yeah, only that's just it—I don't have it yet. Maybe Vegas does it different, but a two-bit slot joint in KC don't exactly hand over that kind of coin right on the spot. I gotta go back Thursday to pick it up."

A puzzle piece clicked into place. "Let me guess: big crowd, oversized novelty check—that sort of deal?"

"That's right," he said.

"Yeah, that's where they're going to hit you."

Rigby didn't look too happy to hear that, but he was skeptical still. "What makes you so sure?"

"Their instructions were to make it public."

Even in the dim light of the garage, I could see him go pale.

"Fuck," he muttered. "Fucking motherfucking fuck." Then he brightened. "But you said that you could stop 'em, right?"

"I said if you paid me, I could stop them."

"Right, but if you stop 'em, I can get my money, and then I'll have more than enough to pay you."

I shook my head. "I don't work that way. I get my money up front, or no deal."

"I dunno, dude—that sounds pretty fucking hinky to me. If you're as good as you're puttin' on, why's it matter if I pay you after?"

"Well, for one, there's no guarantee you ever would, in which case I'd have to kill you—and that makes two hits I don't get paid for. And for two, an attempt on your life is going to attract all kinds of attention from the authorities, which makes any subsequent transfer of funds a whole lot riskier than it would have been beforehand. But all of that pales in comparison to the fact that I don't kill without good reason. No money, no reason. So take it or leave it, but my offer's nonnegotiable."

"Everything's negotiable, dude."

"Not this."

"So what then? You're just gonna leave me here to die?"

"No," I said, handing him a scrap of paper on which was scrawled the number of a disposable cell, "I'm going to leave you here to make a choice. You can choose to run—to leave this place to-night—and who knows? Maybe you'll manage to disappear again. You can choose to spend the next three days getting my fee to-gether. If you're successful, you give me a ring on that number there, and you have my word no harm will come to you. Or you can choose to do nothing and see how long your luck holds. It's up to you."

Rigby was silent a long while. Then he shook his head and swore. "Damn—all I figured on getting when I came out here was a break-fast sandwich from the gas station on the corner. Instead, I get you, and all the sudden I ain't so hungry anymore." He paused and licked his lips. "But I could sure as shit use something to drink."

Thursday morning, Rigby called. I knew he would. What I hadn't figured on was what he'd say.

"You get my money?" I asked.

"Not exactly," he said.

"Then this conversation is over."

"Wait—don't hang up!"

I didn't hang up. God knows why, but I didn't. Now, of course, I wish to hell I had.

"I'm listening."

"I want you to take it all."

"Excuse me?"

"The whole two mil. Every fucking penny. Just get these guys off my ass long enough for me to rabbit, and it's yours."

Two million dollars.

Two *million* dollars.

It was more than I could make in three jobs—in five. And it was just sitting there in front of me for the taking. All I had to do was pop some lowlife Syndicate button man, and bam.

I wanted to do a backflip. To happy-dance around the fucking room. But Rigby didn't need to know that. So I played it calm, cool. "And how do you propose to get me this money?"

"That's the beauty part," he said, relief apparent in his tone. "We just have the casino give it straight to you. See, that big check is just for show—I'm supposed to give 'em my account info ahead of time so they can transfer the funds directly once the dog-and-pony show is over. But I figure a big-shot hitman like you has probably got a numbered account somewhere, all nice and anonymous-like, am I right? So who's to say for the purpose of this transaction that account ain't mine?"

I should have said no. Should have up and walked away. But I got greedy. I got stupid. Two million dollars buys a lot of bad decisions. So what I said instead was, "You try to screw me, and I'll kill you—you know that, right?"

I swear, I could damn near hear him smiling. "That mean we got a deal?"

Two. Million. Dollars.

"Yeah, we got a deal."

"Cool—let me grab a pen."

Pendleton's Resort and Casino was a tacky riverboat-themed complex overlooking the Missouri River from an industrial park just north of KC proper. And old-timey marquee awash in the light of a thousand bulbs gave way to an interior whose décor was as loud and jarring as the din rising from its endless banks of garish, clanking slots.

Rigby's ceremony was in a banquet hall just off the gaming floor, sandwiched between a hypnotist's matinee performance and some country act I'd never heard of. The room was big and dark, with plush carpeting of nauseating green and red and floor-to-ceiling curtains on each wall. A small stage was set up at one end of the room, surrounded by a smattering of linened tables with folding chairs to match. The chairs were mostly occupied, full of drunks and barflies and compulsive gamblers who'd run out of dough, tossing back free drinks and snatching apps from silver platters as they passed. To one side of the stage was a short, stout bar, people crowded all around. At each of the two exits was a security guard—husky, uniformed, armed. Another couple stood just offstage at either side.

I didn't like it.

The hall was too full, had too few exits and way too much security. Not to mention the half-domes of tinted plastic that protruded downward at regular intervals from the ceiling—security cameras, watching every inch of the room.

The room I was about to pop a guy in.

I told myself that I should walk. That the chances of success—as defined by both me and Rigby getting out of here alive—were slim to none. That to do this job right, I would've had to scout the place a week, maybe identify the button man ahead of time. And I wasn't wrong.

Problem was, I had two million reasons to try anyway.

Least I'd come prepared. Job like this, the key is blending in, so I'd gone full-on gambling cliché. A red-and-white-checked cowboy shirt with white trim. Dark blue boot-cut jeans over a pair of alligator boots. Brown leather jacket with a ceramic knife stashed in the lining of its right sleeve, and a homemade pen-light zip gun in its left-hand pocket. On my head, an off-white Stetson, a pair of BluBlockers, and a big-ass fake mustache. Did I look ridiculous? Absolutely—but then, so did everyone else in here. If I'd walked in dressed for stealth, any hitter worth his salt would've made me in an instant. Just like I made the guy I was gunning for.

Seems he went the cliché route too. Black turtleneck. Black jeans. Black jacket, beneath which lurked the telltale bulk of a shoulder holster. Coarse, grim features, and hair so slick it glistened beneath the lights. He was sitting down in front, his hands under the table, casting surreptitious glances around the room while waiting for Rigby to take the stage. In front of him a gin and tonic sat untouched. As I watched him from behind my tinted lenses, he glanced back my way a moment, but his eyes just slid right off me. And why wouldn't they? I was just another two-bit gambler playing cowboy, one of thirty in the room.

Seemed to me the key was tagging him all quiet-like, then getting out of here before the crowd got wise he'd died. Figured I'd sidle up beside him acting tipsy while everyone was still milling about, then lean in quick and slice his femoral. He'd bleed out onto the floor beneath his table in seconds, and the floor-length linens would hide the worst of it. Long as he didn't fall out of his chair, he'd probably just look like another sloppy drunk too soused to play the tables. By the time the room cleared and his body was discovered, I'd be half a state away from here.

That's what I told myself, at least.

But that's not quite how it went down.

Oh, sure, I sidled up just like I'd planned, dropped the knife into my palm with a practiced flick. Spied Rigby standing in the wings as I approached the stage, straining to see the audience past the stage lights and looking like he had a king-fuck case of stage fright. Then something kind of weird happened.

And by "something kind of weird happened," I mean my target doubled over coughing, and then the room erupted in a hail of gunfire.

When the shots rang out, Rigby hit the deck, drywall pocking just behind where he'd been standing. I hit the floor as well, but not quickly enough—a bullet tore through my right side and spilled blood all over where my target should've been. But he wasn't there anymore. He'd turned his double-over into a roll, vacating his chair just before his buddies blew it all to hell and taking cover behind the bar as its patrons fled.

Did I say "target"? I should've said "bait." And did I say "Rigby"? I should've said "shit-bag." Because as I said before, by the time you hear the shot, the bullet's come and gone, only Rigby managed to duck those ones just fine. And no way could he have seen someone pull a gun past all the stage lights. Besides, it was clear my would-be target's cough had been the go-ahead to open fire. The fact that Rigby ducked in time meant he hadn't reacted to the gunfire, he'd reacted to the cough—which meant that he'd been tipped to listen for it.

Which meant the fucker'd set me up.

I kicked a table over, darted behind it. The shooting continued unabated. Staccato, automatic, and so fucking loud I could barely hear the screaming of the crowd. I counted three shooters, alternating fire so that each could reload in turn. Two guards were down, and maybe a dozen civilians, all for the sin of standing too damn close to me.

My wayward target poked his head out around the bar and popped off a couple shots my way. I yanked the zip gun from my pocket and discharged it at him, its single .22 round hitting the bullet-riddled bar just inches from his face. Damn. As he ducked back behind the bar, I tossed the spent penlight casing aside. Then I spotted all the ruined, shattered bottles atop the bar and smiled. Grabbed the tacky red-glass candleholder from the table beside me, the candle still flickering inside, and lobbed it toward the bar. It shattered on impact, and there was a whoosh as all that spilled liquor caught fire. For a few seconds the dude behind the bar shrieked so loud I could hear him over all the automatic fire. Then he fell silent, and the sickly sweet scent of burning flesh filled the room.

One down. Three to go.

Pop, pop from somewhere far away, and one of the shooters was silenced. That made two. Then a manic spray of bullets from his compatriots, and the guard who bagged him was repaid in kind. Kid should've turned tail and run—this was way above his pay grade. Still, I knew a good diversion when I heard one.

I stood and threw my knife at the nearest shooter, aiming to bury it in his eye. Guess I was a little rusty, though—it wound up three-deep in his throat.

One to go.

I dove across the floor to the nearest fallen guard and grabbed his piece out of his holster. Had to pry his fingers off the still-closed snap. Poor bastard hadn't even unfastened the damn thing before they got him.

The last shooter returned his attention to me, or tried. Wound up ventilating the bodies sprawled out in the spot I'd just vacated. In the dim banquet hall light, I could barely see him against the backdrop of the curtains, but I caught his muzzle flash just fine. Squeezed off six quick rounds, and he went down. Pretty sure I landed five at least.

My ears rang in the quiet that followed, so bad it took me a few seconds to realize that the quiet wasn't quiet at all. Gunfire and gaming had given way to shrieking and wailing, and over it all, I could hear the shout of security drawing closer. Iffy as my hearing was, I couldn't tell which door they'd be coming through—just that they were headed this way. So I did the only thing I could think to do.

My gun hand pressed tight to my bleeding gut, I sprinted for the stage. Damn near stepped right over Rigby, who lay cowering where he fell. Then I figured maybe I ought to take him with me. I grabbed his collar and yanked him to his feet.

Eight uniforms sprinted into the room, four through each door. When they spotted me, they opened fire. Looked like it was time to make my exit.

To one side of the stage, a half-assed backstage area had been set up. Looked to me they put it there to take advantage of a door that led to a service hallway, allowing easy access to the stage for employees and talent both. Like every service door in this place, it had a PIN pad and a spot to swipe your employee ID badge. I had neither. Good thing for me, then, it was propped.

I kicked the chair that held the door open out of the way, and then I threw Rigby into the hall after it. The guards converged on us, firing shots off all the while. Thirty yards, twenty. I dove through the open door as, just behind me, one of them shouted into his radio, "Suspect retreating to south hall! Lock down! Repeat — *LOCK DOWN THE SOUTH HALL!*"

And as I pulled the door shut behind me, I heard the snick of thirty bolts locking, trapping me and Rigby inside.

So I'd been shot. That was bad. It was a through-and-through, though, and it looked to me like it had missed my major organs, which wasn't too shabby. But then again, I was trapped inside a casino chock full of security guards who, along with the entire Chicago Syndicate, seemed to really want me dead. I guess on the balance I'd have to say my day wasn't going all that well.

Least I'd managed to snag that turncoat douchebag Rigby by the collar and drag his ass with me when I'd made my exit from the banquet hall. Score that one in the plus column. At first he was biting and scratching at me like a rabid raccoon, so it wasn't all roses, but once I slammed his head into the wall a couple times, he got docile in a hurry. Which was good, because I couldn't afford to kill him yet.

Emergency lights strobed all around us, though the main hall lights stayed lit. There were no cameras I could see, which was a plus, but as promised, every door leading from the hall was locked, their PIN pads blinking red. After the bloodbath in the banquet hall, I figured security aimed to sit on us till Kansas City SWAT arrived. Which I figured meant I had three minutes to get out of here — maybe less.

Plenty of time to teach Rigby a little lesson about loyalty.

I pinned him against the wall, got up in his face.

"You set me up, you son of a bitch."

"Dude, I got no idea what you *UNGFH!*"

Truth is, I've got no idea what I *UNGFH* either, but I don't think it was so much a question as the noise he made when I punched him in the solar plexus. I let him go. He doubled over but kept his feet. Then he puked, which I could have done without, but at least it stopped him lying.

"You want to try again?" I asked.

"Okay, okay," he said once his breath returned, "I set you up. But they got to me just after you did, and they offered me a deal. Said they knew you were tapped into their communiqués. Said they made sure you'd think they were gonna pop me here, and that if I helped them draw you out, maybe did a little digging for 'em, they'd let me walk."

"Digging? What *kind* of digging?"

"You know—bank shit. That's why I needed your account info."

This day kept getting better and better.

"Don't worry, though, dude—you covered your tracks pretty good. I mean, this shit is my bread and butter, and I couldn't hardly find nothing—no name, no address, hardly even any cash. Aside of that Evelyn chick you've been paying off, you're a fucking ghost, dude."

All the air drained from the room. I thought I was going to faint. I pulled Rigby close—so close I could have bit his fucking face off. And right then, I had half a mind to do it.

"What do you know about Evie?"

"Nothing, really—I swear it! Name and address, that's it!"

Son of a bitch. "And did you pass along that information to your friends at the Syndicate?"

"They said if I didn't help 'em they were gonna kill me! The fuck was I supposed to do?"

I swallowed hard, willed myself to stay calm. But I knew then I couldn't let them take me here. That I had to get to Evie before the Syndicate did. Even if it meant I had to let this fuckwit live.

I let go of said fuckwit. Smoothed out his shirt a bit. "It's cool," I said. "I understand. What's done is done."

Rigby flashed me a cautious smile. "Yeah?"

That's when I hit him again—in the face this time. Broke his nose. Blood sprayed crimson down his shirt and onto the institutional tile floor. When Rigby saw the blood, his eyes fluttered, and he went down. Barely got an arm out in time to catch himself from smacking his forehead.

I kicked him, hard. Heard ribs snap. He screamed, and rolled onto his side. Eyes wide with fear, snot and blood pouring from his nose as he cried like a child.

That was good.

That was how I needed him if I was going to get out of here alive.

I knelt next to him, slapped him once or twice. "No, you stupid shit, it isn't cool. My line of work, it doesn't pay to be forgiving. I ought to put you in the ground for what you've done. But the fact is, I need your help to get out of here, and if you cooperate like a good little boy, then maybe—just maybe—I'll let you live."

His head bobbed up and down, and he blubbered something unintelligible I assumed was a heartfelt pledge of undying allegiance. Which should hold until he got a better offer.

"Good. Now I'm going to need you to override the casino's lockdown—can you do that?"

"Are you fucking nuts?"

I grabbed his ruined nose and pinched. He thrashed like I'd hit him with a live wire. I let go and asked again. He just stared at me all mute and big-eyed, too terrified to even answer.

That was no good. I needed to keep him calm enough to do the job. So I changed my tone, replacing steel with what I hoped would pass for warmth. "Listen, Rigby, you can do this. I mean working for the Mob, you've dealt with systems a thousand times scarier than this one."

"Yeah, but—"

"And you beat Pendleton's system once before, right?"

"Well, yeah, but I had time—time and tools . . ."

I pulled a Leatherman from my pocket, handed it to him. Then I jammed the dead guard's Glock under his chin, barrel aiming upward toward his brain.

Warmth has never been my strong suit.

"That right there is all the tools you've got to work with. That and a couple minutes. You fail, or try to stall until the cops arrive, and I swear to you the last thing I do before they take me is blow your fucking head off, you understand? But if you get that door open, you have my word I'll let you live. I'll just walk on through and you'll never see me again, okay?"

Rigby nodded.

"Good—now get moving."

He got moving, prying the cover off the PIN pad for the stairwell door we'd stopped beside. Even shaking as he was, I could see the kid was good. Give me an hour or two, and maybe I could pop a lock like that. Rigby had it open in just under ninety seconds.

When the light went green and the locking mechanism clicked, I let out a yelp of joy that set my bullet wound throbbing. But Rigby didn't look like he was up for celebrating. He was just kneeling there beside the door lock, face pale, eyes clenched. After a moment of watching him, I had to ask.

"Rigby, what the hell are you doing?"

He opened one eye and looked at me. "Waiting for you to kill me."

"I told you, you get that open, you're free to go."

Color flooded his cheeks. "Yeah, but I didn't figure you were serious!"

I shoved him aside. Stepped through the door into a dingy fire stairwell, dimly lit and obviously unused.

"I always keep my word," I said. "Besides, once the Syndicate catches up with you, you're dead anyway."

"What? No! They cut me a deal!"

"Yeah, and you figure they aim to honor it? You stole damn near thirty million dollars from them—they can't just let you live. My guess is, you'll be dead within the week."

"You don't know that," he said, but there was no force behind it.

"Hey," I said. "Maybe I'm wrong. It's been known to happen." *Just look at this gig,* I thought. "Either way, guess you'll know soon enough."

Then I closed the door and fled, leaving a weeping Rigby in my wake.

Getting out of the stairwell was a breeze. Security figured they had me dead to rights, locked up in the south hall, and since the hallway contained no cameras, they had no idea I'd gotten out. And sure, they were probably watching all the building's exits, but that was only a problem if I headed down. So instead I headed up.

The upper floors of Pendleton's were nothing but hotel rooms. By the time I got there, most of them were empty, on account of some folks downstairs had started shooting at each other and the building was being evacuated. Found a room abandoned midclean-ing by the housekeepers and helped myself to a clean pillowcase to dress my wound and a change of clothes, swapping my silly cowboy getup for a pair of khakis and a crisp blue oxford. Even with the ad hoc bandages, the oxford was a hair too big for me, and a little loose about the neck, so I left the collar undone and threw on my unwitting benefactor's charcoal sport coat. Then it was a matter of peeling off the fake mustache and walking out the front door look-ing confused and frightened like the rest of the good people with the misfortune to be caught up in this sordid mess.

My phone clocked Springfield to Morgantown at sixteen hours. I figured I could make it in eleven. Stole an Audi from one of the ca-sino's satellite lots, kept the needle pinned at eighty-five the whole way. Even chance they'd try to pull me over, I knew. Even chance I didn't care. They could chase my ass the whole damn way. All that mattered now was Evie. All that mattered was I kept her safe. And leading a parade of cops to her front door was as good a way as any to do it.

But they didn't. Didn't try to pull me over. Didn't chase my ass at all. And so I wound up on Evie's front porch alone.

The Syndicate hadn't beaten me here—that much I knew. If they had, they would have made a show of it—trashing the place, causing a scene, maybe leaving me a grisly souvenir. A finger, or perhaps an ear. But all looked normal, and quiet, and dark.

Still, they'd be here soon enough. And I had to be ready for them when they did.

My head was throbbing. My stomach churned. A sheen of cold, acrid sweat covered every trembling inch of me, and the gunshot in my side itched and burned. Moving hurt. Hell, standing hurt.

And still I kept on pounding on that door.

"Evie!" I shouted, my voice hoarse from exertion, and oddly tinny and distant to my own ears. Loss of blood. Lack of sleep. But I'd had worse. Least, that's what I told myself. "God damn it, Evie—open up!"

Did I mention it was late? Well, it was. Pushing five A.M. So late I guess you'd have to call it early.

If I were Evie and had some nutjob banging on my door at five A.M., shouting my name, I might be reluctant to answer too. Which is to say, I should've figured on what happened next.

The inside light came on, spilling yellow through the decorative panel in the door. Then the door flew open. As I squinted against the sudden light, a hand grabbed a fistful of my new shirt, its medium starch no match for Stuart's angry, sweat-slick grip. Next thing I knew, I was up against the doorjamb, the business end of a baseball bat in my face.

Fucking Stuart.

It was all I could do not to end his ass right then and there.

But I didn't. Instead I tried to talk. To calm him down. It didn't take.

He was all riled up, the king defending his castle. Lots of "Who the fuck are you?" and "The fuck you think you're doing, pounding on our goddamn door in the dead of fucking night?" And I admit, I was a little bummed he didn't recognize me. Guess Evie didn't keep too many pictures of me around.

Then again, maybe I should go a little easier on the guy—it's not like anyone expects their wife's dead first husband to come knocking in the middle of the night. But he just kept on working himself up—spit flying, veins pulsing, nose almost touching mine—and the whole time, all I could think was, *This is the guy who gets to sleep with Evie.*

So I took the bat. Pushed him back into the house and closed the door. And okay, I might have pushed him a little harder than was strictly necessary. He toppled backward into the hallway, crashing ass over teakettle through the console table along the wall and coming to rest amid a hail of keys and cell phones and spare change.

Of course that's when Evie showed up.

When Stuart took the table out, Evie half ran, half stumbled down the stairs calling his name as though she'd been listening from just out of sight the whole time. Then she spotted me standing over him with the bat, and the air around me seemed to gel. I couldn't move, couldn't speak, couldn't breathe—I just stood there staring as fear turned to confusion, as recognition turned to shock.

"Jake?" she said, her voice thin and frail, like that of a frightened child.

Hearing her say my name—a name I'd walked away from long ago—tore at my insides worse than any bullet could. It hurt like love. Like dying.

Her hand to her mouth, she sank to her knees. Slowly, as if through water. Seeing her like that—mouth open, chest hitching beneath her husband's borrowed undershirt, no noise coming out—she looked like a scream set on mute. And all I could think was, *I did this. I made her feel this way.*

The bat clattered to the floor, forgotten. The distance between us melted away. And for a few blissful moments, I held her—her swollen belly warm against my own, her face buried in the crook of my neck as she cried.

"So let me get this straight," she said, gripping her coffee mug in both hands, her bare legs curled under her on the couch. "There are men coming. Coming for you. And you don't know when they'll get here. But you mean to kill them when they do."

"Coming for you," I corrected.

"But to get to you."

"Yes," I said. "But that distinction doesn't make you any safer."

"No, I imagine it doesn't."

"But I can protect you. Protect you both. You just have to trust me and do exactly as I say."

"Oh, for fuck's sake!" This from Stuart. "I don't know why the hell we're even listening to this bullshit! You let her think you fucking *died*—why in God's name should we trust you now?"

"Because I have no reason to lie. I let Evie think I was dead to protect her. From this life. From this job. Why the hell would I show up and ruin that now, if it wasn't to keep her safe?"

Stuart snorted, rolled his eyes. And it's not like I didn't see where he was coming from. I'd just told them both that I kill people for a living. That I'd been hiding from my wife and from the law for the better part of the last decade. That I'd been funneling Evie blood money for years. And that by doing so, I'd put her life in danger—both their lives in danger. I'm pretty sure I wouldn't have trusted me either.

So I told him the bit that I'd left out. The bit I didn't want to say aloud. The bit that, once he'd heard it, he couldn't dare ignore.

"Look, Stuart, you want the truth? Fine, here it is. They *need* Evie. They need her alive, because they think that they can use her to get to me. Now that doesn't mean they need her in good condition. And the guys they send on missions like this, these are not nice guys. In all likelihood, they'll beat her. Rape her. Torture her, just to hear her scream. And you won't be able to do a thing about it, because you'll be dead. See, they need Evie, but you? You they don't give a shit about. They don't give a shit about you because they figure you're not worth a thing to me—you're just the guy who's been fucking my wife."

Stuart made like he was going to object, but I raised a hand to silence him. "I know, I know, that's not how it really is. Any claim I had on the title of husband died in the desert a long time ago. But you've got to understand just what we're up against."

Evie's face darkened in thought. "Say you kill these men," she said. "Their employers will only send more, won't they? And they'll keep sending more until they finish the job. We'll never be safe."

She was right. I knew she was. And suddenly I realized what I had to do.

"There is one way," I said. "One way to end this all for good."

Stuart looked confused. Evie didn't, though; tears brimmed anew in her eyes, streaking down her cheeks, and the hand she raised to brush them away shook like a leaf in the wind. It was clear she understood.

"Jake," she said, "you can't."

"I have to. It's the only way."

Stuart looked to her, and then to me. "What? What's the only way?"

It was Evie who answered. "He means to let them kill him."

Stuart laughed. There was no humor to it, only incredulity. "Hey, good riddance, I say!" Then he saw my face—her face—caught on it was no joke. "Wait—you're serious? You're going to let them gun you down?"

"It's the only way I can be sure they never come back. Once I'm gone, they've got no use for you. You'll be safe. All three of you," I said, my gaze pulled toward Evie's swollen belly.

"But you only just . . ." she said. The sentiment died on her lips, though. It was for the best, I guess. She had a new life, a new love, a new path. All I had was the beginnings of a plan, and a pretty shitty one at that.

"Look, if this is going to work, we have to get you out of here, and fast. You remember my family's old camp?" Evie nodded. "Good. I want you to pack a bag and head up there, okay? Take only what you need, and leave your cell phones so you can't be tracked. I've holed up there a time or two myself—there's food enough in the cupboards for at least a week, and the generator's all gassed up."

"How do we know when you're . . . how do we know when it's over?"

"There's a radio. Keep it on. If I'm going out, I'm taking as many of those fuckers with me as I can. When it's over, you're sure to hear it."

"And what do we tell the police?"

I shrugged. "Tell them the truth. Tell them whatever you like."

"Jake, this is crazy."

"Maybe. But it's the way it's got to be."

She didn't want to listen. Didn't want to leave. But eventually she acquiesced; she and Stuart packed a bag, hopped in her truck, and together they disappeared into the hills.

I watched until they vanished from sight, and then a couple minutes more.

Then I went inside and made my call.

Rigby answered on the seventh ring.

"H-hello?"

"Oh, good," I said, "They haven't come to kill you yet."

He swallowed hard, made a little keening noise in the back of his throat. "Dude, you don't know for sure they're gonna."

"Sure I don't. Listen, I want you to do me a favor, on account of I let you live."

"Yeah? What's that?"

"When your Mob friends come to kill you, I want you to tell them if they go after Evie I'll be waiting. That if they plan to take me, they'd best send every guy they've got. And that if I were them, I'd bring a fucking armory."

A long pause. "Uh, you sure you really wanna tell 'em that?"

"Yeah, I'm sure. Now say it back."

He said it back. "But really, dude, they might not come for me—"

I hung up. I had nothing more to say to him. And I had no interest in anything he could say to me. What was the point in wasting either of our time? Soon enough, we'd both be dead.

My call made, I wandered Evie's empty house, drinking in the

scent of her that lingered in the air. I closed blinds. I shut off lights.
I busted stemware up in a paper bag and spread the broken shards
across the windowsills. I nailed shut the front and back door both,
and barricaded the French doors I'd watched Evie through with
the kitchen table and Evie's grandma's china hutch.

I stuck a can of cooking spray and a couple tins of Sterno in the
microwave. Then I tossed in the contents of the silverware drawer
for good measure, and set the timer for ten seconds. I figured
maybe when the shit went down, I'd have a chance to trigger it.

I hoped so. Dying didn't seem so scary, but I'd be damned if I
was going to do it alone.

In the living room, I spied Evie's dad's old hi-fi and smiled to
find it working after all these years. She'd lost him to cancer our
sophomore year of high school; we'd sit and listen to his records
for hours, tears streaming down her smiling face as, for a little
while at least, he lived among the vinyl's hiss and scratch.

I fired it up and dropped the needle. The opening strains of *Ex-
ile* filled the house. For one beautiful, painful moment, it felt like
Evie was standing right beside me—she always had a soft spot for
the Stones.

Took me clean through "Sweet Virginia" to make Molotov cock-
tails of Evie and Stuart's liquor cabinet. When I finished, I made a
quick trip to the kitchen to fetch a chef's knife and one of Stuart's
longneck PBRs. I tested the heft and balance of the knife in my
hand and decided it'd do. Then I cracked the beer and retired to
the couch, to sit and listen in the darkness.

As I sat there—eyes closed, listening—I wondered if Rigby'd
pass along my message, or if they'd pop him from afar before he
got the chance. I wondered if they'd think that I was bluffing. I
wondered if they'd come in full-force or sideways—some way I
hadn't thought of.

But in the end, I knew, it didn't matter.

Eventually, message or no, they'd come.

Could be it took them hours. Could be it took them days. But
soon enough, I knew, they'd be here; all I had to do was wait.

HARRY HUNSICKER

West of Nowhere

FROM *Ellery Queen Mystery Magazine*

DANNY THE DUMB-ASS fires once into the ceiling of the bar.

Plaster and slivers from a ruined fan shower the room, a slurry of dust and wood fragments.

I cringe, grip my pistol tighter, face hidden by a Ronald Reagan Halloween mask.

Rule One: The guns are for show only; don't shoot unless absolutely necessary.

"N-n-n-nobody move." Danny's voice, muffled by his own rubber mask, sounds shrill, scared. "Ha-ha-hands where I can see them."

Rule Two: Let me do the talking. Especially if you're a stutterer.

In the middle of the room, a half-dozen men in overalls and work clothes sit around a felt-covered gaming surface. The table is between a bar on one wall and a shuffleboard game on the other. Nobody else in the place except for a scared-looking bartender by the beer taps.

In the middle of the table: a pile of chips and cash, and a spray of playing cards, trapped by a circular fence of longneck bottles and ashtrays.

Danny the Dumb-ass moves to one side of the front door and unplugs the jukebox.

Toby Keith and Willie Nelson stop singing in midverse. *"Whiskey for my men —"*

Silence. The bartender is shaking. A mug in one hand, beer slops over onto his fingers. Danny looks at me and nods, apparently now remembering to be quiet.

I resist the urge to slap him. Instead, I flip the deadbolt on the door, stride to the table.

Outside, it's early afternoon and the sign on the bank around the corner reads ninety-three degrees. Inside it's balmy, the narrow room thick with air conditioning and smoke, lit only by a handful of neon beer signs.

"Put the cash in here." I drop a canvas bag in the middle of the card pile. "All of it."

The guy at the head of the table is about seventy. He has work-gnarled hands and a leathery face, evidence of a lifetime in the sun, most likely working the rocky soil of Central Texas.

"Boy, you are making a big mistake." He exhales a plume of smoke from his nostrils.

"Less talk, more money." I fire a round into a framed picture of John Wayne. The photo hangs next to a deer's head with a dusty bra dangling from the antlers.

What the heck; the don't-shoot rule has already been broken and my other wingman is a no-show. Time to crank this cash-and-dash up to eleven and get out.

Five of the six people at the table flinch and duck. The old man with the gnarled hands doesn't move, not even a blink. He smiles instead.

Danny hobbles to the table, dragging his foot in the special shoe, the one he told me would allow him to walk normally but clearly doesn't. He grabs a wad of currency and a manila envelope that sits in front of the old man. He stuffs both into the sack.

The old guy tenses, the tiniest movement in an otherwise still room. Losing that much cash hurts. Danny doesn't notice. I do, and the old man knows it.

"The rest of it," I say. "Get a move on."

The other players shove money toward Danny.

"You know whose game this is?" the old man says.

"W-w-w-wouldja just shut the hell up." Danny's voice is louder than necessary. He jams the muzzle against the man's temple. "It's our ga-ga-game now."

"You nervous or something?" The old guy raises one eyebrow. "People stutter when they get nervous."

Danny's gloved hands shake. He doesn't handle stress well, not the best attribute for the sidecar on an armed robbery, even one as easy as this. Sometimes, however, you've got to run with whoever's on the playground, even if he comes to school on the short bus and has one leg longer than the other.

The old man shrugs. He stares at me. His eyes seem to pierce my mask.

Danny scoops up the rest of the money with his free hand, shoves it in the bag.

Lots of high-denomination bills, a big game. The stopwatch in my head says we've been inside for about fifteen seconds. Another fifteen to wrap things up, and we'll be in the stolen pickup just outside the front entrance.

Danny limps toward the door, sack in hand.

"Don't anybody be stupid." I back away, weapon pointing at the men. "It's just money."

Danny is at the entrance when the back door we'd locked earlier opens.

A woman in her mid-thirties wearing a denim miniskirt and a halter top bounces in, cigarette dangling between her lips.

Everybody turns her way.

She stares at me and screams, a keening sound like the gates of hell just opened up for an instant or maybe *American Idol* has been canceled. The cigarette falls to the floor.

Danny startles. Fires his pistol again for no apparent reason. The bullet hits the floor.

Several of the men at the table jump up. The bartender reaches under the bar.

The old guy moves faster than everybody. A gun appears in his hand. An orange spit of flame. *BOOM.* The bullet hits the wall about a foot from my head.

In the same movement, I fire twice and turn to the door. I'm not really aiming, only pointing in the general direction of the table, hoping not to hit anybody, especially the girl, just trying to make the old man quit shooting.

Another round hits the wall near my face. Shouts from behind me. A grunt of pain too, maybe.

I grab Danny, push him outside. Slam the door behind us.

The joint is on a side street in a little town in the Texas hill country, between an antique shop that's always closed for lunch and an abandoned feed store. No traffic or people visible. Yet.

I rip off the mask and blink at the sun. From the cardboard box we've left sitting by the front of the bar, I grab a battery-powered nail gun.

Thwack-thwack-thwack. Three nails in the door and frame, almost as good as a deadbolt.

Danny takes off his mask too. Sweat drips down his nose. "S-s-sorry about that."

"Get in the truck." I walk as fast as possible to the driver's side of the Chevy parked by the curb.

Inside, we buckle up, all legal. I head to Main Street, driving well under the speed limit.

"Don't forget Chris." Danny's tone has returned to default, a whine somewhere between petulant and pathetic. "We g-g-gotta go to the rendezvous to get Chris."

The urge to rip out a clump of Danny the Dumb-ass's red hair rises in my gorge like week-old anchovy pizza eaten too quickly. I reach over. Danny backs away. I mutter, lean back, keep driving.

We're in the clear so far. There looks to be enough money in the canvas bag to pay off a few debts with some left over to send to the kid and hopefully make the she-beast that is my ex-wife go away.

A sheriff's car idles by in the other direction. The driver's window is down and a uniformed guy who looks like Jabba the Hutt but bigger sits behind the wheel. He pays us no mind.

I don't look at him either. I keep my hands at ten and two on the wheel. At the next stop sign, I turn toward the rendezvous point, the parking lot of the Baptist church. A few moments later, we stop by a Dumpster behind the sanctuary, windows down. The air stinks of grease from the trash and a charcoal fire nearby.

Thirty nervous seconds stretch to a panic-filled minute before Chris appears, running around the corner of the church.

She's wearing a denim skirt and a halter top, the girl from the bar, our lookout who was supposed to be inside *before* we got there, sending a text or three on the situation.

"Sorry I was late." She hops in, scoots Danny between us. "But I dropped the key to the back door and then my parole officer called. Figured I'd scream to distract everybody."

"That's okay, Chrissie." Danny smiles, a goofy look on his face. "It's all good."

Danny would give another inch from his bad leg if she'd acknowledge him as something more than a lopsided stump with eyes. He'd give his entire leg if she'd sleep with him. Chrissie, who's made a career out of going to bed with authority figures and dope-addled musicians, would rather French-kiss an armadillo than let Danny touch her.

I pull away from the Dumpster, marveling at the stupidity of my cohorts.

"The old guy's hurt." Chrissie lights a cigarette. "One of your shots hit him in the gut."

"All good" just morphed into something less, more like "all screwed."

"W-w-w-what are we gonna do?" Danny looks at me. "That guy said the operation was connected."

"Somebody owned that game?" Chrissie leans forward, stares at me. "I thought this was an indie?"

I don't reply, trying to process it all. Only so many people who could control a poker table like that, none of them folks you want to mess with. One in particular is especially vigilant when it comes to keeping a watch on his investments: Sinclair, a psychopathic Pole whose problem-solving techniques start with a blowtorch and then get nasty.

"Jesus H." Chrissie flicks her cigarette out the window. "I thought that guy was familiar. I've seen him before. In Waco."

I keep driving, vision tunneling at the news. We pass the city-limit sign on a narrow two-lane farm-to-market road that heads west.

"Waco?" Danny starts to shake.

Waco is Sinclair's base. Which means the game we just robbed was his.

And so was the guy I had shot.

Houston belongs to what's left of the Italian mob, mostly the aging wise guys based in Louisiana. Dallas has gone from an independent region controlled by local mom-and-pop thugs to being run by the Russians advancing across the country from the East Coast. The border region, everything from the Rio Grande to San Antonio, is controlled by the cartels.

That leaves Central Texas, the swath of foothills and blackland prairie between Dallas and the Alamo.

The heartland of the Lone Star State belongs to the Bohunk Mafia, the descendants of the Central European immigrants who arrived in the middle of the nineteenth century. The Krauts and Slovaks, Czechs and Poles. In addition to a taste for beer and sausage, they brought the vices of the motherland: whores and gambling, numbers rackets that appealed to their Teutonic sense of order. And a wicked style of loan sharking picked up over the years from the Jews as they herded them into the ghettos.

The three of us are Czechs from the same town, a little place near the Brazos River famed for its oompah band, sausage house, and second-generation meth labs, the latter of which are run by Chrissie's family. We grew up together and—if we'd stayed in school—would have graduated in the same class, coming up on twenty years ago.

We used to work for the Nemeceks, a local crew recently dispersed by prison and a nasty strain of syphilis too long untreated. I was muscle and transport, moving the weekly take to a friendly bank in Austin. Chrissie ran a strip club and hotsheet joint by the interstate. Danny, dumb as cut hair, worked as the point guy at a Nemecek dope operation, essentially directing customers to the right aisle of the store, sort of like a greeter at Wal-Mart.

But that was then. Now we are scared and a long way from home, cruising down a farm-to-market road in the western fringes of Central Texas, open territory, or so we thought. The terrain itself is sparse, rocky outcroppings topped with cedars, craggy hills that jut from barren pastures. Wood and stone farmhouses bleached by the elements.

Chrissie pounds the dash with both palms. She is angry.

"Sinclair," she says. "What the fricassee do we do now?"

My cell rings. The caller ID shows the number of an attorney in Dallas, a rabid weasel hired by my ex to get even on the child support. I turn the ringer off.

"We don't know it was his game for sure." I turn onto a gravel road that leads to a grove of wind-stunted live oaks. "Let's keep a positive thought."

The truck shimmies over rain-carved ruts in the caliche surface.

"Don't worry, Chrissie. I-I-I-I'll take care of you." Danny bounces, presses against her shoulder, then chest. He doesn't bounce back.

"Are you copping a feel, you little pervert?" She elbows him in the ribs.

Danny yelps, jumps away.

On the other side of the live oak trees is a clearing at the base of a small hill. A double-wide trailer with a rotting wooden deck sits in the middle of the open area. The sides are faded metal, once white, half of the windows either broken or weathered plywood.

"Nice place." I park by a rusted-out barrel smoker.

"You wanted somewhere to lie low." Chrissie flings open the passenger door. "Next time I'll get us a suite at the Motel Six."

We navigate the crumbling steps to the front of the trailer. Step inside.

The interior has orange shag carpet that smells like cat piss. A purple leather sectional sofa. Avocado green tile in the kitchen area. Through the back window I can see a shed and a narrow path leading around the hill.

I sit on the sofa, dump the contents of the canvas bag onto the wagon-wheel coffee table.

A pile of currency dotted with the occasional chip and scrap of paper. And the envelope.

Danny offers to count.

"No offense, Dumbo." Chrissie rolls her eyes. "But two plus two does not equal 'a bunch more than two.'"

Danny looks like she just kicked him in the nuts.

"Go outside." I point to the door. "Keep watch."

"I can do 'rithmetic, you know." He puffs up his chest. "I'm not s-s-s-stupid."

"Add up how long you'd last with Sinclair making s'mores out of your fingers." I throw a handful of chips at him. "Now get outside."

He grumbles, limps out.

I sort and then count. Twenties and fifties and the occasional ten-spot. And lots of hundreds. I open the manila envelope that had been sitting in front of the old guy and dump out another ginormous pile of c-notes. Chrissie licks her lips, smokes.

"Holy crap." I gulp at the final tally. "There's over sixty grand here."

"And this." Chrissie holds up a key that looks like the kind used to lock a storage locker at a bus station.

The key had been in the envelope.

"What do you think it goes to?" Chrissie purses her lips.

"Beats me." I'd been expecting a take somewhere around five thousand.

Chrissie drops the key on the pile of money. She takes the envelope and discarded scraps of paper and chips into the kitchen, drops them in the trash. When she comes back, she carries two bottles of Bud Light.

"We can't stay here." I accept a beer. "That's too much cash. They're gonna come looking."

"This place belongs to my cousin." Chrissie takes a drink. "No way Sinclair can find us here."

"Let's go west." I check the magazine in my pistol, sorry not to have brought more bullets.

"You ever been west?" she says.

I don't reply. Neither Chrissie nor Danny has ever left Texas. I've been the farthest. I've seen the ocean at Galveston twice, New Orleans once.

"We're west of nowhere already," she says. "And look what's happened to us."

We could head toward California, but where? And then what do we do?

"They won't find us," I say, more to myself than to her.

Chrissie shakes her head, drinks beer. "I'm gonna call my parole officer, see if he can get me in one of those witness protection programs."

I head to the back. In the narrow confines of the bathroom, my cell vibrates, a text message from a number in the Waco area code.

Give me envelope & ur partners. u can keep cash. Sinclair.

That didn't take long. Who knew it would be so easy to track down a stuttering gimp of a stickup guy and his partners?

I flush, walk to the living area.

Chrissie is still sitting on the couch. She holds her cell phone like it's hot, looking at the front door, an expression of shock on her face.

Danny stands in the entryway, his cell in one hand, pistol in the other.

"S-s-sit by her." He aims at me.

"Easy, partner." I raise my hands. "Let's be cool."

"The mo-mo-money's mine." He wags the phone at me. "And Sinclair gets you two."

When I was about twelve—right before he left to get some Skoal and never came back—my old man told me to look out for Danny the Dumb-ass.

"Anybody that stupid's gonna need all the help he can get." Pop cuffed me on the head and walked out.

I suppose, looking back, I was a little unclear on the concept, because later that week some buddies and I knocked over a Porta-Potty while Danny was inside taking a dump. Seemed like a good idea at the time.

Danny no longer looks stupid and befuddled. He looks angry. Hope he's forgotten about the Porta-Potty.

"Go in the kitchen." He waves the pistol. "Both of you."

"You just told me to sit down." I point to the sofa.

Chrissie nods in agreement. Her face is white.

Danny—saddled with the unfortunate nickname since grade school—frowns.

Chrissie and I don't move. Sweat beads on my forehead.

Danny's frown morphs into something else, a dark spot on the far side of his soul, the cold and brittle crevice where thirty years of insults and playground beatings have been brewing.

His mouth twitches, eyes darken. He grips the pistol tighter, knuckles turning white, muzzle shaking.

"I got the same message from Sinclair." I hold up my phone. "He's on to us."

Danny's eyes narrow, finger tightens on the trigger.

"Ah jeez, c'mon, Danny. Don't shoot us." Chrissie holds up her hands, voice panicky. "We're your friends."

"F-f-friends?" He limps inside. "You treat me like d-d-dirt."

Neither of us responds.

"How much?" He points to the money.

"A lot." I ease a step closer. "Enough to get us gone from this part of the world."

Danny stops by the table. "Where's the envelope?"

"In the trash." Chrissie points to the kitchen, obviously ignoring the key that sits next to her pack of Capris, a few inches from the pile of cash.

Danny turns that way but hesitates. Indecision etches itself across his face.

"Put your piece on the table." He waves his gun at my waistband. "And get the envelope."

"He's not gonna let any of us go," I say. "He's just playing us against each other."

"Nuh-uh." Danny shakes his head. "He's gonna give me a job, a full-time gig at one of his cathouses."

Sinclair is not stupid. He's offered the two things most important to Danny: steady employment and women who have no choice but to pay attention to him.

My phone is still in my hand. It buzzes again.

The same Waco number: Too late, sucker.

"He's lying to you." Chrissie stands.

"Shut up." Danny's face is red, mottled like a moldy tomato. "SHUTTHEHELLUP."

His phone buzzes, a text message. He looks at the screen and his face turns gray.

I lunge across the small living area, grab for his gun.

He lets me take it, offers no resistance.

Chrissie runs to the door, slams it shut. Her phone rings, a call coming in. She looks at the screen. "It's my cousin."

Danny stares at me, a blank look on his face. He seems to get smaller, shoulders falling in on themselves.

"Why are you calling?" Chrissie answers and peers out the remaining window, moving aside a gingham curtain. "I told you we'd be gone in a couple of days."

The room gets very quiet, nothing but the low rumble of the asthmatic air conditioner.

"You told him WHAT?" Chrissie lets the curtain drop, looks at me. "'Course I know what a blowtorch can do." She rubs her eyes. "How long do we have?"

I throw money in the bag. Grab the key to the storage locker.

She hangs up. "Sinclair knows where we are."

Danny begins to hyperventilate.

"What do we do now?" Chrissie lights a cigarette, takes one puff, and stubs it out.

"He doesn't care about the money. That's what the messages said." I look at her. "He wants the envelope."

"The key." She nods, points to the item in my hand. "It was in the envelope."

A car door slams outside.

"We give him the key, then." I peer out the window.

Sinclair Wachowski stands by the front of a late-model Chevy dual-axle pickup, beefy arms crossed. He's wearing a faded pair of overalls and a wife-beater T-shirt. A large man, if by large you mean obscenely overweight, Sinclair would field-dress three hundred pounds if you were to gut him like a deer.

"Stay here." I hand Danny's gun to Chrissie, leave the money on the table. "Cover us."

To one side of the truck stands a younger, fitter man about the same girth but taller. He's holding a gun. His skin is ruddy and hairless, and he looks like a side of beef straining the thin material of his sleeveless T-shirt.

"W-w-w-what do I do?" Danny says.

"You're going with me." I push him toward the door. "Safety in numbers."

Outside, I blink at the glare. The key is in my pocket, gun in one hand.

Sinclair watches us descend the rickety stairs, eyes like slits. He doesn't move except to work his jaws around a wad of chewing tobacco in one cheek.

A blowtorch sits on the hood of the truck.

"I didn't know it was your game." I stop a few feet away.

Danny is behind me, out of direct view, whimpering.

"Uppity Czech trash, that's what you are." Sinclair spits a stream of brown tobacco juice into the dust. "Your old man thought he was sumpin' special too."

His accent is pure Brazos bottom drawl, as country as smoked brisket.

"I wouldn't have hit one of your games." I keep the gun pointed down, next to my thigh.

"Give it to me." He holds out a fat hand. "And the money too." He smiles. "You didn't think I was really gonna let you keep all that cash, didya?"

I toss him the key, try to squelch my anger. I think about the Dallas lawyer, my bitchy ex-wife. The son I'm not gonna get to see anymore.

"What the hell is this?" He holds up the key.

I don't reply. My skin gets cold despite the heat.

"Hey, Danny the Dumb-ass." Sinclair peers around my shoulder. "What is this bull crap you're pulling, huh?"

Danny moans but doesn't reply. He leans against me like he's gonna faint.

"That's what you wanted," I say. "The key."

"You're as dumb as Danny." Sinclair shakes his head. "I don't want some dang old key."

I blink, running through options, the adrenaline in my system making my brain mushy.

Danny figures it out, once in a row.

"You want the envelope," he says. "That's what your text said." He pauses. "It's inside."

"You better hope so." Sinclair picks up the blowtorch, points to the trailer. "Let's go."

The envelope is not inside.

Neither is Chrissie or the money.

The door on the shed out back that was closed is open now, the storage space empty.

Sinclair takes my gun and watches us while his bodyguard, the slab of meat who'd been standing by the truck, searches the double-wide. After a few minutes, Slab-O-Meat returns to the living room and shakes his massive head.

"Start talking." Sinclair turns on the blowtorch, and a blue tongue of heat emerges.

"Chrissie." I lick my lips. "She was in on it. She took the cash and the envelope."

"That's funny." He turns up the flame. "Who do you think put me on to you two?"

"Chrissie?" Danny looks at me. "She s-s-screwed us?"

I nod, the fear a physical presence in the pit of my stomach, a lead brick that sits there.

She screwed us and good. She came in late and screamed so there would be no way she could be tied to the robbery. She arranged the hideout and apparently the getaway car hidden in the shed. She told me the key was important, not the envelope itself.

"Where is she?" Sinclair approaches, my gun in one hand, the blowtorch in the other.

"I don't know." I shake my head. "Honestly, have no idea."

"That's too bad." He waves the blowtorch. "Because I *really* need that envelope."

I don't say anything. All I can do is stare at the blue flame. The fire consumes my consciousness to a point that I almost don't react when he tosses me my handgun.

I catch the weapon, look at Sinclair and his guard.

The Slab-O-Meat holds a pistol by his side but is not aiming it at me.

"You're gonna get that envelope back," Sinclair says.

I nod slowly.

"If you don't"—he holds up the torch—"then I'm gonna start on your toes and work my way up."

I look at my gun, afraid it's a trick. The magazine is still there, a round in the chamber.

Then I get it. Sinclair knows I won't do anything. I'm just poor dumb Czech trash that's been given a lifeline, a slim chance for redemption. His power and reach in my world is all-consuming.

I start to shake and sweat uncontrollably.

He smiles at me like I'm a three-legged dog, his face reflecting the utter self-confidence one gets when dealing with lesser life forms, a look of supreme control.

I grip the gun, think about bringing it up.

"That ain't the way this plays." Sinclair shakes his head. "You coulda taken me out a dozen times over the years, but you didn't. You're not gonna grow a set now."

I lower the gun.

"Just in case you don't get the gist of what I'm talking about," he says, "I'll give you a little demonstration on Danny the Dumb-ass."

Danny gasps, runs for the door.

Slab-O-Meat grabs him with one hand, holds out a skinny arm. His other hand brings up the pistol my way. Danny yells, struggles.

"Not like anybody's gonna miss him anyway." Sinclair walks toward my friend, blowtorch at the ready. He pauses, looks my way. "You ain't got a problem with this, do you?"

I hesitate, breath caught in my throat. Then I shake my head and wait for hell to commence.

Two Weeks Later

The darkness is all-consuming, even in the bright light of day. The permanent night that is in the center of my mind never rests. I have a tiredness about me that no sleep will ever cure, not even death.

But I do have a goal, and that's important, according to the guidance counselor at juvie lockup way back when and a self-help book I read one time. The counselor had said, "A goal is a good way to break free from lowered expectations that people place on you."

My goal is Chrissie, and I am as close as fleas on a pound dog to reaching her.

I stand outside the end unit of a motel a block from the beach in Port Aransas, at the north end of Padre Island. Peeling paint, rusty window frames, a couple of old cars and sand in the parking lot. A flickering neon display that reads "Vacancy."

Early November, and there's only one occupied room and barely anybody in town, most places closed since the season ended months ago.

I grip the shotgun and kick in the door.

Sunlight spills into a darkened room that smells like cigarettes, burned metal, and sweat.

Chrissie screams, pulls the sheet up to her neck.

A man in his forties with a week-old beard sits in an easy chair by the desk. He's comatose, mouth slack, eyes rolled back in his head. A bent and blackened spoon is on the desk next to a lighter and a syringe.

"Where's my money?" I cross the room and slam the barrel down on her legs underneath the sheet, aiming for a knee.

She screams and babbles, words unintelligible.

I let her cry.

The guy in the chair doesn't move, doesn't appear to breathe. He is thin, cheeks hollowed. His skinny, needle-scarred arms look like twigs sticking out of a San Antonio Spurs T-shirt.

"Please-don't-hurt-me-please-please." Chrissie shivers even though the room is warm.

"The money," I say. "And the envelope."

She cries harder, shakes her head.

I raise the barrel of the gun.

She holds up a hand. "D-d-don't. Please."

I stop.

She rolls off the bed, naked. Wraps herself in the dirty sheet, pads across the room to a dresser, limping from my blow.

"Don't try anything." I shoulder the gun, aim at her torso.

She shakes her head. Tears stream down her face. From a duffel bag on the dresser, she pulls out the envelope. She crosses the room and hands it to me. It's empty.

"Where's the money?"

"What money?" She wipes her eyes, sniffs. "Look around, willya."

A wallet sits by the bent spoon and the syringe on the desk. I open it. No cash. The ID reads "Joel MacIntosh, Parole Officer."

"He promised me we'd leave Texas," she says. "We were gonna start over in California."

"Where did it all go?" I mentally slap myself as soon as the words leave my mouth.

"Where do you think?" She points to the spoon. "Up his arm. At the dog track. Hell, it just blew away like the damn wind."

I read the outside of the envelope, the name of a bank in Atlanta, a phone number, some other cryptic marks. The information so important to Sinclair.

"Please don't hurt me," she says. "I just want to go home."

I point the muzzle at her stomach, and an anger blacker than the darkness in my mind oozes from my pores.

"Jesus please no." She shakes. The sheet drops, and she makes no move to cover her nakedness.

"We've known each other since we were kids." I tighten my finger around the trigger. "And this is what you do to me?"

"I just wanted out." She crosses her arms, covering her breasts now. "I wanted to go somewhere new."

"You finally got to see the ocean at least." I close one eye, aim at her face.

"I could buy my way back home with the envelope, couldn't I?" she says. "It's all I've got. Please tell me I could."

And then, like a light extinguished, the anger is gone.

"I'm sorry about Danny," she says. "But Sinclair told me he needed to make an example out of somebody, you know, to keep people in line."

"You're not fit to say his name." I sling the shotgun over my shoulder by its strap and pick up the lighter.

"You and me," she says. "We could ransom the envelope to Sinclair. Use the money to start over."

I smile, the decision made. I flick the lighter, hold the flame under the envelope.

"NOOOO." She lunges toward the fire.

I kick her away, hold the envelope up high until the flames singe my fingers and the precious slip of paper is consumed.

"See you around, Chrissie." I let the ashes flutter to the dirty carpet.

Two blocks down is the car I've left parked by the seawall. I leave and walk there, the permanent darkness in my mind lessening just a fraction.

The ocean is cold and gray, a line of storms visible on the southern horizon. The beach is empty except for a couple of people surf-fishing and an old guy with a metal detector. The air smells like seawater. Gulls trill overhead.

Danny the Dumb-ass sits on the hood of the car, watching a tanker steam by in the distance. I sit next to him.

"Did you find her?" he says.

I nod.

"What do we do now?"

"I don't know." I sigh. "Maybe we should go to California."

They say every dog has its day, so I guess every uppity piece of Czech trash has a chance to break free from the burden of lowered expectations.

Sinclair, of course, is dead. Every night in my dreams I picture the surprise on his face as I shot both him and the guard right before they went to work on Danny with the blowtorch.

"Yeah, that's a good idea." Danny smiles. He slides off the hood and gets in the car.

I look at the Texas coast one last time and do the same.

An hour later, we're on the highway by the cutoff.

I ignore the road west and point the car toward our place in this world, the little corner of Central Texas where we'd both been born and would die.

Danny doesn't say anything. Neither do I.

RICHARD LANGE

Baby Killer

FROM *Slake*

PUPPET SHOOTING THAT BABY comes into my head again, like a match flaring in the dark, this time while I'm wiping down the steam tables after the breakfast rush at the hospital.

Julio steps up behind me with a vat of scrambled eggs, and I flinch like he's some kind of monster.

"*Que pasa?*" he asks as he squeezes by me to drop the vat into its slot.

"Nothing, *guapo*. You startled me is all."

I was coming back from the park and saw it all. Someone yelled something stupid from a passing car, Puppet pulled a gun and fired. The bullet missed the car and hit little Antonio instead, two years old, playing on the steps of the apartment building where he lived with his parents. Puppet tossed the gun to one of his homies, Cheeks, and took off running. He shot that baby, and now he's going to get away with it, you watch.

Dr. Wu slides her tray over and asks for pancakes. She looks at me funny through her thick glasses. These days everybody can tell what I'm thinking. My heart is pounding, and my hand is cold when I raise it to my forehead.

"How's your family, Blanca?" Dr. Wu asks.

"Fine, doctor, fine," I say. I straighten up and wipe my face with a towel, give her a big smile. "Angela graduated from Northridge in June and is working at an insurance company, Manuel is still selling cars, and Lorena is staying with me for a while, her and her daughter, Brianna. We're all doing great."

"You're lucky to have your children close by," Dr. Wu says.

"I sure am," I reply.

I walk back into the kitchen. It's so hot in there, you start sweating as soon as the doors swing shut behind you. Josefina is flirting with the cooks again. That girl spends half her shift back here when she should be up front, working the line. She's fresh from Guatemala, barely speaks English, but still she reminds me of myself when I was young, more than my daughters ever did. It's the old-fashioned jokes she tells, the way she blushes when the doctors or security guards talk to her.

"Josefina," I say. "Maple was looking for you. *Andale* if you don't want to get in trouble."

"*Gracias, señora,*" she replies. She grabs a tray of hash browns and pushes through the doors into the cafeteria.

"*Que buena percha,*" says one of the cooks, watching her go.

"Hey, *payaso,*" I say, "is that how you talk about ladies?"

"*Lo siento, Mamá.*"

Lots of the boys who work here call me *Mamá*. Many of them are far from home, and I do my best to teach them a little about how it goes in this country, to show them some kindness.

At twelve I clock out and walk to the bus stop with Irma, a Filipina I've known forever. Me and Manuel Senior went to Vegas with her and her husband once, and when Manuel died she stayed with me for a few days, cooking and cleaning up after the visitors. Now her own Ray isn't doing too good. Diabetes.

"What's this heat?" she says, fanning herself with a newspaper.

"And it's supposed to last another week."

"It makes me so lazy."

Irma and I share the shade from her umbrella. There's a bench under the bus shelter, but a crazy man dressed in rags is sprawled on it, spitting nonsense.

"They're talking about taking off Ray's leg," Irma says.

"Oh, honey," I say.

"Next month, looks like."

"I'll pray for you."

I like Ray. Lots of men won't dance, but he will. Every year at the hospital Christmas party he asks me at least once. "Ready to rock 'n' roll?" he says.

My eyes sting from all the crap in the air. A frazzled pigeon lands and pecks at a smear in the gutter. Another swoops down to join it, then three or four smaller birds. The bus almost hits them when it pulls up. Irma and I get a seat in front. The driver has a fan that blows right on us.

"I heard about the baby that got killed near you yesterday," Irma says.

I'm staring up at a commercial for a new type of mop on the bus's TV, thinking about how to reply. I want to tell Irma what I saw, share the fear and sorrow that have been dogging me, but I can't. I've got to keep it to myself.

"Wasn't that awful?" I say.

"And they haven't caught who did it yet?" Irma asks.

I shake my head. No.

I'm not the only one who knows it was Puppet, but everybody's scared to say because Puppet's in Temple Street, and if you piss off Temple Street, your house gets burned down or your car gets stolen or you get jumped walking to the store. When it comes to the gangs, you take care of yours and let others take care of theirs.

There's no forgiveness for that, for none of us coming forward, but I hope—I think we all hope—that if God really does watch everything, he'll understand and have mercy on us.

Walking home from my stop, I pass where little Antonio was shot. The news is there filming the candles and flowers and stuffed animals laid out on the steps of the building, and there's a poster of the baby too, with "RIP Our Little Angel" written on it. The pretty girl holding the microphone says something about grief-stricken parents as I go by, but she doesn't look like she's been sad a day in her life.

This was a pretty nice block when we first moved onto it. Half apartments, half houses, families mostly. A plumber lived across the street, a fireman, a couple of teachers. The gangs were here too, but they were just little punks back then, and nobody was too afraid of them. One stole Manuel Junior's bike once, and his parents made him bring it back and mow our lawn all summer.

But then the good people started buying newer, bigger houses in the suburbs, and the bad people took over. Dopers and gangsters and thieves. We heard gunshots at night, and police helicopters hovered overhead with their searchlights on. There was graffiti everywhere, even on the tree trunks.

Manuel was thinking about us going somewhere quieter right before he died, and now Manuel Junior is always trying to get me to move out to Lancaster where he and Trina and the kids live. He worries about me being alone. But I'm not going to leave.

This is my little place. Three bedrooms, two bathrooms, a nice, big backyard. It's plain to look at, but all my memories are here. We added the dining room and patio ourselves, we laid the tile, we planted the fruit trees and watched them grow. I stand in the kitchen sometimes, and twenty-five years will fall away like nothing as I think of my babies' kisses, my husband's touch. No, I'm not going to go. "Just bury me out back when I keel over," I tell Manuel Junior.

Brianna is on the couch watching TV when I come in, two fans going and all the windows open. This is how she spends her days now that school's out. She's hardly wearing anything. Hootchie-mama shorts and a tank top I can see her titties through. She's fourteen, and everything Grandma says makes her roll her eyes or giggle into her hand. All of a sudden I'm stupid to her.

"You have to get air conditioning," she whines. "I'm dying."

"It's not that bad," I say. "I'll make some lemonade."

I head into the kitchen.

"Where's your mom?" I ask.

"Shopping," Brianna says without looking away from the TV. Some music and dancing show.

"Oh, yeah? How's she shopping with no money?"

"Why don't you ask *her?*" Brianna snaps.

The two of them have been staying with me ever since Lorena's husband, Charlie, walked out on her a few months ago. Lorena is supposed to be saving money and looking for a job, but all she's doing is partying with old high school friends—most of them divorced now too—and playing around on her computer, sending notes to men she's never met.

I drop my purse on the kitchen table and get a Diet Coke from the refrigerator. The back door is wide open. This gets my attention, because I always keep it locked since we got robbed last time.

"Why's the door like this?" I call into the living room.

There's a short pause, then Brianna says, "Because it's hot in here."

I notice a cigarette smoldering on the back step. And what's that on the grass? A Budweiser can, enough beer to slosh still in it. Somebody's been up to something.

I carry the cigarette and beer can into the living room. Lorena doesn't want me hollering at Brianna anymore, so I keep my cool when I say, "Your boyfriend left something behind."

Brianna makes a face like I'm crazy. "What are you talking about?"

I shake the beer can at her. "Nobody's supposed to be over here unless me or your mom are around."

"Nobody was."

"So this garbage is yours then? You're smoking? Drinking?"

Brianna doesn't answer.

"He barely got away, right?" I say. "You guys heard me coming, and off he went."

"Leave me alone," Brianna says. She buries her face in a pillow.

"I don't care how old you are, I'm calling a babysitter tomorrow," I say. I can't have her disrespecting my house. Disrespecting me.

"Please," Brianna yells. "Just shut up."

I yell back, I can't help it. "Get in your room," I say. "And I don't want to see you again until you can talk right to me."

Brianna runs to the bedroom that she and her mom have been sharing. She slams the door. The house is suddenly quiet, even with the TV on, even with the windows open. The cigarette is still burning, so I stub it in the kitchen sink. The truth is, I'm more afraid for Brianna than mad at her. These young girls fall so deeply in love, they sometimes drown in it.

I change out of my work clothes into a housedress, put on my flip-flops. Out back, I water the garden, then get the sprinkler going on the grass. Rudolfo, my neighbor, is working in the shop behind his house. The screech of his saw rips into the stillness of the afternoon, and I smile when I think of his rough hands and emerald eyes. There's nothing wrong with that. Manuel has been gone for three years.

I make myself a tuna sandwich and one for Brianna, plus the lemonade I promised. She's asleep when I take the snack to the bedroom. Probably faking it, but I'm done fighting for today. I eat in front of the TV, put on one of my cooking shows.

A knock at the front door startles me. I go over and press my eye to the peephole. There on the porch is a fat white man with a sweaty, bald head and a walrus mustache. When I ask who he is, he backs up, looks right at the hole, and says, "Detective Rayburn, LAPD." I should have known, that coat and tie in this heat.

I get a little nervous. No cop ever brought good news. The detective smiles when I open the door.

"Good afternoon," he says. "I'm sorry to bother you, but I'm here about the boy who was killed Sunday, down at 1238?"

His eyes meet mine, and he tries to read me. I keep my face blank. At least I hope I keep it blank.

"Can you believe that?" I say.

"Breaks your heart."

"It sure does."

The detective tugs his mustache and says, "Well, what I'm doing is going door to door and asking if anybody saw something that might help us catch whoever did it. Were you at home when the shooting occurred?"

"I was here," I say, "but I didn't see anything."

"Nothing?" He knows I'm lying. "All that commotion?"

"I heard the sirens afterward, and that's when I came out. Someone told me what happened, and I went right back inside. I don't need to be around that kind of stuff."

The detective nods thoughtfully, but he's looking past me into the house.

"Maybe someone else then," he says. "Someone in your family?"

"Nobody saw anything."

"You're sure?"

Like I'm stupid. Like all he has to do is ask twice.

"I'm sure," I say.

He's disgusted with me, and to tell the truth, I'm disgusted with myself. But I can't get involved, especially not with Lorena and Brianna staying here. A motorcycle drives by with those exhaust pipes that rattle your bones. The detective turns to watch it pass, then reaches into his pocket and hands me a business card with his name and number on it.

"If you hear something, I'd appreciate it if you give me a call," he says. "You can do it confidentially. You don't even have to leave your name."

"I hope you catch him," I say.

"That's up to your neighborhood here. The only way that baby is going to get any justice is if a witness comes forward. Broad daylight, Sunday afternoon. Someone saw something, and they're just as bad as the killer if they don't step up."

Tough talk, but he doesn't live here. No cops do.

He pulls out a handkerchief and mops the sweat off his head as he walks away, turns up the street toward Rudolfo's place.

My heart is racing. I lie on the couch and let the fans blow on me. The ice cream truck drives by, playing its little song, and I close my eyes for a minute. Just for a minute.

A noise. Someone coming in the front door. I sit up lost, then scared. The TV remote is clutched in my fist like I'm going to throw it. I put it down before Lorena sees me. I must have dozed off.

"What's wrong?" she says.

"Where have you been?" I reply, going from startled to irritated in a hot second.

"Out," she says.

Best to leave it there, I can tell from her look. She's my oldest, thirty-five now, and we've been butting heads since she was twelve. If you ask her, I don't know anything about anything. She's raising Brianna differently than I raised her. They're more like friends than mother and daughter. They giggle over boys together, wear each other's clothes. I don't think it's right, but we didn't call each other for six months when I made a crack about it once, so now I bite my tongue.

I have to tell her what happened with Brianna though. I keep my voice calm so she can't accuse me of being hysterical; I stick to the facts, A, B, C, D. The questions she asks, however, and the way she asks them, make it clear that she's looking for a way to get mad at me instead of at her daughter.

"What do you mean the back door was open?"

"She acted guilty? How?"

"Did you actually see a boy?"

It's like talking to a lawyer. I'm all worn out by the time I finish the story and she goes back to the bedroom. Maybe starting dinner will make me feel better. We're having spaghetti. I brown some hamburger, some onions and garlic, add a can of tomato sauce, and set it to simmer so it cooks down nice and slow.

Lorena and Brianna come into the kitchen while I'm chopping lettuce for a salad. They look like they've just stopped laughing about something. I feel myself getting angry. What's there to joke about?

"I'm sorry, Grandma," Brianna says.

She wraps her arms around me, and I give her a quick hug back, not even bothering to put down the knife in my hand.

"That's okay, *mija.*"

"From now on, if she wants to have friends over, she'll ask first," Lorena says.

"And no beer or smoking," I say.

"She knows," Lorena says.

No, she doesn't. She's fourteen years old. She doesn't know a goddamn thing.

Brianna sniffs the sauce bubbling on the stove and wrinkles her nose. "Are there onions in here?" she asks.

"You can pick them out," I say.

She does this walk sometimes, stiff arms swinging, legs straight, toes pointed. Something she learned in ballet. That's how she leaves the kitchen. A second later I hear the TV come on in the living room, too loud.

"So who was he?" I whisper to Lorena.

"A boy from school. He rode the bus all the way over here to see her."

She says this like it's something sweet. I wipe down the counter so I don't have to look at her.

"She's that age," I say. "You've got to keep an eye on her."

"I know," Lorena says. "I was that age once too."

"So was I."

"Yeah, but girls today are smarter than we were."

I move over to the stove, wipe that too. Here we go again.

"Still, you have to set boundaries," I say.

"Like you did with me?"

"That's right."

"And like Grandma did with you?" Lorena says. "'Cause that worked out real good."

We end up here every time. There's no sense even responding.

Lorena got pregnant when she was sixteen and had an abortion. Somehow that makes me a bad mother, but I haven't figured out yet how she means to hurt me when she brings it up. Was I too strict, or not strict enough?

As for myself, the boys went kind of nuts for me when I turned fourteen. I wasn't a tease or anything; they just decided that I was the one to get with. That happens sometimes. I was the oldest girl in my family, the first one to put my parents through all that. My dad would sit on the porch and glare at the guys who drove past hoping to catch me outside, and my mom walked me to school every day. I got a little leeway after my *quinceañera,* but not much.

Manuel was five years older than me. I met him at a party at my cousin's when I was fifteen. He'd only been in the U.S. for a few years, and his idea of dressing up was still boots and a cowboy hat. Not my type at all. I was into lowriders, *pendejos* with hot cars. But Manuel was so sweet to me, and polite in a way the East L.A. boys weren't. He bought me flowers, called twice a day. And after my parents met him, forget it. He went to mass, he could rebuild the engine in any car, and he was already working at the brewery, making real money: they practically handed me over to him right there.

Our plan was that we'd marry when I graduated, but I ended up pregnant at the end of my junior year. Everything got moved up then, and I never went back to school. My parents were upset, but they couldn't say much because the same thing had happened to them. It all worked out fine though. Manuel was a good husband, our kids were healthy, and we had a nice life together. Sometimes you get lucky.

I do the dishes after dinner, then join the girls in the living room. The TV is going, but nobody's paying attention. Lorena is on her laptop and Brianna is texting on her phone. They don't look up from punching buttons when I sit in my recliner. I watch a woman try to win a million dollars. The audience groans when she gives the wrong answer.

I can't sit still. My brain won't slow down, thinking about Antonio and Puppet, thinking about Lorena and Brianna, so I decide to make my rounds a little early. I can't get to sleep if I haven't

checked the lock on the garage door, latched the gate, and watered
my flowers. Manuel called it "walking the perimeter."

"Sarge is walking the perimeter," he'd say.

The heat has broken when I step out into the front yard. The
sun is low in the sky, and little birds chase each other from palm
tree to palm tree, twittering excitedly. Usually you can't hear them
over the kids playing, but since the shooting, everybody is keeping
their children inside.

I drag the hose over to the roses growing next to the chainlink
fence that separates the yard from the sidewalk. They're blooming
like mad in this heat. The white ones, the yellow, the red. I lay the
hose at the base of the bushes and turn the water on low, so the
roots get a good soaking.

Rudolfo is still at work in his shop. His saw whines, and then
comes the *bang bang bang* of a hammer. I haven't been over to see
him in a while. Maybe I'll take him some spaghetti.

I wash my face and put on a little makeup. Lipstick, eyeliner,
nothing fancy. Perfume. I change out of my housedress into jeans
and a nice top. My stomach does a flip as I'm dressing. I guess you
could say I've got a thing for Rudolfo, but I think he likes me too,
the way he smiles. And for my birthday last year he gave me a jewelry box that he made. Back in the kitchen I dig out some good
Tupperware to carry the spaghetti in.

Rudolfo's dog, Oso, a big shaggy mutt, barks as I come down the
driveway.

"*Cállate, hombre,*" Rudolfo says.

I walk to the door of the shop and stand there silently, watching
Rudolfo sand a rough board smooth. He makes furniture—simple, sturdy tables, chairs, and wardrobes—and sells it to rich people from Pasadena and Beverly Hills. The furniture is nice, but aw-
fully plain. I'd think a rich woman would want something fancier
than a table that looks like it belongs in a farmhouse.

"Knock, knock," I finally say.

Rudolfo grins when he looks up and sees me standing there.

"*Hola,* Blanca."

I move into the doorway but still don't step through. Some men
are funny. You're intruding if you're not invited.

"Come in, come in," Rudolfo says. He takes off his glasses and
cleans them with a red bandanna. He's from El Salvador, and so

handsome with that Indian nose and his silver hair combed straight back. "Sorry for sawing so late, but I'm finishing an order," he says. "That was the last little piece."

"I just came by to bring you some spaghetti," I say. "I made too much again."

"Oh, hey, *gracias. Pasale.*"

He motions for me to enter and wipes the sawdust off a stool with his bandanna. I sit and look around the shop. It's so organized, the lumber stacked neatly by size, the tools in their special places. This used to crack Manuel up. He called Rudolfo "the Librarian." The two of them got along fine but were never really friends. Too busy, I guess, both working all the time.

Rudolfo takes the spaghetti from me and says, "Did that cop stop by your house today?"

"The bald one? Yeah," I reply.

"He told me he's sure someone saw who killed that baby."

Someone who's just as bad as the killer. I know. I run my finger over the blade of a saw sitting on the workbench. If this is what he wants to talk about, I'm going to leave.

"Are things getting crazier?" Rudolfo continues. "Or does it just seem that way?"

"I ask myself that all the time," I reply.

"I'm starting to think more like *mi abuelo* every day," he says. "You know what he'd say about what happened to that baby? 'Bring me the rope, and I'll hang the bastard who did it myself.'"

I stand and brush off my pants.

"Enjoy your spaghetti," I say. "I've got to get back."

"So soon?"

"I wake up at two-thirty to be at the hospital by four."

"Let me walk you out."

I wave away the offer. "No, no, finish what you were doing."

Puppet and his homies are hanging on the corner when I get out to the street. Puppet is leaning on a car that's blasting music, that *boom boom fuck fuck* crap. He is wearing a white T-shirt, baggy black shorts that hang past his knees, white socks pulled all the way up, and a pair of corduroy house shoes. The same stuff *vatos* have been wearing since I was a kid. His head is shaved, and there's a tattoo on the side of it, Temple Street.

I knew his mom before she went to prison; I even baby-sat him a couple times when he was young. He went bad at ten or eleven, though, stopped listening to the grandma who was raising him and started running with thugs. The boys around here slip away like that again and again. He stares at me now, like, "What do you have to say?" Like he's reminding me to be scared of him

"Baby killer," I should shout back. "You ain't shit." I should have shut the door in that detective's face too. I've got to be smarter from now on.

I haven't been sleeping very well. It's the heat, sure, but I've also been dreaming of little Antonio. He comes tonight as an angel, floating above my bed, up near the ceiling. He makes his own light, a golden glow that shows everything for what it is. But I don't want to see. I swat at him once, twice, knock him to the floor. His light flickers, and the darkness comes rushing back.

My pillow is soaked with sweat when I wake up. It's guilt that gives you dreams like that. Prisoners go crazy, rattle the doors of their cells and scream out confessions. Anything, anything to get some peace. I look at the clock, and it's past midnight. The sound of a train whistle drifts over from the tracks downtown. I have to be up in two hours.

I pull on my robe to go into the kitchen for a glass of milk. Lorena is snoring quietly, and I close her door as I pass by. Then there's another sound. Whispers. Coming from the living room. The girls left something unlocked, and now we're being robbed. That's my first thought, and it stops the blood in my veins. But then there's a familiar giggle, and I peek around the corner to see Brianna standing in front of a window, her arms reaching through the bars to touch someone—it's too dark to say who—out in the yard.

I step into the room and snap on the light. Brianna turns, startled, and the shadow outside disappears. I hurry to the front door, open it, but there's no one out there now except a bum pushing a grocery cart filled with cans and newspapers down the middle of the street. Brianna is in tears when I go back inside, and I'm shaking all over, I'm so angry.

"So that talk today was for nothing?" I say.

My yelling wakes Lorena, and she finds me standing over Brianna, who is cowering on the couch.

"Let her up," she says.

She won't listen as I try to explain what happened, how frightened I was when I heard those voices in the dark. She just grabs Brianna and drags her back to their room.

I wind up drinking coffee at the kitchen table until it is time to get ready for work. Lorena comes out as I'm about to leave for the bus. She said that the boy from Brianna's school came to see her again, and she was right in the middle of telling him to go away when I came in. She says we're going to forget the whole incident, let it lie.

"That's the best way to handle it," she says. "I want to show that I trust her."

"Okay," I say.

"Just treat her like normal."

"I will."

"She's a good girl, Mom."

"I know."

They've beaten the fire out of me. If all they want is a cook and a cleaning lady, fine.

My stomach hurts during the ride to work the next morning, and I feel feverish too. Resting my forehead against the cool glass of the window, I take deep breaths and tell myself it's nothing, just too much coffee. It's still dark outside, the streets empty, the stores locked tight. Like everyone gave up and ran away and I'm the last to know. I smell smoke when I get off at the hospital. Sirens shriek in the distance.

Irma is fixing her hair in the locker room.

"You don't look so good," she says.

"Maybe it's something I ate," I reply.

She gives me a Pepto Bismol tablet from her purse, and we tie our aprons and walk to the kitchen. One of the boys has cornered a mouse in there, back by the pantry, and pinned it to the floor with a broom. Everybody moves in close, chattering excitedly.

"Step on it," somebody says.

"Drown it," someone else suggests.

"No! No mate el pobrecito!" Josefina wails, trembling fingers raised to her lips. Don't kill the poor little thing! She's about to burst into tears.

The boy with the broom glances at her, then tells one of the dishwashers to bring a bucket. He and dishwasher turn the bucket upside down and manage to trap the mouse beneath it. They slide a scrap of cardboard across the opening and flip the bucket over. The mouse cowers in the bottom, shitting all over itself. The boys free it on the construction site next door, and we get to work.

I do okay until about eight, until the room starts spinning and I almost pass out in the middle of serving Dr. Alvarez his oatmeal. My stomach cramps, my mouth fills with spit, and I whisper to Irma to take my place on the line before I run to the bathroom and throw up.

Maple, our supervisor, is waiting when I return to the cafeteria. She's a twitchy black lady with a bad temper.

"Go home," she says.

"I'm okay," I reply. "I feel better."

"You hang around, you're just going to infect everybody else. Go home."

It's frustrating. I've only called in sick three times in my twenty-seven years here. Maple won't budge though. I take off my gloves and apron, get my purse from my locker.

My stomach bucks again at the bus stop, and I vomit into the gutter. A bunch of kids driving by honk their horn and laugh at me. The ride home takes forever. The traffic signals are messed up for blocks, blinking red, and the skyscrapers shimmer in the heat like I'm dreaming them.

I stop at the store for bread and milk when I get off the bus. Not the Smart & Final, but the little *tienda* on the corner. The Sanchezes owned it forever, but now it's Koreans. They're nice enough. The old lady at the register always smiles and says *gracias* when she gives me my change. Her son is out front painting over fresh graffiti. Temple Street tags the place every night, and he cleans it up every day.

A girl carrying a baby blocks my path. She holds out her hand and asks me in Spanish for money, her voice a raspy whisper. The baby is sick, she says, needs medicine. She's not much older than Brianna and won't look me in the eye.

"Whatever you can spare," she says. "Please."

"Where do you live?" I ask.

She glances nervously over her shoulder. A boy a little older than her pokes his head out from behind a tree, watching us. Maria, from two blocks over, told me the other day how a girl with a baby came to her door, asking for money. The girl said she was going to faint, so Maria let her inside to rest on the couch while she went to the bathroom to get some Huggies her daughter had left behind. When she came back, the girl was gone, and so was Maria's purse.

My chest feels like a bird is loose inside it.

"I don't have anything," I say. "I'm sorry."

"My baby is going to die," the girl says. "Please, a dollar. Two."

I push past her and hurry away. When I reach the corner, I look back and see her and the boy staring at me with hard faces.

The sidewalk on my street has buckled from all the tree roots pushing up underneath it. The slabs tilt at odd angles, and I go over them faster than I should while carrying groceries. If I'm not careful, I'm going to fall and break my neck. I'm going to get exactly what I deserve.

Brianna's eyes open wide when I step through the door. A boy is lying on top of her on the couch. Puppet.

"Get away from her," I yell, and I mean it to be a roar, but it comes out like an old woman's dying gasp.

Standing quickly, he pulls up his pants and grabs his shirt off the floor. Brianna yanks a blanket over her naked body. As he walks out, Puppet sneers at me. He's so close I can feel heat coming off him. I slam the door and twist the deadbolt.

It was one month after my fifteenth birthday, and all everybody was talking about was a party some kid was throwing at his house while his parents were in Mexico for a funeral. Carmen and Cindy said, "You've got to go. We'll sneak out together." Stupid stuff, teenagers being teenagers. "You tell your mom that you're staying at my house, and I'll tell mine I'm staying at yours." We were actually shocked that it worked, to find ourselves out on the streets on a Saturday night.

The crowd at the party was a little older than we were, a little rougher. Lots of gangbangers and their girlfriends, kids who didn't go to our school. Carmen and Cindy were meeting boys there and soon disappeared, leaving me standing by myself in the kitchen.

One of the *vatos* came up and started talking to me. He said his name was Smiley and that he was in White Fence, the gang in that neighborhood. Boys were always claiming to be down with this clique or that, and most of them were full of it. Smiley seemed like he was full of it. He was so tiny and so cute.

Things move fast when you're that age, when you're drinking rum and you've never drunk rum before, when you're smoking weed and you've never smoked weed before. Pretty soon we were kissing right there in front of everybody, me sitting on the counter, Smiley standing between my legs. I was so high I got his tongue mixed up with mine. Someone laughed, and it bounced around inside my head like a rubber ball.

Following Smiley into the bedroom was my mistake. I should have said no. Lying down on the mattress, letting him peel off my T-shirt, letting him put his hand inside my pants—I take the blame for all that too. But everything else is on him and the others. Forever, like a brand. I was barely fifteen years old, for God's sake. I was drunk. I was stupid.

"Stop," I hissed, but Smiley kept going.

I tried to sit up, and he forced me back down. He put his hand on my throat and squeezed.

"Just fucking relax," he said.

I let myself go limp. I gave in because I thought he'd kill me if I didn't. He seemed that crazy, choking me, pulling my hair. Two of his homies came in while he was going at it. I hoped for half a second that they were there to save me. Instead, when Smiley was finished, they did their thing too, took turns grinding away on a scared little girl, murdering some part of her that she mourns to this day.

Afterward they made me wash my face and get dressed. I wasn't even crying anymore. I was numb, in shock.

"White Fence," Smiley said right before he walked back out into the party, into the music and laughter. "Don't you forget." A warning pure and simple. An ugly threat.

I never told my friends what happened, never told my family, never told my husband. What could they possibly have said or done that would've helped? Nothing. Not a goddamn thing. The sooner you learn it, the better: some loads you carry on your own.

They make a big show of it when they come for Puppet. Must be six cop cars, a helicopter, TV cameras. That detective wasn't lying: all it took was an anonymous phone call. "I saw who killed the baby."

One minute Puppet is preening on the corner with his homies, acting like he owns the street; the next he's face-down on the hot asphalt, hands cuffed tight behind his back.

I run outside as soon as I hear the commotion. I want to see. Lorena and Brianna come too, whispering, "Oh my God, what's happening?"

"It's the bastard who shot little Antonio," says an old man carrying a bottle in a bag.

We stand at the fence and watch with the rest of the neighborhood as they lift Puppet off the ground and slam him against a police car. Then, suddenly, Brianna is crying. "No," she moans and opens the gate like she's going to run to him. "No." Lorena grabs her arm and yanks her back into the yard.

"José," Brianna yells. His real name.

He can't hear her, though, not with all the shouting and sirens and the *chop chop chop* of the helicopter circling overhead. And I'm glad. He doesn't deserve her tears, her reckless love. Instead, I hope the last thing he sees before they drive him off is my satisfied smile and the hatred in my eyes, and I hope it burns him like fire, night and day, for as long as he fouls this earth.

It's Friday evening, and what a week. The freezer at work broke down, Maple changed the rules on vacation time, and one of the boys cut his finger to the bone, chopping onions. There was some good news too: looks like Puppet isn't going to be back. As soon as they picked him up, his boy Cheeks flipped on him and told the cops everything. A few punks still hang out on the corner and stare the neighborhood down, but none of them know that it's me who took out their homie.

I fall asleep on the couch when I get home and don't wake up until a few hours later, but that's okay, because I'm off tomorrow, so I can go to bed whenever I want tonight and sleep in. I couldn't do that when Lorena and Brianna were here. They'd be banging around in the kitchen or blasting the TV every time I tried to rest. Or I'd be cooking for them or doing their laundry.

I love them, but I wasn't sad to see them go when they moved out last week. They're in Alhambra now, living with a fireman Lorena met on the computer. He's really great, she says, with a big house, a swimming pool, and an RV. And so good with Brianna. I was thinking she should ask him about his ex-wife, find out why she's not around anymore, but I kept it to myself.

When I get up, I finish watering the garden and pick a bunch of tomatoes. The sun has just set, leaving the sky a pretty blue, but it's going to be one of those nights when it doesn't cool down until past midnight. The kids used to sleep out in the yard when it was like this. Manuel would cut up a watermelon he'd kept on ice all day, and the juice would run down their faces and drip onto the grass.

I sit on the back porch and watch the stars come out. There's a little moon up there too, a little silver smile in the sky. Oso barks next door, and another dog answers. Music floats over from Rudolfo's shop, old ranchero stuff, and I think, You know, I'll never eat all these tomatoes myself.

Rudolfo looks up from the newspaper he's reading as I come down the driveway, trailed by Oso.

"Blanca," he says. *"Buenas noches."*

He reaches out and turns the radio down a bit. He's drinking a beer, and a cigar smolders in an ashtray on the workbench. Picking up the ashtray, he moves to carry it outside.

"Go ahead and smoke," I say.

"You're sure?"

"No problem."

He lived next door for years before I found out that he had a wife and son back in El Salvador. He got in trouble with the government there and had to leave. The plan was that he'd go to the U.S. and get settled, then his family would join him. But a few years later, when it was time, his wife decided that she was happy where she was and refused to move north. I remember he told this like it had happened to another person, but I could see in his eyes how it hurt him.

"I brought you some tomatoes," I say, setting the bag on the workbench. "I've got them coming out of my ears."

"You want a beer?" he asks.

"Sure," I say, and lower myself onto a stool.

He reaches into a cooler and lifts out a Tecate, uses his bandanna to wipe the can dry.

"I'm sorry I don't have any lime," he says as he passes it to me.

"It's good like this," I reply.

He lifts his can and says, *"Salud."*

I take a sip, and boy, does it go down easy. Oso presses his cold nose against my leg and makes me jump. I'm wearing a new skirt. A new blouse too.

"Another wild Friday night, huh?" I say.

Rudolfo laughs. He runs his fingers slowly through his hair and shakes his head. "I might have a few more in me," he says. "But I'm saving them up for when I really need them."

He asks about Lorena and Brianna, how they're doing at the new place, and wonders if I'm lonely now that they're gone. I admit that I'm not.

"You get used to being by yourself," I say.

"Yeah, but that's not the same as enjoying it," he replies, something sad in his voice.

I like the way we talk to each other. It feels honest. Things were different with Manuel. One of us always had to win. Husbands and wives do that, worry more about being right than being truthful. What goes on between Rudolfo and me is what I always imagined flirting would be like. It's kind of a game. We hint at what's inside us, each hoping the other picks up on the clues.

I didn't learn to flirt when I was young. I didn't have time. One year after that party I was engaged to Manuel, and the last thing I wanted him to know were my secrets.

A moth flutters against the bare light bulb suspended above us, its wings tapping urgent messages on the thin glass. Rudolfo tells me about something funny that happened to him at Home Depot, how this guy swiped his shopping cart. It's his story I'm laughing at when he finishes, but I'm also just happy to be here with this handsome man, drinking this beer, listening to this music. It feels like there are bubbles in my blood.

A song my mom used to play comes on the radio.

"Hey," I say. "Let's dance."

"I don't know, it's been years," Rudolfo replies.

"Come on." I stand and wiggle my hips, reach out for him.

He puts down his beer and wraps his arms around me. I pull him close and whisper the lyrics to the song in his ear as we sway so smoothly together. You forget what that feels like. It seems impossible, but you do.

"Blanca," he says.

"Mmmmmm?" I reply.

"I'm seeing a lady in Pacoima."

"Shhh," I say.

"I've been seeing her for years."

"Shhh."

I lay my head on his chest, listen to his heart. Sawdust and smoke swirl around us. *Qué bonita amor,* goes the song, *qué bonita cielo, qué bonita luna, qué bonita sol.* God wants to see me cry. He must have his reasons. But for now, Lord, please, give me just one more minute. One more minute of this.

JOE R. LANSDALE

The Stars Are Falling

FROM *Stories*

BEFORE DEEL ARROWSMITH came back from the dead, he was crossing a field by late moonlight in search of his home. His surroundings were familiar, but at the same time different. It was as if he had left as a child and returned as an adult to examine old property only to find the tree swing gone, the apple tree cut down, the grass grown high, and an outhouse erected over the mound where his best dog was buried.

As he crossed, the dropping moon turned thin, like cheap candy licked too long, and the sun bled through the trees. There were spots of frost on the drooping green grass and on the taller weeds, yellow as ripe corn. In his mind's eye he saw not the East Texas field before him or the dark rows of oaks and pines beyond it, or even the clay path that twisted across the field toward the trees like a ribbon of blood.

He saw a field in France where there was a long, deep trench, and in the trench were bloodied bodies, some of them missing limbs and with bits of brains scattered about like spilled oatmeal. The air filled with the stinging stench of rotting meat and wafting gun smoke, the residue of poison gas, and the buzz of flies. The back of his throat tasted of burning copper. His stomach was a knot. The trees were like the shadowy shades of soldiers charging toward him, and for a moment, he thought to meet their charge, even though he no longer carried a gun.

He closed his eyes, breathed deeply, shook his head. When he opened them the stench had passed and his nostrils filled with the nip of early morning. The last of the moon faded like a melting snowflake. Puffy white clouds sailed along the heavens and light tripped across the tops of the trees, fell between them, made shadows run low along the trunks and across the ground. The sky turned light blue and the frost dried off the drooping grass and it sprang to attention. Birds began to sing. Grasshoppers began to jump.

He continued down the path that crossed the field and split the trees. As he went, he tried to remember exactly where his house was and how it looked and how it smelled, and most important, how he felt when he was inside it. He tried to remember his wife and how she looked and how he felt when he was inside her, and all he could find in the back of his mind was a cipher of a woman younger than he was in a long, colorless dress in a house with three rooms. He couldn't even remember her nakedness, the shape of her breasts and the length of her legs. It was as if they had met only once, and in passing.

When he came through the trees and out on the other side, the field was there as it should be, and it was full of bright blue and yellow flowers. Once it had been filled with tall corn and green bursts of beans and peas. It hadn't been plowed now in years, most likely since he left. He followed the trail and trudged toward his house. It stood where he had left it. It had not improved with age. The chimney was black at the top and the unpainted lumber was stripping like shedding snakeskin. He had cut the trees and split them and made the lumber for the house, and like everything else he had seen since he had returned, it was smaller than he remembered. Behind it was the smokehouse he had made of logs, and far out to the left was the outhouse he had built. He had read many a magazine there while having his morning constitutional.

Out front, near the well, which had been built up with stones and now had a roof over it supported on four stout poles, was a young boy. He knew immediately it was his son. The boy was probably eight. He had been four years old when Deel had left to fight in the Great War, sailed across the vast dark ocean. The boy had a bucket in his hand, held by the handle. He set it down and raced toward the house, yelling something Deel couldn't define.

A moment later she came out of the house and his memory filled up. He kept walking, and the closer he came to her, standing framed in the doorway, the tighter his heart felt. She was blond and tall and lean and dressed in a light-colored dress on which were printed flowers much duller than those in the field. But her face was brighter than the sun, and he knew now how she looked naked and in bed, and all that had been lost came back to him, and he knew he was home again.

When he was ten feet away the boy, frightened, grabbed his mother and held her, and she said, "Deel, is that you?"

He stopped and stood, and said nothing. He just looked at her, drinking her in like a cool beer. Finally he said, "Worn and tired, but me."

"I thought . . ."

"I didn't write 'cause I can't."

"I know . . . but . . ."

"I'm back, Mary Lou."

They sat stiffly at the kitchen table. Deel had a plate in front of him and he had eaten the beans that had been on it. The front door was open and they could see out and past the well and into the flower-covered field. The window across the way was open too, and there was a light breeze ruffling the edges of the pulled-back curtains framing it. Deel had the sensation he'd had before when crossing the field and passing through the trees, and when he had first seen the outside of the house. And now, inside, the roof felt too low and the room was too small and the walls were too close. It was all too small.

But there was Mary Lou. She sat across the table from him. Her face was clean of lines and her shoulders were as narrow as the boy's. Her eyes were bright, like the blue flowers in the field.

The boy, Winston, was to his left, but he had pulled his chair close to his mother. The boy studied him carefully, and in turn Deel studied the boy. Deel could see Mary Lou in him, and nothing of himself.

"Have I changed that much?" Deel said, in response to the way they were looking at him. Both of them had their hands in their laps, as if he might leap across the table at any moment and bite them.

"You're very thin," Mary Lou said.

"I was too heavy when I left. I'm too skinny now. Soon I hope to be just right." He tried to smile, but the smile dripped off. He took a deep breath. "So, how you been?"

"Been?"

"Yeah. You know. How you been?"

"Oh. Fine," she said. "Good. I been good."

"The boy?"

"He's fine."

"Does he talk?"

"Sure he talks. Say hello to your daddy, Winston."

The boy didn't speak.

"Say hello," his mother said.

The boy didn't respond.

"That's all right," Deel said. "It's been a while. He doesn't remember me. It's only natural."

"You joined up through Canada?"

"Like I said I would."

"I couldn't be sure," she said.

"I know. I got in with the Americans, a year or so back. It didn't matter who I was with. It was bad."

"I see," she said, but Deel could tell she didn't see at all. And he didn't blame her. He had been caught up in the enthusiasm of war and adventure, gone up to Canada and got in on it, left his family in the lurch, thinking life was passing him by and he was missing out. Life had been right here and he hadn't even recognized it.

Mary Lou stood up and shuffled around the table and heaped fresh beans onto his plate and went to the oven and brought back cornbread and put it next to the beans. He watched her every move. Her hair was a little sweaty on her forehead and it clung there, like wet hay.

"How old are you now?" he asked her.

"How old?" she said, returning to her spot at the table. "Deel, you know how old I am. I'm twenty-eight, older than when you left."

"I'm ashamed to say it, but I've forgotten your birthday. I've forgotten his. I don't hardly know how old I am."

She told him the dates of their births.

"I'll be," he said. "I don't remember any of that."

"I . . . I thought you were dead."

She had said it several times since he had come home. He said, "I'm still not dead, Mary Lou. I'm in the flesh."

"You are. You certainly are."

She didn't eat what was on her plate. She just sat there looking at it, as if it might transform.

Deel said, "Who fixed the well, built the roof over it?"

"Tom Smites," she said.

"Tom? He's a kid."

"Not anymore," she said. "He was eighteen when you left. He wasn't any kid then, not really."

"I reckon not," Deel said.

After dinner, she gave him his pipe the way she used to, and he found a cane rocker that he didn't remember being there before, took it outside and sat and looked toward the trees and smoked his pipe and rocked.

He was thinking of then and he was thinking of now and he was thinking of later, when it would be nighttime and he would go to bed, and he wasn't certain how to approach the matter. She was his wife, but he hadn't been with her for years, and now he was home, and he wanted it to be like before, but he didn't really remember how it was before. He knew how to do what he wanted to do, but he didn't know how to make it love. He feared she would feel that he was like a mangy cat that had come in through the window to lie there and expected petting.

He sat and smoked and thought and rocked.

The boy came out of the house and stood to the side and watched him.

The boy had the gold hair of his mother and he was built sturdy for a boy so young. He had a bit of a birthmark in front of his right ear, on the jawline, like a little strawberry. Deel didn't remember that. The boy had been a baby, of course, but he didn't remember that at all. Then again, he couldn't remember a lot of things, except for the things he didn't want to remember. Those things he remembered. And Mary Lou's skin. That he remembered. How soft it was to the touch, like butter.

"Do you remember me, boy?" Deel asked.

"No."

"Not at all?"

"No."

"'Course not. You were very young. Has your mother told you about me?"

"Not really."

"Nothing."

"She said you got killed in the war."

"I see . . . Well, I didn't."

Deel turned and looked back through the open door. He could see Mary Lou at the washbasin pouring water into the wash pan, water she had heated on the stove. It steamed as she poured. He thought then he should have brought wood for her to make the fire. He should have helped make the fire and heat the water. But being close to her made him nervous. The boy made him nervous.

"You going to school?" he asked the boy.

"School burned down. Tom teaches me some readin' and writin' and cipherin'. He went eight years to school."

"You ever go fishin'?"

"Just with Tom. He takes me fishin' and huntin' now and then."

"He ever show you how to make a bow and arrow?"

"No."

"No, sir," Deel said. "You say, no, sir."

"What's that?"

"Say yes, sir or no, sir. Not yes and no. It's rude."

The boy dipped his head and moved a foot along the ground, piling up dirt.

"I ain't gettin' on you none," Deel said. "I'm just tellin' you that's how it's done. That's how I do if it's someone older than me. I say no, sir and yes, sir. Understand, son?"

The boy nodded.

"And what do you say?"

"Yes, sir."

"Good. Manners are important. You got to have manners. A boy can't go through life without manners. You can read and write some, and you got to cipher to protect your money. But you got to have manners too."

"Yes, sir."

"There you go . . . About that bow and arrow. He never taught you that, huh?"

"No, sir."

"Well, that will be our plan. I'll show you how to do it. An old Cherokee taught me how. It ain't as easy as it might sound, not to make a good one. And then to be good enough to hit somethin' with it, that's a whole nuther story."

"Why would you do all that when you got a gun?"

"I guess you wouldn't need to. It's just fun, and huntin' with one is real sportin', compared to a gun. And right now, I ain't all that fond of guns."

"I like guns."

"Nothin' wrong with that. But a gun don't like you, and it don't love you back. Never give too much attention or affection to somethin' that can't return it."

"Yes, sir."

The boy, of course, had no idea what he was talking about. Deel was uncertain he knew himself what he was talking about. He turned and looked back through the door. Mary Lou was at the pan, washing the dishes; when she scrubbed, her ass shook a little, and in that moment, Deel felt, for the first time, like a man alive.

That night the bed seemed small. He lay on his back with his hands crossed across his lower stomach, wearing his faded red union suit, which had been ragged when he left, and had in his absence been attacked by moths. It was ready to come apart. The window next to the bed was open and the breeze that came through was cool. Mary Lou lay beside him. She wore a long white nightgown that had been patched with a variety of colored cloth patches. Her hair was undone and it was long. It had been long when he left. He wondered how often she had cut it, and how much time it had taken each time to grow back.

"I reckon it's been a while," he said.

"That's all right," she said.

"I'm not sayin' I can't, or I won't, just sayin' I don't know I'm ready."

"It's okay."

"You been lonely?"

"I have Winston."

"He's grown a lot. He must be company."

"He is."

"He looks some like you."

"Some."

Deel stretched out his hand without looking at her and laid it across her stomach. "You're still like a girl," he said. "Had a child, and you're still like a girl . . . You know why I asked how old you was?"

"'Cause you didn't remember."

"Well, yeah, there was that. But on account of you don't look none different at all."

"I got a mirror. It ain't much of one, but it don't make me look younger."

"You look just the same."

"Right now, any woman might look good to you." After she said it, she caught herself. "I didn't mean it that way. I just meant you been gone a long time . . . In Europe, they got pretty women, I hear."

"Some are, some ain't. Ain't none of them pretty as you."

"You ever . . . you know?"

"What?"

"You know . . . While you was over there."

"Oh . . . Reckon I did. Couple of times. I didn't know for sure I was comin' home. There wasn't nothin' to it. I didn't mean nothin' by it. It was like filling a hungry belly, nothin' more."

She was quiet for a long time. Then she said, "It's okay."

He thought to ask her a similar question, but couldn't. He eased over to her. She remained still. She was as stiff as a corpse. He knew. He had been forced at times to lie down among them. Once, moving through a town in France with his fellow soldiers, he had come upon a woman lying dead between two trees. There wasn't a wound on her. She was young. Dark-haired. She looked as if she had laid down for a nap. He reached down and touched her. She was still warm.

One of his comrades, a soldier, had suggested they all take turns mounting her before she got cold. It was a joke, but Deel had pointed his rifle at him and run him off. Later, in the trenches he had been side by side with the same man, a fellow from Wisconsin, who like him had joined the Great War by means of Canada. They had made their peace, and the Wisconsin fellow told him it was a poor joke he'd made, and not to hold it against him, and Deel said it was all right, and then they took positions next to each other and talked a bit about home and waited for the war to come. During the battle, wearing gas masks and firing rifles, the fellow from Wisconsin had caught a round and it had knocked him down. A moment later the battle had ceased, at least for the moment.

Deel bent over him, lifted his mask, and then the man's head. The man said, "My mama won't never see me again."

"You're gonna be okay," Deel said, but saw that half the man's head was missing. How in hell was he talking? Why wasn't he dead? His brain was leaking out.

"I got a letter inside my shirt. Tell Mama I love her . . . Oh, my god, look there. The stars are falling."

Deel, responding to the distant gaze of his downed companion, turned and looked up. The stars were bright and stuck in place. There was an explosion of cannon fire and the ground shook and the sky lit up bright red; the redness clung to the air like a veil. When Deel looked back at the fellow, the man's eyes were still open, but he was gone.

Deel reached inside the man's jacket and found the letter. He realized then that the man had also taken a round in the chest, because the letter was dark with blood. Deel tried to unfold it, but it was so damp with gore it fell apart. There was nothing to deliver to anyone. Deel couldn't even remember the man's name. It had gone in one ear and out the other. And now he was gone, his last words being, "The stars are falling."

While he was holding the boy's head, an officer came walking down the trench holding a pistol. His face was darkened with gunpowder and his eyes were bright in the night and he looked at Deel, said, "There's got to be some purpose to all of it, son. Some purpose," and then he walked on down the line.

Deel thought of that night and that death, and then he thought of the dead woman again. He wondered what had happened to her body. They had had to leave her there, between the two trees. Had someone buried her? Had she rotted there? Had the ants and the elements taken her away? He had dreams of lying down beside her, there in the field. Just lying there, drifting away with her into the void.

Deel felt now as if he were lying beside that dead woman, blond instead of dark-haired, but no more alive than the woman between the trees.

"Maybe we ought to just sleep tonight," Mary Lou said, startling him. "We can let things take their course. It ain't nothin' to make nothin' out of."

He moved his hand away from her. He said, "That'll be all right. Of course."

She rolled on her side, away from him. He lay on top of the covers with his hands against his lower belly and looked at the log rafters.

A couple of days and nights went by without her warming to him, but he found sleeping with her to be the best part of his life. He liked her sweet smell and he liked to listen to her breathe. When she was deep asleep, he would turn slightly, and carefully, and rise up on one elbow and look at her shape in the dark. His homecoming had not been what he had hoped for or expected, but in those moments when he looked at her in the dark, he was certain it was better than what had gone before for nearly four horrible years.

The next few days led to him taking the boy into the woods and finding the right wood for a bow. He chopped down a bois d'arc tree and showed the boy how to trim it with an ax, how to cut the wood out of it for a bow, how to cure it with a fire that was mostly smoke. They spent a long time at it, but if the boy enjoyed what he was learning, he never let on. He kept his feelings close to the heart and talked less than his mother. The boy always seemed some yards away, even when standing right next to him.

Deel built the bow for the boy and strung it with strong cord and showed him how to find the right wood for arrows and how to collect feathers from a bird's nest and how to feather the shafts. It took almost a week to make the bow, and another week to dry it and to make the arrows. The rest of the time Deel looked out at what had once been a plowed field and was now twenty-five acres of flowers with a few little trees beginning to grow, twisting up among the flowers. He tried to imagine the field covered in corn.

Deel used an ax to clear the new trees, and that afternoon, at the dinner table, he asked Mary Lou what had happened to the mule.

"Died," Mary Lou said. "She was old when you left, and she just got older. We ate it when it died."

"Waste not, want not," Deel said.

"Way we saw it," she said.

"You ain't been farmin', how'd you make it?"

"Tom brought us some goods now and then, fish he caught, vegetables from his place. A squirrel or two. We raised a hog and smoked the meat, had our own garden."

"How are Tom's parents?"

"His father drank himself to death and his mother just up and died."

Deel nodded. "She was always sickly, and her husband was a lot older than her . . . I'm older than you. But not by that much. He was what? Fifteen years? I'm . . . Well, let me see. I'm ten."

She didn't respond. He had hoped for some kind of confirmation that his ten-year gap was nothing, that it was okay. But she said nothing.

"I'm glad Tom was around," Deel said.

"He was a help," she said.

After a while, Deel said, "Things are gonna change. You ain't got to take no one's charity no more. Tomorrow, I'm gonna go into town, see I can buy some seed, and find a mule. I got some muster-out pay. It ain't much, but it's enough to get us started. Winston here goes in with me, we might see we can get him some candy of some sort."

"I like peppermint," the boy said.

"There you go," Deel said.

"You ought not do that so soon back," Mary Lou said. "There's still time before the fall plantin'. You should hunt like you used to, or fish for a few days . . . You could take Winston here with you. You deserve time off."

"Guess another couple of days ain't gonna hurt nothin'. We could all use some time gettin' reacquainted."

Next afternoon when Deel came back from the creek with Winston, they had a couple of fish on a wet cord, and Winston carried them slung over his back so that they dangled down like ornaments and made his shirt damp. They were small but good perch and the boy had caught them, and in the process shown the first real excitement Deel had seen from him. The sunlight played over their scales as they bounced against Winston's back. Deel, walking slightly behind Winston, watched the fish carefully. He watched them slowly dying, out of the water, gasping for air. He couldn't help but want to take them back to the creek and let them go. He had seen injured men gasp like that, on the field, in the trenches. They had seemed like fish that only needed to be put in water.

As they neared the house, Deel saw a rider coming their way, and he saw Mary Lou walking out from the house to meet him.

Mary Lou went up to the man and the man leaned out of the saddle, and they spoke, and then Mary Lou took hold of the saddle with one hand and walked with the horse toward the house. When she saw Deel and Winston coming, she let go of the saddle and walked beside the horse. The man on the horse was tall and lean with black hair that hung down to his shoulders. It was like a water-fall of ink tumbling out from under his slouched gray hat.

As they came closer together, the man on the horse raised his hand in greeting. At that moment the boy yelled out, "Tom!" and darted across the field toward the horse, the fish flapping.

They sat at the kitchen table. Deel and Mary Lou and Winston and Tom Smites. Tom's mother had been half Chickasaw, and he seemed to have gathered up all her coloring, along with his Swed-ish father's great height and broad build. He looked like some kind of forest god. His hair hung over the sides of his face, and his skin was walnut-colored and smooth and he had balanced features and big hands and feet. He had his hat on his knee.

The boy sat very close to Tom. Mary Lou sat at the table, her hands out in front of her, resting on the planks. She had her head turned toward Tom.

Deel said, "I got to thank you for helpin' my family out."

"Ain't nothin' to thank. You used to take me huntin' and fishin' all the time. My daddy didn't do that sort of thing. He was a farmer and a hog raiser and a drunk. You done good by me."

"Thanks again for helpin'."

"I wanted to help out. Didn't have no trouble doin' it."

"You got a family of your own now, I reckon."

"Not yet. I break horses and run me a few cows and hogs and chickens, grow me a pretty good-size garden, but I ain't growin' a family. Not yet. I hear from Mary Lou you need a plow mule and some seed."

Deel looked at her. She had told him all that in the short time she had walked beside his horse. He wasn't sure how he felt about that. He wasn't sure he wanted anyone to know what he needed or didn't need.

"Yeah. I want to buy a mule and some seed."

"Well, now. I got a horse that's broke to plow. He ain't as good as a mule, but I could let him go cheap, real cheap. And I got more seed than I know what to do with. It would save you a trip into town."

"I sort of thought I might like to go to town," Deel said.

"Yeah, well, sure. But I can get those things for you."

"I wanted to take Winston here to the store and get him some candy."

Tom grinned. "Now, that is a good idea, but so happens, I was in town this mornin', and —"

Tom produced a brown paper from his shirt pocket and laid it out on the table and carefully pulled the paper loose, revealing two short pieces of peppermint.

Winston looked at Tom. "Is that for me?"

"It is."

"You just take one now, Winston, and have it after dinner," Mary Lou said. "You save that other piece for tomorrow. It'll give you somethin' to look forward to."

"That was mighty nice of you, Tom," Deel said.

"You should stay for lunch," Mary Lou said. "Deel and Winston caught a couple of fish, and I got some potatoes. I can fry them up."

"Why, that's a nice offer," Tom said. "And on account of it, I'll clean the fish."

The next few days passed with Tom coming out to bring the horse and the seed, and coming back the next day with some plow parts Deel needed. Deel began to think he would never get to town, and now he wasn't so sure he wanted to go. Tom was far more comfortable with his family than he was, and he was jealous of that and wanted to stay with them and find his place. Tom and Mary Lou talked about all manner of things, and quite comfortably, and the boy had lost all interest in the bow. In fact, Deel had found it and the arrows out under a tree near where the woods firmed up. He took it and put it in the smokehouse. The air was dry in there and it would cure better, though he was uncertain the boy would ever have anything to do with it.

Deel plowed a half-dozen acres of the flowers under, and the next day Tom came out with a wagonload of cured chicken shit and helped him shovel it across the broken ground. Deel plowed it under and Tom helped Deel plant peas and beans for the fall crop, some hills of yellow crookneck squash, and a few mounds of watermelon and cantaloupe seed.

That evening they were sitting out in front of the house, Deel in the cane rocker and Tom in a kitchen chair. The boy sat on the ground near Tom and twisted a stick in the dirt. The only light came from the open door of the house, from the lamp inside. When Deel looked over his shoulder, he saw Mary Lou at the washbasin again, doing the dishes, wiggling her ass. Tom looked in that direction once, then looked at Deel, then looked away at the sky, as if memorizing the positions of the stars.

Tom said, "You and me ain't been huntin' since well before you left."

"You came around a lot then, didn't you?" Deel said.

Tom nodded. "I always felt better here than at home. Mama and Daddy fought all the time."

"I'm sorry about your parents."

"Well," Tom said, "everyone's got a time to die, you know. It can be in all kinds of ways, but sometimes it's just time and you just got to embrace it."

"I reckon that's true."

"What say you and me go huntin'?" Tom said, "I ain't had any possum meat in ages."

"I never did like possum," Deel said. "Too greasy."

"You ain't fixed 'em right. That's one thing I can do, fix up a possum good. 'Course, best way is catch one and pen it and feed it corn for a week or so, then kill it. Meat's better that way, firmer. But I'd settle for shootin' one, showin' you how to get rid of that gamey taste with some vinegar and such, cook it up with some sweet potatoes. I got more sweet potatoes than I know what to do with."

"Deel likes sweet potatoes," Mary Lou said.

Deel turned. She stood in the doorway drying her hands on a dish towel. She said, "That ought to be a good idea, Deel. Goin' huntin'. I wouldn't mind learnin' how to cook up a possum right. You and Tom ought to go, like the old days."

"I ain't had no sweet potatoes in years," Deel said.

"All the more reason," Tom said.

The boy said, "I want to go."

"That'd be all right," Tom said, "but you know, I think this time I'd like for just me and Deel to go. When I was a kid, he taught me about them woods, and I'd like to go with him, for old time's sake. That all right with you, Winston?"

Winston didn't act like it was all right, but he said, "I guess."

That night Deel lay beside Mary Lou and said, "I like Tom, but I was thinkin' maybe we could somehow get it so he don't come around so much."

"Oh?"

"I know Winston looks up to him, and I don't mind that, but I need to get to know Winston again . . . Hell, I didn't ever know him. And I need to get to know you . . . I owe you some time, Mary Lou. The right kind of time."

"I don't know what you're talkin' about, Deel. The right kind of time?"

Deel thought for a while, tried to find the right phrasing. He knew what he felt, but saying it was a different matter. "I know you ended up with me because I seemed better than some was askin'. Turned out I wasn't quite the catch you thought. But we got to find what we need, Mary Lou."

"What we need?"

"Love. We ain't never found love."

She lay silent.

"I just think," Deel said, "we ought to have our own time together before we start havin' Tom around so much. You understand what I'm sayin', right?"

"I guess so."

"I don't even feel like I'm proper home yet. I ain't been to town or told nobody I'm back."

"Who you missin'?"

Deel thought about that for a long time. "Ain't nobody but you and Winston that I missed, but I need to get some things back to normal . . . I need to make connections so I can set up some credit at the store, maybe some farm trade for things we need next year. But mostly I just want to be here with you so we can talk. You and Tom talk a lot. I wish we could talk like that. We need to learn how to talk."

"Tom's easy to talk to. He's a talker. He can talk about any-thing and make it seem like somethin', but when he's through, he ain't said nothin' . . . You never was a talker before, Deel, so why now?"

"I want to hear what you got to say, and I want you to hear what I got to say, even if we ain't talkin' about nothin' but seed catalogs or pass the beans, or I need some more firewood or stop snoring. Most anything that's got normal about it. So, thing is, I don't want Tom around so much. I want us to have some time with just you and me and Winston, that's all I'm sayin'."

Deel felt the bed move. He turned to look, and in the dark he saw that Mary Lou was pulling her gown up above her breasts. Her pubic hair looked thick in the dark and her breasts were full and round and inviting.

She said, "Maybe tonight we could get started on knowing each other better."

His mouth was dry. All he could say was, "All right."

His hands trembled as he unbuttoned his union suit at the crotch and she spread her legs and he climbed on top of her. It only took a moment before he exploded.

"Oh, God," he said, and collapsed on her, trying to support his weight on his elbows.

"How was that?" she said. "I feel all right?"

"Fine, but I got done too quick. Oh, girl, it's been so long. I'm sorry."

"That's all right. It don't mean nothin'." She patted him stiffly on the back and then twisted a little so that he'd know she wanted him off her.

"I could do better," he said.

"Tomorrow night."

"Me and Tom, we're huntin' tomorrow night. He's bringin' a dog, and we're gettin' a possum."

"That's right . . . Night after."

"All right, then," Deel said. "All right, then."

He lay back on the bed and buttoned himself up and tried to

decide if he felt better or worse. There had been relief, but no fire. She might as well have been a hole in the mattress.

Tom brought a bitch dog with him and a .22 rifle and a croaker sack. Deel gathered up his double barrel from out of the closet and took it out of its leather sheath coated in oil and found it to be in very good condition. He took it and a sling bag of shells outside. The shells were old, but he had no cause to doubt their ability. They had been stored along with the gun, dry and contained.

The sky was clear and the stars were out and the moon looked like a carved chunk of fresh lye soap, but it was bright, so bright you could see the ground clearly. The boy was in bed, and Deel and Tom and Mary Lou stood out in front of the house and looked at the night.

Mary Lou said to Tom, "You watch after him, Tom."

"I will," Tom said.

"Make sure he's taken care of," she said.

"I'll take care of him."

Deel and Tom had just started walking toward the woods when they were distracted by a shadow. An owl came diving down toward the field. They saw the bird scoop up a fat mouse and fly away with it. The dog chased the owl's shadow as it cruised along the ground.

As they watched the owl climb into the bright sky and fly toward the woods, Tom said, "Ain't nothin' certain in life, is it?"

"Especially if you're a mouse," Deel said.

"Life can be cruel," Tom said.

"Wasn't no cruelty in that," Deel said. "That was survival. The owl was hungry. Men ain't like that. They ain't like other things, 'cept maybe ants."

"Ants?"

"Ants and man make war 'cause they can. Man makes all kinds of proclamations and speeches and gives reasons and such, but at the bottom of it, we just do it 'cause we want to and can."

"That's a hard way to talk," Tom said.

"Man ain't happy till he kills everything in his path and cuts down everything that grows. He sees something wild and beautiful and wants to hold it down and stab it, punish it 'cause it's wild. Beauty draws him to it, and then he kills it."

"Deel, you got some strange thinkin'," Tom said.

"Reckon I do."

"We're gonna kill so as to have somethin' to eat, but unlike the owl, we ain't eatin' no mouse. We're having us a big fat possum and we're gonna cook it with sweet potatoes."

They watched as the dog ran on ahead of them, into the dark line of the trees.

When they got to the edge of the woods the shadows of the trees fell over them, and then they were inside the woods, and it was dark in places with gaps of light where the limbs were thin. They moved toward the gaps and found a trail and walked down it. As they went, the light faded, and Deel looked up. A dark cloud had blown in.

Tom said, "Hell, looks like it's gonna rain. That came out of nowhere."

"It's a runnin' rain," Deel said. "It'll blow in and spit water and blow out before you can find a place to get dry."

"Think so?"

"Yeah. I seen rain aplenty, and one comes up like this, it's traveling through. That cloud will cry its eyes out and move on, promise you. It ain't even got no lightnin' with it."

As if in response to Deel's words it began to rain. No lightning and no thunder, but the wind picked up and the rain was thick and cold.

"I know a good place ahead," Tom said. "We can get under a tree there, and there's a log to sit on. I even killed a couple possums there."

They found the log under the tree, sat down, and waited. The tree was an oak, and it was old and big and had broad limbs and thick leaves that spread out like a canvas. The leaves kept Deel and Tom almost dry.

"That dog's done gone off deep in the woods," Deel said, and laid the shotgun against the log and put his hands on his knees.

"He gets a possum, you'll hear him. He sounds like a trumpet."

Tom shifted the .22 across his lap and looked at Deel, who was lost in thought. "Sometimes," Deel said, "when we was over there, it would rain, and we'd be in trenches, waiting for somethin' to happen, and the trenches would flood with water, and there was big ole rats that would swim in it, and we was so hungry from time to time we killed them and ate them."

"Rats?"

"They're same as squirrels. They don't taste as good, though. But a squirrel ain't nothin' but a tree rat."

"Yeah? You sure?"

"I am."

Tom shifted on the log, and when he did Deel turned toward him. Tom still had the .22 lying across his lap, but when Deel looked, the barrel was raised in his direction. Deel started to say somethin', like, "Hey, watch what you're doin'," but in that instant he knew what he should have known all along. Tom was going to kill him. He had always planned to kill him. From the day Mary Lou had met him in the field on horseback, they were anticipating the rattle of his dead bones. It's why they had kept him from town. He was already thought dead, and if no one thought different, there was no crime to consider.

"I knew and I didn't know," Deel said.

"I got to, Deel. It ain't nothin' personal. I like you fine. You been good to me. But I got to do it. She's worth me doin' somethin' like this . . . Ain't no use reaching for that shotgun, I got you sighted; twenty-two ain't much, but it's enough."

"Winston," Deel said, "he ain't my boy, is he?"

"No."

"He's got a birthmark on his face, and I remember now when you was younger, I seen that same birthmark. I forgot but now I remember. It's under your hair, ain't it?"

Tom didn't say anything. He had scooted back on the log. This put him out from under the edge of the oak canopy, and the rain was washing over his hat and plastering his long hair to the sides of his face.

"You was with my wife back then, when you was eighteen, and I didn't even suspect it," Deel said, and smiled as if he thought there was humor in it. "I figured you for a big kid and nothin' more."

"You're too old for her," Tom said, sighting down the rifle. "And you didn't never give her no real attention. I been with her mostly since you left. I just happened to be gone when you come home. Hell, Deel, I got clothes in the trunk there, and you didn't even see 'em. You might know the weather, but you damn sure don't know women, and you don't know men."

"I don't want to know them, so sometimes I don't know what I know. And men and women, they ain't all that different . . . You ever killed a man, Tom?"

"You'll be my first."

Deel looked at Tom, who was looking at him along the length of the .22.

"It ain't no easy thing to live with, even if you don't know the man," Deel said. "Me, I killed plenty. They come to see me when I close my eyes. Them I actually seen die, and them I imagined died."

"Don't give me no booger stories. I don't reckon you're gonna come see me when you're dead. I don't reckon that at all."

It had grown dark because of the rain, and Tom's shape was just a shape. Deel couldn't see his features.

"Tom—"

The .22 barked. The bullet struck Deel in the head. He tumbled over the log and fell where there was rain in his face. He thought just before he dropped down into darkness: It's so cool and clean.

Deel looked over the edge of the trench where there was a slab of metal with a slot to look through. All he could see was darkness except when the lightning ripped a strip in the sky and the countryside lit up. Thunder banged so loudly he couldn't tell the difference between it and cannon fire, which was also banging away, dropping great explosions near the breastworks and into the zigzagging trench, throwing men left and right like dolls.

Then he saw shapes. They moved across the field like a column of ghosts. In one great run they came, closer and closer. He poked his rifle through the slot and took half-ass aim and then the command came and he fired. Machine guns began to burp. The field lit up with their constant red pops. The shapes began to fall. The faces of those in front of the rushing line brightened when the machine guns snapped, making their features devil red. When the lightning flashed they seemed to vibrate across the field. The cannons roared and thunder rumbled and the machine guns coughed and the rifles cracked and men screamed.

Then the remainder of the Germans were across the field and

over the trench ramifications and down into the trenches themselves. Hand-to-hand fighting began. Deel fought with his bayonet.
He jabbed at a German soldier so small his shoulders failed to
fill out his uniform. As the German hung on the thrust of Deel's
blade, clutched at the rifle barrel, flares blazed along the length of
the trench, and in that moment Deel saw the soldier's chin had
bits of blond fuzz on it. The expression the kid wore was that
of someone who had just realized this was not a glorious game after all.

And then Deel coughed.

He coughed and began to choke. He tried to lift up, but couldn't,
at first. Then he sat up and the mud dripped off him and the rain
pounded him. He spat dirt from his mouth and gasped at the air.
The rain washed his face clean and pushed his hair down over his
forehead. He was uncertain how long he sat there in the rain, but
in time the rain stopped. His head hurt. He lifted his hand to it
and came away with his fingers covered in blood. He felt again,
pushing his hair aside. There was a groove across his forehead. The
shot hadn't hit him solid; it had cut a path across the front of his
head. He had bled a lot, but now the bleeding had stopped. The
mud in the grave had filled the wound and plugged it. The shallow
grave had most likely been dug earlier in the day. It had all been
planned out, but the rain was unexpected. The rain made the dirt
damp, and in the dark Tom had not covered him well enough. Not
deep enough. Not firm enough. And his nose was free. He could
breathe. The ground was soft and it couldn't hold him. He had
merely sat up and the dirt had fallen aside.

Deel tried to pull himself out of the grave but was too weak, so
he twisted in the loose dirt and lay with his face against the ground.
When he was strong enough to lift his head, the rain had passed,
the clouds had sailed away, and the moon was bright.

Deel worked himself out of the grave and crawled across the
ground toward the log where he and Tom had sat. His shotgun was
lying behind the log where it had fallen. Tom had either forgotten
the gun or didn't care. Deel was too weak to pick it up.

Deel managed himself onto the log and sat there, his head held
down, watching the ground. As he did, a snake crawled over his
boots and twisted its way into the darkness of the woods. Deel
reached down and picked up the shotgun. It was damp and cold.

He opened it and the shells popped out. He didn't try to find them in the dark. He lifted the barrel, poked it toward the moonlight, and looked through it. Clear. No dirt in the barrels. He didn't try to find the two shells that had popped free. He loaded two fresh ones from his ammo bag. He took a deep breath. He picked up some damp leaves and pressed them against the wound and they stuck. He stood up. He staggered toward his house, the blood-stuck leaves decorating his forehead as if he were some kind of forest god.

It was not long before the stagger became a walk. Deel broke free of the woods and onto the path that crossed the field. With the rain gone it was bright again, and a light wind had begun to blow. The earth smelled rich, the way it had that night in France when it rained and the lightning flashed and the soldiers came and the damp smell of the earth blended with the biting smell of gunpowder and the odor of death.

He walked until he could see the house, dark like blight in the center of the field. The house appeared extremely small then, smaller than before; it was as if all that had ever mattered to him continued to shrink. The bitch dog came out to meet him but he ignored her. She slunk off and trotted toward the trees he had left behind.

He came to the door, and then his foot was kicking against it. The door cracked and creaked and slammed loudly backward. Then Deel was inside, walking fast. He came to the bedroom door, and it was open. He went through. The window was up and the room was full of moonlight, so brilliant he could see clearly, and what he saw was Tom and Mary Lou lying together in mid-act, and in that moment he thought of his brief time with her and how she had let him have her so as not to talk about Tom anymore. He thought about how she had given herself to protect what she had with Tom. Something moved inside Deel and he recognized it as the core of what man was. He stared at them and they saw him and froze in action. Mary Lou said, "No," and Tom leaped up from between her legs, all the way to his feet. Naked as nature, he stood for a moment in the middle of the bed, and then plunged through the open window like a fox down a hole. Deel raised the shotgun and fired and took out part of the windowsill, but Tom was out and away. Mary Lou screamed. She threw her legs to the side of the bed and made as if to stand, but couldn't. Her legs were too weak. She sat back down and started yelling his name. Something called from deep inside Deel, a long call, deep and dark and certain. A bloody leaf dripped off his forehead. He raised the shotgun and fired. The shot tore into her breast and knocked her sliding across the bed, pushing the back of her head against the wall beneath the window.

Deel stood looking at her. Her eyes were open, her mouth slightly parted. He watched her hair and the sheets turn dark.

He broke open the shotgun and reloaded the double barrel from his ammo sack and went to the door across the way, the door to the small room that was the boy's. He kicked it open. When he went in, the boy, wearing his nightshirt, was crawling through the window. He shot at him, but the best he might have done was riddle the bottom of his feet with pellets. Like his father, Winston was quick through a hole.

Deel stepped briskly to the open window and looked out. The boy was crossing the moonlit field like a jackrabbit, running toward a dark stretch of woods in the direction of town. Deel climbed through the window and began to stride after the boy. And then he saw Tom. Tom was off to the right, running toward where there used to be a deep ravine and a blackberry growth. Deel went after him. He began to trot. He could imagine himself with the other soldiers crossing a field, waiting for a bullet to end it all.

Deel began to close in. Being barefoot was working against Tom. He was limping. Deel thought that Tom's feet were most likely full of grass burrs and were wounded by stones. Tom's moon shadow stumbled and rose, as if it were his soul trying to separate itself from its host.

The ravine and the blackberry bushes were still there. Tom came to the ravine, found a break in the vines, and went over the side of it and down. Deel came shortly after, dropped into the ravine. It was damp there and smelled fresh from the recent rain. Deel saw Tom scrambling up the other side of the ravine, into the dark rise of blackberry bushes on the far side. He strode after him, and when he came to the spot where Tom had gone, he saw Tom was hung in the berry vines. The vines had twisted around his arms and head and they held him as surely as if he were nailed there.

The more Tom struggled, the harder the thorns bit and the better the vines held him. Tom twisted and rolled and soon he was facing in the direction of Deel, hanging just above him on the bank of the ravine, supported by the blackberry vines, one arm outstretched, the other pinned against his abdomen, wrapped up like a Christmas present from nature, a gift to what man and the ants liked to do best. He was breathing heavily.

Deel turned his head slightly, like a dog trying to distinguish what it sees. "You're a bad shot."

"Ain't no cause to do this, Deel."

"It's not a matter of cause. It's the way of man," Deel said.

"What in hell you talkin' about, Deel? I'm askin' you, I'm beggin' you, don't kill me. She was the one talked me into it. She thought you were dead, long dead. She wanted it like it was when it was just me and her."

Deel took a deep breath and tried to taste the air. It had tasted so clean a moment ago, but now it was bitter.

"The boy got away," Deel said.

"Go after him, you want, but don't kill me."

A smile moved across Deel's face. "Even the little ones grow up to be men."

"You ain't makin' no sense, Deel. You ain't right."

"Ain't none of us right," Deel said.

Deel raised the shotgun and fired. Tom's head went away and the body drooped in the clutch of the vines and hung over the edge of the ravine.

The boy was quick, much faster than his father. Deel had covered a lot of ground in search of him, and he could read the boy's sign in the moonlight, see where the grass was pushed down, see bare footprints in the damp dirt, but the boy had long reached the woods, and maybe the town beyond. He knew that. It didn't matter anymore.

He moved away from the woods and back to the field until he came to Pancake Rocks. They were flat, round chunks of sandstone piled on top of one another and they looked like a huge stack of pancakes. He had forgotten all about them. He went to them and stopped and looked at the top edge of the pancake stones. It was twenty feet from ground to top. He remembered that from when he was a boy. His daddy told him, "That there is twenty feet from top to bottom. A Spartan boy could climb that and reach the top in three minutes. I can climb it and reach the top in three minutes. Let's see what you can do."

He had never reached the top in three minutes, though he had tried time after time. It had been important to his father for some reason, some human reason, and he had forgotten all about it until now.

Deel leaned the shotgun against the stones and slipped off his boots and took off his clothes. He tore his shirt and made a strap for the gun, and slung it over his bare shoulder and took up the ammo bag and tossed it over his other shoulder, and began to climb. He made it to the top. He didn't know how long it had taken him, but he guessed it had been only about three minutes. He stood on top of Pancake Rocks and looked out at the night. He could see his house from there. He sat cross-legged on the rocks and stretched the shotgun over his thighs. He looked up at the sky. The stars were bright and the space between them was as deep as forever. If man could, he would tear the stars down, thought Deel.

Deel sat and wondered how late it was. The moon had moved, but not so much as to pull up the sun. Deel felt as if he had been sitting there for days. He nodded off now and then, and in the dream he was an ant, one of many ants, and he was moving toward a hole in the ground from which came smoke and sparks of fire. He marched with the ants toward the hole, and then into the hole they went, one at a time. Just before it was his turn, he saw the ants in front of him turn to black crisps in the fire, and he marched after them, hurrying for his turn, then he awoke and looked across the moonlit field.

He saw, coming from the direction of his house, a rider. The horse looked like a large dog because the rider was so big. He hadn't seen the man in years, but he knew who he was immediately. Lobo Collins. He had been sheriff of the county when he had left for war. He watched as Lobo rode toward him. He had no thoughts about it. He just watched.

Well out of range of Deel's shotgun, Lobo stopped and got off his horse and pulled a rifle out of the saddle boot.

"Deel," Lobo called. "It's Sheriff Lobo Collins."

Lobo's voice moved across the field loud and clear. It was as if they were sitting beside each other. The light was so good he could see Lobo's mustache clearly, drooping over the corners of his mouth.

"Your boy come told me what happened."

"He ain't my boy, Lobo."

"Everybody knowed that but you, but wasn't no cause to do what you did. I been up to the house, and I found Tom in the ravine."

"They're still dead, I assume."

"You ought not done it, but she was your wife, and he was messin' with her, so you got some cause, and a jury might see it that way. That's something to think about, Deel. It could work out for you."

"He shot me," Deel said.

"Well now, that makes it even more different. Why don't you put down that gun, and you and me go back to town and see how we can work things out."

"I was dead before he shot me."

"What?" Lobo said. Lobo had dropped down on one knee. He had the Winchester across that knee and with his other hand he held the bridle of his horse.

Deel raised the shotgun and set the stock firmly against the stone, the barrel pointing skyward.

"You're way out of range up there," Lobo said. "That shotgun ain't gonna reach me, but I can reach you, and I can put one in a fly's asshole from here to the moon."

Deel stood up. "I can't reach you, then I reckon I got to get me a wee bit closer."

Lobo stood up and dropped the horse's reins. The horse didn't move. "Now don't be a damn fool, Deel."

Deel slung the shotgun's makeshift strap over his shoulder and started climbing down the back of the stones, where Lobo couldn't see him. He came down quicker than he had gone up, and he didn't even feel where the stones had torn his naked knees and feet.

When Deel came around the side of the stone, Lobo had moved only slightly, away from his horse, and he was standing with the Winchester held down by his side. He was watching as Deel advanced, naked and committed. Lobo said, "Ain't no sense in this, Deel. I ain't seen you in years, and now I'm gonna get my best look at you down the length of a Winchester. Ain't no sense in it."

"There ain't no sense to nothin'," Deel said, and walked faster, pulling the strapped shotgun off his shoulder.

Lobo backed up a little, then raised the Winchester to his shoulder, said, "Last warnin', Deel."

Deel didn't stop. He pulled the shotgun stock to his hip and let it rip. The shot went wide and fell across the grass like hail, some twenty feet in front of Lobo. And then Lobo fired.

Deel thought someone had shoved him. It felt that way. That someone had walked up unseen beside him and had shoved him on the shoulder. Next thing he knew he was lying on the ground looking up at the stars. He felt pain, but not like the pain he had felt when he realized what he was.

A moment later the shotgun was pulled from his hand, and then Lobo was kneeling down next to him with the Winchester in one hand and the shotgun in the other.

"I done killed you, Deel."

"No," Deel said, spitting up blood. "I ain't alive to kill."

"I think I clipped a lung," Lobo said, as if proud of his marksmanship. "You ought not done what you done. It's good that boy got away. He ain't no cause of nothin'."

"He just ain't had his turn."

Deel's chest was filling up with blood. It was as if someone had put a funnel in his mouth and poured it into him. He tried to say something more, but it wouldn't come out. There was only a cough and some blood; it splattered warm on his chest. Lobo put the weapons down and picked up Deel's head and laid it across one of his thighs so he wasn't choking so much.

"You got a last words, Deel?"

"Look there," Deel said.

Deel's eyes had lifted to the heavens, and Lobo looked. What he saw was the night and the moon and the stars. "Look there. You see it?" Deel said. "The stars are fallin'."

Lobo said, "Ain't nothin' fallin', Deel," but when he looked back down, Deel was gone.

CHARLES McCARRY

The End of the String

FROM *Agents of Treachery*

I FIRST NOTICED the man I will call Benjamin in the bar of the
Independence Hotel in Ndala. He sat alone, drinking orange soda,
no ice. He was tall and burly—knotty biceps, huge hands. His
short-sleeved white shirt and khaki pants were as crisp as a uniform.
Instead of the usual third-world Omega or Rolex, he wore a cheap
plastic Japanese watch on his right wrist. No rings, no gold, no
sunglasses. I did not recognize the tribal tattoos on his cheeks. He
spoke to no one, looked at no one. He himself might as well have
been invisible as far as the rest of the customers were concerned.
No one spoke to him or offered to buy him a drink or asked him
any questions. He seemed poised to leap off his barstool and kill
something at a moment's notice.

He was the only person in the bar I did not already know by
sight. In those days, more than half a century ago, when an American was a rare bird along the Guinea coast, you got to know everyone in your hotel bar pretty quickly. I was standing at the bar, my
back to Benjamin, but I could see him in the mirror. He was watching me. I surmised that he was gathering information rather than
sizing me up for robbery or some other dark purpose.

I called the barman, put a ten-shilling note on the bar, and asked
him to mix a pink gin using actual Beefeater's. He laughed merrily as he pocketed the money and swirled the bitters in the glass.
When I looked in the mirror again, Benjamin was gone. How a
man his size could get up and leave without being reflected in the
mirror I do not know, but somehow he managed it. I did not dismiss him from my thoughts, he was too memorable for that, but I

didn't dwell on the episode either. I could not, however, shake the feeling that I had been subjected to a professional appraisal. For an operative under deep cover, that is always an uncomfortable experience, especially if you have the feeling, as I did, that the man who is giving you the once-over is a professional who is doing a job that he has done many times before.

I had come to Ndala to debrief an agent. He missed the first two meetings, but there is nothing unusual about that even if you're not in Africa. On the third try, he showed up close to the appointed hour at the appointed place—two A.M. on an unpaved street in which hundreds of people, all of them sound asleep, lay side by side. It was a moonless night. No electric light, no lantern or candle even, burned for at least a mile in any direction. I could not see the sleepers, but I could feel their presence and hear them exhale and inhale. The agent, a member of parliament, had nothing to tell me apart from his usual bagful of pointless gossip. I gave him his money anyway, and he signed for it with a thumbprint by the light of my pocket torch. As I walked away I heard him ripping open his envelope and counting banknotes in the dark.

I had not walked far when a car turned into the street with headlights blazing. The sleepers awoke and popped up one after another as if choreographed by Busby Berkeley. The member of parliament had vanished. No doubt he had simply laid down with the others, and two of the wide-open eyes and one of the broad smiles I saw dwindling into the darkness belonged to him.

The car stopped. I kept walking toward it, and when I was beside it the driver, who was a police constable, leaped out and shone a flashlight in my face. He said, "Please get in, master." The British had been gone from this country for only a short time, and the locals still addressed white men by the title preferred by their former colonial rulers. The old etiquette survived in English and French and Portuguese in most of the thirty-two African countries that had become independent in a period of two and a half years—less time than it took Stanley to find Livingstone.

I said, "Get in? What for?"

"This is not a good place for you, master."

My rescuer was impeccably turned out in British tropical kit—blue service cap, bush jacket with sergeant's chevrons on the shoulder boards, voluminous khaki shorts, blue woolen knee socks, gleaming oxfords, black Sam Browne belt. A truncheon dangling from the belt seemed to be his only weapon. I climbed into the backseat. The sergeant got behind the wheel and, using the rearview mirror rather than looking behind him, backed out of the street at breathtaking speed. I kept my eyes on the windshield, expecting him to plow into the sleepers at any moment. They themselves seemed unconcerned, and as the headlights swept over them they lay down one after the other with the same precise timing as before.

The sergeant drove at high speed through back streets, nearly every one of them another open-air dormitory. Our destination, as it turned out, was the Equator Club, Ndala's most popular nightclub. This structure was really just a fenced-in space, open to the sky. Inside, a band played highlife, a kind of hypercalypso, so loudly that you had the illusion that the music was visible as it rose into the pitch-black night.

Inside, the music was even louder. The air was the temperature of blood. The odors of sweat and spilled beer were sharp and strong. Guttering candles created a substitute for light. Silhouettes danced on the hard dirt floor, cigarettes glowed. The sensation was something like being digested by a tyrannosaurus rex.

Benjamin, alone again, sat at another small table. He was drinking orange soda again. He too wore a uniform. Though made of finer cloth, it was a duplicate of the sergeant's, except that he was equipped with a swagger stick instead of a baton and the badge on his shoulder boards displayed the wreath, crossed batons, and crown of a chief constable. Benjamin, it appeared, was the head of the national police. He made a gesture of welcome. I sat down. A waiter placed a pink gin with ice before me with such efficiency, and was so neatly dressed, that I supposed he was a constable too, but undercover. I lifted my glass to Benjamin and sipped my drink.

Benjamin said, "Are you a naval person?"

I said, "No. Why do you ask?"

"Pink gin is the traditional drink of the Royal Navy."

"Not rum?"

"Rum is for the crew."

I had difficulty suppressing a grin. Our exchange of words sounded so much like a recognition code used by spies that I wondered if that's what it really was. Had Benjamin got the wrong

American? He did not seem the type to make such an elementary mistake. He looked down on me—even while seated he was at least a head taller than I was—and said, "Welcome to my country, Mr. Brown. I have been waiting for you to come here again, because I believe that you and I can work together."

Brown was one of the names I had used on previous visits to Ndala, but it was not the name on the passport I was using this time. He paused, studying my face. His own face showed no flicker of expression.

Without further preamble, he said, "I am contemplating a project that requires the support of the United States of America."

The dramaturgy of the situation suggested that my next line should be, "Really?" or "How so?" However, I said nothing, hoping that Benjamin would fill the silence.

Frankly, I was puzzled. Was he volunteering for something? Most agents recruited by any intelligence service are volunteers, and the average intelligence officer is a sort of latter-day Marcel Proust. He lies abed in a cork-lined room, hoping to profit by secrets that other people slip under the door. People simply walk in and for whatever motive—usually petty resentment over having been passed over for promotion or the like—offer to betray their country. It was also possible, unusual though that might be, that Benjamin hoped to recruit me.

His eyes bored into mine. His back was to the wall, mine to the dance floor. Behind me I could feel but not see the dancers, moving as a single organism. Through the soles of my shoes I felt vibration set up by scores of feet stamping in unison on the dirt floor. In the yellow candlelight I could see a little more expression on Benjamin's face.

Many seconds passed before he broke the silence. "What is your opinion of the president of this country?"

Once again I took my time answering. The problem with this conversation was that I never knew what to say next.

Finally I said, "President Ga and I have never met."

"Nevertheless you must have an opinion."

And of course I did. So did everyone who read the newspapers. Akokwu Ga, president for life of Ndala, was a man of strong appetites. He enjoyed his position and its many opportunities for pleasure with an enthusiasm that was remarkable even by the usual standards for dictators. He possessed a solid gold bathtub and bedstead. He had a private zoo, and it was said that he was sometimes seized by the impulse to feed his enemies to the lions. He had deposited tens of millions of dollars from his country's treasury into personal numbered accounts in Swiss banks.

Dinner for him and his guests was flown in every day from one of the restaurants in Paris that had a three-star rating in the Guide Michelin. A French chef heated the food and arranged it on plates, an English butler served it. Both were assumed to be secret agents employed by their respective governments. Ga maintained love nests in every quarter of the capital city. Women from all over the world occupied these cribs. The ones he liked best were given luxurious houses formerly occupied by Europeans and provided with German cars, French champagne, and "houseboys" (actually undercover policemen) who kept an eye on them.

"Speak," Benjamin said.

I said, "Frankly, chief constable, this conversation is making me nervous."

"Why? No one can bug us. Listen to the noise."

How right he was. We were shouting at each other in order to be heard above the din. The music made my ears ring, and no microphone then known could penetrate it. I said, "Nevertheless, I would prefer to discuss this in private. Just the two of us."

"And how then will you know that I am not bugging you? Or that someone else is not bugging both of us?"

"I wouldn't. But would it matter?"

Benjamin examined me for a long moment. Then he said, "No, it wouldn't. Because I am the one who will be saying dangerous things."

He got to his feet — *uncoiled* would be the better word. Instantly the sergeant who had brought me here and three other constables in plain clothes materialized from the shadows. Everyone else was dancing, eyes closed, seemingly in another world and time. Benjamin put on his cap and picked up his swagger stick.

He said, "Tomorrow I will come for you."

With that, he disappeared, leaving me without a ride. Eventually I found a taxi back to the hotel. The driver was so wide awake, his taxi so tidy, that I assumed that he too must be one of Benjamin's men.

The porter who brought me my mug of tea at six A.M. also brought me a note from Benjamin. The penmanship was beautiful. The note was short and to the point: "Nine o'clock, by the front entrance."

Through the glass in the hotel's front door, the street outside was a scene from Goya—lepers and amputees and victims of polio or smallpox or psoriasis, and among the child beggars a few examples of hamstringing by parents who needed the income that a crippled child could bring home. A tourist arrived in a taxi and scattered a handful of change in order to disperse the beggars while he made his dash for the entrance. Clearly he was a greenhorn. The seasoned traveler in Africa distributed money only after checkout. To do so on arrival guaranteed your being fondled by lepers every time you came in or went out. One particularly handsome, smiling young fellow who had lost his fingers and toes to leprosy caught coins in his mouth.

At the appointed time exactly—was I still in Africa?—Benjamin's sergeant pulled up in his gleaming black Austin. He barked a command in one of the local languages, and once again the crowd parted. He took me by the hand in the friendly African way and led me to the car.

We headed north, out of town, horn sounding tinnily at every turn of the wheels. Otherwise, the sergeant explained, pedestrians would assume that the driver was trying to kill them. In daylight when everyone was awake and walking around instead of sleeping by the wayside, Ndala sounded like the overture of *An American in Paris*. After a hair-raising drive past the brand-new government buildings and banks of downtown, through raucous streets lined with shops and filled with the smoke of street vendors' grills, through labyrinthine neighborhoods of low shacks made from scraps of lumber and tin and cardboard, we arrived at last in Africa itself, a sun-scorched plain of rusty soil dotted with stunted bush, stretching from horizon to horizon. After a mile or so of emptiness, we came upon a policeman seated on a parked motorcycle. The sergeant stopped the car, leaped out, and, leaving the motor running and the front door open, opened the back door to let me out. He gave me a map, drew himself up to attention, and, after stamping his right foot into the dust, gave me a quivering British hand salute. He then jumped onto the motorcycle behind its rider, who revved the engine, made a slithering U-turn, and headed back toward the city trailed by a corkscrew of red dust.

I got into the Austin and started driving. The road soon became a dirt trail whose billowing ocher dust stuck to the car like snow and made it necessary to run the windshield wipers. It was impossible to drive with the windows open. The temperature inside the closed vehicle (air conditioning was a thing of the future) could not have been less than one hundred degrees Fahrenheit. Slippery with sweat, I followed the map and, after making a right turn into what seemed to be an impenetrable thicket of rubbery bushes, straddled a footpath which in time opened into a clearing containing a small village. Another car, a dusty black Rover, was parked in front of one of the conical mud huts. This place was deserted. Grass had grown on the footpaths. There was no sign of life.

I parked beside the other car and ducked into the mud hut. Benjamin, alone as usual, sat inside. He wore national dress—the white togalike gown invented by nineteenth-century missionaries to clothe the natives for the benefit of English knitting mills. His feet were bare. He seemed to be deep in thought and did not greet me with word or sign. A .455-caliber Webley revolver lay beside him on the floor of beaten earth. The light was dim, and because I had come into the shadowy interior out of intense sunlight, it was some time before I was able to see his face well enough to be absolutely certain that the mute tribesman before me actually was the chief constable with whom I had passed a pleasant hour the night before in the Equator Club. As for the revolver, I can't explain why I trusted this glowering giant not to shoot me just yet, but I did.

Benjamin said, "Is this meeting place sufficiently private?"

"It's fine," I replied. "But where have all the people gone?"

"To Ndala, a long time ago."

All over Africa were abandoned villages like this one whose inhabitants had packed up and left for the city in search of money and excitement and the new life of opportunity that independence promised. Nearly all of them now slept in the streets.

"As I said last night," Benjamin said, "I am thinking about doing something that is necessary to the future of this country, and I would like to have the encouragement of the United States government."

"It must be something impressive if you need the encouragement of Washington."

"It is. I plan to remove the present government of this country and replace it with a freely elected new government."

"That *is* impressive. What exactly do you mean by *encouragement?*"

"A willingness to stand aside, to make no silliness, and afterward to be helpful."

"Afterward? Not before?"

"Before is a local problem."

The odds were at least even that afterward might be a large problem for Benjamin. President Ga's instinct for survival was highly developed. Others, including his own brother, had tried to overthrow him. They were all dead now.

I said, "I recommend first of all that you forget this idea of yours. If you can't do that, then you should speak to somebody in the American embassy. I'm sure you already know the right person."

"I prefer to speak to you."

"Why? I'm not a member of the Ministry of Encouragement."

"But that is exactly what you are, Mr. Brown. You are famous for it. You can be trusted. This man in the American embassy you call 'the right person' is in fact a fool. He is an admirer of President for Life Ga. He plays ball with President Ga. He cannot be trusted."

I started to answer this nonsense. Benjamin showed me the palm of his hand. "Please, no protestations of innocence. I have all the evidence I would ever need about your good works in my country, should I ever need it."

That made me blink. No doubt he did have an interesting file on me. I had done a good deal of mischief in his country, even before the British departed, and for all I knew his courtship was a charade. He might very well be trying to entrap me.

I said, "I'm flattered. But I don't think I'd make a good assistant in this particular matter."

Something like a frown crossed Benjamin's brow. I had annoyed him. Since we were in the middle of nowhere and he was the one with the revolver, this was not a good sign.

"I have no need of an assistant," Benjamin said. "What I need is a witness. A trained observer whose word is trusted in high places in the U.S. Someone who can tell the right people in Washington what I have done, how I have done it, and most of all, that I have done it for the good of my country."

I could think of nothing to say that would not make this conversation even more unpleasant than it already was.

Benjamin said, "I can see that you do not trust me."

He picked up the revolver and cocked it. The Webley is something of an antique, having been designed around the time of the Boer War as the standard British officer's sidearm. It is large and ugly but also effective, being powerful enough to kill an elephant. For a long moment Benjamin looked deeply into my eyes and then, holding the gun by the barrel, handed it to me.

"If you believe I am being false to you in any way," he said, "you can shoot me."

It was a wonder that he had not shot himself, handling a cocked revolver in such a carefree way. I took the weapon from his hand, lowered the hammer, swung open the cylinder, and shook out the cartridges. They were not blanks. I reloaded and handed the weapon back to Benjamin. He wiped it clean of fingerprints—my fingerprints—with the skirt of his robe and put it back on the floor.

In the jargon of espionage, the recruitment of an agent is called a seduction. As in a real seduction, assuming that things are going well, a moment comes when resistance turns into encouragement. We had arrived at the moment for a word of encouragement.

I said, "What exactly is the plan?"

"When you strike at a prince," Benjamin said, "you must strike to kill."

Absolutely true. It did not surprise me that he had read Machiavelli. At this point it would not have surprised me if he burst into fluent Sanskrit. Despite the rigmarole with the Webley, I still did not trust him and probably never would, but I was doing the work that I was paid to do, so I decided to press on with the thing.

"That's an excellent principle," I said, "but it's a principle, not a plan."

"All the right things will be done," Benjamin said. "The radio station and newspapers will be seized, the army will cooperate, the airport will be closed, curfews will be imposed."

"Don't forget to surround the presidential palace."

"That will not be necessary."

"Why?"

"Because the president will not be in the palace," Benjamin said.

All of a sudden Benjamin was becoming cryptic. Frankly, I was just as glad, because what he was proposing in words of one syllable scared the bejesus out of me. So did the expression on his face. He was as calm as a Buddha.

He rose to his feet. In his British uniform he had looked impressive, if slightly uncomfortable. In his gown he looked positively majestic, a black Caesar in a white toga.

"You now know enough now to think this over," he said. "Do so, if you please. We will talk some more before you fly away."

He ducked through the door and drove away. I waited for a few minutes, then went outside myself. A large black mamba lay in the sun in front of my car. My blood froze. The mamba was twelve or thirteen feet long. This species is the fastest-moving snake known to zoology, capable of slithering at fifteen miles an hour, faster than most men can run. Its strike is much quicker than that. Its venom will usually kill an adult human being in about fifteen minutes. Hoping that this one was not fully awake, I got into the car and started the engine. The snake moved but did not go away. I could easily have run over it, but instead I backed up and steered around it. Locally this serpent was regarded as a sign of bad luck to come. I wasn't looking for any more misfortune than I already had on my plate.

After dinner that evening I spent an extra hour in the hotel bar. I felt the alcohol after I went upstairs and got into bed, but fell almost immediately into a deep sleep. Cognac makes for bad dreams, and I was in the middle of one when I was awakened by the click of the latch. For an instant I thought the porter must be bringing my morning tea and wondered where the night had gone. But when I opened my eyes it was still dark outside. The door opened and closed. No light came in, meaning that the intruder had switched off the dim bulbs in the corridor. He was now inside the room. I could not see him but I could smell him: soap, spicy food, shoe polish. *Shoe polish?* I slid out of bed, taking the pillows and the covers with me and rolling them into a ball, as if this would help me defend myself against the intruder who I believed was about to attack me in the dark with a machete.

In the dark, the intruder drew the shade over the window. An instant later the lights came on. Benjamin said, "Sorry to disturb you."

He wore his impeccable uniform, swagger stick tucked under his left arm, cap square on his head, badges and shoes and Sam Browne belt gleaming. The clock read 4:23. It was an old-fashioned wind-up alarm clock with two bells on top. It ticked loudly while I waited until I was sure I could trust my voice to reply. I was stark naked. I felt a little foolish to be holding a bundle of bedclothes in my arms, but at least this preserved my modesty.

Finally I said, "I thought we'd already had our conversation for the day."

Benjamin ignored the Bogart impersonation. "There is something I want you to see," he said. "Get dressed as quick as you can, please." Benjamin never forgot a please or a thank-you. Like his penmanship, Victorian good manners seemed to have been rubbed into his soul in missionary school.

As soon as I had tied my shoes, he led the way down the back stairs. He moved at a swift trot. Outside the back door, a black Rover sedan waited with the engine running. The sergeant stood at attention beside it. He opened the back door as Benjamin and I approached, and after a brief moment as Alphonse and Gaston, we got into the backseat.

When the car was in motion, Benjamin turned to me and said, "You seem to want to give President Ga the benefit of the doubt. This morning you will see some things for yourself, and then you can decide whether that is the Christian thing to do."

It was still dark. As a usual thing there is no lingering painted sunrise in equatorial regions; the sun, huge and white, just materializes on the rim of the earth, and daylight begins. In the darkness, the miserable of Ndala were still asleep in rows on either side of every street, but little groups of people on the move were caught in our headlights.

"Beggars," Benjamin said. "They are on their way to work." The beggars limped and crawled according to their afflictions. Those who could not walk at all were carried by others.

"They help each other," Benjamin said. He said something to the sergeant in a tribal language. The sergeant put a spotlight on a big man carrying a leper who had lost his feet. The leper looked over his friend's shoulder and smiled. The big man walked onward as if unaware of the spotlight. Benjamin said, "See? A blind man will carry a crippled man, and the crippled man will tell him where to go. Take a good look, Mr. Brown. It is a sight you will never seen in Ndala again."

"Why not?

"You will see."

At the end of the street an army truck was parked. A squad of soldiers armed with bayoneted rifles held at port arms formed a line across the street. Benjamin gave an order. The sergeant stopped the car and shone his spotlight on them. They did not stir or open their eyes as when the sergeant drove down this same street the night before. Whatever was happening, these people did not want to be witnesses. The soldiers paid no more attention to Benjamin's car than the people lying on the ground paid to the soldiers.

When the beggars arrived, the soldiers surrounded them and herded them into the truck. The blind man protested, a single syllable. Before he could say more, a soldier hit him in the small of the back with a rifle butt. The blind man dropped the crippled leper and fell down unconscious. The soldiers would not touch them, so the other beggars picked them up and loaded them into the truck, then climbed in themselves. The soldiers lowered the back curtain and got into a smaller truck of their own. All this happened in eerie silence, not an order given or a protest voiced, in a country in which the smallest human encounter sent tsunamis of shouting and laughter through crowds of hundreds.

We drove on. We witnessed the same scene over and over again. All over the city, beggars were being rounded up by troops. Our last stop was the Independence Hotel, my hotel, where I saw the beggars I knew best, including the handsome, smiling leper who caught coins in his mouth, being herded into the back of a truck. As the truck drove away, gears changing, the sun appeared on the eastern horizon, huge and entire, a miracle of timing.

Benjamin said, "You look a little sick, my friend. Let me tell you something. Those people are never coming back to Ndala. They give our country a bad image, and two weeks from now hundreds of foreigners will arrive for the Pan-African Conference. Thanks to President Ga, they will not have to look at these disgusting creatures, so maybe they will elect him president of the conference. Think about that. We will talk when you come back."

In Washington, two days later at six in the morning, I found my chief at his desk, drinking coffee from a chipped mug and reading the *Wall Street Journal.* I told him my tale. He knew at once exactly who Benjamin was. He asked how much money Benjamin wanted, what his timetable was, who his coconspirators were, whether he himself planned to replace the abominable Ga as dictator after he overthrew him, what his policy toward the United States would be—and, by the way, what were his hidden intentions? I was unable to answer most of these questions.

I said, "All he's asked for so far is encouragement."

"Encouragement?" said my chief. "That's a new one. He didn't suggest one night of love with the first lady in the Lincoln bedroom?"

A certain third-world general had once made just such a demand in return for his services as a spy in a country whose annual national product was smaller than that of Cuyahoga County, Ohio. I told him that Benjamin had not struck me as being the type to long for Mrs. Eisenhower.

My chief said, "You take him seriously?"

"He's an impressive person."

"Then go back and talk to him some more."

"When?"

"Tomorrow."

"What about the encouragement?"

"It's cheap. Ga is a bad 'un. Shovel it on."

I was cheap too—a singleton out at the end of the string. If I got into trouble, I'd get no help from the chief or anyone else in Washington. The old gentleman himself would cut the string. He owed me nothing. "Brown? *Brown?*" he would say in the unlikely event that he would be asked what had become of me. "The only Brown I know is Charlie."

The prospect of returning to Ndala on the next flight was not a very inviting one. I had just spent eight weeks traveling around Africa, in and out of countries, languages, time zones, identities. My intestines swarmed with parasites that were desperate to escape. There was something wrong with my liver: the whites of my eyes were yellow. I had had a malaria attack on the plane from London that frightened the woman seated next to me. The four aspirins I took, spilling only twenty or so while getting them out of the bottle with shaking hands, brought the fever and the sweating under control. Twelve hours later I still had a temperature of 102; I shuddered still, though only fitfully.

To the chief I said, "Right."

"This time get *all* the details," my chief said. "But no cables. Your skull only, and fly the information back to me personally. Tell the locals nothing."

"Which locals? Here or there?"

"Anywhere."

His tone was nonchalant, but I had known this man for a long time. He was interested; he saw an opportunity. He was a white-haired, tweedy, pipe-smoking old fellow with a toothbrush mustache and twinkling blue eyes. His specialty was doing the things that American presidents wanted done without actually requiring them to give the order. He smiled with big crooked teeth; he was rich but too old for orthodontia. "Until I give the word, nobody knows anything but us two chickens. Does that suit you?"

I nodded as if my assent really was necessary. After a breath or two, I said, "How much encouragement can I offer this fellow?"

"Use your judgment. Take some money too. You may have to tide him over till he gets hold of the national treasure. Just don't make any promises. Hear him out. Figure him out. Estimate his chances. We don't want a failure. Or an embarrassment."

I rose to leave.

"Hold on," said the chief.

He rummaged around in a desk drawer and, after examining several identical objects and discarding them, handed me a large bulging brown envelope. A receipt was attached to it with Scotch tape. It said that the envelope contained $100,000 in hundred-dollar bills. I signed it with the fictitious name my employer had assigned to me when I joined up. As I opened the door to leave, I saw that the old gentleman had gone back to his *Wall Street Journal.*

Benjamin and I had arranged no secure way of communicating with each other, so I had not notified him that I was coming back to Ndala. Nevertheless, the sergeant met me on the tarmac at the airport. I was not surprised that Benjamin knew I was coming. Like all good cops, he kept an eye on passenger manifests for flights in and out of his jurisdiction. After sending a baggage handler into the hold of the plane to find my bag, the sergeant drove me to a safe house in the European quarter of the city. It was five o'clock in the morning when we got there. Benjamin awaited me. The sergeant cooked and served a complete English breakfast—eggs, bacon, sausage, fried potatoes, grilled tomato, cold toast, Dundee orange marmalade, and sour gritty coffee. Benjamin ate with gusto but made no small talk. Air conditioners hummed in every window.

"Better that you stay in this house than the hotel," Benjamin said when he had cleaned his plate. "In that way there will never be a record that you have been in this country."

That was certainly true, and it was not the least of my worries. I was traveling on a Canadian passport as Robert Bruce Brown, who had died of meningitis in Baddeck, Nova Scotia, thirty-five years before at age two. Thanks to the sergeant, I had bypassed customs and passport control. That meant that there was no entry stamp in the passport. In theory I could not leave the country without one, but then again, I was carrying $100,000 American in cash in an airline bag, and this was a country in which money talked. If I did disappear, I would disappear without a trace. One way or another, so would the money.

"There is something I want you to see," Benjamin said. Apparently this was his standard phrase when he had something unpleasant to show me. After wiping his lips on a white linen napkin, folding it neatly, and dropping it onto the table, he led me into the living room. The drapes were drawn. The sun was up. A sliver of white-hot sunlight shone through. Benjamin called to the sergeant, who brought his briefcase and pulled the curtains tighter. Before leaving us he started an LP on the hi-fi and turned up the volume to defeat hidden microphones. Sinatra sang "In the Still of the Night."

Benjamin took a large envelope from the briefcase and handed it to me. It contained about twenty glossy black-and-white photographs—army trucks parked in a field, soldiers with bayonets fixed; a large empty ditch with two bulldozers standing by; beggars getting down from the truck; beggars being tumbled into the ditch; beggars, hedged in by bayonets, being buried alive by the bulldozers; bulldozers rolling over the dirt to tamp it down with their treads.

"The army is very unhappy about this," Benjamin said. "President Ga did not tell the generals that soldiers would be required to do this work. They thought they were just getting these beggars out of sight until after the Pan-African Conference. Instead the soldiers were ordered to solve the problem once and for all."

My throat was dry. I cleared it and said, "How many people were buried alive?"

"Nobody counted."

"Why was this done?"

"I told you. The beggars were an eyesore."

"That was reason enough to bury them alive?"

"The soldiers were supposed to shoot them first. But they refused. This is good for us, because now the army is angry. Also afraid. Now Ga can execute any general for murder simply by discovering the crime and punishing the culprits in the name of justice and the people. The generals have not told the president that the solders refused to follow his orders, so now they are in danger. If he ever finds out, he will bury the soldiers alive. Also a general or two. Or more."

I said, "Who would tell him?"

"Who indeed?" asked Benjamin, stone-faced. I handed the pictures back to him. He held up a palm. "Keep them."

I said, "No, thank you."

The photos were a death warrant for anyone who was arrested with them in his possession.

Benjamin ignored me. He rummaged in his briefcase and handed me a handheld radio transceiver. Technologically speaking, those were primitive days, and the device was not much smaller than a fifth of Beefeater's, minus the neck of the bottle. Nevertheless, it was a wonder for its time. It was made in the U.S.A., so I supposed it had been supplied by the local chief of station, the man who played ball with Ga, as a trinket for a native.

Benjamin said, "Your call sign is Mustard One. Mine is Mustard. This for emergencies. This too." He handed me a Webley and a box of hollow-point cartridges.

I was touched by his concern. But the transceiver was useless—if the situation was desperate enough to call him, I would be a dead man before he could get to me. The Webley, however, would be useful for shooting myself in case of need. Shooting anyone else in this country would be the equivalent of committing suicide.

Benjamin rose to his feet. "I will be back," he said. "We will spend the evening together."

When Benjamin returned around midnight, I was reading Sir Richard Burton's *Wanderings in West Africa,* the only book in the house. It was a first edition, published in 1863. The margins were sprinkled with pencil dots. I guessed that it had been used by some romantic Brit for a book code. Benjamin was sartorially correct as usual—crisp white shirt with paisley cravat, double-breasted naval blazer, gray slacks, gleaming oxblood oxfords. He cast a disapproving eye on my wrinkled shorts and sweaty shirt and bare feet.

"You must wash and shave and put on proper clothes," he said. "We have been invited to dinner."

Benjamin offered no further information. I asked no questions. The sergeant drove, rapidly, without headlights on narrow trails through the bush. We arrived at a guard shack. The guard, a very sharp soldier, saluted and waved us through without looking inside the car. The road widened into a sweeping driveway. Gravel crackled under the tires. We reached the top of a little rise and I saw before me the presidential palace, lit up like a football stadium by the light towers that surrounded it. The flags of all the newborn African nations flew from a ring of flagstaffs.

The soldiers guarding the front door—white belts, white gloves, white bootlaces, white rifle slings—came to present arms. We walked past them into a vast foyer from which a double staircase swept upward before separating at a landing decorated by a huge floodlit portrait of President Ga wearing his sash of office. A liveried servant led us up the stairs past a gallery of portraits of Ga variously uniformed as general of the army, admiral of the fleet, air chief marshal, head of the party, and other offices I could not identify.

We simply walked into the presidential office. No guards were visible. President Ga was seated behind a desk at the far end of the vast room. Two attack dogs, pit bulls, stood with ears pricked at either side of his oversize desk. The ceiling could not have been less than fifteen feet high. Ga, not a large person to begin with, was so diminished by these Brobdingnagian proportions that he looked like a puppet. He was reading what I supposed was a state paper, pen in hand in case he needed to add or cross something out. As we approached across the snow-white marble floor, our footsteps echoed. Benjamin's were especially loud because he wore leather heels, but nothing, apparently, could break the president's concentration.

About ten feet from the desk we stopped, our toes touching a bronze strip that was sunk into the marble. Ga ignored us. The pit bulls did not. Ga pressed a button. A hidden door opened behind the desk, and a young army officer in dress uniform stepped out. Behind him I could see half-a-dozen other soldiers, armed to the teeth and standing at attention in a closetlike space that was hardly large enough to hold them all.

Wordlessly, Ga handed the paper to the officer, who took it, made a smart about-face, and marched back into the closet. Ga stood up, still taking no notice of us, and strolled to the large window behind his desk. It looked out over the brightly lit, shadowless palace grounds. At a little distance I could see an enclosure in which several different species of gazelle were confined. In other paddocks—too many to be seen in a single glance—other wild animals paced. Ga drank in the scene for a long moment, then whirled and approached Benjamin and me at quick-march, as if he wore one of his many uniforms instead of the white bush jacket, black slacks, and sandals in which he actually was dressed. Benjamin did not introduce me. Apparently there was no need to do so, because Ga, looking me straight in the eye, shook my hand and said, "I hope you like French food, Mr. Brown."

I did. The menu was a terrine of gray sole served with a 1953 Corton-Charlemagne, veal stew accompanied by a 1949 Pommard, cheese, and grapes. The president ate the food hungrily, talking all the while, but only sipped the wines.

"Alcohol gives me bad dreams," he said to me. "Do you ever have bad dreams?"

"Doesn't everyone, sir?"

"My best friend, who died too young, never had bad dreams. He was too good in mind and heart to be troubled by such things. Now he is in my dreams. He visits me almost every night. Who is in your dreams?"

"Mostly people I don't know."

"Then you are very lucky."

During the dinner Ga talked about America. He knew it well. He had earned a degree from a Negro college in Missouri. Baptist missionaries had sent him to the college on a scholarship. He graduated second in his class, behind his best friend, who now called on him in dreams. When Ga spoke to his people, he spoke standard Africanized English, the common tongue of his country, where more than a hundred mutually incomprehensible tribal languages were in use. He spoke to me in American English, sounding like Harry S. Truman. He had had a wonderful time in college — the football games, the fraternity pranks, the music, the wonderful food, homecoming, the prom, those American coeds! His friend had been the school's star running back; Ga had been the team manager; they had won their conference championship two years in a row. "From the time we were boys together in our village, my friend was always the star, I was always the administrator," he said. "Until we got into politics and changed places. My friend stuttered. It was his only flaw. It is the reason I am president. Had he been able to speak to the people without making them laugh, he would be living in this house."

"You were fond of this man," I said.

"Fond of him? He was my brother."

Tears formed in the president's eyes. Despite everything I knew about his crimes, I found myself liking Akokwu Ga.

Servants arrived with coffee and a silver dessert bowl. "Ah, strawberries and crème fraîche!" said Ga, breaking into his first smile of the evening.

After the strawberries, another servant offered cigars and port, discreetly showing me the labels. Ga waved these temptations away like a good Baptist. I did the same, not without regret.

"Come, my friend," said Ga, rising to his feet and suddenly speaking West African rather than Missouri English, "it is time for a walk. Do you get enough exercise?"

I said, "I wish I got more."

"Ah, but you must make time to keep up to snuff," said Ga. "I ride horseback every morning and walk in the cool of the evening. Both things are excellent exercise, and also, to start the day, you have the companionship of the horse, which never says anything stupid. You must get a horse. If you are too busy for a horse, a masseur. Not a masseuse. They are too distracting. Massage is like hearty exercise if the masseur is strong and has the knowledge. Bob Hope told me that. Massage keeps him young."

By now we were at the front door. The spick-and-span young army captain who had earlier leaped out of the closet behind Ga's desk awaited us. Standing at rigid attention, he held out a paper for Ga. Benjamin immediately went into reverse, walking backward as he withdrew from eyeshot and earshot of the president while the latter read his document and spoke to his orderly. I followed suit.

Staring straight ahead and barely moving his lips, Benjamin muttered, "He is charming tonight. Be careful." These were the first words he had uttered all evening. Throughout dinner, Ga had ignored him entirely, as if he were a third pit bull lying at his feet.

Outside, under the stadium lights, Ga led the way across the shadowless grounds to his animal park. Three men walked in front, sweeping the ground in case of snakes. As I knew from rumor and intelligence reports, Ga had a morbid fear of snakes. Another bearer carried Ga's sporting rifle, a beautiful weapon that looked to me like a Churchill, retail in London £10,000.

The light from the towers was so strong that everything looked like an overexposed photograph. Ga pointed out the gazelles, naming them all one by one. "Some of these specimens are quite rare," he said, "or so I am told by the people who sell them. I am preserving them for the people of this nation. Most of these beasts no longer live in this part of Africa, but before the Europeans came with their guns and killed them for sport, we knew them as brothers."

Ga was a believer in raising a mythical African past to the status of reality. The public buildings he had built during his brief reign featured murals and mosaics depicting Africans of a lost civilization inventing agriculture, mathematics, architecture, medicine, electricity, the airplane, even the postage stamp. In his mind it was only logical that the ancients had also lived in peace with the lion, the elephant, the giraffe—everything but the serpent, which Ga had exiled from his utopia.

We tramped on a bit, to an empty paddock. "Now you will see something," he said. "You will see nature in the raw."

This paddock was unlighted. Ga lifted his hand, and the lights went on. Standing alone in the middle of the open space was an animal that even I was able to recognize as a Thomson's gazelle from its diminutive size, its lovely tan-and-white coat, the calligraphic black stripe on its flank. This one was a buck, something like three feet tall, a work of art like so many other African animals.

"This type of gazelle is common," Ga said. "There are hundreds of thousands of them in herds in Tanganyika. They can outrun a lion. Watch."

The word *suddenly* does not convey the speed of what happened next. Out of the blinding light in which it had somehow been concealing itself as it stalked the Tommy, a cheetah materialized, moving at sixty miles an hour. A cheetah can cover a hundred meters in less than three seconds. The Tommy saw or sensed this blur of death that hurtled toward him and leaped three or four feet straight up into the air, then hit the ground running. The Tommy was slightly slower than its predator, but far more nimble. When the cheetah got close enough to attack, the little gazelle would make a quick turn and escape. This happened over and over again. The size of the paddock — or playing field, as Ga must have thought of it — was an advantage to the Tommy, who would lead the cheetah straight at the fence, then make a last-second turn. One or twice the cheetah crashed into the wire.

"This is almost over," Ga said. "Usually it lasts only a minute or so. If the cat does not win very quickly, it runs out of strength and gives up."

A second later the cheetah won. The gazelle turned in the wrong direction, and the cat brought it down. A cheetah is not strong enough to break the neck of its prey, so it kills by suffocation, biting the throat and crushing the windpipe. The Tommy struggled, then went limp. The cheetah's eyes glittered. So did Ga's.

Beaming, he threw an arm around my shoulders. He said, "Wonderful, eh?"

I smelled the food and wine on his breath, felt his excited heart beating against my shoulder. Then, without a good night or even a facial expression, Ga turned on his heel and, surrounded by his snake sweepers and his gun bearer, marched away and disappeared into the palace. The evening was over. His guests had ceased to exist.

We lost no time in leaving. Minutes later, as we rolled toward the wakening city in Benjamin's Rover, I asked a question.

"Is he always so hospitable?"

"Tonight you saw one Ga," Benjamin said. "There are a thousand of him."

I could believe it. In this one evening I had seen him in half-a-dozen incarnations: Mussolini redux, gourmet, Joe College, tender friend, zoologist, mythologist, and a fun-loving god who stage-managed animal sacrifices to himself.

The Rover purred along a smoothly paved but deserted road, bush to the left and right, the sticky night dark as macadam. Headlights appeared behind us and approached at high speed. The sergeant switched off the Rover's lights and pulled off the road. The tires bit into soft dirt. Benjamin and I were slammed together hip and shoulder. We were being overtaken by a motorcade. A Cadillac, the lead car, swept by at high speed, then a Rolls-Royce, then another Cadillac as chase car.

"The president," Benjamin said calmly when the Rover stopped bouncing. "He always has a woman or two before the sun rises. He is quick with them, never more than fifteen minutes, then he goes back to the presidential palace. He never goes to the same woman twice in the same month."

"He keeps thirty-one women?"

"More, in case one of them is not clean on a certain night."

"How does he choose which one?"

"Each woman has a number. Each month Ga receives from somebody in St. Louis, Missouri, what is called a dream book. It is used in America to play the numbers game. He uses the number in the dream book for the day."

I said, "So if you want to find him on any given night, you match the woman's number to the number for that particular day in the dream book."

"Yes, if you know the address of every woman, that is the key," Benjamin said.

He smiled and placed a hand on my shoulder, pleased as a proud father with the quickness of my mind.

For the next several days there was no sign of Benjamin. I was not locked up, but as a practical matter this meant that I was confined to the safe house during daylight hours. There was nowhere to go at night. Like any other prisoner I invented ways to pass the empty hours. Solitude and time-wasting did not bother me; I was used to them; both were occupational hazards. I was concerned by the lack of exercise, because I did not want to run out of breath in case I had to make a run for it. This seemed a likely outcome. How else could this situation end?

I jogged in place for an hour every morning, and in the afternoon ran the 100- and 220-yard dashes, also in place but flat out. I did pushups and sit-ups and side-straddle hops. I punched and karate-chopped the sofa cushions until I had beaten every last mote of dust from them. I jitterbugged in my socks to cracked 78 rpm records I found in a closet: Louis Armstrong, the Harmonica Rascals, the Andrews Sisters. Satchmo's "Muskrat Ramble" and the sisters' "Boogie Woogie Bugle Boy of Company B" provided the best workouts.

The sergeant stopped by every day to cook lunch and dinner and wash up afterward. He brought quality groceries, and he was a good cook, specializing in curries and local piripiri dishes loaded with cayenne pepper that made the heart beat in the skull. I asked him to bring me books. He refused money to pay for them or the groceries—apparently I was covered by a budget in secret funds—and came back from the African market the next day with at least one Penguin paperback by every writer I had named and a few more besides. The books were dog-eared and food- and coffee-stained, and most were missing pages.

I was in bed, reading a W. Somerset Maugham short story about adulterers in Malaya, when Benjamin finally showed up. As usual he chose the wee hours of the morning for his visit. He was as stealthy as he had been when he visited me in the hotel, and I heard no car or any other sound of his approach.

All the same I felt his presence before he materialized out of the darkness. He seemed to be alone. He carried a battered leather valise, the kind that has a hinged top that opens like a mouth when the catch is released. The valise seemed to jump in his hand, as if it contained a disembodied muscle. I rationalized this by thinking that he must be trembling for some reason. Maybe he had had a bout of fever and was not quite recovered. That would explain why I hadn't seen him for a week.

Then, at the instant when I realized that there was something alive inside the valise and it was trying to get out, Benjamin held the bag upside down over my bed and pressed the catch. The bag popped open and a huge blue-black mamba uncoiled itself from within. It landed on my legs. With blinding speed it coiled and struck. I felt the blow, a soft punch but no sting, on my chest just above the heart. I knew that I was a dead man. So apparently did the mamba. It stared into my eyes, waiting (or so I thought) for my heart to stop, for the power of thought to switch off. No more than a second had passed. Already I felt cold. An ineffable calm settled upon me. The laboring air conditioner in the window was suddenly almost silent. My hearing seemed to be going first. Next, I thought, the eyes. I felt no pain. I thought, Maybe after all there is a God, or was a God, if the last moment of life has been arranged in such a kindly and loving way.

Dreamily I watched as Benjamin's hand, black as the mamba, seized the snake behind the head. The serpent struggled, lashing its body and winding itself around Benjamin's arm. The sergeant appeared, stepping out of the darkness and into the light of my reading lamp just as Benjamin had done. It took the combined strength of these two powerful men to stuff the thing back into the valise and close it. They did so without the slightest sign of fear. In the half-light, with their faces close together, they looked more than ever like brothers. How strange it was, I thought, that this surreal scene in this misbegotten place should be the last thing I would ever see. Benjamin handed the valise to the sergeant. It jumped violently in his hand. The sergeant produced a key and with a perfectly steady hand locked the valise. His eyes were fixed on me. He was grinning in what I can only describe as total delight. Make that unholy delight.

To me, an unsmiling Benjamin said, "You must be wondering why you are not dead yet."

He was not grinning. The sergeant, watching me over Benjamin's shoulder, did it for him, big white teeth reflecting more light than there seemed to be in the room.

Up to this point I had not looked at my fatal wound. In fact, I had not moved at all since the snake had struck me. Something told me that any movement might quicken the action of the venom and rob me of whatever split seconds of life I might have left. Besides, I did not want to see the wound that I imagined: twin punctures made by the mamba's fangs, perhaps a drop of two of blood, and, most horribly, venom oozing from the holes in my skin. Finally I found the courage to glance at my chest. It was unmarked.

I leaped out of bed, dashed into the bathroom, and examined

my sweating torso. I stripped off my boxer shorts, the only garment I was wearing, and twisted and turned in the stingy light, looking for what I still feared was a mortal wound. But I saw no break in my skin, no bruise even. The symptoms of death I had been feeling—the lightheadedness, the shortness of breath, and a sense of loss so intense that it felt like the shutdown of the heart—went away.

Without bothering to put my shorts back on, I went back into the bedroom.

"Look at him!" the sergeant cried, pointing a finger at me.

At first I thought he was making fun of my nakedness. I had spent time on a beach in South Africa, and the part of me formerly covered by my shorts was dead white. I soon realized that he was laughing at something other than my tan line. I was the victim of the most sadistic practical joke since Harry Flashman was kicked out of Rugby College, and these two were the jokers. There is no mirth like African mirth, and both Benjamin and the sergeant were doubled over by it. They howled with laughter, their eyes were filled with tears, they gasped for breath, they hugged each other as they danced a jig of merriment, they lost their balance and staggered to regain it.

"Look at him!" they said over and over again. "Look at him!"

The locked valise had been placed on the bed. The contortions of the infuriated six-foot-long muscle that was trying to escape from it caused it to skitter across the sheets. I tried to get around the helpless men, but they kept lurching into my path, so I was not able to reach the Webley, Benjamin's gift to me, that was stashed under the mattress. My plan was to empty the revolver, if I could get my hands on it, into the pulsating valise. I was in no way certain that I could stick to this plan if I actually had the gun in my hands and this comedy team at point-blank range.

Breath by breath, I got hold of myself. So did Benjamin and the sergeant, though it took them a little longer. It was obvious what had happened. Some juju man had captured the snake and removed its fangs and venom sac. Knowing Benjamin—and by now I felt that I knew him intimately despite the brevity of our friendship—he had commissioned the capture and the veterinary surgery. Knowing also how terrified President Ga was of snakes, I could only surmise that the defanged mamba was going to be a player in the overthrow of the tyrant. Maybe, if the coup succeeded, Benjamin would make the mamba part of the flag, as an earlier group of patriots had done a couple of hundred years ago with another poisonous snake in another British colony.

Benjamin offered no explanations for the prank. I was damned if I was going to ask him any questions. I was by no means certain that I could control my voice. By now the joke had cooled off. Benjamin had stopped smiling. His grave dignity had returned. He made a minimal gesture. The sergeant picked up the valise.

Benjamin said, "I will be back soon."

With a scratchy throat, I said, "Good."

The two of them let themselves out the front door. I locked it behind them, and as I tried to put the key into my pants pocket I remembered that I was stark naked. Nakedness was deeply offensive to Christianized Africans like Benjamin. Maybe that was why he had stopped laughing before the joke had really worn off.

I reached under the mattress and pulled out the Webley and cocked it. It is a very heavy weapon, weighing almost three pounds when fully loaded, and when I felt its heft in my hand I began to tremble. I could not stop. I was afraid that the gun might go off, but I had so little control over my muscles that I could not safely put it down. Teeth chattering, my body chilling in a room where the temperature was not less than ninety degrees, I understood fully and for the first time just what a brilliant son of a bitch Benjamin was.

Two days later, at five in the morning, he showed up at the safe house for breakfast. He said he had been up all night. There was no outward sign of this. He was fresh from the shower, his starched uniform still smelled of the iron, and he sat up straight as a cadet in his chair. However, he was not his usual masked self. There was an air of excitement about him that he did not bother to conceal.

He ate the yolks of his fried eggs with a spoon, then touched the corners of his mouth with his napkin. "The president of the republic is very upset," he said.

He spoke in a low tone. It was difficult to hear him because a Benny Goodman record was playing on the phonograph—the usual precaution against eavesdroppers—and Harry James and the rest of the trumpet section were playing as if their four or five horns were a single instrument.

I said, "Upset? Why?"

"He has discovered the fangs and the poison sac of a black mamba on his desk."

"Good Lord," I said. "No wonder he's upset."

"Yes. He found these things when he came back from one of his women last night. They were right in the center of the blotter, in his coffee cup. If someone had poured coffee into the cup he might well have drunk it absentmindedly. He said so himself."

I could think of nothing to say. Certainly Benjamin needed no encouragement to go on with his story.

He said, "He flew off the handle and called me immediately. He screamed into the telephone. He was surrounded by traitors, he said. How could anyone have gained access to his office in his absence, let alone smuggled in the coffee cup? How could no one have noticed this coffee cup and what was in it? There are soldiers everywhere in the presidential palace. Or were."

"They are there no longer?"

"Naturally he has dismissed them. How could he trust them after this? He also ordered the arrest of the army chief of staff. His order has of course been carried out."

"The army chief of staff is in your custody?"

"For the time being, yes. It gives us an opportunity to talk frankly to each other."

"Who is handling security if not the army?"

"The national police. This is an honor, but it is a strain on our manpower, especially with the Pan-African festival beginning the day after tomorrow. Thousands will flood into Ndala, including twenty-six heads of state and who knows how many other dignitaries and nobodies. But of course the safety of our own head of state and government is the number-one priority."

"You are investigating, of course."

"Oh, yes," Benjamin said. "Suspects, some of them of very high rank, are being interviewed, quarters are being searched, every safe in the nation is being opened, information is being gathered, fingerprints and other physical evidence have been assembled, all the usual police procedures are in place, but on a much larger and more urgent scale than usual. The presidential palace is off-limits to everyone except the president and the police."

He was in complete control of his voice and his facial muscles. But underneath his unflappable behavior, he glowed with joy. He was within reach of something that he wanted very much indeed.

"The fangs and so on are not all that we have to worry about," Benjamin went on. "The president for life has also received an anonymous letter, mysteriously placed under his pillow by an unknown hand, stating that a sample of his bodily secretions has been given to a famous juju man in the Ivory Coast."

This was momentous news. Playing the naif, my assigned role in this charade, I said, "Bodily secretions?"

"We believe they were obtained from one of Ga's women. He is deeply concerned. This can only mean that a curse has been put upon him by an enemy. The curse can be reversed only if we can find the culprit who hired the juju man."

Imparting this news, he remained impassive. No smile, no equivalent of a wink, no expression of any kind came to the surface. Benjamin himself had, of course, engineered everything he was reporting to me—the fangs, the venom, the anonymous letter with its chilling message. But he described these things as if he had no more idea than the man in the moon who was responsible for tormenting President Ga.

The juju curse was the keystone of the plot. I had known Africans, one of them an agent of mine who possessed a first-class degree from Cambridge, who had withered and died from witchcraft. The bodily secretion was the vital element in casting a juju spell. Some product of the victim's body was needed to invoke a truly effective curse—a lock of hair, an ounce of urine, a teaspoon of saliva, feces. The more intimate the product, the greater its power. Nothing could be a more effective charm than a man's semen. No wonder Ga was beside himself. And no wonder that he was now in Benjamin's power.

By now more than thirty African heads of state had flown into Ndala for President Ga's Pan-African Conference. This was the day on which they would all ride through the city in their Rolls-Royces and Mercedes-Benzes and Cadillacs, waving to the vast crowd that had been assembled to greet them. Whether any of these spectators had the faintest idea who the dignitaries were or what they were doing in Ndala were separate questions. Whole tribes had been bused or trucked or herded on foot into the city from the interior. Many were dancing. Chiefs had brought warriors armed with shields and spears to protect them against enemies, wives to service them, dwarves to keep them entertained. Every single one of these human beings seemed to be grunting or shouting or singing or, mostly, laughing, and the noise produced by all those voices, added to the beating of drums and the sound of musical instruments and the tootling of automobile horns, made the air tremble. Palm wine and warm beer flowed, and the spicy aroma of stews and roasting goats rose from hundreds of cook fires.

At last the sergeant found the exact spot he had been looking for, an empty space in front of the parliament building, and parked the car in the shadow of a huge baobab tree. A couple of constables were already on hand, and they cleared away the crowd so that we had an unobstructed view.

"They will come soon," the sergeant said.

It was a little before five in the afternoon. The parade was already about ninety minutes behind schedule, but there was no such concept as "on time" in Ndala or any other place in Africa. Maybe forty minutes later, we heard the faraway warped sound of a brass band playing "The British Grenadiers." The music grew louder and the band marched by, drum major brandishing a baton that was as tall as he was, every musician's eye seemingly fixed on the Austin as the marching men turned eyes left on the parliament and the flags of the African nations that flew from its circle of flagpoles. A battalion of infantry then marched smartly by, drenched in sweat, arms swinging, boots kicking up powdery dust. The infantry were followed by several tanks and armored cars and howitzers. Finally came a platoon of bagpipers, tartan kilts and sporrans swinging, "Scotland the Brave" splitting the sun-scorched air. If the Brits had taught these people nothing else in a century of colonialism, they had taught them how to organize a parade.

"Now come the presidents," the sergeant said. "President for Life Ga will be first, then the others." Then, even though we were alone in the car with the windows rolled up, he dropped his voice to a whisper and added, "Watch very carefully the road ahead of his car."

Ga's regal snow-white Rolls-Royce materialized out of the dust. There were a few grunts from onlookers but no ululations or other such behavior. The masses merely watched this strange alien phenomenon, and no doubt they would have reacted in the same way if a spaceship had been landing among them. Not that the occasion was wholly lacking in ceremony. The soldiers posted along the street at ten-foot intervals came to present arms. The sergeant leaped out of the car, and he and the two constables stood to attention, saluting. I got out too. No one paid the slightest attention to me. But then, only a few of the onlookers were paying very much attention to President Ga. The Rolls-Royce continued its stately approach, flags flying, headlights blazing. The crowd stirred and muttered.

Then, without warning, the crowd suddenly broke and began to run in all directions—men, women, children, the decrepit old borne aloft by their sons and daughters, everyone except the dancers, who had by now fallen into a collective trance and went right on dancing, oblivious to the panic all around them. Everyone else scattered as fast as their legs would carry them. The presidential Rolls-Royce slammed on its brakes and stood on its nose. Inside it, President Ga or one of his doubles, dressed in a white uniform, was thrown about like a rag doll.

It was impossible not to see Benjamin's hand in all this. A single thought filled my mind: assassination. He was going to kill his man in full view of thirty other presidents for life.

I leaped onto the hood of the Austin, then scrambled to the roof. From that vantage point I saw what all the fright was about. A black mamba at least ten feet long was slithering with almost unbelievable swiftness across the road in the path of the white Rolls-Royce. Suddenly half-a-dozen brave fellows, half-naked all of them, leaped out of the crowd and attacked the serpent with pangas, cutting it into pieces that writhed violently as if trying to reconnect themselves into a living reptile. The crowd uttered a loud, collective basso grunt. This was a huge yet subdued sound, like a whisper amplified to the power of ten thousand on some enormous hi-fi speaker yet to be invented.

The Rolls-Royce, klaxon sounding, sped away. The sergeant said, "Get into the car. We must go."

I did as he ordered. Inside the sweltering, buttoned-up Austin, I asked if the mamba crossing President Ga's path on his day of triumph would be seen as a bad omen.

"Oh, yes," the sergeant said, grinning into the mirror. "*Very* bad. No one who saw will ever forget."

Darkness fell. The sergeant did not take me home but drove me to a different safe house on the outskirts of the city. As soon as we were inside I switched on the English-language radio. The opening ceremonies of the Pan-African Conference were now in progress at the soccer stadium. Announcers shouted to be heard above the blare of bands and choirs, the boom of fireworks, and the noise of the crowd. Needless to say, not a word was uttered over the airways about the meeting between the mamba and Ga's white Rolls-Royce. Everyone knew all about it anyway by word of mouth or talking drum or one of the many Bantu tongues that could be signed or whistled as well as spoken.

In all those minds, as in my own, the questions were, What happens next and when will it happen? I left the radio on, knowing that the first word of the coup would come from its speakers. Second only to the capture or murder of the prince, the broadcasting station was the most important objective in any coup d'état. Obviously Benjamin and his coconspirators—assuming that he had any—must strike tonight. Never again would he have such an opportunity to destroy the tyrant before the very eyes of Africa. He would want to kill Ga in the most humiliating way possible. He would want to show him as weak, impotent, and alone, without a single person willing or able to defend him.

Promptly at eight o'clock, the sergeant carried a cooler into the house, rattled pots and pans in the kitchen, and served my dinner, all five courses at once. The food was French. "This is the same food that all the presidents will be eating at the state dinner," the sergeant said. I ate only the heated-up entrée, medallions of veal in a cream sauce that had separated because the sergeant had let it boil.

Around two in the morning, the sergeant's walkie-talkie squawked. He lifted it to his ear, heard what sounded to me like a single word, and replied with what also seemed to be a single word. The conversation lasted less than a second. He said, "Come, Mr. Brown. It is time to go."

We drove through a maze of streets, but on this night of revelry saw no sleepers by the wayside. Everybody was still celebrating. Oil lamps and candles glowed in the blackness like red and yellow eyes, as if the entire genus *Carnivora* was drawn up in a hungry circle on the outskirts of the party. Music blared from loudspeakers, people danced, thousands of shouted conversations stirred the stagnant, overheated air. The city had become one enormous, throbbing Equator Club. The sergeant maneuvered the Austin through the pandemonium with one hand on the steering wheel and the other on the hooter, constantly beeping to let people know that he wasn't trying to sneak up on them and kill them. Not since Independence Night, I thought, could there have been so many witnesses awake at this hour, ready to observe whatever Benjamin was going to do next.

At last we drove out of the crowd and into the European quarter. Through the rear window I could see the distorted smoky-red glow of the city. I imagined I could feel the earth quivering in rhythm to the innumerable bare feet that were pounding it in unison a mile or so away. The music and the shouting were very loud even at such a distance.

The sergeant drove at his usual brisk pace, lights off as usual. He parked the car and switched off the engine. By now my eyes had adjusted, and I could see another police car parked a few yards away. We were parked on a low hilltop, and the red glow of the city caught in the mirror-shine of its metal. Soon a third car drove up and parked close beside us. It was Benjamin's Rover, identifiable by the baritone throb of its engine. The driver's cap badge caught a little light. A large man who might have been Benjamin sat in the backseat alone.

Moving swiftly, Benjamin got into the backseat with me. The dome light blinked. He wore the dress uniform I supposed he had worn to the state dinner—long pants, white shirt with necktie, short epauletted mess jacket that the Brits call a bum freezer, decorations. Benjamin smelled as usual of starch, brass polish, soap, his own musk.

Headlights swept up the hill, turned sharp left into the street that paralleled the one on which our own cars were parked, then stopped. Car doors slammed, men moved quick-time, a key turned in a lock, a door squeaked as it was opened, a scratchy Edith Piaf LP played five or six bars of *"Les amants de Paris."*

We were parked behind the house into which Ga had gone to keep his rendezvous for tonight. Jumpy light showed in an upstairs

window, dim and yellowish, as if filtering down a hallway from another room. The back door opened. A flashlight blinked. The Rover's headlights flashed in reply.

"Come," Benjamin said. He got out of the car and strode into
the darkness. I followed. The sergeant got something out of the
trunk, then slammed the lid. Behind me I heard his brogans at a
run. We went through the open door. Inside the house, the record
changed on the hi-fi and Piaf's recorded voice began to sing *"Il
Pleut."* Benjamin, entirely at home, strode down a hallway, then up
a stairway. At the top, in half-shadow outside a half-open bedroom
door, a policeman stood at attention as if he did not quite know
exactly what was expected of him or what would happen next.

In a mirror I saw a man and a woman engaged in vigorous coitus
and heard the woman's moans and outcries. The sergeant marched
into the room. Benjamin gave me a little push, and I marched in
behind him. The room was full of burning candles. The smell of
incense was strong. Smoke hung in the air. The woman shouted
something in what sounded to me like Swedish. She was quite
small. President Ga, lying on top of her, covered her completely.
Her legs were wound around his waist, ankles crossed, feet in gilt
shoes with stiletto heels. I looked into the mirror in hope of seeing
the girl's face. My eyes met Ga's. The candlelight exaggerated the
size of his startled, wide-open eyes. His face twisted into a mask of
furious anger, and he rolled off the woman, knocking off one of
her shoes. Now I saw her face, smeared lipstick and tousled hair.
She was a cookie-cutter blonde, as flawless as a dummy in a store
window.

I knew what was coming next, of course. The sergeant took one
step forward. In his outstretched hands he held the valise that I remembered so well. Evidently that was what he had retrieved from
the trunk of the Austin. The snap of brass latches sounded like the
metallic *one-two* of the slide of an automatic pistol. The sergeant
opened the valise and turned it upside down. The mamba flowed
out of the bag with the same unbelievable swiftness, as if it were
coming into being before our eyes. I tried to leap backward, but
Benjamin stood immediately behind me, blocking the way. President Ga and the blonde froze as if captured in a black-and-white
photograph by the flash of a strobe light.

The snake, a blur as it attacked, struck at the nearest target, President Ga. He grunted as if a bullet had entered his body. His mouth opened wide and he shouted, in English, "Oh, Jesus, sweet Jesus!" It was a prayer, not a blasphemy. In the same breath he uttered a tremendous sob. Between these two primal sounds, the woman, screaming, threw her body over the foot of the bed. Somehow she landed behind us on all fours in the hallway. Still shrieking, still wearing one gilt shoe, she sprinted down the hallway. The constable in the hall pursued her for a step or two, picked up the shoe after she kicked it off, and caught her by the hair, which was very long. Her head jerked back, but she kept going, leaving the constable with a handful of blond threads in his hand. He stared at these in puzzlement, then blew his whistle. At the head of the stairs the woman was captured by a second constable, a man almost as large as Benjamin. He carried her, squirming, kicking, screaming, back toward the bedroom. Her skin was so white that I half expected powder to fly from it. She bit his face. He twisted her jaw until she let go, and when he saw his own blood on her teeth he slammed her twice against the wall, then let go of her, throwing his hands wide in disgust that a woman should have attacked him, should have *bitten* him. Her limp, unconscious body slid to the floor. She landed with a thump on her round bottom, her back against the wall, her head lolling inside its curtain of hair. She twitched as if dreaming, and I wondered if her spine was broken. She had shapely breasts, pretty legs, peroxided delta, and it looked as though she had lipsticked her nipples. For some reason — maybe because this touch of perversity was so unimaginative, so innocent, such a learner's trick — my heart went out to her, if only for a moment.

Behind me I heard a gunshot. In the confined space of the bedroom it sounded like an artillery round going off. The stink of cordite mingled with the incense. Benjamin stood over the bed with a smoking Webley in his hand. The headless snake in its death throes whipped uncontrollably over the bed, spraying blood on Ga and the sheets. With his hands protecting his genitals, Ga scooted rapidly backward over the bed to escape the serpent, even though he must have known that it was now harmless. What a seed God planted in the human mind on the day that Adam ate the apple! From the look on Ga's face it was clear that he believed that he himself was dying almost as fast as the snake had just done, but his instincts, from which he could not escape, instructed him to cover his nakedness and flee for his life.

Ga's eyes were now fixed on Benjamin. The question in them was easy to read: Had Benjamin murdered him or rescued him? Benjamin made a gesture to Ga: *Come.*

Ga, strangling on the words, said, "Doctor!"

Benjamin ignored him. Silently he pointed a finger first at the sergeant, then at Ga. Then he whirled on his heel and left the room. The sergeant picked up the writhing snake and threw it into the hallway, then grasped Ga's left arm, turned him onto his stomach, and expertly cuffed his hands behind him.

Surprised, then outraged, Ga shouted, "I order you—"

The sergeant punched him hard in the kidney. Ga shrieked in pain and subsided, gasping. The sergeant shouted an order in his own language. Two constables—the one who had been posted in the hallway all along and the one the blonde had bitten—came into the room, pulled Ga to his feet, and marched him naked down the hallway, past the headless mamba, past the crumpled blonde, and out the back door. The mamba, still twitching, would be the first thing the girl would see when she opened her eyes.

In the bedroom the hi-fi played the last words of the Piaf song that had begun as we entered the house. It had taken Benjamin three minutes and twenty seconds to carry out his coup d'état.

Outside, Ga struggled with the two constables who were trying to stuff him into the trunk of Benjamin's Rover. He kicked, squirmed, butted. One of the constables struck him on the hipbone with his baton. Ga collapsed like a marionette whose strings had been cut. The constables heaved him into the trunk and slammed it shut. One of them locked it, and then, in his jubilation, knocked on it to make a little joke. The sergeant spoke an angry word to him.

Benjamin had already taken his place in the backseat of the Rover. I expected to be put into another car or to be left behind, but the sergeant opened the door for me and I got in and sat beside Benjamin. We heard Ga in the trunk behind us—groans, childlike sobs, whisperings, appeals to Jesus, an explosive shout of Benjamin's name, so throat-scraping in its loudness that I imagined spit flying from Ga's mouth. If Benjamin derived any satisfaction from these proofs that his enemy was entirely in his power, he did not show it by sign or sound. He sat at attention in his Victorian dress uniform—silent, unmoving, eyes front.

The sergeant's Austin, driven by one of the constables, tailgated us as we rolled through the wide-awake city. It was just as noisy as before but more drunken, more out of control. What must Ga be thinking as he lay in pitch darkness in his tiny cell, folded like a fetus, naked and in shackles? Ten minutes ago he had been the most powerful man in Africa. Not now. He was silent. Why? Did he fear that the crowd would discover him and drag him out of the trunk and parade him naked through the howling mob? Did he imagine photographs and newsreels of this appalling humiliation being seen by the entire world?

We arrived at a darkened building I did not recognize. Somewhere above us a red light pulsed, and when I got out of the car I looked upward and realized that it was the warning beacon on the tower of the national radio transmitter. I made out the silhouettes of an armored car and maybe a dozen men in uniform.

The constables hauled Ga out of the trunk. He struggled and shouted words in a language I did not understand. A door opened and emitted a shaft of light. To my eyes, which had seen nothing brighter than a candle flame all evening, it was blindingly bright. We went through the door, a back entrance, into a cramped stairwell. A young chief inspector came to attention and saluted. He looked and behaved remarkably like the spick-and-span army captain I had met at the presidential palace. Other constables were posted on the stairway, one man on every other step. Incongruously for men who dressed like British bobbies and were trained to behave like them, each was armed with a submachine gun. I wondered what would happen if they all started shooting at once in this concrete chamber.

Ga screamed a question: "Do you know who I am?"

No one answered.

In a different, commanding tone, Ga said, "I am the president of this republic, elected by the people. I have been kidnapped by these criminals. I order you to arrest them at once."

Ga sounded like his newsreel self, voice like a church bell, and in spite of his abject state looked like that old self, blazing eyes, imperious manner. However, the reality was that two large policemen had hold of his arms. He was naked and in chains and spattered with the blood of the mamba. A string of spittle hung from the corner of his mouth. The constables gave him a shove in the direction of the stairs. He stubbed his naked toes on the concrete step and sucked a sharp breath through his clenched teeth. This sound turned into a sob of frustration. The men to whom he was giving orders would not look at him.

I wondered if the next event in this Alice in Wonderland scenario might involve sitting Ga down at the microphone and ordering him to tell the nation that he had been removed from power. But no, he was frog-marched up the stairs and into the control room by his escorts. I remained with Benjamin and the sergeant in the studio. The control room was brightly lit. It was strange to gaze through the soundproof glass and see the wild-haired, glaring, unclothed Ga looking like one of his ancestors from the Neolithic.

The engineer switched on his mike and said, "Ready when you are, chief constable."

Into the open mike Ga shouted, "You will die, all of you! Your families will die! Your tribes, all of you will die!"

The engineer, quaking with fear, switched off the microphone, but Ga's mouth kept moving until the bigger constable put his hand over it, gagging him. Eyes rolling, chest heaving as he fought for breath, he kept on shouting. The constable pinched his nostrils shut, and the dumb-show noise behind the soundproof glass ceased.

Detecting movement near at hand, I shifted my gaze. A man in nightclothes was seated at the microphone. He was at least as nervous as the engineer. Benjamin handed him a sheet of paper. It was covered by Benjamin's perfect penmanship. Benjamin, a man who delegated nothing except, apparently, the most important announcement ever made over Radio Ndala, gave the engineer a thumbs-up signal. The engineer counted off seconds on raised fingers. He pointed to the announcer, who began reading in mellifluous broadcaster's English.

"Pay attention to this message from the high command of Ndala to all the people of our country," he said, voice steady but head twitching and hands trembling. "The tyrant Akokwu Ga is no longer the president of Ndala. He has been charged with mass murder, with treason, with corruption, and with other serious crimes and will be tried and punished according to the law. The functions of the government have been assumed for the time being by the high command of the armed services and the national police. The United Nations and the embassies of friendly nations have been informed of these developments. The people are to remain calm, obey the police, and return to their homes at once. An election to select a new head of state will be held in due course. The people are safe. The nation is safe. Investments by foreign nationals are safe. The treasure stolen by Akokwu Ga from the people is being recovered. All guests in our country are safe, and they are at liberty to remain in Ndala or leave Ndala whenever they wish. Additional communiqués will be issued from time to time by the high command. Long live Ndala. Long live independence and freedom. Long live justice. Long live democracy."

As the announcer read, Ga, listening intently, became very still, very attentive, his gaze fixed on what must have been a loudspeaker inside the control room. He might have been a child listening to a bedtime story about himself, so complete was his absorption in what was being said. His eyes were wide, his face bore a look of wonder, his mouth was slightly open. A police photographer took several pictures of him. Ga drew himself up and posed, head thrown back, one shackled foot advanced, as if he were wearing one of his resplendent uniforms.

After that, he was marched back to the Rover and again dumped into its trunk. He did not struggle or make a sound. The camera, it seemed, had given him back his dignity.

Roadblocks manned by soldiers had been erected on the road to the presidential palace. At the approach of Benjamin's Rover they opened the barricades and saluted as we passed. We were a feeble force—two ordinary sedans not even flying flags, four police constables and an American spy with a defective passport, plus the prisoner in the trunk of the car who was the reason for the soldiers' awe.

The palace came into view, illuminated as before by the megawatts that flooded down from the light towers. A dozen stretch limousines, seals of high office painted on their doors, were parked in the circular drive of the presidential palace. The palace doors were guarded by police constables armed with Kalashnikovs. On the roof of the palace, more constables manned the machine guns and antiaircraft guns that they had taken over from the army.

Benjamin waited for the constables in charge to haul Ga from the trunk, then he got out of the car. He gave me no instructions, so I followed along as he strode into the palace with his usual lack of ceremony. We climbed the grand stairway. All busts and statues and portraits in oil of Ga in his many uniforms had been removed. Less than an hour before, he had walked down these stairs as president of the republic for life. Now he climbed them as a prisoner dragging chains. There was a dreamlike quality to this scene, as if we did not belong in it or deserve it, as if it were a reenactment of an event from the life of some other tyrant who had lived and died in some other hour of history. Did Caesar as he felt the knife remember some assassinated Greek who had died a realer death?

A courtroom of sorts had been organized in Ga's vast and magnificent office. His desk and all his likenesses had been removed from this room too. The Ndalan flag remained, flanked by what I took to be the flags of the armed forces and other government entities, but not by the presidential flag. The presidential conference table, vast and gleaming and smelling of wax, stood crosswise where Ga's desk had formerly been. Through the window behind it Ga's antelopes and gazelles could be seen, bathed in incandescent light, as they bounded across the paddocks of his game park. Half-a-dozen grave men in British-style army, navy, and air force uniforms sat at the table like members of a court-martial. They were flanked by a half-dozen others in black judicial robes and white wigs, clearly members of the supreme court, and a handful of other dignitaries wearing national dress or European suits.

All but the military types seemed to be confused by the entrance of the prisoner. In some cases this was obviously the last thing they had expected to see. Some, if not all, of them probably had not been told why they were here. Maybe some simply did not recognize Ga. Who among them had ever imagined seeing in his present miserable state the invulnerable creature the president of the republic had been?

If in fact there were any doubts about his identity, Ga removed them at once. In his unmistakable voice he shouted, "As president for life of the republic, I command you, all you generals, to arrest this man on a charge of treason."

He attempted to point at Benjamin but of course could not do so with his wrists chained to his waist. Nevertheless, it was an impressive performance. Ga's voice was thunderous, his eyes flashed, he was the picture of command. For an instant he seemed to be fully clothed again. He gave every possible indication that he expected to be obeyed without question. But he was not obeyed, and when he continued to shout, the large constable did what he had done before, at the radio station. He clapped a hand over Ga's mouth and pinched his nostrils shut, and this time prolonged the treatment until Ga's struggle for breath produced high-pitched gasps that sounded very much like an infant crying.

The trial lasted less than an hour. Some might have called it a travesty, but everyone present knew that Ga was guilty of the crimes with which he was charged, and guilty too of even more heinous ones. Besides that, they knew that they must kill Ga now that they had witnessed his humiliation, or die themselves if he regained power. The trial itself followed established forms. Benjamin, as head of the national police, had prepared a bundle of evidence that was presented by a prosecutor and objected to by a lawyer appointed to defend Ga. Both men wore barrister's wigs. Witnesses were duly sworn. They testified to the massacre of the beggars. The spick-and-span young captain testified that Ga had embezzled not less than $50 million from the national treasury and deposited it in secret accounts in Geneva and Zurich and Liechtenstein. The court heard tape recordings of Ga, in secret meetings with foreign ambassadors and businessmen, agreeing to make certain high appointments and award certain contracts in return for certain sums of money. Damning evidence was introduced that Ga had ordered the death of his own brother and had perhaps fed him alive to hyenas in the game park.

Without retiring to deliberate, the court returned a unanimous verdict of guilty on all counts. Benjamin, who was not member of the court-martial, did not join the others at the table and was not called to testify. He spoke not a single word during the proceedings. When Ga, who had also been silent, was asked if he had anything to say before sentence was pronounced, he laughed. But it was a very small laugh.

The prisoner was delivered to Benjamin for immediate execution. After this the court-martial reconvened as the Council of the High Command, and in Ga's presence—or, more accurately, as if Ga no longer existed and had been rendered invisible—elected the chief of staff of the army as acting head of state and government. Benjamin kept his old job, his old title, his old powers, and presumably his pension.

I wish I could tell you for the sake of symmetry that Ga died the kind of barbarous death that he had decreed for others, that Benjamin fed him like a Thomson's gazelle to the cheetahs or gashed his flesh and set a pack of hyenas on him under the stadium lights. But nothing of the sort happened.

What happened was this. The generals and admirals and justices and the others got into their cars and drove away. Ga, Benjamin, the sergeant, the two constables, and I went outside. We walked across the palace grounds, Ga limping in his chains, walked away from the palace, over the lawns. Animals in the zoo stirred. Something growled as it caught our scent. Only the animals took an interest in what was happening. The constables guarding the palace stayed at their posts. The servants had vanished. Looking back at the palace, I had the feeling that it was completely empty.

When we came to a place that was nearly out of sight of the palace — the white mansion glowed like a toy in the distance — we stopped. The constables let go of Ga and stepped away from him. Ga said something to Benjamin in what sounded to me like the same language that Benjamin and the sergeant spoke to each other. Benjamin walked over to Ga and bent his head. Ga whispered something in his ear.

Benjamin made a gesture. The sergeant vanished. So did the two constables. I made as if to go. Benjamin said, "No. Stay." The stadium lights went out. The sun was just below the horizon in the east. I could feel its mass pulling at my bones and, even before it became visible, its heat on my skin.

We walked on, until we could no longer see the presidential palace or light of any kind, no matter where we looked. Only moments of darkness remained. Ga sank to his knees, with difficulty because of the chains, and stared at the place where the sun would rise. Briefly Benjamin placed a hand on his shoulder. Neither man spoke.

The rim of the sun appeared on the horizon. And then with incredible buoyancy and radiance, as if slung from the heavens, the entire star leaped into view. Benjamin stepped back a pace, pointed his Webley at the back of Ga's head, and pulled the trigger. The sound was not loud. Ga's body was thrown forward by the impact of the bullet. Red mist from his wound remained behind, hanging in the air, and seemed to shoot from the edge of the sun, but that was a trick of light.

Benjamin did not examine the corpse or even look at it. I realized he was going to leave it for the hyenas and the jackals and the vultures and the many other creatures that would find it.

Benjamin said to me, "You have seen everything. Tell them in Washington."

"All right," I said. "But tell me why."

Benjamin said, "You know why, Mr. Brown."

He walked away. I followed him, not sure I could find my way out of this scrubby wilderness without him but not sure either whether he was going back to civilization or just going back.

DENNIS McFADDEN

Diamond Alley

FROM *Hart's Grove*

THE YEAR WE WERE SENIORS in high school, a girl in our class was murdered and the Pittsburgh Pirates won the World Series. Which was the more momentous event? No contest, of course; how could a game, a boys' game at that, compete with the death of a classmate, a girl who was our friend? Yet somehow, despite our lip service to the contrary, these two happenings seemed to attain a shameful equality in our minds. And if anything, now that so many years have passed, Mazeroski rounding the bases in jubilation after his homer had vanquished the big, bad Yankees is more vivid in our memories than the image of Carol Siebenrock, young, beautiful, and naked, as seen from the darkness beyond her window.

The Pirates were with us everywhere that autumn. They filled the air. Every evening when we went out, we didn't need our transistors—we could hear Bob Prince calling the game all over town, his friendly baritone drifting from radios on porches, in kitchens and living rooms, pervasive as the scent of burning leaves. We would often pause, interrupting whatever nonsense we were up to, holding a hand in the air to signify an at-bat worthy of our attention: maybe Smoky Burgess coming up to pinch-hit with the tying run in scoring position, or Clemente connecting, sending a screamer through the gap, or big, dumb Dick Stuart approaching the plate with enough runners on to win the game with one mighty swing of his lumber. And every time they played the Pirates' jingle, we would sing along:

> Oh, the Bucs are going all the way,
> All the way, all the way,

> Oh, the Bucs are going all the way,
> All the way this year!

We might have been anywhere in Hartsgrove, the hilly, leafy town of our youth that most of us have long since abandoned. We came out after dark, after our homework was done, savoring our first heady taste of freedom—seniors now! When we weren't at Les's Pizza Palace down by the bridge over Potters Creek, we were at the elementary school playground on the north side, back in by the swings and seesaws near the trees, watching the stars, smoking the Winstons and Luckies we'd pilfered from our old man's pack on the kitchen counter. Or walking down East Main Street, by all the crowded houses sorely in need of paint and repair, or trudging up Pine, where the leaves on the trees were burnt orange in the scattered streetlights. We might have been crossing the swinging bridge over the Sandy Lick Creek by Memorial Park, seeing how perilously we could get it to sway in the dark, or taking the shortcut down Rose Hill, shrieking like ghosts in the woods on the rutted, littered path that had been a turnpike a hundred years before. Everywhere we went, we smelled the burning leaves and listened to the Voice of the Pittsburgh Pirates. The darker it got, the better we liked it.

Many nights found us in the pine shadows of Carol Siebenrock's backyard on Diamond Alley, waiting for the light in her window.

Her house was on a hill—Hartsgrove was built on seven hills—the backyard at eye level with her second-floor bedroom. We didn't venture there till late summer, when the days were getting shorter, the concealing nighttime longer. We'd heard the rumors a year or two before, from older guys, guys since graduated and gone, but we were younger then, our curfews earlier, it was the fifties, and we were timid; peeping was a serious offense in Hartsgrove, Pennsylvania—that and running stop signs were about all the cops had to live for. But now we were seniors, bulletproof, brave, bold and fast, our ears attuned to the slightest hint of a cruiser on Diamond Alley, a dozen escape routes mapped out in our minds.

On the good nights, her light would come on. And there she was. "Ladies and gentlemen, it is now showtime," Wonderling would whisper. At the foot of her bed she unbuttoned her blouse, looking out at the darkness hiding any number of eager eyes; then she turned, blouse open. Steadying herself, hand on the dresser, she stepped from her shoes, loosened her belt. Then the snaps and crackles would begin, as we positioned ourselves in the pine needles for a better view, louder than dancing elephants. She stepped from her pants, shrugged from her blouse. White bra and panties. Heavenly curves and crevices. Her bra fell away, nipples staring us down like little red eyes. Her thumbs went to the sides of her panties.

The nights were rare and precious when the planets aligned to allow us the perfect sighting. She might have gone to bed too early, or too late, or it was raining, or we were spotted on Diamond Alley, or we heard a car, or we had too much homework, or we were simply giving it a rest. But when the planets finally did align, it was ecstasy, nearly unbearable.

"You're blocking my view!" Wonderling whispered hoarsely, shoving Nosker. But his inflated state amplified the whisper, and the ensuing chorus of shushes must have sounded to Carol as though her backyard had sprung a leak.

She came to the window holding a pillow over her tits, and yelled through the screen, "Why don't you guys grow up! Go get a girlfriend!"

We were gone. Down Diamond Alley in the dark, wind whistling past our ears, coming out on Pine beneath the streetlight, where we slowed, ambling down toward Valley Street. Suddenly we stopped. In the air we heard Rocky Nelson line a shot up the right-field alley, scoring Groat all the way from first with the winning run — *How sweet it is!* cried Bob Prince; *How sweet it is!* — and we pumped our fists and yelled, falling to our knees on the sidewalk, nearly weeping.

Next time the curtains would be closed. They would inch open again over the next few nights, first a visible sliver, followed by a gradual widening. We wondered if Carol could guess we were there, and we tried to believe she was willing to play the game, willing to be seen as long as we didn't let her know we were seeing. That was what we wanted to believe. It never occurred to us that she might simply have felt she had the right to fresh air, that she might have believed that we had given up, or, better, that we had grown up now and respected her privacy and were above crawling on our bellies in the dirt and darkness for a cheap glimpse of flesh.

She stood out from the other girls in our class. Other girls were pretty, sexy, smart, and popular, but none of them packaged it quite the way she did. None of us had been her boyfriend, but we'd all been her confidant at one time or another, the one chosen to rub her back between classes, to sit with her at lunch, to dance with her at Les's, to have those privileged, personal conversations when her clear blue eyes would mesmerize you.

When we rubbed her back, she would put her arms on her desk, her head down as if she were going to sleep. "Higher," she would say. "Right there—between the shoulder blades." And she would moan. That moan. That skin. We would have to pretend our heavy breathing was caused by the physical exertion of rubbing. And we would have to cross our legs.

"Do you have a date for the record hop?" she would ask.

"I hadn't really thought about it," we said, panting.

She was concerned about our social life. She didn't want any of us left out, left behind. It was as though she wanted us all to experience life in the same expansive, wonderful way that she was. She was always offering helpful advice: *Bobby, you should be more serious—everything's not always a joke, you know.* Or, *Jimmy, how come you never smile? You look so serious all the time.* Or, *Doug, why don't you comb your hair in a DA? You'd look really sharp with a DA.* Or, *Don't squeeze that, John. If you squeeze it, it'll leave a scar.*

"Why don't you ask Brenda?" Carol said. "She likes you."

"I don't know. I'll think about it." We wanted to play it cool. "You going with Bucky?" Bucky was her boyfriend. Her boyfriends were always three or four years older than us, always with cars and the coolest of reputations.

"Yeah. Wait'll you see his car." Bucky had a new midnight-blue GTO, leather seats, four on the floor, competition clutch. She told us all about it. Then she put her hand on ours, leaning close, adding conspiratorially, "But I don't like it—the back seat's too small."

A comment such as that could fuel our masturbatory fantasies for a month. She was mature, sexy without being slutty, no easy feat in 1960. Her silky blond hair and clear blue eyes seem almost suspect now, as if our memories have polished them to perfection, but her picture in our yearbook—which we dedicated to her—bears out the truth of it. She always seemed to wear the skimpiest briefs beneath her cheerleader's outfit, and Nosker in fact claimed that once she wore none at all, swears to this day he saw her beaver that fateful Friday night. We insisted he was full of shit, secretly allowing ourselves to entertain the possibility, masturbatory fuel for another month.

The teachers seemed to hold her apart as well. She challenged Mrs. Ishman, an elegant and earthy lady, over the amount of trigonometry she assigned. Mrs. Ishman, grim and determined, defended herself as she would to an adult—the rest of us would have ended up in detention. Carol debated Mr. Zufall, our social studies teacher: Why should we bother watching the presidential debate? Everyone knew Kennedy didn't have a snowball's chance in heck anyway, because then the pope would be running the country, so it was all just a waste of time. Mr. Zufall laughed, shook his head. He let her get away with it. Mr. Zufall, in fact, almost seemed to encourage her.

He almost seemed to be in Carol's confidant rotation along with the rest of us. He was one of those teachers who try to be one of the guys, and he came close. We liked him. He had a habit of rocking up on his toes while he was teaching, which we often mimicked but secretly admired. He was graceful, athletic; he'd been a pretty good basketball player for Hartsgrove High, then got a medal in the war. He used to make fun of the nonathletic types behind their backs, the same as we did, mimicking their pigeon-toed strut across the front of his classroom. He told us dirty jokes and gossip, the only teacher who did. And every day he could talk to us about how the Pirates had fared the night before.

He pulled us aside before class. "I came in the back way this morning," he said. "No sooner do I open the door than who do I see standing there, behind the back stairwell, but a good friend of ours, with her boyfriend—I won't mention any names, but you know her well. And her boyfriend is holding her breasts! One in each hand! Buoying them up!" Mr. Zufall was positively gleeful. He repeated the phrase—*Buoying them up!*—holding out his hands, buoying a pair of imaginary tits. We shared his zeal, wondering exactly who he was talking about, when we noticed Carol Siebenrock across the room, watching us.

The last place we saw her was Les's, the evening she disappeared. Les's was overflowing with the usual afterschool crew. Carol was sitting with some of the other cheerleaders, planning a bonfire and pep rally for Friday night. We had a big game Saturday against Cranberry.

"Hey," Carol yelled over to us. The music was too loud for talking. Everybody yelled. "Do you guys know where we can get any wood?"

"I know where you can get some," Wonderling said, snickering.

"I don't know," Nosker said. "I haven't been getting any either."

"Get your minds out of the gutter," Carol said.

"I'd like to lay the wood to her," Knapp whispered, and we grinned.

Plotner dropped a nickel, reaching down to get it so he could look up their skirts, smacking his head against the table on the way back up, good for another laugh. He swore Brenda Richards had jerked her legs apart while he was down there, displaying her crotch for his viewing pleasure. "Sure, sure," we said, refusing to allow the remotest possibility it was true, believing it all the while, because it's what we wanted to believe. We were hooked on the implications of a free peek willingly given. The cheerleaders kept talking wood and fire, while we lapsed into our typical topics: who was getting bare tit off whom, who was getting bare ass, who was finger-fucking whom, and who was actually getting laid. And, most importantly, with whom. The jukebox stopped playing, but no one stopped yelling. Allshouse chased Judy Lockett around the pinball machine, and Les Chitester, his long white apron bloody with sauce, yelled from beside his pizza oven, "Hey! Take a cold shower!" Linda Pence was dancing, shaking her perfect ass in our general direction, and Nosker said, "Say this five times real fast: Tiny Tim tickled Tillie's tit till Tillie's twat twitched," and we were up to the challenge. Many times. And every time we looked at Carol Siebenrock, all we could see were her nipples.

Les brought out the cheerleaders' pizza, and Carol, taking her first bite, dropped sauce on her white blouse, close enough to her boob to prompt another outbreak of hilarity on our part. She tried to wipe it off with her napkin, but only smeared it around. She stood to leave, shoulders back, making no effort to conceal her sullied boob. "Grow up, you guys," she said.

We wanted to run after her. We wanted to leapfrog over the parking meters down Main Street, fly up the hill, get to her backyard before she got home, but we didn't. It was still light out, and we wondered why she was leaving so early, assuming it was the stain on her blouse, never guessing she might have had a date. It was a school night. So we stayed, laughing, leering, the occasional erection springing to life on our young, healthy bodies, and later we walked home listening to the Pirates' magic number dwindling down toward zero. The last thing Carol ever said to us was "Grow up." We remembered that later, smitten by the twist, sure that we were the only ones on the face of the earth ever to witness an irony so deep and true as that.

Carol's two older sisters, Dottie and Mary, were married and gone. She was the baby. Some years before, her mother had tried to commit suicide with her father's rifle—trying to pierce her ears, went the old, black joke. She'd managed only to graze her brain, leaving her more or less lobotomized. Mr. Siebenrock was a chubby, earnest fellow who owned a shoe store down on Main Street, and we all knew him pretty well—he'd been one of our Little League coaches, even though he'd apparently never held a bat in his own two hands before taking over the reins of Sterck's Terriers. He cheered enthusiastically—maybe the source of Carol's talent. As a coach, he made a pretty good shoe salesman.

He'd left Little League about the same time we had, when his wife had shot herself with his .22, which he'd kept in a closet and seldom touched. He was not a hunter, but for some reason thought he should own a gun. Everyone else did. Now, when he wasn't selling shoes he spent most of his time taking care of his wife, bringing her to church and school events, trying to maintain some semblance of a social life.

The night Carol disappeared he'd taken his wife to the Hartsgrove Businessmen's Association Banquet out at the country club. Home late, he'd assumed Carol was upstairs asleep. Next morning he discovered his mistake, along with her bloodstained blouse.

By the time we learned the blood was pizza sauce, a hundred different rumors had swept through town: Her bracelet had been found here, her shoe there, a stranger spotted here, Carol herself there. She'd run away with her boyfriend; she'd run away by herself. She'd been abducted from her bedroom; she'd been abducted walking up the hill from Les's. She'd gone kicking and scratching;

she'd gone willingly with someone she knew. She'd been raped; she'd eloped; she was being held for ransom. The rumors were flimsy, yet they lived and died and were born again, endlessly, it seemed. In the end, she was simply missing.

Her empty desk filled every classroom. Every blond head we saw in the hallway brought an instant of expectation, which dissolved again just as quickly. Mr. Zufall seemed as stricken as any of us. *She'll be fine,* he told the class. *Leave her alone and she'll come home, wagging her tail behind her.* And he grinned a rueful grin.

Shuffling down Main Street one afternoon on our way to Les's, we saw Mr. Zufall coming out of Siebenrock's Shoes with his arms full. It looked as though he'd bought half-a-dozen pairs of shoes. Seeing us across the street, he only nodded a greeting, his arms too full to wave. It struck us at the time as some sort of magnanimous, mature gesture, a show of support, the sort of thing we'd have been incapable of. We wouldn't have had the slightest idea of what to say to Mr. Siebenrock in a circumstance such as that.

Evenings at Les's were quiet, filled with the whisper of rumors. The pep rally and bonfire at Memorial Park were canceled; we lost to the Cranberry Rovers the next afternoon, 45–6. The cheerleaders' efforts were halfhearted, as were the team's, although the outcome of the game wasn't all that far from the norm. No one was in the mood for a pep rally the next week either, but there was a large pile of lumber that had to be disposed of somehow, so the pep rally was rescheduled for the next Friday night, before the Harmony Mills game.

Like the crowd, the fire was large and nervous, shooting jittery red trails of sparks and shape-shifting plumes of smoke into the night over the black running waters of Potters Creek. The speakers—the captain of the cheerleaders, the football team captain, the school principal—all spoke about our team, our school, our town, our pride, about giving our best and winning. No one mentioned the big white elephant sitting just beyond the bonfire. It was a decidedly pepless rally.

All the while Carol stayed missing.

The rumors grew silly and cruel. She was living with beatniks in New York City. She was living with cousins in Oil City, having been knocked up. She'd run away to join the circus girlie show. She'd run off to become a Playboy Bunny. She'd had to leave town because someone had spotted her in a skin flick. All the silly, cruel rumors tried to imagine where she was. None of them imagined her dead.

All the while the Pirates kept winning.

Carol's disappearance, magnificent mystery that it was, never distracted us from the heat of the pennant race. There was plenty of room in our hearts and minds for both. When the Pirates finally clinched on a Sunday afternoon in late September, joy erupted and settled back over the town like a golden mist. It was the only topic of conversation at school Monday morning—*How sweet it is! How sweet it is!* We sang, *Oh, the Bucs are going all the way!* The first fifteen minutes of Mr. Zufall's class were devoted to nothing but Hoak, Groat, Mazeroski and Stuart, Clemente, Virdon, Skinner and the boys. By the end of class, however, it was business as usual; Mr. Zufall reminded us—warned us, really—that the Kennedy-Nixon debate was taking place that evening.

"Who watched the debate?" he asked next morning. "Raise your hands."

No one was foolish enough not to. Mr. Zufall rocked up on his toes, his approving smile turning wistful as he glanced at the empty desk. "I'm only sorry Carol wasn't here to see it," he said. "History in the making. I think even Carol would have appreciated that."

The collective sigh was audible, the moment of silence spontaneous. It was the first time anyone had spoken of her as though she weren't coming back.

They found her two weeks later. Evan Shields and his grandson, hunting squirrel in the woods along Potters Creek just north of town, spotted her body snagged on a log in the water. Her skull was fractured, and she'd probably been dead since the day she disappeared. That was about all the coroner could determine, given the state of her body.

It was assumed she'd been raped. She was naked from the waist down.

Every generation or so there's a murder in Hartsgrove above and beyond the usual run-of-the-mill, heat-of-the-moment killing, a murder with a certain cachet. About twenty-five years earlier, before we were born, a lady had been raped and stabbed to death in the railroad yard signal tower on the south side of town, where she worked. Les Chitester, manning his pizza oven with his long-handled paddle, remembered it well, though he'd been only ten at the time; the town had been in a frenzy of fear till the killer had finally been caught. Years later, after we'd scattered and were slogging toward the end of our own middle ages, a pack of drunken, drugged-up kids stripped and hanged a girl in a clearing in the woods by Potters Creek. The young always think these flashy crimes are unique, that life has devised this outstanding drama just for them, and them alone. That's what we thought. Now we know better. Now we know it's just part of the cycle, just another run-of-the-mill murder that happens to have a certain cachet.

Girls cried in the classrooms. Boys shook their heads. There were hollow-eyed stares down the hallways of the school. *Gone but not forgotten;* Mr. Zufall must have uttered that hackneyed phrase a hundred times. Les's was even quieter. We hugged self-consciously, in solemn unawareness of what else we could possibly do. We talked about it, tried to exorcize it. We talked about Carol, every last little thing we'd ever done with her, every last little minute we'd ever spent with her, competing to have known her best, as if whoever had been closest to her would be closest to this new mortality, and therefore the most worthy among us.

Who had done it? Who could have done such a thing? Bucky Morrison, her boyfriend, naturally came to mind, but Bucky was away at college, and though his alibi wasn't airtight, he was reputed to be a gentle creature, who, Brenda Richards let it be known, kept a kitten in his dorm room against all regulations. Mark Schoffner, the boy Carol had dumped for Bucky? In the army now, at Fort Drum. There were the usual local toughs in Hartsgrove, the high school dropouts and misfits, but we inventoried and dismissed them one by one, group by group. The crime was a quantum leap from picking a fight on a street corner with a bellyful of beer, from stealing hubcaps or keying the car of an antagonist. It was beyond them, just as it was beyond any of us, beyond anyone, really, that we knew. It would have to be a stranger. No one we'd ever laid our eyes upon could possibly commit such an evil.

She was buried on a Wednesday, the same day as the sixth game of the World Series. We were conflicted, to say the least, though we never dared suggest we'd have preferred spending the afternoon in front of a television, rooting for the Pirates to wrap it up; they led the series three games to two. But the Buccos made it easy on us that day. Their resounding 12–0 loss dovetailed perfectly with the tragedy, reflecting ominously on the future. We were sure they'd lose tomorrow too. It was how the planets were aligned.

Mr. Siebenrock looked softer than we remembered, like a marshmallow that had been stepped on. He followed Carol's casket down the wide aisle of the Presbyterian church, his jowls inflated, his comb-over glistening with sweat, his hand fidgeting in his pocket like a squirming mouse; we could hear the coins jingle in the sniffle-filled silence. His wife, her hand clutching his coat sleeve, her hair too black, her gaze unanchored, looked as though she were wandering through a fog. Carol's two older sisters, Dottie and Mary, not nearly as pretty as Carol, followed with their husbands. Our hearts ached at how sad they looked, and at the fact that we were missing the game, and as soon as the service was over we rushed out to Nosker's car and turned on the radio—the Pirates were trailing 6–0 after two and a half! Crushed, we joined the funeral procession to Chapel Cemetery, a couple miles south of town, Bob Prince filling us in: Bob Friend, in whose right arm we'd trusted, had lasted only two innings. Clouds swelled with gloom over the cemetery at the top of the hill.

We did our best to say goodbye to Carol there. The view from the cemetery was wide, but the sweep of bright trees was dulled by the gray of the day. We were too far away to hear the words of the preacher, a skinny man with white hair and big ears. When it was over we drifted away. We weren't in a hurry to get back to the game; we knew a lost cause when we saw one. Over our shoulders we watched Carol's mother, her hand fluttering at the pile of dirt like a toddler just learning to wave bye-bye.

Next morning during homeroom, they interrupted the announcements over the PA system to call for a moment of silence for Carol. We felt it applied just as much to the Pirates. That afternoon they suspended classes, and we gathered in the auditorium to watch the seventh game of the series on the televisions they'd set up on the stage. We were absorbed from the first flickering image of Forbes Field, immersed for the next four hours, emotions soaring and plummeting, as the lead went back and forth, ecstasy and anguish in the balance. The Pirates blew a four-run lead and trailed, 5–4, after seven. When the Yankees tacked on two more in the top of the eighth, Allshouse actually snuffled and blew his nose, and we were actually too upset to ridicule him for being such a baby. We were on the verge ourselves.

In the bottom of the eighth, a routine ground ball took a bad hop and hit the Yankee shortstop in the neck. We rejoiced, Tony Kubek's evident agony notwithstanding. This could be the break — pun intended — we needed; this might be the omen, the sign we'd been waiting for, and sure enough, when Hal Smith capped the five-run rally with a three-run homer, joy once again erupted, echoing through the cavernous old auditorium. With a two-run lead in the top of the ninth, and Bob Friend coming in to nail it down, it was all but over.

Incredibly, impossibly, the Yankees tied it up.

Blackness settled over the congregation. The wooden seats never felt harder. "I can't watch," Plotner said, and he was the stoic one among us. The big, bad Yankees were bearing down on us like an oncoming freight train. Nosker buried his head in his hands. And Carol Siebenrock revisited us, tragedy in all its guises, as we went to the bottom of the ninth.

Then, when Mazeroski homered, we were born again. We leaped in the aisles, teachers and students alike, hugging, cheering, delirious with bliss. Clover and Mrs. Ishman were dancing. Plotner and Nosker were dancing. Wonderling hugged Brenda Richards and Judy Lockett, every girl he could find, copping as many feels as he possibly could. Mr. Zufall, at the peak of his powers, lifted Allshouse over his head. And Carol was gone again.

Gone but not forgotten. Less than a week later we paid our final respects. It was a spontaneous tribute, unpremeditated. Leaving Les's, we crossed the crumbling bridge over Potters Creek, heading up toward Main Street in the dwindling twilight. At the Court House, we turned up Pershing, still paved with bricks as all of Hartsgrove's streets had been at one time, onto Coal Alley, and up the concrete steps that climbed the hill through the trees. The steps were tilted, old, and uneven. By the time we reached the top we were winded, our thighs aching.

The mansards and gables high on the school were nearly invisible in the dark. The streetlights couldn't throw much light up through the trees, only a glint off a window here and there. We cut through the schoolyard. Mary Lou Allgier lived on Maple, just beyond the baseball field. We checked out her windows: the lights were on, but the shades were down, and we couldn't see a thing. Halfway up Pine, we cut across to Diamond Alley. The best place to pay our last respects was not in the graveyard but in the backyard.

Solemnly we filed in, taking our places among the pines. From the shadows we stared at her darkened window, remembering. Everything was black. We spoke in whispers. "Remember how she used to piss off Mrs. Ishman?" we said. We thought, *Bobby, don't try so hard—if you pretend you're not interested, you'll have her eating out of the palm of your hand.* "How about the way she argued with Zufall?" *Jimmy, your teeth aren't that bad—is that why you never smile? You have a nice smile.* "Remember the time she called Mrs. Stockdale a bitch? Man, she had balls." We stared at her window as though the light might come on at any moment, as though she might appear. *Doug, you have to work harder on your grades. You have to get into college. Do you need any help studying?* "Remember the time she was cheering without any tights on?" *You should learn how to dance, John. It's easy. Want me to teach you?* "What a body." The shadows sighed. "What a shame."

You have such beautiful hair, Jimmy. You're going to get taller. By next year at this time, the girls are going to be chasing you like a hawk. Her clear blue eyes were still gazing into ours, holding us hostage, verifying the truth of every word she said. Her beautiful face was still resting on her hands as we rubbed her back, the warm, soft, living heat of her.

The whispering desisted. The moment of silence was long and true. The air was empty, except for the scent of burning leaves, the sound of crickets. No Bob Prince. It was over. We began to stir, our tribute paid, our obligation fulfilled, feeling a little ennobled, a little restless.

The light came on. Carol's mother appeared in her window, looking around the room as if she'd never seen it before. "Ladies and gentlemen, it is now showtime," Wonderling whispered, and at that moment we hated him. Carol's mother came toward the window and we crabbed back farther into the shadows. Absently she raised a hand to her ear, looking around again with a frown, then to her other ear, taking off her earrings. She placed them on the dresser, straightened the tilted mirror, then began to unbutton her blouse. The look on her face was as though she were trying to recognize a song, a song that no one else could hear. We watched, uncomfortable with the hollow thumping in our chests. A pinecone dropped with a soft plump that jolted through us like a shot. We watched Carol's mother step out of her slacks.

We watched. Not watching was no more of an option than speaking. We watched until she was naked, until every inch of her aging flesh had been revealed in all its faded splendor, and she stood bewildered, looking around the room again, perhaps for her nightgown, perhaps for nothing at all. Carol's father came in, a look of relief on his face, and we watched him gather up his wife's clothes, put his arm around her shoulder, and guide her toward the doorway. There he paused, looking around the room again. Spotting something, he came back, crossing our field of vision; when he returned he was carrying a doll that appeared to be quite old, a well-worn, well-loved doll with yellow hair. Putting his arm around his wife again, he led her out of the room. We watched him reach back and flick off the light with a nervous glance toward the window.

We watched the dark of the house again, in silence, until our erections and galloping blood, our shame, had finally subsided enough to allow us the freedom to leave.

They arrested Blinky Mumford a month later, but it wasn't the closure we needed. It was anticlimactic. We never suspected him; furthermore, we never really believed he did it. One of the school janitors, Blinky Mumford was sullen and ill-tempered, with a facial tic that animated his scowl. He had no family and was often seen walking up and down Main Street muttering to himself. The story was that he'd been left in Hartsgrove when he was six by one of the orphan trains that used to stop on the south side in the early years of the century, but no one had taken him in. As with the other candidates we'd inventoried and dismissed, a crime like this was beyond him—too important, too notable. Despite his conviction, we were never convinced. They found what they said were strands of her hair in his battered old wreck of a Ford, and the key piece of evidence was a pair of panties found hidden in the janitors' closet near Blinky's buckets, brooms, and mops. Her father identified them as Carol's.

We wondered how he could possibly have been so sure, so Bruner came up with a theory: skid marks are like fingerprints, he hypothesized, no two exactly alike.

Not much is left now. The old high school on the hill came tumbling down, and a whole generation of kids has graduated from the new school out by the new interstate, neither of which is new anymore. Les Chitester built a new place too, the Colonial Eagle Interchange Hotel Restaurant, not far from the new school, and our old hangout by Potters Creek was razed, a hardware store built in its place. For over thirty-five years, its motto has been "Buy by the Bridge." Even Memorial Park was buried, all the towering elms and oaks along the banks of the creeks cut down and burned, victims of Hartsgrove's flood control project.

We scattered. The teachers are gone too, retired and died, most of them. A few years after we left, Zufall quit teaching to become a carpenter. That didn't surprise us; we figured he must have wanted a manlier profession, something more in line with his athletic sensibilities.

And Blinky Mumford? He faded away in his cell, a self-proclaimed innocent man.

We still gather in Hartsgrove now and then for reunions and funerals. Tomorrow we're burying Nosker's mother. We'll be next in line. Unlike Carol, we're waiting our turn. Thanks to Carol, we know how to die.

We talk about the Pirates. They won two more titles in the seventies but haven't come close since; it's beginning to look as though they never will. We complain about the state of baseball, the small-market quandary, convinced the sport will never be the same. We don't complain about our own aging bodies, however, which will never be the same again either. We don't ogle and leer at the pretty girls like we used to, because we're mature now—unlike Carol, we got to grow up. At least that's what we tell ourselves. The truth is, ogling and leering would only be mocking our own aging bodies. The truth is, we miss it, everything about it; we miss our young, healthy selves, the dependable, Eveready erections of our youths.

Sooner or later, as if to atone, we set aside the Pirates, put to rest the small talk, and Carol Siebenrock arises from the grave. We speak of her reverently, honoring her. We never speak of our adolescent indiscretions, the nights we spent on our bellies in the black shadows of her yard, the primordial thrill we felt at the sight of her lush, naked flesh.

But in our minds she is naked. In our minds she will always be naked.

She is naked even as she sits in a classroom a lifetime ago, raising her hand, sunlight streaming through the window, touching her with grace and radiance. Where is our place in this picture? Where is our place in this world? We maintain our innocence. We blow away any trace of guilt, like blowing dust off the top of a locked box, but the dust swirls and swirls in the sunlight, swirls and swirls, refusing to disperse and disappear. And so we talk about the Pirates. We talk about Carol as if we never loved her. And always it ends up the same. "Who do you suppose really killed her?" we always say, never looking ourselves in the eye.

CHRISTOPHER MERKNER

Last Cottage

FROM *The Cincinnati Review*

WE KNOW THE LARSONS. They come to Slocum Lake each summer. We would like them to stop, but they do not stop. For fifteen years they have come to Slocum Lake to stay at their place on the waterfront. They own the only cottage remaining on the lake; they possess the only waterfront property that has not been developed commercially. Here, in Slocum Lake, we could use that development. We desperately wish they would sell. Instead, they bring their children and teach them the ways of traditional summertime Slocum Lake living. It's very depressing, it's very outmoded, and our tolerance is pressed.

In June someone paid to have someone electrocute Slocum Lake, to stun and then kill some of the fish. It wasn't terribly expensive. A collection was taken. The more expensive part of the process involved gathering the dead fish and corralling them into the part of the lake that runs about twenty yards out from the Larsons' beachfront and approximately fifty yards across. The expensive part, actually, was installing the concealed netted cage that would keep the dead fish where we wanted them—mysteriously pent up against the Larsons' beach.

The Larsons always arrive on one of the first days of July. They roll in at nighttime. We presume they are sheepish people. It is possible their drive down from the north of Wisconsin is longer than we know it to be, because perhaps their children make them stop frequently. We don't exactly know. We know they arrive late at night, as a general annual rule. We know they carry their children into the cottage, put them in their respective bunk beds, knock off the bedroom lights, lock up, and walk down to the beach-front.

This year they arrived this way again. When they walked down to the beachfront, they held hands. Their hot truck engine was still ticking in their gravel drive. Locusts were scorching the ears of the trees on their property, the only native trees remaining on the waterfront, inglorious poplars. Summer had come very early to Slocum Lake. The locusts had hatched early also. The nights were very warm and still. The Larsons exchanged a few inaudible remarks. Their shoulders were rubbing.

Once they had reached the waterfront, they turned to face one another, held one another, and kissed. They kissed for quite some time. They have kissed before, in years previous, and they usually stop kissing and go into the water together. This year they did not go into the water. They dropped onto their knees and continued kissing. Then Robert Larson took his shirt off, and we thought this signaled a move they might make toward the water. We were wrong. Robert embraced his wife very hard. Then he slipped his wife's shirt over her head.

They were kissing with great force, it seemed, and it seemed they would not stop kissing. Then they stopped kissing. We thought this was it. Instead of rising from his knees, however, Robert lowered himself onto his back. His wife, Penny Larson, laughed and put herself on top of him. It was dark, and we believe they then made love in this position. We watched it, thinking they would go swimming after, but instead they only made docile, unremark-able love, gathered their clothes, and ran naked back toward their cottage. They were laughing, but when they stepped onto the porch, they stopped laughing and were very quiet as they slipped in through their screen door. They never turned on any house lights. They simply vanished into the dark of their lit-tle dwarfish cottage that everyone on Slocum Lake wanted to blow up.

We would not want to hurt the Larsons. We certainly would not want to hurt children. The Larsons are good people with good in-tentions. They leave their home in northernmost Wisconsin and head south just as everyone in Illinois not affiliated with Slocum Lake and its general and perpetual state of impoverishment goes north to summer on the largely virgin beachwater up there. No doubt the Larsons know exactly what it feels like to have strange people perching on your property, behaving as though it were their own just because they had purchased it from you. We actually feel for the Larsons as people.

We feel for them enough, in any case, that we try not to be awkward about our determination to ouster them. We believe confronting them would be awkward and, in the end, because it would likely change nothing, needless. Instead, we have for years determined to be chilly and unwelcoming. We believed this would be enough. Then they had the children, and we could see the future we imagined — fiscal and otherwise — being denied us.

Two years ago, facing this reality, someone who did not identify himself vandalized the Larson's boat launch. Last year, we decided as a community to vandalize their roof. We tore large holes in their shingles with hammers late at night, in February. We believed the water damage from spring runoff would give them pause. They came in early July, studied the damage, left to stay at a hotel, and simply had someone come and rebuild the roof and interior. It was Bernie Benson they hired to do it, and he could not be bribed to do shoddy work, as no one outside of Chicago can be bribed in this way, and their roof is now better than any roof of ours and their interior looks like a catalog image.

The Larsons could not be heard at their windows, so we retired; we returned just after dawn. The children were awake. They are darling children, twins, towheaded beauties. They ate breakfast in their pajamas, careful not to wake their parents. They poked each other without laughing, covering their mouths with their hands, and spoke about their dreams for their vacation. They are good children, and we decided on the dead fish because it would impact them directly. We knew the Larsons would not like their children impacted. We did not want to harm children, and yet the stakes were very high. We believed we could impact the children without devastating them.

The sun had risen over the buildings on the eastern shore, and it was already blasting the buildings on the western shore. The insects had moved from the water to the grasses, because the water was warmer than the air temperature. The insects were horrific biting savages. You never get used to that. Time waiting in such conditions is not terribly pleasant. You look at your watch a lot.

Even in their central air conditioning, installed the year of the children's arrival, the twins had become a little restless. They had already dressed for swimming—at the age of four years, these remarkable, delightful twins had dressed all by themselves. Then they slipped out of the cottage, careful not let the screen door slam. They ran to the boat, which was still hitched to the Larsons' car. They pulled back the protective covering and went down inside the boat, under the covering. We do not know what they do in there. We presume they play make-believe games. Every year they play inside the boat. We think it is peculiar that children from so far north play with boats the way that children from down here do. We often think that, for children and adults from the north, boats are just like old wallpaper.

They were laughing and giggling in the boat for the better part of an hour. Eventually they slid out from under the covering, hopped off the boat, and returned to the cottage. They were inflating their flotation toys just as their parents emerged from their bedroom and sat down beside them on the renovated floor. The Larsons kissed their children on their heads and their hands and petted their hair, and you could see the sort of bliss in the eyes of the Larsons we desired very determinedly to remove.

Shortly thereafter, the children at last received approval to go down to the beachfront, and Robert and Penny stood up to watch their children run from the porch of their cottage down to their sandy beach. The children ran as quickly as four-year-olds can run, shoeless and in minimal swimming wear: both were topless, and the girl's bottoms were nearly obscene, and the boy wore only a baggy pair of briefs. We recognize that the Larsons felt they were alone on their property, and we believe, had they realized the public dimension of their daily events, they likely would have dressed their children differently. Certainly they would have exercised greater restraint in letting their children run down to the beach and plunge half nude into the infested water. We know the Larsons well enough to grasp that they are not reckless, thoughtless types. Like many people from Wisconsin, actually, they are prudent and wry. They remind us of our grandparents.

The Larson children tumbled face-first into the water. For approximately two minutes they rolled and played in innocence.

They laughed and splashed and spread themselves lengthwise in the water. Then the boy screamed. Then the girl screamed. The two of them burst into a series of unpleasant sounds.

The Larsons sprinted from the cottage. They were pained. Their robes were encumbrances. The situation was tense, mortal. We had never seen Robert Larson move so swiftly. He shed his robe as he neared the water; Penny Larson's leg gave out, just at that moment, and she slipped, bent awkwardly, slid several feet, then lifted herself, clutching her knee, and continued running, hopping toward the children. Robert by then had hoisted them from the water. Penny took the girl. Penny and Robert exchanged only a few words in agitation, but we heard what we needed Robert to say: The beach is covered in dead fish.

Indeed. We waited. They walked quickly to the cottage, the twins in their arms. They went inside. There was very little to be heard. We believed we could see Robert pacing, if briefly, before emerging again and walking down to the water, where he kicked the fish with his sandaled foot. He covered his mouth and nose with his hand. The fish smelled even worse once you realized what you were smelling. Robert then shielded his eyes with his other hand and surveyed the water. From that vantage, dead fish carcasses spread out for what must have seemed miles. We'd paid good money for this.

There had been a fair bit of talk about the way to kill the fish. Plenty of the lake's sportsmen felt the need for careful electronic culling, separating the game fish—bass, bluegill, catfish—from those fish whose role in the lake seemed, by sportsmen standards, unclear. The mayor's office and Parks and Recreation, who in the end were footing the largest portion of the bill, contended that such careful culling would require an exorbitant amount of additional cash, and that it was cheaper to restock the game fish than to cull them and restore them once the electrocution was completed. Poets and local liberal activists like myself argued that the impact would be lessened if we merely blitzed the Larsons and their children with dead fish of all types; rather, we argued, if the fish were carefully selected—bottom-dwellers, suckers, waterway leeches all of the same genus—there would be no mistaking the message we were trying to send. It would be difficult, in other words, for the Larsons not to recognize a careful plan at work and to see themselves symbolized as sucking fish, disgusting bottom-dwellers left for dead on their beach.

Robert Larson moved slowly back up the sand, his hands in his pockets. He entered the cottage. He looked at his wife and shrugged. Then Penny shrugged. Then Robert Larson shrugged again. Then he said, Nature down here is funky, and he clicked his tongue and sat down.

The children, these fine and very sweet and well-mannered twins, were glancing back and forth between their parents, very forlorn and very anxious. Larson looked at his wife, and Penny looked at him. Larson nodded. The children darted through the screen door and ran to the beachfront again. They plunged into the water and seized the fish in large quantities, held them against their bodies, and threw them at one another. They lobbed them in various ways—like footballs, like hand grenades. They kissed them, and pretended to fall in love with them, and then they threw them back into the water, jilted. They rode on top of the big ones like dolphins. They pitched them onto the beach; some of the carp were more than five feet long, and by working together, the children were able to drag them onto the sand. The twins then began making forts and castles with them. We held our mouths.

We might have kept holding our mouths had Larson not sped out of the driveway. We turned to see him go. He drove quickly, but the stop signs slowed him. He had his arm out the window. He spat tobacco onto the road. He had his music on loudly—a local radio channel, country-western, not from the Chicago towers but from those in Kankakee. He turned into the Cat rental facility on the north end of Route 176, went inside, and according to Davis, the manager, rented a small skid steer loader for one half day at a holiday rate of $175. Davis also covered the cost of delivery, which would take place later that afternoon, as there was no demand for skid steers at that time. Repelling open or clandestine bribes is one thing; facilitating the enemy is really something entirely different. We sometimes look at Davis and wonder what Slocum Lake would feel like without him.

Larson stopped off at the Island Foods grocery. He called his wife two times on his cellular phone while he stood, looking uneasy, in the meats and seafood department. He bypassed the local bakery doughnuts and took three boxed Danish rings, the national brand. He brought his items to the counter and had the clerk fill several paper bags. He used coupons. He slid his credit card. He pushed his cart to the truck, dropped the bags in the back, and then returned the cart to the rack by the store entry. We never doubted Larson's goodness. He drove back to the cottage and joined his wife, who was sitting on the porch watching the twins bury each other in fish carcasses.

That night the Larsons barbecued the carp on an open grill and somehow managed to swallow it. Penny served the fillets with a mayonnaise and dill relish. We had not seen Robert purchase the dill. After dinner the kids climbed into their bunk beds, and the Larsons went down to the beach and rearranged the carp the kids had strewn across the sand. Given our distance, we did not know they had organized the fish into a sort of soft bed until, as they had the night before, they lay down to make sustained love.

Words cannot bring clarity to the feelings we had while watching the Larsons make love on top of the carp. *We felt very depressed* might be about as close as we can get. We left the Larsons' cottage to have meals with our own families. We figured we were back to the drawing board. We figured we had not impacted the children in the right way, and we therefore had failed to alter the Larsons' iron grip on their ownership of Lake Slocum waterfront property. Because of our depression, we had not foreseen Robert Larson's critical error.

Thankfully, we were not so depressed that we did not return the next morning, just after dawn. The twins were again playing in the boat, and Robert was already awake, running the skid steer, scooping large quantities of the carp and shunting them from the waterfront to the back of his property, where he had—apparently before sunrise—dug a massive grave for the fish. It did not strike all of us at the same time, but the image of Larson hoisting the fish and steering them away from our water gave one of us, and then every one of us, a rather brutal jolt.

We called Princess at the Parks and Recreation office to confirm the limit of carp a person could take from Slocum Lake on any single fishing day. Princess told us what we all well knew from the bylaws of the constitutional charter on fish reparation: one hundred carp is the maximum any one licensed person can catch and keep on a given day. We asked nicely if Princess would send someone over to have a look at the load of carp Mr. Robert Larson had taken from our Slocum Lake.

The fine for violating the charter ran $1,000 alone; the fine for each violating fish ran $100 per fish; the fine for not having a license issued by the state of Illinois for taking any fish from the water, $100. Princess herself came over with a clutch of Slocum Lake police officers to hand the Larsons their ticket for $250,000. She explained that the police estimated Larson had extracted no fewer than twenty-five hundred carp from Slocum Lake, and she pointed down into the massive pit. It would be difficult to doubt that estimate, certainly. She continued in explaining that Parks and Recreation was actually, probably, estimating low, and they were willing, also, to give the Larsons a break on the other violations and round off at a quarter of a million dollars, due October first of the current fiscal year. She touched Robert's shoulder and said, We only take money orders for fines that exceed one hundred thousand, Mister Larson, but we know we can trust your personal checks around here. Princess winked.

Robert Larson winced and recoiled from her hand. He attempted to explain that the fish were already dead, but Princess waved him down—irrelevant and subjective. Robert protested a second time. Princess simply extended the ticket. Robert refused to take it. Princess placed it on the ground near his feet. Robert raised his voice. The children came out from the boat to watch. The police officers adjusted their belts and crossed their arms. Princess withdrew. Robert picked up the ticket. He was sweating so completely, the sunlight glinted wildly off his face.

Robert took the ticket to the porch, where he had a brief conversation with Penny. They shook their heads. They retreated inside. Their children—so bright and sensitive—grasped the gravity of the situation and went inside, settled down into Indian-style sitting, and played cards with one another for the duration of the afternoon. The Larsons held protracted, at times heated dialogues inside the cottage. The skid steer simply sat out in the sun. Some of the carp baked in their pit, and still more lapped against the shoreline.

The sun shifted its weight against the east-facing side of the shore. Evening came and went. Night tumbled in. We were pretty drunk by then. Someone had brought tequila. We had a great deal to celebrate. We took a shot every time Robert Larson rubbed his eyes. We breathed very easily when the house went dark. We assumed we would retire early to our families. But then we heard the Larsons slip out of their screen door and head down to the beach again. The minxes! They took each other's clothes off and made love in the sand. They experimented a little bit. The locusts were screaming. The insects were loathsome. The Larsons rolled about for forty minutes, then ran naked back into their cottage. We wondered if we had all seen this, or if the most drunk of us had imagined it. How strange, these Larsons. What was Slocum Lake property to the kind of people who could make love in the face of its certain loss?

How brazen. We'd had someone at our bank evaluate the Larsons' portfolio: there was no way they could afford the fines. We shook our heads. These people from the northern fringe of Wisconsin were very much like our grandparents in so many ways. We knew them, and yet we knew them not at all.

We drank to this. Then we had a few more drinks. We became increasingly easy with one another as the night wore on. We did not return to our homes and families. We kissed a little bit ourselves, touching each other's limbs in the night. We became stupid in lust and mouthed one another. We did not hear Robert Larson leave the cottage. We did not at first hear the skid steer ignition. Sensuality creates a noise that cannot be rapidly punctured, but in time it became clear we were not hearing the thrumming of our bodies but rather Robert and the skid steer shifting gears in the middle of the night.

We cleared our throats and straightened. We had to adjust our eyes. We tapped our watches. Robert Larson was scooping out the grave of dead fish and, it became clear, trundling his scoops back down to the beach, where he was dumping them into his Shamrock 270 diesel. He had launched the Shamrock in the afternoon. It was a detail that meant very little to us while we were drinking. He was working very quickly with the skid steer. No sooner had he dumped a load into the Shamrock than he was racing back up toward the cottage, behind it, to the grave, to collect another scoop. Then back down to the beach and the boat. We tried to divine the meaning of this activity.

We discovered Penny Larson had also left the cottage and gone down to the water. She was in over her waist. She was wearing only a bra. She appeared to be moving the fish closer to the sand. She did not speak. She did not luxuriate. She seemed entirely devoted to the fish, a sort of shepherd, and we were perplexed until Robert emptied the grave and turned his scoop to the shoreline. Then the Larsons' intentions were made horribly clear and vivid to us. As Robert Larson loaded carp into the Shamrock—hoisting all our work and money very high in the air, water pouring from the hinges in the metal scoop, and dumping them with heavy thuds inside of the gunwales—we could see, very plainly, that Robert Larson planned to scuttle his fiscal and moral obligations to Slocum Lake. We were just sick. If the insects were draining us at that point, we were entirely unaware. We held each other.

And in what was surely less than thirty minutes, while we looked on, Robert Larson had filled his boat with every last fish from the grave and our mostly invisible netted cage. The sun was just beginning to illuminate Slocum Lake. The Larsons' boat sat low against the mooring. Robert killed the skid steer engine and hopped out. He walked the dock and stepped into the boat. With Penny's help, he proceeded to snap the canvas top over the entire boat, covering the fish with a sort of tightly fitted pall.

That's when one of us lost it. It was unspeakably hot. Heat like that, even under less demanding circumstances, it's cruel. Half of us were naked or drunk. All of us were slick with sweat. It is not surprising that one of us would break from our cover and rush the Larsons' cottage with a burning poplar branch in his arms.

Perhaps he thought the rest of us would join him. Perhaps the heat had harmed him. Perhaps he could just no longer operate in clandestine rage, as we all were, and let the Larsons prolong our suffering and embarrassment another year. But there he was— the Kubicka kid, we believed—thrusting a burning, limpid poplar branch at the Larsons' kitchen window, yelling the word *crimes* over and over again at the top of his childish pitch. Try as he might, he could not in the end break through the window with this flaming branch. The limb bent and splayed each time he thrust. But the boy kept at it, jabbing, stepping back a few steps, and charging, jousting, shouting *crimes!*

It was painful to watch, and we did what we could: we called him away. We tried to flag him down. We implored him to drop the

branch and return to us. But Robert Larson ran quickly to appre-
hend the Kubicka boy. Had Larson been faster, he might have
stopped the fire from torching the wooden shingles of the cottage.
In that heat, the siding and the roof went up like gasoline. Penny
had followed Robert and slipped inside the cottage. She emerged
with their beautiful children, groggy, and pointed them down to
the beachfront, away from the cottage.

The Larson kids, so precious, walked down toward the dock in
silence and did not raise their eyes. Had the cottage not caught
fire, the children would probably never have gone down to the water. But it did, and they did, and we owe a great debt to the Kubicka
kid, whom we have never since seen. Robert Larson grappled with
the lithe Kubicka boy in the grass beside the burning cottage until
the boy broke from Robert's grip and fled into the dark glow of
dawn.

Robert did not follow. He grabbed the hose, turned on the house
spigot, and began dousing the fire before it could race to the other
side of the cottage. Penny took down a pickax from the porch.
She yanked the burned and burning siding away from the house
and spread it across the lawn. She whacked at the flames when they
flared up. To watch these two was like watching junior amateur
firefighters in earnest judged competition, a sort of marvel of
meticulous and urgent care, and all the while their children,
those wonderful blond twins, stood in pajamas by the dock, looking upon the smoke rising from the last cottage on our Slocum
Lake.

Those beautiful children, dear God, to think of them. So good.
What we loved most were their good natures. They never knew mistrust. They never asked questions or doubted strangers. You could
tell them to go inside the boat, lie down among the carp, that their
mother had instructed you to help them bed down inside the boat,
beneath the cover of the boat, and to close their eyes. And they
would not doubt you. They would not fuss. They would not fear.

You could sing them a quiet song, hum a melody, and you could
touch their fine hair, brush it from their cheeks, over their ears,
and they would curl to the feel of your knuckles, and they would
smile as their sleep took them back. You don't always know what
you are doing in this sort of Slocum Lake midsummer heat, but the
Larson kids could just slip beneath the canopy of a boat and never

say a word, even as you snapped their covers securely over their heads. Those tender kids, the last thing you'd ever see of them, their hands folded beneath their chins, and that image could just shake you to the core, shatter your soul in a million ways.

And then we receded, and we watched Robert descend to the beach and the dock, and there we held our breath. Penny was scrambling about the inside of the house, working the interior wood paneling and insulation for any trace of smoldering. Robert Larson unmoored the boat, unlashed the tethers from its side, and hopped into the water. From there he pushed on the stern and, straining, moved the heavy, low-riding boat into deeper water. He pushed and built momentum until Slocum Lake was over his neck and nearly in his mouth. Then he let the boat go. In the placid water, it skated silently over our nearly invisible netted cage and into open water. No breeze touched its gentle, steady wake. Out it went.

Robert pulled himself on the dock and watched it go. Then he bent down, dripping, and lifted a rifle to his shoulder. He closed his eye. He aimed and, from his knee, fired two quick, resonant shots. We turned. We saw the boat pitch. It lurched, dropped, then plunged into the depths of Slocum Lake with enormous emissions of escaping air, like the blowing of cattle gas.

Then silence. Just like that. The hot Slocum Lake water was still. Our carp were gone, returned to the gunk of our lake bottom, and with them all our efforts to fleece and harry the Larsons. We felt some remorse. We do not like to devastate children, after all. But the sun was coming up. It shone on the Larsons' cottage. We waited. We watched Robert Larson walk inside, shower, and then sit down on the cottage's fine wood floor beside his wife. They talked as the sun rose. Penny had poured coffee. They wiped their eyes and their foreheads. They studied the fire damage to their interior wall. It was minor. They smiled and shook their heads. Then, as if pricked, Penny stuck up her head. We could see in her eyes the sudden flaming of awareness. She opened her mouth and ran to the empty bunk beds. She returned to Robert. She trembled. She took his shoulder. They began calling out the children's names. They searched the cottage. They moved outside to search the property. They yelled out. They shouted. They screamed in ways we could not have predicted. They ran to the water. They shielded their eyes from the sun in searching. Robert waded in several steps, and then he turned around to look at Penny. His face, we could see, was rent. He yelled to the skies above us all for states around. He entered and left our chests. We know the Larsons, yes. We have known them for years. Now we know they know loss. Now we know they know us.

ANDREW RICONDA

Heart Like a Balloon

FROM *Criminal Class Review*

DENNY FINAFRIGGINALLY NOTICED that the blonde serving us drinks and Cajun fries at Fiddlesticks was missing a finger, the finger that traditionally bears a wedding ring.

It was an Irish pub in the Village, always busy as hell for happy hour. But it was three in the afternoon, a time for nonworking drunks mostly, the dour hour. I flicked a pistachio down and around the horseshoe-shaped bar and it silently disappeared. If people still smoked in bars (like they should), it would've pinged off a metal ashtray.

"How should I know? Maybe she's real commitment-phobic."

"But don't you want to know?" He implored with both hands, shaking those nicely manicured fingernails in my face on the *you*. And he always said shit like that with a guilt-provoking inflection because you didn't agree with what he wanted right then and there.

"I don't. But I will ask anyway. By the way, your cuticles are lovely in this light."

I knew he wouldn't ask. That's the Denny way. If Denny wants an answer, he asks somebody to get it for him. If he wants some business done, he gets a subordinate to handle it. And everybody's a subordinate in Denny's world. He's very successful, owns his own (big) contracting firm, but he's gotten everywhere by having others provide for him. He was like that even in high school. And even before, I'd hazard. Hell, as an infant he probably outsourced for tit milk.

So when the defingered blonde came by, I said, "My friend here is wondering what happened to your finger."

Denny was shooting me a look, quick-tilted head and all, but she didn't mind. You can tell sometimes when someone's the type who's going to be bothered by any little thing or nothing in the world, and she was the latter. And quite from being commitment-phobic, her story was that she had been married all of a week and had been tending bar when her eye caught a cobweb on some ornamental woodwork above the shelves of booze. She jumped up to "swish" the cobweb away, the ring caught on the woodwork, and when she came down to the ground, the finger was literally ripped from her hand. Denny winced. I followed suit with a wince of my own—a courtesy wince. She provided more graphic details: doctors had cut her open at the hip—she peeled back enough of her jeans to show us the scar—and had sewn the severed digit up inside her, hoping to make it more amenable to a bid for future reattachment. Alas . . .

"Did you take it as a sign," Denny asked, "that you shouldn't have gotten married?"

"No, but it put me off cobwebs like forever."

She went to serve others, leaving us to each other, to it.

First he made a superficial inquiry about if things were working out for me on the West Coast, work- and women-wise; and then he made an equally superficial dig about my appearance—my hair had gotten long and hippy-straight and I was long in the beard, too—linking it rather adeptly with that initial inquiry, and how nice it must be that things were so laid back out there in California that I could just let myself go like this. I caught my reflection in the mirror behind; maybe he had a point: I kind of looked like I was living on a Brussels sprouts commune or something. And then it all got to being about him again.

"Things are good here," he said, "you'll be happy to hear."

"I'm overjoyed. What did you want to talk about?"

Denny jacked a smile onto his face and speared the Jim Beam–infused cherry at the bottom of his manhattan with a swizzle stick. When he got it to the glass rim, he grabbed it by the stem and dangled it in front of his mouth forever. It had to be big, and probably dirty. We hadn't sat together for a good three years. We'd been friends of sorts until I did a favor for him to keep him out of jail. Subsequently, he got leery of our association. Denny could deal with the blood on his hands as long as he didn't have a daily reminder of it. Shit, it wasn't all that much blood. And it wasn't even like someone had been killed. That being said, I certainly didn't mourn the loss of our friendship. I'd mainlined enough Dr. Phil while unemployed to recognize the toxic people in my life, and when this bastard broke wind, the room smelled of almonds and burned Legos. He finally popped the cherry, chewed, and swallowed. I'd only be guessing if I told you it tasted like anything to him.

He said, "I wonder where she keeps her ring now."

"Denny . . ."

"There's this guy . . ."

And if Denny wants some bit of dirty business done, he gets me, Brian Rehill.

"Christ, Den. Any time you begin a sentence, 'There's this guy.' Christ on a hand truck."

"I have no right to ask. I owe you. I remember."

He owed me. He remembered. California must be doing wonders for my disposition, because even that didn't get me worked up. And even though I suspected Denny had quietly put a few bad words in for me here and there, after I did him his little favor, putting the kibosh on jobs I should've gotten, including a couple of big sheetrocking contracts that would've put me into a whole other tax bracket, I didn't care now. This pariah's subsequent relocation westward turned out to be the best move I'd ever made. And L.A., much to the bemusement of my condescending New Yorker mentality, turned out to be paradise—professionally, romantically, and even, God help me, spiritually (I hadn't done anything I was ashamed of in nearly two years). I was even thinking about buying my first house, although I still needed to somehow come up with a big chunk for a down payment. Somehow . . .

I scanned the practically empty bar. No one at the other side was looking past their standard three-foot beer stare.

"I need to pat you down. Don't give me that look. I don't hear from you for two years, and six minutes into my Seven and Seven, 'There's this guy.' Again."

He clenched the bar rail, and I moved a hand around his body, quickly, efficiently. "Okay. Finish your fries and let's go for a stroll."

We walked out on Greenwich and headed east to Sixth, passing a bunch of specialty shops, an accessories store with Tibetan fur hats in its window, a mystery-book store, and a novelty shop selling the kinds of cheap, ironic gifts no one ever really needs, bobble-headed Jesus and Dick Cheney dolls. Denny did most of the talking.

There's this guy, it turns out, who happens to be the soon-to-be ex-husband of Denny's girlfriend-slash-administrative assistant. They separated over a year ago, but he won't stop calling, following her, showing up at her job (Denny's shop in Brooklyn), and threatening her if she doesn't take him back. He broke into her apartment a month ago, smacked her around, and she had gotten a restraining order. And things were getting even crazier now that he'd received his walking papers. Threats against her, Denny, and even himself—the ole hat trick of marital rage.

It was February in the city. I shivered as we walked.

"I know. Scary shit, right?"

"It's freaking freezing, Denny."

"Jesus, gone two years and you've already lost your cold-bloodedness. Is that a word?"

"Have somebody look it up for you."

We stopped on the next corner, in front of the Jefferson Market Garden, which had been the site of a women's prison in the 1930s. It was seasonal, and there was a big padlock and chain on the wrought iron gates. *Everything's dead now, thank you, come again!*

The wind was in our face, so we turned back the way we came, passing a graffiti-blighted playground I had not noticed on the first pass because of a fleeting redhead. I pointed out my car rental, and we stood next to it.

Denny said, "You know how these things go, Brian. If someone doesn't . . ."

"Intervene."

"You see it on the news all the time. The victim had a restraining order against her deranged husband. He kills her, himself . . . et cetera."

"I hate suicidal-homicidal guys the most. Make up your mind."

He didn't so much as crack a smile. Despite present circumstances, though, that was more his nature than situational. Denny never had much of a sense of humor. Cheap bastards rarely do. They don't give it up to charities, they cut corners on jobs at the customer's expense, if you sit with them during dinner and have only a drink, they expect you to pay for half of their shell steak and garlic mashed potatoes, and they don't yuck it up, cheap bastards, as if chuckles were something to be hoarded. Hell, ten seconds ago he wouldn't even let go of a second *et cetera*.

"This guy—he found Jesus last year too. But threatening your estranged wife, breaking into her place and smacking her around, this stuff Jesus doesn't object to."

"He's very understanding that way. That's why no one else has won the title."

"He left messages for her at work, disguising his voice. Saying Valentine's Day is coming up and he's got a big surprise for her. He's ruining our lives."

"Well, may I query, how does your wife feel about all this?"

He bristled. "I don't need you judging me. This girl—she fills me up. She makes my heart swell. It swells, just like a big red—"

"Okay, okay. In an ideal world, what kind of restraint would you put on the guy?"

"A talking-to won't work. I'm sure of that. He's proven that. He's way past . . ."

"So, we're talking about a permanent restraint."

His eyes went away from mine.

"Whatever you deem . . . most permanent."

He peered into my Avis midsize. He probably didn't want to look in my eyes—looking into mine might be like looking into his own soul, or lack thereof. And I must admit I'm kind of stunned that this is Denny's lump-sum estimate of me, that I am employable for such a grave task, capable of such a deed—past deeds notwithstanding. I'm slightly less stunned, however, by my agreeing to it—future deeds, specifically the one to the Santa Barbara ranch with the FOR SALE sign on its front lawn and fig tree in the backyard, coming to mind.

He was done looking into the front seat and moved on to some back-seat gazing.

"Are you gonna be guessing the contents of my trunk soon? Maybe win a kewpie doll or big comb?"

"Sorry. You got Wet Ones on the back seat? My hands are sticky from the ketchup."

"It's empty."

I was hoping he would beg off when I asked, "Look, I'm going in for another round. And to stare longingly at that nine-finger wonder. You want another?" I lit up a cigarette.

"I ought to head home."

"This isn't a favor, Denny. You and I are done with favors. Understand?"

"You're . . . like a subcontractor."

"Yeah, like I'm doing some facade restoration work for you. Or sheetrocking."

"What does a facade restoration cost these days?"

I gave him my estimate. He flinched but agreed. Rather too easily. I figured that would come back to haunt me, having seen first-hand the way Denny treats his subcontractors.

Details.

"He lives in Long Island City, in his mother's house, alone. She died last year and he moved in. There's a key. In Sucrete's purse. She won't even know it's gone."

"Just tell me his name and where he works and lives. And stay away from the girl—for now, and until things are done. I know she works for you, but don't be messing around with her in public. Close your office door and nail her on your desk blotter if you have to."

His eyes narrowed.

"Don't get crude. I love her. She fills my heart big like a . . ."

"Bite me. You want the thing done with savoir-faire, or do you want the thing done?"

He looked away again.

"I want the thing done."

We were quiet for a bit.

"Your girlfriend's name is Sucrete, huh?"

"What of it?"

"Nothing."

We shook on something. And he left. I unlocked the door to the car and removed the container of hand wipes. It didn't feel like he had transferred any stickiness to me on the shake, ketchupy and/or ethical, but just in case, I took one out, sniffed at the fresh lemony scent, and sighed. Whatever I deemed.

It's a type of fig, Sucrete is.

And his name was Joe.

I drove to the Bronx to say hello to my mother and, unbeknown to her, get the .38 that was stashed up in her attic; over the years there had been a lot of attic-relegated unbeknown-to-her shit stored in that house. I honked to alert her that I was in her driveway, and while I waited for her to show her face, I called a guy I knew in Williamsburg who used to own a crappy white van with tinted windows. He didn't really want to hear from me again and he still had the van. I honked again and my mother parted the curtains. She opened the window, looking smaller than ever, and threw me down the key.

I kissed her on her sad, tired cheek, sat with her at the kitchen table, told her I wasn't hungry, heard the latest on my junkie sister, went upstairs to the bathroom, pissed, snuck up the attic ladder for the gun, went back down to the kitchen, told her I still wasn't hungry, let her make me a grilled cheese, kissed her on her other equally saddened/exhausted cheek, and was on my way.

Joe lived in an industrial scab of a neighborhood in Long Island City, a flank of beaten-up warehouses mottled with exhausted sky-blue and lime-green two-family frame homes. It was sandwiched between a crap-drab housing project to the east and, to the west, a monstrously huge power plant with three candy-striped smokestacks that were constantly pluming a gray spool over the whole wound like a bad salve. This was all blocks from where developers were putting up 900K lofts and condos—and yet miles away. All the blocks were numbered out here, 46th Roads and 48th Avenues, as if the NYC planners took one look around and decided the streets weren't worth naming. Once the warehouses were done for the day, the streets fell into a coma, and the residents were too busy drawing their curtains and dead-bolting out nightfall to be concerned about a crappy, nondescript white van with tinted windows that had been parked on this broken-beer-bottle corner on and off for a few days now.

Joe's house was adjacent to a small playground that was always locked by dusk. He would come and go, not greeting any of the few neighbors passing his way; and, for their part, said neighbors usually quickened their pace when they spotted Joe. Several had gone so far as to cross to the other side of the street to avoid any contact with him.

An ancient minivan had collapsed into his driveway from four slashed tires, probably the result of Joe's sparkling demeanor, an example of which was stenciled on the side of the vehicle in letters the size of plums: "Notice to Parents: Please do not teach the children that same sex couples is okay. It is Wrong, it is an Abomination before God and Man." And then he'd added a quote from Leviticus, which went a little something like this: "If a man lie with another, their blood shall be upon them."

It was all very, very subtle, but I surmised Joe had some tolerance issues.

Joe didn't really need the vehicle. He never went anywhere but a few blocks in any direction. He made daily trips to the video rental, to the Chinese takeout or the pizza joint, and loads of trips to the liquor store around the corner. He hadn't been to work since I'd been following him. For some people, a broken heart is a full-time job.

The benefits suck, though, Joe. The benefits suck.

It was early in the evening and he had been inside with a bottle for a couple of hours when he stuck his head out the side door that faced the empty park. He put his head against the doorjamb, drunk as a skunk, and looked out onto the playground, maybe for ghosts of someone else's happiness, and a mostly drained bottle of Old Smuggler slipped from his hand and broke on the stoop. From the van, I looked at the other houses. No one came to their windows. They were probably inured to the sound of Joe's broken bottles by now. He stepped back inside, leaving the entrance and screen door open, and then reappeared with a jacket. He slammed the wooden door shut but didn't lock it. He stumbled down the steps on the side of the house, leaving the screen door ajar to the wiles of the Queens wind. He made his way to the sidewalk and up the street.

He needed another bottle, which I ascertained, because as he passed by my van he bellowed to the rest of his inattentive world, "I'm getting another bottle! Judge me!"

Inside the van, I raised my hand, volunteering for the duty. "Will do," I said.

I would have to move fast: if he made no other stops, he could be back in ten minutes. I waited until he turned the corner, waited a minute, and then I crawled up to the front seat. I picked up my satchel, peered up the block, and then down it with the rearview.

I had planned on waiting until tomorrow night, but this was an opportune moment and I could see it all transpiring in my mind's eye: I could get in now without a hassle, wait for him to come home, and before he even had a chance to swill his next swill, come up from behind and stab him right through the fucking heart. Wow, I thought; my la-la land girlfriend was right about this power of visualization crap she was always spouting. I reached for the door handle planning on banging her thankfully and violently when I got back.

Suddenly headlights were coming at me. A red Camaro, a boy and a girl up front, pulled up across the street from me. He was yelling at her and she was just staring straight ahead, saying nothing. After a while he fell silent and gazed out alongside her. She tapped him on the shoulder, he turned his head, and she gave him the finger. He intensely returned to staring out the windshield, started the car up again, and pulled away. I waited. More headlights, this time from behind. A black Lincoln Navigator passed me by and pulled up in front of the house next to Joe's. A man and woman got out, slamming their doors in synchronicity. The woman tried to open the back door.

She yelled at someone inside, "Unlock the door!"

The man stepped up to the car and yelled, "Stop messing around and open the door for your mother."

Nothing happened.

The husband said, "I can't get the groceries if she doesn't unlock the door."

"I know that. Do you think I'm stupid?"

Using telepathy, I messaged hubby: Don't say, No, I don't think you're stupid.

"No, I don't think you're stupid," he said.

"Just wouldn't listen," I said.

Mom and Pop had convinced the kid to unlock the door, and by the time each of them had enthusiastically contributed to a round robin of verbal abuse and had finally gotten the Corn Pops, Pop Tarts, and one-percent-fat milk out of the vehicle, Joe came stumbling back down the street with his black plastic bag. The men exchanged subzero glances, and Joe staggered to the side entrance of his house. He dug around in his pockets looking for his keys but did not find them.

"It's unlocked, Joe," I sighed to the windshield.

He stepped up the stoop, pushed aside the screen door, and put his fist right through a pane of glass on the other door. He stood there on his wobbly drunk legs, watching, as the door creaked open on its own.

"You know, Joe," I laughed, "I think my personal favorite quote from the Bible is, God retards those who retard themselves. You fucking retard."

The man with the groceries dropped his bag to the sidewalk and went to Joe's yard and yelled, "What the hell you doing, man?"

Joe yelled right back, "Jesus loves me anyway!" and pushed open his door and went in.

I needed things to settle down a bit and I didn't want to take the chance of just sitting there while Joe replenished his blood with liquor, so I drove off, figuring he was in for the rest of the night anyway, and the more stewed he got, the better. I went to a White Castle drive-in a few blocks away and got a bag of murder burgers, pulled out of the drive-in lane, and parked in the lot.

It didn't really seem that wrong to me, I had to admit. I had always felt a tinge of guilt over the last guy, the one who was going to testify against Denny about bid-rigging. I was only supposed to persuade him to change his story, but at gunpoint the man had grabbed his chest and vapor-locked right in the front seat of his car. He might not have been a bad guy, I don't know; we really hadn't had the opportunity for getting acquainted. I remember the fear in his eyes. When the gun was against his left temple, he bit into his bottom lip so hard the skin broke and doused his chin with blood, his hands went clutching at his chest—

But this was different. I wasn't anticipating much residual guilt. I tried to suck some chocolate shake through a straw. Different. Except for them both being named Joe, of course.

But this Joe was subhuman. Now, I had two years of college and took a few psychology courses. So I know what the mind does. When you plan to kill somebody, you convince yourself that the guy doesn't have the right to live because he's not human; this rationalization allows you to proceed with the murder. But this was different because this guy just really wasn't human.

There were no other similarities I could recall. Except that, I remembered, I had eaten Whitey one-bites before going to see the whistleblower too. Maybe they were pre-penance. Whatever it was, I was getting too contemplative about the whole thing and had now lost my appetite and was barely able to finish the onion rings.

About an hour later, I parked two blocks away from Joe's, put on some gloves, and headed over with my satchel. No one was on the street when I entered his yard. I moved quickly to the cracked concrete path that led to the side entrance. I went up the stoop, pressed the door, and it opened. I could hear Sinatra singing about Saturday being the loneliest night of the week from somewhere in the basement. A trail of Joe's blood led from the broken window-pane and up the stairs to an open door through which I could see the kitchen. I took out my .38. I was really hoping I wouldn't have to use it—I wanted to use a knife of Joe's—but I might bump into him at any moment. I walked down the steps and gently pushed open the door which led to the garage. A CD player sat on the hood of Sucrete's Miami Beach–edition, cranberry-red Cougar, playing Ol' Blue Eyes. There was no sign of Joe. There was, how-ever, a taped-up garden hose running from the exhaust pipe to the driver's window of the vehicle. It never occurred to me that I might have something in common with a piece of shit like Joe, but here we were: neither one of us was planning on him living through the night.

"Peachy," I said.

I entered the kitchen, listening, and heard a shower running up-stairs. I looked around. There was a brown stove and a matching fridge circa 1972. The warped laminate countertops were a faded blue. A toaster oven on the white, chipped dinette table had to have belonged to Alice on *The Brady Bunch* at some point in time. Scattered around the toaster oven were sheets of balled paper. I unfurled one. It was a suicide note. All it said was *Goodbye, bitch.* It looked like I wouldn't have to wait for the CliffsNotes. I returned the note to an orb and bocce-balled it into the others, banking it off the saltshaker.

The living room was dimly lit by a cheap, bulky candle which was burning horribly uneven and a little street light filtering through bent Venetian-blind slats. And strewn everywhere, on the worn sectional sofa, the love seat, the coffee table, and covering all of the tacky burgundy wall-to-wall carpeting, were hundreds of heart-shaped balloons stenciled *I LOVE YOU.* The only thing not covered with the hearts was a wobbly TV dinner/folding table, upon which the candle, and a few other mementos, stood. There was a piece of paper under the candle. I bent over to look. It was their marriage certificate, covered in dark red wax. The wax had also adhered his marriage band to the document. On the bottom of the certificate was a childish scrawl in black Sharpie: *Its All For You, Darling!* The only other thing on the table was a bloodied paring knife. *Its All For You, Darling!* That kind of shit drove me crazy. You'd think the fucker would try to be grammatically correct for the last and most important memo of his life. I found the Sharpie on a nearby end table and added an apostrophe.

The running water was louder from here. I looked at the staircase leading to the second floor, and waded through the balloons.

I found him dangling in the bathroom, naked down to his shorts, a brown extension cord wrapped around his neck and tied to the shower fixture. His left leg was hanging straight down to the drain, but his right had shot over the side of the tub, wedging his foot between porcelain and sink. Though skunk drunk, he must've panicked at the moment of truth—his right hand had gone up and worked its way under the cord, three fingers stuck underneath it. The tub was about half full. Some people might've seen it as being half empty, but I was seeing no reason for pessimism. I pocketed my gun with a smile and a dimple on my right cheek.

I took it all in.

"Never wear white underwear to your own suicide, Joe."

At the sound of his name, his body suddenly spazzed. He kicked out violently, wrenching the shower fixture out of the wall, which sent him down into the tub, smashing his head viciously against its side when he landed. Water spewed out of the broken wall fixture. Joe gagged and pulled himself over the tub's side and collapsed onto the shower mat, motionless. Since he was lying on his side, I saw what he had been doing with the paring knife. On his right shoulder there was a butchered flap of skin hanging loosely from his flesh where her name was tattooed, presumably during happier times. He had done a half-ass job. The story of his life.

"Joe?"

He raised his head, gagged, and spewed vomit over the little bathroom rug—blood and macaroni and cheese, from what I could see.

"Joe?"

He was barely able to lift up his head to look at me, and his eyes were barely open due to the blood and hard water.

"Is it you? Finally?" he grumbled. "Jesus?"

And I said, "Sure."

Fifteen minutes later we had a pretty solid God/Sinner rapport going on and Joe was giving me the lowdown on his exit strategy. I asked why he hadn't just gassed himself in the garage. He said he was just turning the engine over when he decided he needed a purifying shower. In the shower, he just went with the hanging, a spur-of-the-moment kind of thing.

"She always said I wasn't spontaneous."

I almost felt sympathy: they *were* always saying that.

I convinced him that the gassing was still a good plan, and with me coaching, he began to crawl back to the basement. We were out of the bathroom and halfway down the dark hall to the stairs that were barely illuminated by the bathroom light at the other end. He stopped and buried his head in the hallway carpeting.

"Help, help me, Jesus. I've been . . . waiting."

He lay there in his soiled underwear, half pulled down to his butt crack from the crawling. I was pretty sure I was about to pity him when I caught my reflection in a hallway mirror, and even though it was dark, much darker than usual, I also knew it was God's reflection too, and the one thing I did know about the two of us was that we pitied nobody.

I crouched down.

"Listen, Joe. You know the rules. Jesus only helps those who help themselves. Or God. One of the two. You've got to help yourself."

"Jesus, Jesus, your breath stinks of onions."

"I had some White Castle on the way over."

"Don't you know what that crap does to your body?"

"Hey, Joe, I'm a bachelor. My whole diet consists of takeout. Let's not get too critical of the Lord, here. What?"

His eyes filled with mistrust. "You . . . look like Jesus. But you don't dress like him."

Great, this is going to blow up now because I'm on Blackstone's 10 Worst-Dressed Messiahs list. Without even thinking, my left hand went into my jacket and felt the butt of the gun.

But then I said, "Joe, I can't go around in my normal work clothes—you don't want to get me crucified again, do you?"

He thought about it, "No, of course not, Jesus. Still . . ."

I stood up.

"Fine. I'm leaving." I walked away.

He cried, "Don't abandon me, Jesus! How can you abandon me?"

"Listen, Joe, if I only help those who help themselves, doesn't it stand to reason that I abandon those that abandon themselves, their goals, their God-given destinies?"

"This is my destiny?"

"Sure!"

"Okay." He sighed.

Wet and bloodied, stinking of booze, he crawled again, this time making it to the landing.

He cried, "No, no, no, no," he sobbed, "I can't—I can't go to you, not with her name."

"Forget her. Remember who you are, Joe, but mostly remember who I am. I am, you know, who am."

For a moment he was filled with faith. But then— "It's on my back! Her name! And I can't get it off! It will always be a part of me unless it's not!"

I took my name in vain. "Okay, change of plans. Get your ass back into the tub. I'll get the paring knife."

That seemed to placate him. He smiled and his eyes welled up.

I went downstairs. He called to me twice while I was collecting the knife from the living room and that relic of a toaster oven from the kitchen, but I decided to go deep into character and not answer. He was in the tub when I got back up.

"Good boy."

He beamed at me. I plugged the oven into the extension cord and ran it over to the outlet above the medicine cabinet. The water already covered his legs.

"Her name."

"I'll help you with that."

"I thought I had to help myself."

"Hey." He was really starting to irk me. "What's my name?"

He told me and calmed down by reiterating it. I gave him a toothbrush to put between his teeth. I went to work on his back,

sucking my own bile back down, and as luck would have it, he shivered, convulsed, and lost consciousness as the blade found the corner of the flap of skin he'd been working on. I could faintly make
out the CD player in the basement. It must've been on repeat; it
kept playing that same Sinatra song over and over. I was feeling
even queasier now as I finished flaying off his skin, could feel the
burgers getting ready for their second coming. I was pretty sure
Sinatra was going to be ruined for me forever too. I finished up,
shaking but not vomiting.

I sat down, my back against the tub, and closed my eyes.

"Shit, there was nothing about this in that *Real Estate Investing for
Dummies* book, shit."

Joe was stirring again.

I got up.

"Now, just stay there, Joe. And close your eyes. Joe? Joe?"

He whispered something. I had to lean in.

"Do you—do, do you think she'll know? That it's all for her?"

"I think you've made that pretty clear."

I handed him the toaster oven. I depressed the switch to the on
position, and for some unfathomable reason turned the dial to Bagel. I went over to the outlet and picked up the other end of that
suicide cord. He raised the toaster over his head.

"I'm ready when you are, Jesus."

"Well, okay, then."

His eyes popped open.

"Wait!"

"What?"

"I did want her to see me in her car, dead. We had some good
memories in that car."

"We all have to get over the past, Joe. That's what Dr. Phil says."

"I like Dr. Phil."

"It's good television."

"Wait!" He lowered the toaster several inches.

"What now?"

"Up there. Who's to hang with? People . . . people like me?"

Poor Joe. I knew exactly what he needed to hear right then.

"I only handle the day-to-day down here, Joe. My father—our
Father—runs the shop upstairs. You let him worry about sorting
out the queers and the wife-beaters. Now buck up and get ready."

He arched his back, getting ready. There was pounding at the front door, someone screamed Joe's name. I looked at Joe and he looked at me.

"I called a couple of friends. Earlier. I thought I might do something stupid tonight."

God, I thought, he wanted someone to stop him.

But that wasn't me.

I plugged him in.

"I'm the only friend you'll ever need. In the name of the father, and of the son: dunk."

He closed his eyes and whispered, "Amen. And here I come!"

He dunked, sparks flew as he fried, and the lights blew out in the entire house.

"Jesus!" a man's voice screamed from outside.

I could hear him kicking at the front door. I put my hand out to the walls and started to make my way out into the hallway.

"The lights, Trini, the lights! Oh, Jesus!" the voice cried again.

"All right, that's the name," I whispered. "Don't wear it out."

It was almost as if the Holy Spirit, who hadn't gotten any billing yet, spoke to me: I took my hand away from the wall and put it out to the darkness, and I found my way downstairs without a trip or stumble.

"The side door's open, Manny!" another voice screamed.

I quickly blew out the candle on the little table.

I sat down in the darkness. It seemed very familiar.

My right hand rested on a heart next to me on the sofa, my left on the gun in my lap.

The man and the woman crashed through the kitchen and then into the living room, bumping into things, cursing.

I sat perfectly still. The woman was crying. Joe had someone who cared—amazing.

"Oh, Manny!"

"I hear water running. Upstairs! Stay here!"

"Manny!"

"Stay here!"

Manny went upstairs. I could hear her stepping closer to me, and suddenly she tripped over something and landed on the sectional, mere feet from me. The gun, pointed roughly at the sound of her breathing, became a part of my extended arm; both were rigid and cold now, my finger on the trigger. Somewhere in some separate part of me I thought: I won't ever even know what color her eyes were.

She sat for a moment, still, then whispered, "Something's here. *Dios mio.*"

A scream of "Ahhh Gawd!!!" came from upstairs, and Trini bolted away from me and the sofa, stumbling up the stairs, screaming Manny's name.

Still holding a heart, I put the gun away, threw my bag over my shoulder, unlatched the front door, and slipped out of the house. A couple of lights in nearby houses were on now—we only ever once get the full darkness we ask for—and I moved quickly to the sidewalk and away.

At the van, I took off the latex gloves.

"Jesus needs a smoke," I sighed.

I went to a Cuban deli and bought us each a pack.

I went by Denny's Brooklyn office on Monday. The Red Hook area was showing slow signs of gentrification. It had once been labeled the "crack capital of America," but now they had an Ikea. For most of the residents, I imagine the reality was somewhere in the middle: you can buy your nice red Ektorp sofa, but you might get raped on it by the time you got it home.

Denny was on the loading platform yelling at a bunch of laborers, some Pakistanis whose names he didn't even know. His back stiffened when he laid eyes on me; he put on his most superficial, full-of-shit Denny smile, and raised a finger in the air indicating he'd be with me in one minute. He turned his attention back to his workers, making sure the three men secured some scaffolding equipment properly to the roof of one of his vans. He looked at a knot and shook his head.

"That's gonna roll off on the BQE and decapitate somebody. Look, Charlie . . ."

"My name is not Charlie, sir," the man told him.

"You work for me, right? Then you're Charlie One, he's Charlie Two, and he's Charlie Three. Understand?"

He came over to me and shook my hand. "You shaved off the beard."

"I had an epiphany."

"What was that?"

"It was itchy."

He looked around his warehouse.

"I ought to get a new place. This one is falling apart. I got to go take a look at the chimney. Somebody's complaining it's about to fall down to the street. Come on."

We took a staircase to the roof. A couple of Puerto Ricans, who were fast at work on the chimney, got barked at; I made my way to the edge and looked at the Manhattan cityscape, all those tall buildings except for those two that were still missing. It was windy, and when I put my bag down, I made sure it was tight between my ankles.

Denny came over to the edge with me.

"Hey, you know that thing that I mentioned to you? It actually resolved itself."

"Did it?"

"Yeah. She'll be safe now. Turns out he was really only a threat to himself. And what a threat. I mean, you should have heard the details."

"The devil's in them."

"All for the best. No outside, you know, intervention."

"You know, Denny, some people need a helping hand. In life. And death."

His brow furrowed. "What are you saying?"

"I'm not religious, but maybe when people pray for help, sometimes it just shows up at their door. In Queens even."

"I don't stay in business by paying people for work they haven't done, Brian."

"I would think, just on the basis of our long friendship, you'd grant me the courtesy of believing in such divine interventions."

"But this wasn't about friendship. Or courtesy. It was a business contract, for—" he glanced over to his employees at the chimney, but they barely spoke English anyway, and he took out his finger quotes— "for 'facade restoration.' And there's no proof you performed any of the contracted work. Are you really asking me to believe"—his voice went lower—"what . . . He didn't kill himself?"

"Oh, he committed suicide. Let's not take that away from him."

He looked at his watch. And offered to take me to lunch later.

"I'm more than willing to fairly compensate for whatever time you spent . . . estimating."

"I have a flight to catch. You know, people who really believe, they don't need proof. But maybe it helps to alleviate doubt."

He was barely listening.

"Well, I got to go and see Sucrete anyways. She's pretty upset. I mean, she wanted him out of her life, but she's not without a . . . What's in the bag?"

"It's Valentine's Day, Denny."

"I know that, Brian."

"And Joe wanted her to have a final gift from him. Go ahead and open it. I can rewrap."

Denny turned to his workers. "Vamoose! Get the other van ready to go!"

They made their way to the roof door and left.

I picked up the bag and held it open. Denny retrieved the red, satiny-papered box from within. He held it in his hands. He ripped the paper off and let it drop. I shot my foot out to it, saving it from the wind. I lit a cigarette up as he gingerly opened the lid. I peeked over his shoulder, still somewhat marveled by its contents. Inside, one of those red balloon hearts sat, still completely inflated, and Scotch-taped three times around its center was a small swath of flayed skin with a woman's name on it. He took a step away from me.

"Denny."

He turned, looked at me. I kicked the wrapping paper his way.

"Litter."

Denny picked it up, hands compressing, crushing it into the reddest, bloodiest of balls, while all signs of blood drained from his face. He slowly made his way over to the chimney, put his back against it, and slid down to the asphalt-covered roof. He held on to the box with his right hand, its lid still open, keeping it in his lap, and his other hand went to the guy wires secured to the chimney. He closed his eyes. On the street below, Sinatra was singing on a car radio about making it here and therefore anywhere. I felt a warm sensation.

I crouched down in front of Denny. He refused to look at me, eyes still closed; he seemed to be growing smaller and smaller.

I whispered, "And Sucrete—Joe told me she's got a birthday

coming up too, doesn't she? I'm sorry, did I say this was a final gift?"

I removed the lit cigarette from my mouth and pressed its red hot tip against the balloon. When it burst, he shuddered, his eyes popped open, and they found me only—and I felt sorry for him. We had been friends once, maybe that was why. Or maybe being Christ for a night had made me soft. Softer.

So I provided for my old friend. Everybody always does for Denny.

"Hey? That bartender? She wears her ring around her neck. On a chain. FYI."

S. J. ROZAN

Chin Yong-Yun Takes a Case

FROM *Damn Near Dead 2*

MY DAUGHTER IS a private eye.

You see? It even sounds ridiculous. She follows people. She asks the computer about them as though it were a temple fortuneteller. She pulls out their secrets like dirt-covered roots to hand to the people who hire her. What is private about that? And always involved with criminals, with police! My only good luck, she is not a real police officer, like her best friend Kee Miao-Li. Whenever I see Miao-Li's mother, we give each other sympathy, though I give her the greater amount because her daughter's choice of profession is even more unacceptable than mine.

Although her daughter, at least, is engaged to be married, to a boy of good family, in Chinatown for three generations.

Mine is not.

Not that I believe marriage is the answer to all a woman's problems. I am not a fool, no matter what my daughter thinks. Marriage, if handled badly, can be a source of great distress. This has been the case for Tan Li-Li, a mahjong player of my own age — a fact she tries to hide behind black hair dye and crimson lipstick. I would not call Tan Li-Li "friend," although she is among the women I regularly meet with under the trees in the park or at the folding tables of the senior center. It is not easy to be the friend of a woman who eats so much bitterness. Difficulties make many people more kind than formerly; but some are like Tan Li-Li, thinking they can rid themselves of troubles by giving them to others. Tan Li-Li's gloom stems from marriage, though not her own. She is a widow, and as she will be the first to tell you, a widow's lot is sad, to be always alone. I am also a widow, and although I miss my husband, gone these many years, I do not find myself alone. Perhaps that is because I have five children and five grandchildren, all nearby. My daughter, in fact, though her profession is a disgrace, is filial in this: she still lives with me in the family apartment. But Tan Li-Li has only one son, and one grandson, and the marriage that is so bitter for her is her son's.

My daughter, who follows American ways, knows Tan Li-Li and how difficult she can be. She asks me, "Why do you play with her, Ma? When she's there, why don't you sit at another table or something?" If she had a true Chinese understanding, of course she would never say such things. Tan Li-Li was brought into our mahjong group by Feng Guo-Ha, with whom she shared a village childhood in China. Even a poor village has its social order. The poorest can be the worst: the smaller the treasure at the top of the staircase, the more fierce the battle on the steps. The Tans were a merchant family, while the Fengs labored in the fields. Feng Guo-Ha, a small, shy woman, tells us that Tan Li-Li was sour even as a child; and Tan Li-Li treats Feng Guo-Ha imperiously to this day. One thing that galls Tan Li-Li is the contrast between their sons. Feng Guo-Ha's son, like his mother, is friendly and eager to please. He treats his mother well, living nearby, taking her shopping and to the doctor. Often she looks after her granddaughter while her son and his wife are at work. Tan Li-Li's son, in contrast, has for four years ("Such an unlucky number!" Tan Li-Li sighs) been living on the other side of the world, in Beijing, and raising her grandson there.

Feng Guo-Ha cannot enjoy being criticized and given orders by Tan Li-Li; nevertheless, loyalty to childhood friends is never wrong, no matter their behavior, and she remains loyal. Loyalty to friends from adulthood is also virtuous. Feng Guo-Ha and I sewed together in the garment factory for many years, when our children were young. She's my friend, and I won't abandon her to Tan Li-Li's sneering voice.

You can understand, however, what a surprise it was for me when that voice, which I rarely hear beyond the mahjong table, issued from the red telephone in my own kitchen.

"Chin Yong-Yun," Tan Li-Li said decisively, as though my name were something I didn't know and would be grateful to be told. "I hope you are well. I am looking for your daughter."

I recovered myself and answered calmly, "Quite well, thank you, Tan Li-Li." Politeness suggested I inquire after her health also before reaching the substance of our conversation, but she had not allowed me that courtesy. "I'm sorry, but my daughter is not at home."

"She is not in her office either. How can I speak to her?"

"If you've left a message, as I'm sure you have, she will no doubt call you as soon as she is able." Unless I spoke to her first myself. Perhaps I could discourage her from plunging into the cloud of bitterness that surrounds Tan Li-Li.

"That is not soon enough. Our matter is urgent."

"Our matter?"

"It concerns my son. As you know, he is visiting me here."

I could not help but know. As if it were not enough to see Tan Li-Li daily parading her three-year-old grandson in the park— grasping the child's hand so firmly I feared it would grow misshapen—she also had spoken of nothing but this impending visit for weeks before Tan Xiao-Du and his son arrived from Beijing. I had expected the visit to lighten her humor, especially since her daughter-in-law had remained in China, but her sourness did not abate. Probably I had been foolish. I had expected pleasure and pride to mark her reactions to many events involving her son: his posting to an important position in China with his American firm, his marriage to a kind and beautiful Beijinger, the birth of their son. Each time, however, Tan Li-Li's reaction had been only darkness. Of his return to the homeland: "How can he leave me here to grow old alone?" Of his marriage: "Now he will never come home!" Of his child: "My only grandson, growing up so far from me!" Xiao-Du had offered to bring his mother to Beijing as often as she wanted, even to settle her there for as long as he stayed. But still, around the mahjong table we heard only complaint and recrimination.

"I'm sorry, Tan Li-Li," I said. "I cannot—"

"There, you see?" Tan Li-Li interrupted with a voice of vinegared triumph. I started to ask, "See what?" but she wasn't speaking to me. "I told you, Xiao-Du, that calling Chin Yong-Yun was useless."

I did not want my daughter involved with Tan Li-Li's endless problems, but this insult was unacceptable. Before I could properly respond, however, a man's voice came into my ear.

"Chin Yong-Yun, I hope you and your family are well. This is Tan Xiao-Du."

"Tan Xiao-Du, I and my family are quite well, thank you. I hope your family is also." The son, teaching the mother courtesy. His Cantonese was good, also. I'm sure his skill didn't make his mother grateful for her luck, although it should have. Many American-born children are poor in Cantonese. My children all speak well, of course. They are talented in languages. I'm sure my choice not to learn English, which made it necessary for them to speak Cantonese at home, played only a very small part.

"I'm sorry my daughter is not available," I told Tan Xiao-Du, "but her services are much in demand, you understand."

"Yes, of course. But this is a very important matter. Isn't there any way we can contact her?" I was reluctant to share my daughter's cell phone number with the Tans, but I couldn't help hearing Xiao-Du's strained tones of distress. Especially when he announced, "It's my son. My son has been kidnapped."

I was briefly speechless, hearing this news. The despair in Xiao-Du's voice, and the situation's dire nature, changed my thinking. It did not, however, change the humor of his mother. "Never mind," I heard her sneer behind him. "I told you, there is only one solution. You will give them whatever they want and all will be well. Do as I say!"

"No!" Xiao-Du responded desperately. "Mother, I can't!"

"Foolish boy! You will not—"

"There must—"

"You are—"

"Come speak to me," I said loudly, into his ear.

"What? I'm sorry, Chin Yong-Yun, what did you say?" I could hear the son shushing the mother as he waited for my response.

"I often work with my daughter on her cases." I am not the sort of person to be unscrupulous with the truth, but circumstances were pressing. "I will collect your evidence, and brief it to her when she is available." My daughter thinks I never listen when she talks about her work. If that were so, would I know the words of her profession?

"Chin Yong-Yun—I don't think—"

"Come, you must hurry if your child is in danger." I hung up the phone. I find this often helps people make decisions.

Ten minutes had not passed before mother and son were at my door. Of course I had put the kettle on the stove and set out tea-cups. I might have expected a small gift of almond cookies or bean cakes, as is customary when visiting, but the Tans arrived empty-handed. Making allowances for the son's distraction and the moth-er's customary lack of civility, without comment I added a plate of macaroons to the table. As the tea steeped I seated myself in my armchair, instructed them to sit also, and requested that they tell their story.

"I blame myself," Tan Li-Li began, but her son interrupted.

"No, Mother. It is not your fault, and this is the time for action, not for blame."

"Nevertheless, I—"

"Please," I said to stop this tiresome argument. "We never involve ourselves in the personal lives of our clients."

"We?" Tan Li-Li's plucked eyebrows arched.

"My daughter and myself. In our investigations. Xiao-Du, just tell me what has happened."

I asked to hear the story from the son, but I had little hope. I poured the tea—first for mother, then for son, and last for my-self—and discovered that my assessment had been correct.

"It is, as I said, my fault." Tan Li-Li's shake of the head might have expressed self-disgust, or at least disbelief. However, it was more likely a denial of her son's request not to blame herself, as well as of mine to remain uninvolved in her personal life. "I was in the park with little Bin-Bin while Xiao-Du attended to business for his firm. His position requires him to be available to give instruc-tions to his subordinates at all times. Even when he is overseas with his family." She gave Xiao-Du a look full of maternal suffering and accusation.

"In the park," I repeated firmly. "With Bin-Bin. When was this?"

She turned back to me with narrowed eyes. "Forty minutes ago." She paused before resuming her tale. "Bin-Bin was playing with other boys, and I turned away for a moment to buy roasted peanuts for him, for a treat. No more than a moment! When I looked up, he was gone."

She dabbed at her eyes with a handkerchief.

"What makes you think he was kidnapped?" I asked. "Isn't it more likely he wandered away? Maybe some other grandmother found him. He's a small child who's lived his whole life in Beijing. He doesn't speak Cantonese, or English, does he? He could be at the police station right now, unable to tell the officers even his name."

That was clever of me, to think of that, and I might have expected their eyes to light up and one or the other to call the Fifth Precinct immediately. But the mother looked exasperated, and the son merely sad.

"I got a phone call," he said. "A ransom demand."

I blinked. "Oh."

He waited. "Aren't you going to ask me what they said?"

"Yes. Yes, of course," I said with impatience. "I'm waiting for you to tell me." I added, "It's best to allow people to tell their stories in their own way, without prompting." My daughter has said this, though she thinks, just because I don't stop chopping vegetables when she speaks, that I haven't heard her.

"They said not to go to the police. They said if I do what they ask, my son will be returned unharmed."

"What do they ask?"

He breathed deeply. "My firm develops computer software for foreign markets. Since going to China I've been working on a major project, to enhance the ability of scanners to recognize and read character-based languages—" For some reason, looking at my face, he stopped. "I'm sorry," he said respectfully. "That's technical talk and it doesn't matter. The point is, we're not the only firm working in the area. A successful product, because it will greatly increase computer speed, will be worth many, many millions to the company that develops it. We are the closest."

"Because of Xiao-Du's leadership," the mother put in.

The son just looked at her, then said to me, "That was the demand. To get my son back, they want our code."

"And I say, give it to them!" The mother's face went red with indignation, as though her son's intransigence were willful and unreasonable.

"Your code?" I said. "That is, your solution to your project?"

"Yes. But I can't give it away! I'd be betraying my entire team!

Everyone who works for me, trusts me—and my employer, the faith they've shown—"

"You've given them everything they could have asked for!" the mother countered. "You left your home to live on the other side of the world! You work long hours and days, you're exhausted, no time for anyone! Now you must give them your son also?"

"Of course not, never! But there must be another way. That's why I wanted to come to Lydia—to Ling Wan-Ju." He looked at me desperately. "Can you help us? Can your daughter help us?"

"Possibly," I said. "But first you must both answer some questions for me."

"Anything!" said the son. The mother only sniffed and sipped her tea.

"Xiao-Du. First: were you given a deadline for your compliance?"

"Yes, five this afternoon."

"Over two hours from now. Good, we have some time." The mother frowned at that, but I paid her no attention. I asked the son, "Who was it who called you?"

"I don't know. Obviously he represents one of our competitors, but there are a number of them."

"But it was a man?"

"Yes, though he disguised his voice."

"Really? How?"

"He made it low and growling."

"I see. Now tell me, if you do as they ask, what will be the result?"

"Little Bin-Bin will be returned!" The mother could not contain herself.

"My question concerned a different result," I said in a neutral and professional manner. "For you, Xiao-Du. In relation to your employer. What I mean is, why do you not just do as the kidnappers ask, and then explain the dire nature of the situation to your employer?"

The son swallowed. I poured him more tea, in case his throat was dry. "I'd be betraying my firm and my team," he said. "Three years of work, lost. Worse, given away. Even if they understand, they'll have to fire me to save face."

"They will not fire you!" the mother exploded. "Never mind

their face. You will resign without explaining anything. With your talents you'll easily find another position, and your firm will continue their work in ignorance. When the competitor brings their product to market, your firm will realize they've lost the race, and consider themselves unlucky. That will be all."

"Even if I could do that," the son said, "lie like that to people who've been so good to me, when the rival system comes on the market, they'll analyze it and then they'll know."

"What of it? It will never be more than suspicion. By then you'll have an important position elsewhere, and no one will speak against you."

"Not in China. In China I'll be finished. Even if it's just suspicion, no one will trust me enough keep me on."

"So, you will leave China! For your son, is that too big a sacrifice to make?"

Xiao-Du slumped miserably in his chair.

"Thank you," I said. "Tan Li-Li, now I have questions for you."

"This is ridiculous."

"Please, Mother," the son begged.

The mother rolled her eyes but turned to me with pursed lips, awaiting interrogation.

"You say you took your eyes off little Bin-Bin for a moment, when you were buying peanuts."

"Just for a moment!"

"I find it hard to believe, Tan Li-Li, that you took your eyes from him at all. I have seen you together in the park. You are the most assiduous of guardians." Tan Li-Li gave me a tight, smug smile. "A bag of peanuts could hardly divert you from your duty to your son and grandson," I continued. "Surely there must have been something else."

Her penciled brows knit. "What do you mean?"

"I am talking about a diversion." Let my daughter claim I don't listen to her! "A noise, a commotion, perhaps deliberately meant to distract you. Can you recall anything?"

After a moment her eyes lit up. "Yes! Why, Chin Yong-Yun, you are correct! A loud argument, three thuggish young men. Near the peanut vendor. Pushing each other, shouting, almost coming to blows. They drew everyone's attention. Then they ran off." She beamed. "Is that helpful?"

"Most helpful. Thank you. Would you like more tea? If not, I am ready to work on your case."

They both looked at me blankly. The son comprehended first. "Come, Mother." He stood.

"Where are we going?"

"We're leaving Chin Yong-Yun to her work."

"Chin Yong-Yun?" the mother said incredulously. "What are you proposing?"

"You have hired us," I clarified for her. "Have you not?"

"Yes!" the son said. "Whatever your fee is, I'll pay it."

"Of course," I said. "Now, if you'll excuse me?"

"We have . . ." the mother stammered. "It was Ling Wan-Ju we—he—wanted . . ."

"As I said, my daughter is not available, and as I also said, we often work together. Now, come."

"But . . . the deadline . . ."

"Yes." I turned to the son. "At the appointed time, if I have not recovered little Bin-Bin, you must give the kidnappers what they demand. No matter the consequences for you. Do you understand?"

He nodded glumly.

"But I don't believe you have reason to worry," I added, to be kind, though my daughter says she never promises a client she will solve their case, only that she will do her best. "Now. Perhaps you should go home and wait by the telephone in case the kidnappers call again."

This time the son looked blank and the mother answered with a cold smile. "They called him on his cell phone. He has it in his pocket."

"Oh. Yes. Of course, his cell phone," I said. "Yes. Still."

I was astonished at the mother's rudeness in forcing me to be so impolite as to ask guests to leave. But time was moving swiftly and I needed to begin my investigation. I walked across the living room and opened the door for them. With glances at each other—new hope in the son's eyes, impatient disapproval in the mother's—but without another word, they left.

Once they had gone I exchanged my house slippers for tennis shoes. I hoped the investigation would not demand a great deal of walking, because my bunions had been painful lately. But I didn't think it would. Except that I didn't understand what "code" was—a detail I regarded as unimportant—the situation seemed clear.

At the bottom of the three flights of stairs I opened the street door and peered cautiously around. The sidewalk held no one unexpected, so I emerged. I looked over my shoulder a number of times as I hurried to the park. I could not imagine who might follow me, with the exception of Tan Li-Li herself. That would be unfortunate, if not entirely unanticipated—clearly she had no faith in me—but she was nowhere to be seen.

In the park I questioned various women looking after their children and grandchildren. The number of people there was less than it would have been an hour ago, when Tan Li-Li had lost little Bin-Bin. By now many children had been taken home for their afternoon naps. Some of the women I spoke to had recently arrived, but still, I found a few who had been there for an hour or more. None of them, however, could give me any information about Tan Li-Li, little Bin-Bin, or any loud argument among three thuggish young men.

I was trying to decide what to do next when my own cell phone rang. I rarely use it, but I accepted it after my children repeatedly insisted. They claimed it would ease their minds to know I could contact them if I needed to. What kind of mother knowingly causes her children unease of mind?

I unclasped and unzipped my purse and pulled the phone from it. Pressing the green button, I said, "This is Chin Yong-Yun speaking," not too loudly, because it's very small.

"Yes, Ma, I know." It was my daughter, no time for politeness, a busy detective. "Ma, I have a call here from a man named Tan Xiao-Du, who says he's the son of a friend of yours and it's urgent. Then I have another from his mother, who says never mind. What's going on? Are you all right?"

"I? Of course I am. Why would I not be?"

"I don't know. It sounded like there was something wrong."

"Do not worry. I am taking care of their situation."

"Their situation? Not your situation?"

"Of course not. I'm sorry, Ling Wan-Ju, but I'm very busy right now. I'll explain later. Unless you're not coming home for dinner?"

"Yes, Ma, I'll be home. Are you sure you don't need me? Or the Tans don't need me?"

"They do not. I do."

"You do?"

"Yes. On your way home, please stop for cabbage."

It is important, under pressure, to be able to do two things at once. Therefore as I spoke to my daughter a decision had taken shape in my mind. Now, having said all I needed to say, I pressed the red button and replaced the phone in my purse, which I zipped. This was unfortunate, because as I was clasping the purse shut, the phone rang again. Ready to tell my daughter I really had no time for idle conversation, I unclasped and unzipped and took the phone from its pocket. I pressed the green button. "This is Chin Yong-Yun speaking."

I was surprised to hear, not my daughter's voice, but a man's voice, low and growling. "Stay away if you know what's good for you!"

"Who is speaking?"

"You don't need to know! If Tan Xiao-Du wants to get his son back, you'd better leave us alone! Otherwise someone might get hurt."

I asked again who was calling, but the connection had been broken. Many times that is caused by the inefficiency of the telephone company, but I did not think that had happened here.

Once again I replaced the phone in my purse. The voice had been quite threatening, but an investigator cannot allow herself to be intimidated. My daughter has said that many times.

Tan Li-Li's friend, Feng Guo-Ha, lives near the park. I had some questions to ask her, so I proceeded to her apartment without delay.

"Yong-Yun!" Though Guo-Ha smiled quickly, she seemed quite startled to see me. This was unsurprising. I am not the sort of person who appears on doorsteps unannounced; that is rude. However, my investigation demanded certain adjustments and I was doing what was necessary.

"Guo-Ha, good afternoon," I said. "I'm sorry to arrive without an invitation, but I must ask you some questions."

"I'm delighted to see you, of course, Yong-Yun, but perhaps you could return later? My granddaughter Mei is having her nap right now." Guo-Ha nodded in the direction of the hallway that led to the bedrooms.

"Oh, Mei is here with you today? What a fortunate woman you are, Guo-Ha."

"Yes, thank you, I am. But Mei has trouble sleeping, so once she settles for her nap I take great care not to disturb her. The slightest sound—oh, dear, I think I hear her crying now. I'm sorry, Yong-Yun, but if you'll excuse me—"

"I don't hear anything." I cocked my head to listen while delicately placing my foot in the doorway, in case the door shut accidentally. "Oh! Yes, I do. Allow me, Guo-Ha. I'm very successful with children."

"No, Yong-Yun, you mustn't trouble yourself—"

But I was already across the threshold and into the apartment. Guo-Ha's natural courtesy caused her to move aside for me before she quite knew what she was doing. Over her protests I made directly for the rear bedroom, the one that had been her son's. I heard a child's voice behind the door. I have always been able to quiet children when they fuss, but I could hear before I even opened the door that Guo-Ha had been wrong. Her granddaughter wasn't crying. She was laughing. "Hello, Mei," I said, stepping into the room. And to her father, sitting on the floor with her, a picture book on his lap, "Hello, Lao. I'm glad to hear your throat is no longer hoarse." And to the other child, on Lao's other side, "Hello, Bin-Bin."

Since Bin-Bin had had his nap and was refreshed, I took him with me soon after. Really, my visit was almost short enough to be considered impolite, but I had pressing business. Clearly, neither Lao nor his mother had been the moving force behind this abduction; they were merely agents, hired for the crime. This sort of thing happens often in detective work, and, as my daughter would agree, it is pointless to go after the smaller criminal. My next focus would be their employer, because, though I had recovered the child, an investigator does not like to leave a case unresolved. But first I needed to return Bin-Bin to his worried father.

Both Guo-Ha and her son were abashed at what they'd done, but I told them, "We will speak no more about this." I took little Bin-Bin's hand and led him out the door. In the park I stopped to buy him roasted peanuts, but we didn't linger. I considered calling my client on the cell phone, but Tan Li-Li's apartment, where Xiao-Du waited, was not far, and while I understand the value of such mechanical devices for people whose lives are as busy as my children's, still I consider them a poor choice for expressing matters of the heart. Also, it irritates me to press those tiny numbers.

The reunion of father and child was quite satisfying. Bin-Bin, who didn't know he'd been missing, squealed with everyday delight and ran into his father's arms. I'm sure he didn't understand the tears of joy, or the many kisses and hugs, or the large, dinner-spoiling dish of mango ice cream that followed.

Through all that commotion and all of Xiao-Du's repeated questions and thanks, Tan Li-Li regarded me with mascaraed eyes wide in wonder. Finally I was able to convey to Xiao-Du that I was not at liberty to discuss who the miscreants were, but that he had nothing more to fear from them, and also that he would receive a bill for services, payment of which would express sufficient gratitude. After all, would he thank the chef for cooking dinner or the barber for a haircut? Investigating is simply our job at LC Investigations.

Xiao-Du and his son settled down at the kitchen table to happily ruin their appetites together. I said to Tan Li-Li, "I'll be on my way, then. Perhaps you'll see me to the door?"

I should not have had to ask that, but I wasn't sure Tan Li-Li would be courteous enough to accompany me otherwise. She nodded and followed. I stepped into the hallway; she had no choice but to do so too, shutting the door behind her.

"Chin Yong-Yun," she stammered, "how did you—where did you—"

"Tan Li-Li," I said severely, "I think it's time you accepted that your son's decisions about where to live and raise his family have been made."

"I don't understand."

"Of course you do." I'm afraid I spoke more bluntly than our relationship would have normally allowed, but this was not a time for niceties. "It was a clever plan. And you are fortunate to have in the Fengs loyal friends, to get involved in such business at your behest."

She paled. "They told you?"

"They did not. They remain loyal. I discovered the truth by detecting. Why, for example, did the man who called Xiao-Du disguise his voice? It must be a voice Xiao-Du knows. It was bold of you to have him call me also, but I understand your desperation. He was an excellent actor, by the way. If I hadn't been sure of who it was, I might have been frightened. Another thing, no one in the park remembered seeing you with Bin-Bin today. The peanut vendor, whom I spoke to just now, could recall no loud argument among thuggish young men near his stand. You invented that in answer to my question, isn't that correct? Also, I asked myself, why did you leave a message with my daughter telling her to ignore Xiao-Du's call? Finally, I was struck by your insistence that your son resign rather than explain the situation to his employer. That was because, in fact, the code was never going to change hands at all. Xiao-Du's resignation was the solution, but to an entirely different problem."

Tan Li-Li stared at me, her red lips opening and closing like a fish's. It was comical, but laughing would have been unkind and I am not the sort of person who enjoys being heartless.

"You won't tell Xiao-Du?" Tan Li-Li looked truly scared for the first time. If she had appeared at all frightened during our earlier interview, instead of merely short-tempered and aggravated, I might not have understood from the first the situation's true nature.

"I promise I won't," I said. "But you must promise not to interfere with your son's family decisions anymore."

I trained a stern look on her. She nodded.

"Perhaps," I suggested, "you might consider returning to Beijing when your son does, and spending some time with his family there." Uppermost in my mind was how such a decision would strengthen the bonds between mother and son. The prospect of the cheeriness that might result around the mahjong table only occurred to me afterward.

Tan Li-Li nodded again, but said nothing.

I could feel her eyes watching me as I turned and walked away, but a detective has a sense about when she is in danger and I had nothing to fear from Tan Li-Li. I didn't look back. It was time to go home and prepare dinner. I had promised not to tell Xiao-Du the truth about what had happened, but I hadn't promised I wouldn't tell the story at all. It was, I thought, a noteworthy case, and I was sure my daughter would be interested.

MICKEY SPILLANE AND
MAX ALLAN COLLINS

A Long Time Dead

FROM *Strand Magazine*

KRATCH WAS DEAD.

They ran forty thousand volts through him in the stone mansion called Rahway State Prison with eight witnesses in attendance to watch him strain against the straps and smoke until his heart had stopped and his mind quit functioning.

An autopsy had opened his body to visual inspection and all his parts had been laid out on a table, probed and pored over, then slopped back in the assorted cavities and sewn shut with large economical stitches.

One old aunt, his mother's sister, came forth to claim the remains, and, with what little she had, treated him to a funeral. Kratch had left a fortune but it was tied up, and Auntie was on his mother's side of the family, and poor — Dad had married a succession of showgirls, and Kratch's mom had been the only one to produce an heir.

Whether hoping for a bequest or out of a sense of decency her nephew hadn't inherited, the old girl sat beside the coffin for two days and two nights, moving only to replace the candles when they burned down. Her next-door neighbor brought her the occasional plate of food, crying softly because nobody else had come to this wake.

Just before the hearse arrived, a small man carrying a camera entered the room, smiled at the old lady, offered his condolences, and asked if he could take a picture of the infamous departed.

There was no objection.

Quietly he moved around the inexpensive wooden coffin, snapped four shots with a 35 mm Nikon, thanked Auntie, and left. The next day the news service carried a sharp, clear photo of the notorious Grant Kratch, even to the stitches where they had slid his scalp back after taking off the top of his head on the autopsy table.

No doubt about it.

Kratch was dead.

The serial killer who had sent at least thirty-seven sexually defiled young women to early graves was nothing more than a compost pile himself now.

It had been a pleasure to nail that bastard. I had wanted to kill him when I found him, but the chance that he might give up information during interrogation that would bring some peace of mind to dozens of loved ones out there made me restrain myself.

I knew it was a risk — he was a rich kid who had inherited enough loot to bribe his way out of about anything — but I figured the papers would play up the horror show of the bodies buried on his Long Island estate and keep corruption at bay.

So I'd dragged him into the Fourth Precinct station, let the cops have him, then sat through a trial where he got the death penalty, sweated out the appeal lest some softhearted judge drop it to a life sentence, then was a witness to his smoldering contortions in the big oaken hot seat.

Oh, Kratch was dead all right.

Then what was he doing on a sunny spring afternoon, getting into a taxicab outside the Eastern terminal at LaGuardia Airport?

Damn. I felt like I was in an acid dropper's kaleidoscope — it came fast so fast, no warning — just a slow turn of the head and there he was, thirty feet away, a big man in a Brooks Brothers suit with a craggily handsome face whose perversity exposed itself only in his eyes, and the hate wrenched at my stomach and I could taste the bitterness of vomit. I had my hand on the butt of the .45 and almost yanked it out of the jacket when my reflexes caught hold and froze me to the spot.

Those same reflexes kept me out of his line of sight while my mind detailed every inch of him. He wasn't trying to hide. He wasn't doing a damn thing except standing there waiting for a taxi to pick him up. When one came, he told the cabbie to take him to the Commodore and the voice he spoke in was Kratch's voice.

And Kratch was a long time dead.

I flagged down the next cab and told the driver to take me to the Commodore, and gave him the route I wanted. All he had to do was look at my face and he knew something was hot and leaned into the job. I was forty-five seconds behind Kratch at the terminal, but I was waiting in the Commodore lobby a full five minutes before he came in.

At the desk he said his name was Grossman and they put him on the sixth floor. I got to the elevator bank before he did, went up to the sixth, and waited out of sight until he got out and walked away. When he'd gone in his room, I eased past it and noted the number—620.

Downstairs I asked for something on the sixth, got 601, then went up to my room and sat down to try to put a wild fifty minutes into focus.

There are some things so highly improbable that any time considering them is wasted time. All I knew was that I had just seen Kratch and that the son of a bitch was a long time dead. So that put a look-alike on the scene—a possible twin or a relative with an exceptional resemblance.

Bullshit.

That *was* Kratch I saw. Not unless they had developed human clones, after all. I looked around the room I'd laid down eighty bucks for, wondering just what I had been thinking about when I registered. Been a long while since I'd taken off half-cocked on a dead run like this, and I had damned near pushed myself into a corner.

Great plan I had—push his door button, then pull a gun on him, walk inside, and do a dance on his head—maybe I'd pop those autopsy stitches. Only if I had the wrong guy my ass was grass. I'd had to drop a credit card at the registry desk, and a halfway decent description would point a finger right at me.

Aside from a dead guy who was up and walking around, the basic situation wasn't a new one—I wanted to look around somebody else's hotel room. And after a lot of years in the private cop business in New York, I had plenty of options, legal and il. I propped my door open enough to see anybody who might pass by, then dialed the Spider's number and got his terse "Yeah?"

"Mike Hammer, kid."

It had been more than a year since I'd seen him, so I got a special greeting: "Whaddya want?"

"That gimmick you use for not letting a hotel door shut all the way."

"You goin' inta my business?"

"Don't get smart."

"Where are you?"

"The Commodore."

"And you can't rig something up your own self? Hell, you got wire in the furniture, and in the toilet bowl—"

"Look, I haven't got time. Just bring it over."

"Give me till tonight and I'll get you a passkey."

"No. Now."

"Mike—cut a guy a break. Security knows me there."

"Then send Billy. I'm in 601."

"You're a pain in the ass, Mike."

"Tell me that when yours is back in the can again."

"Okay." He let out a sigh that was meant for me to hear. "This better even up the books."

"Not hardly. But it's a start."

Twenty minutes later, Billy Chappey, looking like the original preppie, showed up at my door to hand me a small envelope, winked knowingly, and strutted off. He sure didn't look like one of the best safecrackers in the city.

After three tries on my own door, I had the routine down pat. Once it was in place, the little spring-loaded gimmick was hardly noticeable. I eased out into the hall, walked down to Room 620, slipped the gizmo into the proper spot, then went back to my room.

After two rings, he answered the phone with a pleasant, resonant "Hello?" He sounded curious but not at all anxious.

I put something nasal in my voice. "Mr. Grossman?"

"Yes."

"This is the front desk, sir. When we entered your credit card in our machine, there was a malfunction and the printout was illegible. Strictly our problem, but would it be too much trouble for you to come down and let us do it over?"

"Not at all. I'll be there right away."

"Thank you. The management would like to send a complimentary drink to your room for the inconvenience."

"That's nice of you. Make it a martini. Very dry."

"Yes. Certainly, sir."

He was punctual, all right. His feet came by my door, and I waited until the elevator opened and shut, then went to his room and went the hell on in. Wouldn't be time to shake the place down. All I wanted was one thing, and I lucked out: he had used the water glass in the bathroom and his prints were all over it. I replaced it with one from my room, after wetting it down, then took the gimmick off the door, which I let close behind me.

The hall was still empty when I shut myself up in my own room. I pulled the bed covers down, messed up the sheets, punched a dent in the pillow, and hung a DO NOT DISTURB sign on the doorknob.

When I got to the lobby, the guy calling himself Grossman was just leaving the bell desk with two no-nonsense security types. They both wore frozen expressions, having been through countless scam situations before. Grossman's face seemed to say someone was playing a joke on him, and nothing more.

My pal Pat Chambers was captain of Homicide and couldn't be bothered with chasing wild gooses.

"No, it's *not* Grant Kratch's print," he growled at me over the phone, after running the errand for me. "Jesus, Mike, that guy is dead as hell!"

"I wish *I'd* made him that way. Then I could be sure."

"The print belongs to Arnold Veslo, a small-time hood who hasn't been in trouble with the law since the midfifties."

"What kind of small-time hood, Pat?"

"He had a couple of local busts for burglary, then turned up as a wheelman for Cootie Banners in Trenton. Did a little time and dropped off the face of the earth."

"Dropped off the face of the earth when? About the time the state fried Kratch?"

"I guess. So what?"

"Messenger over Veslo's photo and anything you got on him."

"Oh, well, sure! We aim to please, Mr. Hammer!"

"I pay my taxes," I said, and hung up on him.

Velda had been eavesdropping from the doorway, but now the big beautiful brunette swung her hips into my inner sanctum, pulled up the client's chair, and filled it, crossing long, lovely legs. She could turn a simple white blouse and black skirt into a public decency beef.

"You want me to start checking on this Arnold Veslo?"

I shook my head. "We'll wait and see what Pat sends over. What about the aunt?"

Most people thought Velda was my secretary. They were right, as far as it went—but she was also the other licensed PI in this office, and my partner. In various ways.

"Long time dead," she said. "Some bitterness about that in the old neighborhood—seems Kratch didn't leave the old lady a dime."

I was trying to get a Lucky going with the desk lighter. She got up, thumbed it to life with one try, and lit me up. "Sure you aren't seeing ghosts?"

"Once I've killed this guy—*really* killed him—then maybe I'll see a ghost."

She settled her lovely fanny on the edge of my desk, folded her arms over the impressive shelf of her bosom, and her lush, luscious mouth curled into a catlike smile. "That all it takes to get a death sentence out of you, Mike? Just resemble some long-gone killer?"

I grinned at her through drifting smoke. "That was Kratch, all right, doll. And I don't think there was anything supernatural about it."

I'd already filled her in on what I'd got at the Commodore. It wasn't the kind of hotel where engravings of George Washington could get you much information. But Abraham Lincoln still had a following.

"So you're stalking an insurance salesman from Lincoln, Nebraska," she said, her mouth amused but her eyes worried, "in the big city for a convention."

"Not just a salesman. He has his own agency. And he'll be here through Sunday. So we've got a couple days. And I hung on to my room on the sixth floor. So I have a base of operations."

"So there's no rush killing him, then."

"Shut up."

"Remind me how this pays the overhead again?"

"Some things," I said, "a guy has to do just to feel good about himself."

The file Pat sent over on Arnold Veslo seemed an immediate dead end. During the war, young Veslo had been tossed out of the army for getting drunk and beating up an officer. As Pat indicated on the phone, the lowlife's stellar postwar career ran from burglary to assault, and notes indicated he'd been connected to Cootie Banner, part of a home invasion crew whose members were all either dead or in stir.

But where was Veslo now?

If that fingerprint was to be believed, he was an insurance broker named Grossman staying at the Commodore. But as far as the states of New York and New Jersey knew, Veslo had been released from Rahway a dozen years ago and done a disappearing act.

This time I was in Velda's domain, the outer office, sitting on the edge of her desk, which visually doesn't stack up with her sitting on the edge of my desk, but you can't have everything. I was studying the Veslo file.

"I can't find any connection," I said. "But I do have a hunch."

She rolled her eyes. "Rarely a good sign . . ."

"Stay with me." I showed her the mug shots. "You remember what Kratch looked like, right? Would you say this guy bears a resemblance?"

She squinted at the front-and-side photos I was dangling. "Not really."

"Look past the big nose and the bushy eyebrows. Check out the bone structure."

"Well . . . yeah. It's there, I suppose. What, plastic surgery?"

I shrugged. "Kratch had dough up the wazoo. It's Hollywood bullshit that you can turn anybody into anybody else, under the knife — but if you start out with a resemblance, and the facial underpinning is right . . ."

"Maybe," she said with a grudging nod. "But so what? You aren't seriously suggesting a scenario where Kratch hires Veslo to undergo plastic surgery and then . . . take his place?"

"Kratch had enough dough to pull just about anything off."

For as beautiful as she was, she could serve up an ugly smirk. "Sure. Makes great sense. Here's a million bucks, pal—all you gotta do is die for me. And by the way, let's trade fingerprints!"

"There are only two places in the system where finger-print cards would need switching—Central Headquarters and the prison itself—and suddenly Kratch's new swirls are Veslo's old ones."

She frowned in thought. "Just bribe a couple of clerks . . . It *could* be done. So what now, Mike?"

"Doll," I said, sliding off the desk, "I got things I want you to check out—you'll need the private detective's chief weapon to do it, though."

"What, a .45? You know I pack a .38."

"That's an understatement." I patted the phone on the desk. "Here's your weapon. You walk your fingers. Mike has to follow his nose."

I told her what I wanted done, retrieved my hat from the closet, and headed out.

George at the Blue Ribbon on Forty-fourth Street had a habit of hiring ex-cops for bartenders. It wasn't a rough joint by any means, in fact a classy German restaurant with a bar decorated by signed celebrity photos and usually some of the celebrities who signed them. Still, a bar is a bar, and having aprons who could handle themselves always came in handy.

Lou Berwicki worked afternoons. He was in his midsixties, six-two of muscle and bone and gristle, with a bucket head, stubbly gray hair, and ice-blue eyes that missed nothing.

He was also an ex–cellblock guard from Rahway State Prison.

Lou got off at four-thirty, and I was waiting for him at my usual table in a nook around a corner. I had ordered us both beers, and as his last duty of the shift, he brought them over.

We shook. He had one of those beefy paws your hand can get lost in, even a mitt like mine.

"Great to see you, Lou."

"Stuff it, Mike—I can tell by that shit-eating grin, this is busi-ness. What the hell can an old warhorse like me do to help a young punk like you?"

I liked guys in their sixties. They thought guys in their thirties were young.

I said, "I need to thumb through your memory book, Lou. Need some info about Rahway, and I hate driving to New Jersey."

"Who doesn't?"

"You didn't work death row."

"Hell no. My God, it was depressing enough on the main cell-blocks."

"But you knew the guys who did?"

"Yeah. Knew everybody there. Big place, small staff—we all knew each other. Paid to. What's this about?"

I lighted up a smoke; took some in, let some out. "About ten years ago they gave Grant Kratch the hot squat."

"Couldn't happen to a nicer guy."

"How well did you know the bulls working that block?"

"Enough, I guess. What's this about, Mike?"

"Any rotten apples?"

He shrugged. "You know how it is. Prison pay stinks. So there's always guys willing to do favors."

"How about a big favor?"

"Don't follow . . ."

"I have a wild hair up my ass, Lou. You may need another beer to follow this . . ."

"Try me."

"Say a guy comes to visit Kratch, maybe the day before he's set to take the electric cure. This guy maybe comes in as Kratch's law-yer—might be he's in a beard and glasses and wig."

"I think I *will* have that beer . . ." Lou gulped the rest of his down and waved a waitress over. "I didn't know you were still readin' comic books, Mike."

"Hear me out. Say this guy has had plastic surgery and is now a ringer for Kratch—"

"This may take a boilermaker."

"So they switch clothes, and Kratch walks, and the ringer gets the juice."

Lou shook his head, laughed without humor. "It's a fairy tale, Mike. Who would do that? Who would take a guy's place in the hot seat?"

"Maybe somebody with cancer or some other incurable disease.

Somebody who has family he wants taken care of. Remember that guy in Miami who popped Cermak for the Capone crowd? He had cancer of the stomach."

The old ex–prison guard was well into the second beer now. Maybe that was why he said, "Okay. So what you're saying is, could you pull that off with the help of the right bent screw?"

"That's what I'm saying. Was anybody working on death row at that time that could have been bought? And we're talking big money, Lou—Irish Sweepstakes money."

The beer froze halfway from the table to his face. Lou was a pale guy naturally, but he went paler.

"Shit," he said. "Conrad."

"Who?"

"Jack Conrad. He was only about fifty, but he took early retirement. The word was, he'd inherited dough. He went to Florida. Him and his wife and kids."

"He was crooked?"

"Everybody knew he was the guy selling booze and cigarettes to the inmates. Legend has it he snuck women in. Whether that's true or not, I can't tell you. But I *can* tell you something that'll curl your hair."

"Go, man."

He leaned forward. "Somebody *murdered* Conrad—maybe a year after he moved down there. Murdered him and his whole family. He had a nice-looking teenage daughter who got raped in the bargain. Real nasty shit, man."

I was smiling.

"Jesus, Mike—I tell you a horror story and you start grinning. What's wrong with you?"

"Maybe I know something you don't."

"Yeah, what?"

"That the story might have a happy ending."

Velda was in the client's chair again, but her legs weren't crossed—her feet were on the floor and her knees together. Prim as a schoolmarm.

"How did you know?" she asked.

"I said it was a hunch."

She was pale as death, after hearing what Lou had shared with me.

"Arnold Veslo had a good-looking wife and child, a young boy," she said, reporting what she'd discovered. "Two weeks after Kratch was executed, Mrs. Veslo was found at home—raped and murdered. The boy's neck was snapped. No one was ever brought to justice. What kind of monster—"

"You know what kind."

She leaned in and tapped the fat file folder on my desk. "Like you asked, I checked our file on Veslo—it's mostly clippings, but there's a lot of them. And I put the key one on top."

I flipped the folder open, and they stared back at me, both of them—Arnold Veslo and Grant Kratch. Veslo in a chauffeur's cap and uniform, opening the car door for his employer, Kratch, who'd been brought in for questioning two weeks before I hauled his ass and the necessary evidence into the Fourth Precinct.

"You were right," she said, rapping a knuckle on the yellowed newsprint. "Veslo worked for Kratch. How did you know? What are you, psychic?"

"No. I'm not even smart. But I saw a murderer today, a living, breathing one, and I knew there had to be a way."

She shrugged. "So we bring Pat in, right? You lay it all out, and the investigation begins. If Grossman really is Kratch, then before his 'death,' Kratch had to find a way to transfer his estate into some kind of bank setup where his new identity could access it. That kind of thing can be traced. You can get this guy, Mike."

"Velda, we know for sure Kratch killed and raped thirty-seven women over a five-year period. Mostly prostitutes and runaways. You remember our clients' faces? The parents of the last girl?"

She swallowed and nodded.

"Well, it's a damn sure bet that he also killed that prison guard's family *and* Veslo's, and got his jollies with a couple more sexual assaults along the way. And do you really think that's his whole damn tally?"

"What do you mean, Mike?"

"I mean 'Grossman' has spent the last ten years doing more than selling insurance, you can damn well bet. Think about it—you just *know* there are missing women in unmarked graves all across the heartland."

"God," she said, ashen. "How many more has he killed?"

"No one but that sick bastard knows. But you can be sure of one thing, doll."

"What?"

"There won't be any more."

Back in my hotel room, I was still weighing exactly how I wanted to play this. I'd been seen here, and a few people knew I'd been asking about Grossman, so even if I handled this with care, I'd probably get hauled in for questioning.

And of course Captain Pat Chambers already knew the basics of the situation.

With my door open and me sitting in a chair with my back to the wall, I had a concealed view of the hallway. I wasn't even sure Kratch was in his room. I was considering going down there, and using the passkey I'd taken Spider up on, and just taking my chances confronting the bastard. I'd rigged self-defense pleas before.

Which was the problem. I was a repeat offender in that department, and the right judge could get frisky.

I was mulling this when the bellboy brought the cute little prostitute—because that's surely what she was—up to the door of 620. She had curly blond Annie hair and a sparkly blue minidress and looked about sixteen.

I could see Kratch, in a white terry-cloth Commodore robe, slip into the hall, give the bellboy a twenty, pat him on the shoulder, send him on his way, pat the prostitute on the bottom, and guide her in.

Knowing Kratch's sexual proclivities, I didn't feel I had much choice but to intervene. My .45 was tucked in the speed rig under my sport jacket, the passkey in my hand. It was about ten P.M. and traffic in the hall was scant—too late for people to be heading out, too early for them to be coming back.

So I stood by that door and listened. I could hear them in there talking. He was smooth, with a resonant baritone, very charming. She sounded young and a little high. Whether drugs or booze, I couldn't tell you.

Then it got quiet, and that worried me.

What the hell, I thought, and I used the passkey.

I got lucky—they were in the bathroom. The door was cracked

and I could hear his smooth banter and her girlish giggling, a radio going, some middle-of-the-road station playing romantic strings, mixed with the bubbling rumble of a Jacuzzi.

I got the .45 out and helped myself to a real look around this time—this was a suite, a sprawl of luxury. There was a wet bar, and I could see where he'd made drinks for them. In back of the bar I found the pill bottle, and a sniff of a lipstick-kissed glass told me the bastard had slipped her a mickey.

That wasn't the most fun thing he had in store for her—I checked the three big suitcases, and one had clothes, and another had toys. You know the kind—handcuffs and whips and chains and assorted S&M goodies. Nothing was in the last big, oversize suitcase.

Not yet.

So he had a whole evening planned for her, didn't he? But there's always a party pooper in the crowd . . .

When I burst into the bathroom with the .45 in hand, he practically jumped out of the tub. The hot bubbles were going, and more drinks sat on the edge, but I motioned with the gun for him to sit down and stay put. The girl didn't notice me, or anyway didn't notice me much. She was half unconscious already, leaning back against the tub, a sweet little nude with hooded eyes and pert handfuls with tiny tips poking up out of the froth like flowers just starting to grow.

I held the gun on him as he frowned at me in seeming incomprehension and I leaned over and lifted the girl by a skinny arm out of the tub. She didn't seem to mind. She might have been a child of twelve but for the cupcake breasts. If I hadn't got here when I did, she wouldn't have ever got any older. She managed to stand on wobbly legs, her wet feet slippery on the tile. I took her chin in my free hand. "I'm the cops. You want to leave. Wake up! This bastard doped you."

Life leaped into her eyes, and self-preservation kicked in, and she stumbled into the other room. I left the door open as I trained the gun on Kratch.

He was a handsome guy, as far as it went, with a pockmarked ruggedness. His hair was gray and in tight Roman curls, his chest hair going white too, stark on tanned flesh.

And he frowned at me, as if I were just some deranged intruder—he didn't have to fake the fear.

"My name is Grossman. I'm an insurance salesman from Nebraska. Take my money from my wallet—it's by the bed. You can have it all. Just don't hurt the girl."

That made me laugh.

She stuck her head in. She was dressed now. Didn't take long with those skimpy threads.

"Thank you, mister," she said.

"I never saw you," I said. "And you never saw me."

She nodded prettily and was out the door.

I grinned at him. "Alone at last. Are you really going to play games, Kratch?"

He smiled. "Almost didn't recognize you, Hammer. You're not as young as you used to be."

"No, but I can still recognize a piece of shit when I see one."

"No one else will. I'm a respectable citizen. Have been for a long, long time."

"I don't think so. I think Grossman is just the latest front for your sick appetites. How many young girls like that have you raped and killed in the past ten years or so, Kratch? I will go to my grave regretting I didn't kill you the first time around."

"My name isn't Kratch." The fear had ebbed. He had an oily confidence—if I was going to kill him, he figured, I'd have done it by now. "It's Grossman. And you will never prove otherwise. You can put all your resources and connections behind it, Hammer, and you will never, ever have the proof you need."

"Since when did I give a damn about proof?"

The radio made a simple splash going in, like a big bar of soap, and he did not scream or thrash, simply froze with clawed hands and a look of horror that had come over him as the deadly little box came sailing his way. I held the plug in and let the juice have him and endured the sick smell of scorched flesh with no idea whether he could feel what I was seeing, the all-over blisters forming like so many more bubbles, the hair on his head catching fire like a flaming hat, fingertips bursting like overdone sausages, eyes bulging, then popping, one, two, like plump squeezed grapes, leaving sightless black sockets crying scarlet tears as he cooked in the gravy of his own gore.

I unplugged the thing, and the grotesque corpse slipped under the roiling water.

"*Now* you're fucking dead," I said.

Contributors' Notes

Other Distinguished Mystery Stories of 2010

Contributors' Notes

Brock Adams is the author of *Gulf,* a collection of short stories. His work has appeared in the *Sewanee Review, A capella Zoo,* and *Eureka Literary Magazine,* among many others. He grew up in Panama City, Florida, and studied at the University of Florida and the University of Central Florida, where he received his MFA. He lives with his wife, Jill, in Spartanburg, South Carolina, where they both write and teach at USC Upstate.

- "Audacious" had a simple beginning: I wanted to write a story about crowds. There's something fascinating about the level of anonymity that can exist even when surrounded by hundreds of people. I knew who Gerald was, and I knew who Audi was, but I had nothing of the story planned other than them sensing each other's loneliness in the midst of a crowd. They took it from there.

I'm amazed at the success that "Audacious" has had. When I wrote it, I had no idea if it worked at all. The others in my workshop panned it. They wanted to see Audi steal from Gerald. They wanted to see Gerald and Audi have sex. They wanted lots of things and I ignored them all, and the story works as it is: simple and sad. It taught me the most important thing I learned in school: you have to know when to listen, but sometimes you have to know when to ignore everybody else.

Eric Barnes is the author of the novel *Shimmer* (2009), an IndieNext pick that is a dark and sometimes comic novel about a person who's built a company based entirely on a lie. He also has published short stories in *Raritan, Washington Square Review, North Atlantic Review, Tampa Review,* and a number of other journals. He has been a reporter, editor, and publisher in Connecticut, New York, and now Memphis. Years ago he drove a forklift in Tacoma, Washington, and then in Kenai, Alaska, worked construction on Puget Sound, and froze fish in a warehouse outside Anchorage. He has an MFA from Columbia University and is the publisher of three newspapers covering business and politics in Memphis and Nashville.

▪ I wrote the first version of "Something Pretty, Something Beautiful" a number of years ago, as part of a series of stories about Tacoma, where I grew up, and four friends who lived there. They are all very dark stories, and every time I reread one, I like them even more, yet am also slightly more disturbed that I was ever able to write them in the first place.

Lawrence Block has been doing this long enough to have collected lifetime achievement awards from Mystery Writers of America, Private Eye Writers of America, the Short Mystery Fiction Society, and the (U.K.) Crime Writers Association. He'll be publishing two books in 2011, *A Drop of the Hard Stuff* and *Getting Off*.

▪ I'd written a couple of short stories about a young woman who picked up men for sex, went home with them, had a fine time in bed with them, and capped it off by killing them. I couldn't get her out of my head, and found myself wondering why she was doing this, and how she got this way, and where she was going with it. "Clean Slate" was the result.

Max Allan Collins has earned an unprecedented sixteen Private Eye Writers of America Shamus nominations, winning for *True Detective* (1983) and *Stolen Away* (1993) in his Nathan Heller series, which includes the recent *Bye Bye, Baby*. His graphic novel *Road to Perdition* is the basis of the Academy Award–winning film.

Both Collins and Mickey Spillane (who died in 2006) received the Private Eye Writers Lifetime Achievement Award, the Eye.

▪ Mickey Spillane said to his wife, Jane, just days before his passing, "After I'm gone, there'll be a treasure hunt around here—give everything you find to Max. He'll know what to do." Mickey was the hero of my adolescence, and the direct inspiration for my career. So it's hard for me to think of a greater honor.

Jane, my wife, Barb, and I went through the voluminous files in Mickey's three offices in his South Carolina home. Among the treasures discovered were half-a-dozen incomplete Hammer novels—all running 100 manuscript pages or more—and three of these (thus far) have appeared: *The Goliath Bone, The Big Bang,* and *Kiss Her Goodbye*. We also discovered a number of shorter fragments that I felt would be better served as short stories.

"A Long Time Dead" was one of the most interesting of those fragments, and one that clearly appeared to be intended as a short story, not a novel. For the Spillane fan/scholar, this is particularly exciting, because Mickey published only a handful of Mike Hammer short stories in his lifetime.

David Corbett is the author of four novels: *The Devil's Redhead, Done for a Dime* (a *New York Times* Notable Book), *Blood of Paradise* (nominated for numerous awards, including the Edgar), and *Do They Know I'm Running?*, published in March 2010 ("a rich, hard-hitting epic" — *Publishers Weekly*, starred review). Corbett's short fiction and poetry have appeared in numerous periodicals and anthologies, and his story "Pretty Little Parasite" was selected for inclusion in *The Best American Mystery Stories 2009*. For more, go to www.davidcorbett.com.

▪ When Luis was in San Francisco being feted because *The Hummingbird's Daughter* had been chosen for the One City One Book distinction, we met through a mutual friend, Kathi Kamen Goldmark, discovered we also had a mutual friend in John Connolly, and just basically hit it off. Then Luis, whose tastes are nothing if not eclectic, talked about collaborating on something in the genre realm, using his exhaustive knowledge of the border and Mexican arcana and my instincts for straight-ahead train-wreck plotting. It sounded like fun, but our other obligations kept us from doing anything but talking about it until Bobby Byrd, the editor of *Lone Star Noir*, approached Luis for a story and he (Luis) decided to throw me a bone. He had the main character, Chester Richard, already in mind, as well as the Cajun/zydeco musical background, the Port Arthur locale, and a few other impressionistic details. I added a few things of my own, we tossed a few other ideas back and forth, and then we agreed on a general story idea. I took first whack, Luis batted second, I did some minor cleanup, and we sent it on. It turned out to be strangely hassle-free, since Luis is both wildly imaginative and incredibly easy to work with.

Brendan DuBois of New Hampshire is the award-winning author of twelve novels and more than one hundred short stories. His latest novel, *Deadly Cove*, was published in July 2011. His short fiction has appeared in *Playboy, Ellery Queen's Mystery Magazine, Alfred Hitchcock's Mystery Magazine*, the *Magazine of Fantasy & Science Fiction*, and numerous other magazines and anthologies, including *The Best American Mystery Stories of the Century*, published in 2000 and edited by Tony Hillerman and Otto Penzler. His short stories have twice won him the Shamus Award from the Private Eye Writers of America and have also earned him three Edgar Allan Poe Award nominations from the Mystery Writers of America. Visit his website at www.BrendanDuBois.com.

▪ As a former newspaper reporter, I had scores of opportunities to go with police officers on ride-alongs, where I sat next to them in the front seat of police cruisers and got a firsthand look at "serving and protecting" the general public. Among the things I learned: ride-alongs at night are more productive; always take an anti-motion-sickness pill before leaving the station (cops are aggressive when it comes to braking and accelerating); and when responding at high speed with lights on and sirens racing, just relax—everything is out of your hands.

There are some slow evening shifts when the most important decision is what kind of muffin to buy, and there are other nights when you're responding to an "officer needs assistance" call, barreling down a two-lane road, going one hundred miles an hour.

And you learn other things as well: that during night ride-alongs, when the majority of people are home and asleep, there's a whole different breed of people who are out and about in one's community—the lonely, the drinkers, and the troublemakers. A mixture that often leads to arrests and crime stories. In "Ride-Along," I decided to make the troublemakers the ones inside the police cruiser, and not outside. It was a fun story to write, and I'm honored to have it appear in this anthology.

Loren D. Estleman's first novel was published in 1976. Since that time he has published sixty-five books, including mainstream and historical novels and the Amos Walker series, which debuted in 1980. In 2002 his alma mater, Eastern Michigan University, honored him with a doctorate in humane letters. He lives in Michigan with his wife, the author Deborah Morgan. *Infernal Angels*, the twenty-first Amos Walker novel, was released this past summer.

▪ When Tyrus Books asked me to compose a new story for *Amos Walker: The Complete Story Collection*, I started with the title "Sometimes a Hyena." This was nothing new; most of my ideas start with a title, although years may pass before I come up with a story to stick on the end of it. In this case, a joke I'd heard in several versions led to speculation over how one news story can lead to another, and I began writing with no clear idea where I was going. Of course, the real mystery is, who knows what makes a joke work?

Beth Ann Fennelly is the author of three books of poems (*Open House, Tender Hooks,* and *Unmentionables*) and a book of nonfiction (*Great with Child*). She's won a Pushcart Prize and grants from the National Endowment for the Arts and United States Artists. **Tom Franklin** is the author of one collection of short stories (*Poachers*) and three novels (*Hell at the Breech, Smonk,* and *Crooked Letter, Crooked Letter*). He has won an Edgar and a Guggenheim. Fennelly and Franklin live in Oxford, Mississippi, and teach in the MFA program at Ole Miss. Together they have collaborated on short stories and short people (Anna Claire, nine, Thomas, five, and Nolan, three weeks).

▪ The seeds of "What His Hands Had Been Waiting For" began years ago, when Tommy wrote a bad story about zombies chomping through an apocalyptic wasteland and, thankfully, put it in a drawer. Later, he and Beth Ann were asked to contribute a story to an anthology of Mississippi blues tales. Feeling uninspired, he went to his drawer of failed attempts but couldn't make much happen, though on rereading the zombie story he realized it had some potential. Tommy gave the story to Beth Ann to see if she could help resurrect it. She got rid of the zombies and set about researching the flood of the Mississippi River in 1927, figuring that sometimes what really happened with real live humans is much wilder than anything they could make up for zombies to do. They had so much fun writing this story together that now they are using it as the basis of an as-yet-untitled novel.

Ernest J. Finney is a native Californian and a sympathetic, though often amused and sometimes outraged, observer of daily life within that state. California figures large in all his fiction. His four novels take place in the San Francisco Bay area, the Sierra, and the San Joaquin Valley. His short fiction appears often in literary journals and anthologies, including the *O. Henry Prize Stories,* in which his story "Peacocks" was a first-prize winner. Each of his two story collections received a California Book Award. His third collection, *Sequoia Gardens: California Stories* was published in February 2011. Finney lives and writes on Pliocene Ridge in Sierra County, California.

> • "A Crime of Opportunity" began with a platter of General Tso's chicken in a restaurant on Clement Street in San Francisco and a conversation about a novice public defender known as the Funeral Director by a host of unfortunate felons hoping for a life sentence but anticipating death row. Delilah emerged full-grown by the end of the meal. Renée was inspired by one of my mothers-in-law, who had a lot to say about life lessons.

Ed Gorman has published more than twenty mystery and suspense novels and seven collections of short stories. Over the years he's won a Shamus, twice been nominated for the Edgar, won an Anthony, and been short-listed for a Silver Dagger. Two of his books have been filmed, one as a low-budget feature and one as a TV movie. *Kirkus Reviews* called him "one of the most original crime writers around," while the *San Francisco Examiner* noted that "Gorman has a wonderful writing style that allows him to say things of substance in an entertaining way." Presently he writes the Dev Conrad series, dark political thrillers, and the Sam McCain books, which have followed the life of a young attorney from the late fifties up into the seventies.

• "Flying Solo" is the result of sitting in chemo rooms for the past nine years dealing with my multiple myeloma, an incurable but treatable cancer. You buy as much time as you can. I've been very, very lucky so far. I'd been noticing a sad-eyed nurse for several visits. I'd never dealt with her, but one day she gave me my IVs and I noticed a bruise on her cheek. This day she looked forlorn. She told me she was tired, that she'd moved into an apartment with her two kids late the night before. I assumed she was a battered wife. You hear and see a lot in chemo rooms—usually nothing soap operatic (the rooms I've been in are generally friendly places with a lot of smiling faces) — but every once in a while a mask will slip and you get a glimpse of cancer turmoil. Of fear. And not only of cancer but of personal lives that the disease has only made more difficult. Couples divorcing following a cancer diagnosis is not unheard-of. All this caused me to drag out my nickel notebook one day and start taking notes about a mismatched pair of old cancer patients who decided they'd spend whatever time they had left taking care of the nurses and patients in the chemo room. And I still prefer James Garner.

James Grady is the author of *Six Days of the Condor*, a dozen more novels, and as many short stories, which often appear in "Best of" collections. He's covered politics, crime, spies, and terrorists as a journalist since Watergate, written for TV and the movies, been awarded France's Grand Prix de Roman Noir, Italy's Raymond Chandler Award, Japan's Baku-Misu literature award, and been nominated for a Mystery Writers of America Edgar. London's *Daily Telegraph* named Grady as one of "fifty crime writers to read before you die."

• "Destiny City" let me shed light on the complex mysteries of terrorism and the often messy means we use to fight it. To make sure I got the story as right as writing can, I worked with our good guys and with terrorists— an interesting literary journalism dance. I also wanted to show readers snapshots of America they might not glimpse out the windows of their moving cars, but more than anything, I wanted to bring to life characters—heroes, villains, victims—who, like all of us, navigate through a fog of power politics and personal dreams.

Chris F. Holm was born in Syracuse, New York, the grandson of a cop who passed along his passion for crime fiction. He wrote his first story at the age of six. It got him sent to the principal's office. Since then his work has fared better, appearing in such publications as *Ellery Queen's Mystery Magazine*, *Alfred Hitchcock's Mystery Magazine*, *Needle* magazine, *Beat to a Pulp*, and *Thuglit*. He's been a Derringer Award finalist and a Spinetingler Award winner, and he's also written a novel or two, which he'd likely show you if you asked him nice.

▪ I'm not sure *where* the idea for "The Hitter" came from, but I remember precisely when it arrived. It was late one Sunday night in April of 2010, and I was lying in bed, drifting off to sleep. As my mind wandered, a scene ran through my head. A city square in some nameless banana republic. A teeming crowd, cheering on a petty despot. And above them all, watching through a gun sight, an assassin. Truth be told, I didn't think much of it until that assassin pulled the trigger—three pounds' pressure, no more, no less—and I realized that the petty despot wasn't the target. Once that happened, any pretense of a good night's sleep evaporated, and I leapt from bed, running to my computer to get down everything I could remember before it faded in the way that dreams do. See, a political assassination is straightforward, uncomplicated—a matter of money or of zealotry, nothing more. But my hitter's motives were of a subtler sort, and I knew that, much as I'd like never to meet him, I wanted to know what made him tick.

Three weeks later, the story was written. I thought it too long for most markets, but Steve Weddle, editor of the then not-yet-published *Needle* magazine, assured me that *Needle* was not your average market. Turns out Steve was right—which seems fitting, since Jake is hardly your average hitman.

Harry Hunsicker is the former executive vice president of the Mystery Writers of America and the author of three novels, crime thrillers about a Dallas private investigator with the unfortunate name of Lee Henry Oswald. In 2006 his debut novel, *Still River,* was nominated for a Shamus Award by the Private Eye Writers of America, and in 2010 his short story "Iced" was nominated for a Thriller Award by the International Thriller Writers. Hunsicker lives in Dallas, where, when not working on a book, he is a commercial real estate appraiser and an occasional speaker on creative writing.

▪ "West of Nowhere" came to me in the form of an opening line about a man so inept his friends called him Danny the Dumb-ass. From there I imagined a small crew of robbers, each damaged and ill-functioning in his or her own special way. I placed them in Central Texas, a region where I spent a great deal of time as a child and young adult. For some reason, the relationship between these three lifelong friends solidified itself in my mind early on, and the story grew of its own volition.

Richard Lange is the author of the short story collection *Dead Boys* and the novel *This Wicked World.* His stories have appeared in the *Sun,* the *Iowa Re-*

view, The Best American Mystery Stories 2004, and as part of the *Atlantic Monthly*'s Fiction for Kindle series. He was the 2008 recipient of the Rosenthal Family Foundation Award for Literature from the American Academy of Arts and Letters and a finalist for the William Saroyan International Prize for Writing and was awarded a Guggenheim Fellowship in 2009. He is currently working on a novel and another collection of stories.

▪ Children get shot in Los Angeles. It's a fact. Well, children get shot everywhere, but I live in L.A. and write about the city, so it's our dead children I was thinking of when I wrote "Baby Killer." One child in particular, actually, a four-year-old boy who happened to be walking down the street with his sister one afternoon when the local gangsters opened fire on a passing car. A stray bullet hit the boy in the chest, killing him.

People process tragedies like this in different ways. I'm a writer, so I write. And I resurrected a dead woman to tell this story. Blanca was a character from a failed novel, long laid to rest. I brought her back to life and started her talking, and little by little the tale came out. As with all of my stories, I wasn't sure where it was going until it got there. When it did, I wished it had ended a little better for Blanca. But it didn't. I also wish that little boy had never died, but he did. I hate this goddamn world sometimes, I really do.

Joe R. Lansdale is the author of over thirty novels and twenty short story collections, numerous essays and articles, and scripts. He has edited or coedited more than thirty anthologies. His work has been filmed, turned into comics, and performed on the stage. His story "Bubba Hotep" was turned into a cult film. He has received numerous awards for his work, among them the Edgar, seven Bram Stoker Awards, the British Fantasy Award, the Grinzane Cavour Prize, the Herodotus Award for Historical Fiction, the Inkpot Award for lifetime achievement in the field of comics, fantasy, and science fiction. He has had two *New York Times* Notable Books. A martial artist for forty-nine years, he is the founder of Lansdale's Shen Chuan, Martial Science, has been inducted into the Martial Arts Hall of Fame four times, and owns a martial arts school in Nacogdoches, Texas. He teaches at Stephen F. Austin State University, where he is writer in residence. Currently he is helping produce the low-budget film *Christmas with the Dead,* based on his story of the same name.

▪ I was born in Gladewater, Texas, and my first memory is of a house on a hill overlooking a honky-tonk, a highway, and a drive-in theater. My mother and I watched the drive-in from the windows of our house, and she told me what characters were saying. From then on I was hooked on storytelling and have often written about drive-ins and honky-tonks and the people who kept them in business. I began to learn boxing and wrestling from my father at an early age; he was forty-two years old when I was born. He could neither read nor write, but like my mother, who could, he was a great storyteller. He rode the rails during the Great Depression from one carnival to the next, where he wrestled or boxed for money. My mother encouraged my love for writing, my father my love for all manner of martial arts. I still practice them both. On my way to becoming a writer I've been an aluminum chair worker, farmer, field hand, bodyguard of sorts, and a janitor. I like writing and martial arts best. Follow me on Twitter. My handle is joelansdale.

Charles McCarry, born in 1930 in Pittsfield, Massachusetts, established an international reputation as a novelist with the publication of his worldwide bestsellers, *The Miernik Dossier* (1973) and *The Tears of Autumn* (1975). He is the author of nine other novels, translated into more than thirty languages, and the author, coauthor, or editor of nine nonfiction books, in addition to short stories, poems, and about a million words of journalism in leading American and foreign magazines. As a young man he drafted speeches for a president, a presidential candidate, and other politicians. During the early Cold War, he spent an uninterrupted decade abroad as a CIA agent under deep cover. Later on he was the editor in charge of freelance operations at *National Geographic* and wrote the magazine's official history for its one hundredth anniversary in 1988. He and his wife, Nancy, married since 1953, live in south Florida in winter and the Berkshire Hills of Massachusetts in summer.

• "The End of the String" is autobiographical in the sense that it closely reflects the atmosphere and, to a degree, the reality of some of the things I experienced as a secret agent fifty-odd years ago in Africa. As is true of most works of fiction, parts of this story are invented and parts of it are drawn from vivid memory. I knew places like Ndala and made friends with men like Benjamin, the leading character in this tale, and lived through episodes that were not so very different from the ones in this story. But there is no parallel Ndala or real Benjamin. They are, by design, different enough from the originals to give away no secrets. Even for writers who never took an oath of secrecy, fiction is, after all, what ought to have been, not what actually was. At least, not exactly.

Dennis McFadden lives and writes in an old farmhouse called Mountjoy on Bliss Road, just up Peaceable Street from Harmony Corners in upstate New York. His collection of linked stories, *Hart's Grove*, was published in June 2010, and his fiction has appeared in dozens of publications, including the *Missouri Review, New England Review, Massachusetts Review, Hayden's Ferry Review, CutBank,* and *South Carolina Review.*

• For a writer, the blessing of rejection is the opportunity it affords the rejected story to grow and develop. "Diamond Alley" was afforded ample opportunity. One of my earliest stories, it began as a simple vignette about a teenaged peeping Tom and the Voice of the Pittsburgh Pirates, but it underwent some serious evolution after that humble beginning. Over the years the characters and lore of the small, fictional town of Hart's Grove began to take shape and take over, insinuating themselves into the story from the roots up. "Diamond Alley" probably grew most and developed best, however, the day I decided to shift the narration to the first-person-plural point of view; then, instead of a man remembering a murder that had occurred when he was a boy, I had a Greek chorus singing a Greek tragedy.

As for the mystery in this story, it's not much different from the mystery in every story I write—mystery in the sense that we can never really know everything that is happening in our lives, or anything that will happen after them. It's just that this one is magnified by murder. But mysteries in fiction are seldom as insoluble as those in life, as most writers can't resist the lure of omniscience; given that, and given the nature of the linked collection, it's not surprising that the answer to the primary mystery of "Diamond Alley"—*who do you suppose really killed her?*—lies naked there in *Hart's Grove* for all who care to see.

Christopher Merkner's stories have recently appeared in *Black Warrior Review, Gettysburg Review, Gulf Coast, New Orleans Review,* and *Cincinnati Review.* He teaches creative writing for the University of Colorado, Denver.

• "Last Cottage" started as a touching and lighthearted meditation on my youth and my hometown in Illinois. I don't know what went wrong. At some point it became clear that the story had no interest in being touching or lighthearted. Writing and rewriting, I could not drop the image of the carp that sucked the surface of the lakes and rivers near my hometown. I have so many good memories of my youth in northern Illinois, but those carp—those mouths gasping and sucking, those oily eyes rolling—kept returning instead. So I decided to kill them. "Last Cottage" followed. A huge thanks to Brock Clarke and the amazing people at the *Cincinnati Review* for their help and support and encouragement.

Andrew Riconda lives on City Island in the Bronx. His fiction has appeared in the *Amherst Review, Criminal Class Review, Oyez Review, Phantasmagoria, Rio Grande Review, Watchword,* and *William and Mary Review.* He is currently at work on a novel, *The Three People I Had to Kill Last Year,* featuring the protagonist of the story in this collection.

• "Heart Like a Balloon" was my first attempt at the mystery genre.

Most of my stories are quirky tales about sad, alienated men—just without crimes, guns, paring knives, and the flayed skin. Like many of my characters, the narrator, Brian Rehill, is trying to remain God-oblivious in a world that just won't permit that. Speaking of deities, I like to think that one of the gods of quirky crime tales, Charles Willeford, might have enjoyed this story. Hail Hoke Moseley.

S. J. Rozan was born and raised in the Bronx and is a lifelong New Yorker. She's the author of eleven books in the Lydia Chin/Bill Smith series, the most recent of which is *Ghost Hero.* She also has two standalones, *Absent Friends* and *In This Rain,* and three dozen short stories published in various periodicals and anthologies, including a number of "Best of the Year" collections. She has won the Edgar, Shamus, Anthony, Nero, and Macavity Awards for best novel, as well as the Japanese Maltese Falcon Award and the Edgar for best short story. She lectures and teaches widely and runs an English-language writing workshop in the summers in Assisi, Italy. Visit www.sjrozan.com.

• I get a lot of comments from readers about Lydia Chin's mother. Everyone, it seems, either knows someone with a mother like Chin Yong-Yun or has one. (My favorite comment ever at a book signing: a young Chinese man who said, "I only have one question. When did you meet my mother?") "Chin Yong-Yun Takes a Case" was my first shot at giving Ma Chin her own voice, at seeing things from her side of the kitchen table. It probably won't be the last; I have a feeling she's just getting started.

Mickey Spillane was the best-selling American mystery writer of the twentieth century. He introduced Mike Hammer in *I, the Jury* (1947), which sold in the millions, as did the six tough mysteries that soon followed. The controversial PI has been the subject of a radio show, a comic strip, two television series, and numerous films, notably director Robert Aldrich's seminal film noir, *Kiss Me Deadly* (1955).

Luis Alberto Urrea is the author of several books, among them *In Search of Snow, The Hummingbird's Daughter* (winner of the Kiriyama Prize), and *The Devil's Highway* (a finalist for the Pulitzer and winner of the Lannan Literary Award). He was born in Mexico and currently lives in the Chicago area, where he teaches at the University of Illinois. His story "Amapola," from *Phoenix Noir,* won the Edgar Award in 2010.

• This story began its life as a set of notes dating back to my time as writer in residence at the University of Louisiana at Lafayette. I was taken—as who wouldn't be—by zydeco music and Cajun/Creole culture.

I was a huge Beau Jocque fan, and when I finally met him and talked one night, I knew a zydeco story had to happen. I jotted notes for a "literary" fiction. What is that? I knew ol' Chester Richard was my hero, but beyond that . . . I had no idea. My advice to all lazy writers is to team up with David Corbett. He writes like some well-oiled machine and apparently doesn't mind doing a year's worth of research in one night.

Other Distinguished Mystery Stories of 2010

BEALL, WILL
  The Blood-Dimmed Tide. *Hook, Line & Sinister*, ed. T. Jefferson Parker
    (Countryman)
BRUCHAC, JOSEPH
  Helper. *Indian Country Noir*, ed. Sarah Cortez and Liz Martinez (Akashic)

COHEN, ROBERT
  Our Time with the Pirates. *Ploughshares*, Fall
COLE, DAVID
  JaneJohnDoe.com. *Indian Country Noir*, ed. Sarah Cortez and Liz Martinez
    (Akashic)
COLEMAN, REED FARREL
  Another Role. *Indian Country Noir*, ed. Sarah Cortez and Liz Martinez (Akashic)

EGAN, K. J.
  Black Hole Devotion. *Alfred Hitchcock Mystery Magazine*, June

FINDER, JOSEPH
  Neighbors. *Agents of Treachery*, ed. Otto Penzler (Vintage)

HAYWOOD, GAR ANTHONY
  The Lamb Was Sure to Go. *Alfred Hitchcock Mystery Magazine*, November
HENDRIX, LAURA FRANCES
  Mister Visits. *Kenyon Review*, Summer
HOWARD, CLARK
  Escape from Wolfkill. *Ellery Queen Mystery Magazine*, August
HUDSON, SUZANNE
  All the Way to Memphis. *Delta Blues*, ed. Carolyn Haines (Tyrus)
HUNTER, STEPHEN
  Casey at the Bat. *Agents of Treachery*, ed. Otto Penzler (Vintage)

HYER, BRIAN
Package. *Greensboro Review,* Spring

JACKSON, ALICE
Cuttin' Heads. *Delta Blues,* ed. Carolyn Haines (Tyrus)

KILPATRICK, LYNN K.
Domestic Drama. *Alfred Hitchcock Mystery Magazine,* May
KLAVAN, ANDREW
Sleeping with My Assassin. *Agents of Treachery,* ed. Otto Penzler (Vintage)

LICATA, DAVID
There Is Joy Before the Angels of Good. *Literary Review,* Winter
LINK, WILLIAM
Duel. *Ellery Queen Mystery Magazine,* March/April

MCFALL, PATRICIA
On the Night in Question. *Orange County Noir,* ed. Gary Phillips (Akashic)

PARKER, T. JEFFERSON
Luck. *Hook, Line & Sinister,* ed. T. Jefferson Parker (Countryman)

RAINONE, ANTHONY
Tomb Guardian. *Alfred Hitchcock Mystery Magazine,* September

SCHUTZ, GREG
Joyriders. *Ploughshares,* Fall
STEINHAUER, OLEN
You Know What's Going On. *Agents of Treachery,* ed. Otto Penzler (Vintage)
STRAIGHT, SUSAN
Bee Canyon. *Orange County Noir,* ed. Gary Phillips (Akashic)

VAN DEN BERG, LAURA
The Isle of Youth. *Conjunctions,* no. 54

WARD, ROBERT
Black Star Canyon. *Orange County Noir,* ed. Gary Phillips (Akashic)
WHITE, EDWARD
The Creative Writing Murders. *The Dark Side of the Street,* ed. Jonathan Santlofer
and S. J. Rozan (Bloomsbury)
WIRKUS, TIM
Thirteen Virtues of a Colonial Detective. *Cream City Review,* Spring
WOLVEN, SCOTT
Los Millonarios. *Crime Spree,* January/February

ZEMAN, ANGELA
Skip Trace. *Back Alley,* Spring